Material

Loved by a rich man...

Three passionate novels!

In October 2007 Mills & Boon bring back two of their classic collections, each featuring three favourite romances by our bestselling authors...

MISTRESS MATERIAL

The Billionaire's Pregnant Mistress
by Lucy Monroe
The Married Mistress by Kate Walker
His Trophy Mistress by Daphne Clair

WEDDING BELLS

Contract Bride by Susan Fox
The Last-Minute Marriage
by Marion Lennox
The Bride Assignment by Leigh Michaels

THE BILLIONAIRE'S PREGNANT MISTRESS

by

Lucy Monroe

Lucy Monroe started reading at age four. After she'd gone through the children's books at home, her mother caught her reading adult novels pilfered from the higher shelves on the book case... alas, it was nine years before she got her hands on a Mills & Boon® romance her older sister had brought home. She loves to create the strong alpha males and independent women that people Mills & Boon® books. When she's not immersed in a romance novel (whether reading or writing it) she enjoys travel with her family, having tea with the neighbours, gardening and visits from her numerous nieces and nephews. Lucy loves to hear from readers: e-mail Lucymonroe@Lucymonroe.com or visit www.LucyMonroe.com

Don't miss Lucy Monroe's exciting new novel
What the Rancher Wants...
out now from Mills & Boon® Modern™ Extra.

To my Resident Alpha Male.
You are, and always will be, the hero of my heart. Thank you for believing in me. I love you.

PROLOGUE

THE cold porcelain of the bathroom sink pressed against Alexandra Dupree's forehead as she leaned against it, her stomach still heaving from its third early-morning upset in as many days. She dragged air into lungs starved by the unpleasant moments spent bent over the sink.

After a minute of doing nothing but breathe, she tentatively brought her body erect. A small twinge of nausea hit her, but she was able to control it. Okay, as unpleasant as this new early morning ritual had become, she had something even less pleasant to perform. She stared at the small white stick with all the wariness she would feel for a snake found curled around the base of the commode.

Dimitri had been fanatical about using birth control. So she'd convinced herself one late period didn't mean anything, until she woke up heaving three days ago. At first she'd thought she had the flu, sure there could be no possibility she was pregnant even though the condom had broken a month ago. Her menses had come right on time a week later.

She still didn't understand how this could be possible, but she had too many symptoms to deny. Her breasts were tender. She was tired all the time. She'd cried when Dimitri told her he had to spend more time in Greece and wouldn't be returning to their Paris apartment for several days. She never cried.

She forced herself to do what was necessary for the pregnancy test. Ten minutes later the world went white around the edges as she stared at the blue line confirming she carried the child of Dimitrius Petronides.

Dimitri clenched his fists, refusing to give vent to his frustration.

"You know it is time. You are thirty, heh? You need a wife, some babies, a home." The older man's gray head tilted arrogantly, while he fixed Dimitri with a look that said he would argue this to the ground.

Dimitri had no desire to argue anything with his grandfather. He had barely survived a heart attack five days ago. Dimitri smiled. "I'm hardly in my dotage, Grandfather."

The man who had raised Dimitri and his brother since their parents' deaths snorted. "Don't try to get around me with your charm. It won't work. You're my heir and I need to go to my grave knowing you will do your duty by the Petronides name."

Dimitri's heart contracted. "You are not going to die."

His grandfather shrugged. "Who of us is to say when we will die? But I'm old, Dimitrius. My heart is not as strong as it once was. Is it so much to ask you marry Phoebe now? Why put it off? She's a sweet girl. She'll make you a proper Greek wife. She'll give you Petronides babies."

Eyes sliding shut, the older man breathed shallowly as if his short speech had taken more out of his weakened physical state than he had to give. Dimitri wanted to do something, but he was powerless. His grandfather's doctors wanted the old man to have heart surgery, but he had refused to discuss it.

"Why won't you have the by-pass operation your doctor is recommending?"

"Why won't you marry?" the old man countered. "Perhaps if I had great-grandchildren to look forward to, the pain of such an operation would be worth going through."

Dimitri felt the blood drain from his face. "Are you saying you won't have the operation if I don't marry Phoebe Leonides?"

Dark blue eyes, so much like his own, opened to stare at Dimitri with all the stubbornness a Petronides male had to bear. "Yes."

CHAPTER ONE

ALEXANDRA nervously smoothed the kerchief style silk halter-top over the nonexistent bump where her baby rested under her heart.

The unaccustomed warmth of late spring had allowed her to wear the sexy outfit to boost her flagging morale. She turned to the side and surveyed herself in the full-length mirror in her bedroom. Her willowy body encased in the champagne silk hip-hugging pants and sexy halter looked no different than it had when Dimitri had left for Greece.

The week-old knowledge that she was pregnant with his child might show in her wary hazel eyes, tinted sultry green by colored contacts, but it had not yet affected the shape of her body. She adjusted the gold chain belt resting low on her hips and the multiple thin bangles she wore on her wrist tinkled like small bells as they clinked together. Then in a nervous gesture, she pulled another curling strand of her hair down to frame the soft angles of her face.

Curled and professionally bleached so many shades, it looked like rippling sunlight when she let it down, her hair was a Xandra trademark. Only right now, she didn't feel like Xandra Fortune, popular model and lover to Greek Tycoon, Dimitrius Petronides. She felt like Alexandra Dupree, daughter of an old New Orleans family, convent educated and shocked to be unmarried and pregnant with her lover's child.

"You look beautiful, *pethi mou*."

Alexandra spun away from the mirror. Dimitri stood in the door, masculine appreciation burning in his startling blue eyes. For a moment she forgot her condition. Forgot the many truths she needed to tell him. Forgot her fears. Forgot everything but how much she had missed this man over the past three weeks.

She flew across the room and threw herself against his chest. "*Mon cher*, I have counted the minutes since you left!"

Strong arms locked around her in an almost convulsive movement while his body remained strangely stiff. "It has only been a month and you have been busy with work. You cannot have missed me that much."

His words reminded her how he had resented her refusal to quit modeling when they had become lovers, but she had not wanted to be any man's kept mistress. Nor had she had the option of quitting her job. She needed the money she made to support the family he knew nothing about.

"You are wrong. Nothing can keep me so occupied I do not notice your absence. A day. A week. A month. I grieve them all." She grimaced inwardly at her blatant vulnerability. Where had her sophisticated cool gone, the career model facade that had initially drawn Dimitri to her?

The first crack had appeared when he'd told her he was going to be in Greece longer than anticipated and she'd cried. After two-and-a-half weeks of morning sickness, a positive pregnancy test and her mother's horrified reaction to the news, the Xandra Fortune persona was in definite risk of extinction.

* * *

Dimitri tried to hold on to his self-control, not an easy thing around Xandra. And this was Xandra as he'd never seen her. Clingy. Almost vulnerable, but he knew that could not be true. They had become lovers a year ago and although she shared her body with a generosity that moved him, she kept her heart and parts of her life hidden from him.

Their relationship was modern and free of long-term commitment, something she'd made it clear by her actions she did not expect from him.

She pressed her body to his in blatant invitation and he laughed. "You mean you have grieved my absence from your bed, do you not?"

That was the only place he was convinced she did need him. She wouldn't let him support her, making it obvious she would rather spend time away from him than give up any part of her career. None of this, however, made it easier to say what needed to be said. In fact, he was sure it would be harder for him to say the words than for her to hear them. His sophisticated lover would not appreciate a drawn out, or emotional goodbye any more than he would.

She shook her head, stretching up to link her hands behind his neck and brushed the hair at his nape. "I missed *you,* Dimitri. There was no joy in cooking for myself alone, no pleasure in watching the French Open without you to mutter when your favorite double-faulted on game point."

He frowned, remembering the play. She smiled at him with a look that spelled his doom if he didn't get his news out quickly. It had already wrought an instant response in his body. "I have news I must tell you."

Her arms went stiff in reaction to the seriousness of his tone. "Can it not wait, *mon cher?*"

He reached behind his neck to remove her hands, but she locked her fingers with surprising force.

He clasped her wrists. "We must talk now."

Alexandra did not want to talk. She was not ready to share her news. He'd seduced her from the beginning. She'd given him her heart, her body and her fidelity, as committed to him as any wife could be. Only she wasn't his wife and she didn't know how he'd respond to his lover getting pregnant.

Fear more than desire prompted her hips to grind against him. "No." She kissed his chin, tasting the skin and letting her body absorb the return of its other half. "No talk." She brushed her unfettered breasts behind her thin top back and forth across the crisp white silk of his shirt. "First, this."

"Xandra, no." He pulled her hands away from his neck, but made the mistake of letting them go.

She tunneled under his jacket and pushed it off his shoulders. "Dimitri, yes."

He glared at her, but he did not stop her from pushing his suit coat to a pile of expensive Italian designer fabric on the floor. She smiled in approval. "I want you, Dimitri. We can talk later."

She needed the affirmation that they were two halves of the same whole before she could tell him the truth about the baby she carried and equally as terrifying, the truth about who and what she was.

He grabbed her round the waist and lifted her until her mouth was even with his own. "Heaven help me, I want you, too."

There was something about the angry tone in his voice she did not understand, but she could not focus on it for long, not with his warm lips closing over her own in overwhelming passion.

She tore at his tie while he made quick work of the two hooks holding her top together. He helped her with the buttons on his shirt. The two garments fell to the thick pile carpet together and his lips never separated from hers. He pulled her flush against his body and the naked flesh of her already aroused nipples brushed the heat of his muscular chest.

She shivered in reaction while he groaned.

"We should not be doing this."

The words registered only subliminally, planting a question as to why they should be said, but she could not consciously respond to them. She was too overwhelmed by the feel of his flesh against her own for the first time in over a month. He seemed similarly affected as his arms tightened around her until she could barely take a breath.

Seconds later they lay entwined on the bed, the rest of their clothes discarded, hungry hands touching intimate places, mouths devouring one another. They climbed to the heights together with a speed they never had before. When they tumbled into starbursts and oblivion, masculine shouts mingled with her own cries of pleasure.

Alexandra laid her hand over Dimitri's heart. It still beat with the accelerated pulse of recently spent passion.

"Such a strong heart," she murmured, "such a strong man." Would the news she had to share direct that strength toward her or against her?

His body tensed as if he had some premonition of what was to come. He rolled away and ejected himself from the bed. "I need a shower."

She stared at the six-foot-four-inch sexy giant towering above the bed. Tension was emanating off him in waves.

"I'll join you."

He shook his head. "Stay there. I will be quick."

Her heart squeezed at the small rejection, but she smiled and nodded. "All right." Craven coward that she was, she gladly accepted another excuse to put off telling him her news.

He came out of the bathroom fifteen minutes later dressed in his usual sartorial elegance, but his dark hair was still damp. His choice of another business suit over something less formal made her pause.

"Do you have a meeting?"

The chiseled features of his gorgeous face were set in an unemotional mask. "Xandra, there is something I must tell you."

She scooted into a sitting position, pulling the sheet with her to shield her body from the blue gaze that had mesmerized her from the moment they met. "What?"

"I'm getting married."

Everything inside her went still. Had he said what she thought he had said? No. It wasn't possible. "M-married?"

His hands fisted at his sides, his body stiff with tension she could no longer ignore. "Yes."

She could not take it in. It had to be some kind of joke. "If this is your idea of a marriage proposal, you've got a lot to learn."

Sensual lips twisted in a grimace. "Do not be ridiculous."

"Ridiculous?" She wished her brain would start working again, but she couldn't think in the face of his words.

"You are a career woman as you've shown time and again over the past year." He slashed the air with one cutting hand. "A woman with your ambitions would not make a proper wife for the heir to the Petronides empire."

She shivered with a chill that went clear to the marrow of her bones. "What exactly are you saying?"

"I am getting married and naturally our liaison must come to an end." The sick paleness of his features did nothing to alleviate her personal pain.

"You told me our relationship was exclusive. You told me I could trust you. You would not make love to another woman while I shared your bed." She jumped out of that bed, feeling dirty and used, the passion they had shared soiled with his revelation.

Running his long fingers through the black silk of his hair, he sighed. "I have not had sex with another woman."

"Then who are you marrying?" she practically shrieked.

"No one you know."

"Obviously." Alexandra glared at him, wanting to kill him, wanting to scream, very afraid she would cry.

He sighed again. "Her name is Phoebe Leonides."

Greek. The other woman was Greek and probably meek, proper and brought up to marry money. "When did you meet her?" Though the pain was tearing her apart, she had to know.

"I've known Phoebe most of my life. She is the daughter of a family friend."

"You've known her most of your life and you just decided you loved her?"

A cynical laugh erupted from him. "Love has nothing to do with it."

He said love like it was a dirty word. Neither of them had ever spoken of love, but she adored Dimitri with every fiber of her being and had hoped that he had returned those feelings at least in some small way. Enough to make a marriage and family between them work now that she was pregnant with his child, but he quite obviously didn't believe in the emotion.

"If you don't love this woman, why are you marrying her?"

"It is time."

She swallowed convulsively. "You say that like it's something you'd always planned to do."

"It is."

Blood roared to her head, making her feel flushed and weak. She swayed.

He said something vicious in Greek and grabbed her upper arms to steady her. "Are you all right, *pethi mou?*"

What planet was he from? How could she be all right? He'd just told her he planned to marry another woman, a woman he'd always intended to make his wife while he'd spent the past year using Alexandra as his whore.

"Let. Me. Go," she got out between clenched teeth.

He dropped his hands, his face registering affront and she wanted to slap him so much it was an ache in her muscles. He took a single step back.

She glared up at the face that had been more beloved than any other since they met fourteen months ago. "Let me get this straight. You always planned to marry another woman?"

Indigo eyes narrowed. He didn't like repeating himself. "Yes."

"Yet you seduced me into your bed. You made me your tart knowing you never intended our relationship to be anything more than sexual?"

He reared back as if she'd struck him. "I did not make you my tart. You are my lover."

"Ex-lover."

His jaw clenched. "Ex-lover."

"Why..." She swallowed the bile rising in her throat. She couldn't ask this, but she had to. "Why did you make love, I mean... *have sex* with me just now?"

He spun away from her, his magnificent body sending messages to her own even amidst the carnage of their discussion.

"I couldn't help myself."

She believed him. She hadn't been able to help herself with him from the very beginning. She'd still been a virgin at the ripe age of twenty-two, but her innocence had been no barrier to the feelings he ignited in her.

He'd been shocked by her virginity, but not deterred in his resolve to make her his lover. She'd loved him and after two months of holding him off, she'd given in. It had been fantastic. He had made her feel cherished and there had been times over the past year when she had even felt loved.

"I don't believe you want to let me go." He couldn't.

"It is time," he said again, as if that explained it all.

"Time to marry the woman you intended to marry all along?" she asked, needing to make it very clear in her own mind.

"Yes."

Suddenly she felt her nakedness even through the mists of her anger and it shamed her. She had shared her body without inhibitions with this man for a year... a year during which he knew he planned to marry another woman.

She spun on her heel and headed to the bathroom where she jerked on the toweling robe she kept hanging on the back of the door. When she came back into the bedroom, Dimitri was gone. A search of the apartment revealed he had not merely left the bedroom, he had left her.

She stood in the middle of the living room and let the emptiness of the apartment sink into her consciousness until it was so heavy it forced her to her knees. Her head dropped, feeling too heavy for her neck and the sting of tears began in the back of her throat.

Soon their acid heat burned their way down her cheeks and neck to soak into the lapel of the heavy Turkish robe.

Dimitri was gone.

Dimitri leaned against the wall in the hallway outside the apartment. He'd forced himself to leave when Xandra went into the bathroom. If he hadn't, he would never have made it out the door. Even now, the temptation to go back to her and tell her it was all a mistake rode him hard.

But it was not a mistake. If Dimitri did not marry Phoebe Leonides, an old man whom Dimitri loved more than his own life or personal happiness, would die. His grandfather had refused to back down from his ultimatum and even now sat weakly in a wheelchair, refusing necessary surgery until Dimitri set a wedding date.

His fist jabbed viciously into the palm of his other hand. Why had Xandra mentioned marriage between them? Why taunt him with the impossible? She did not want marriage. She could not. If she had, at least one time over the past year, her career would have come second and he would have come first. It never had. Not once.

Xandra was angry right now, her feminine pride bruised. It had upset her to realize he had planned to marry another woman all along, but he could not take seriously the idea she thought their liaison would end in marriage. She'd made her independence too much an issue for that. However, she had obviously believed he had no plans at all in that direction.

More guilt added to the already swirling cauldron of emotions inside him.

He had not intended to make love with her again, but he'd lost his cool and his control the moment she went into seductive mode. For all her worldly sophistication, Xandra was not an aggressive lover. She was affectionate and responsive, more responsive than any woman he'd ever known, but she initiated lovemaking rarely and even then, she did so subtly. Her seduction just now had been anything but subtle and it had undermined his defenses with the impact of an invading army.

Afterward, it had been harder than he thought possible to tell her of his upcoming marriage while her body remained warm and fragrant from their intimacy.

He forced himself away from the wall and toward the elevator. A clean break was the only way.

Alexandra waited thirty-six hours to call Dimitri's cell phone, sure with the passing of each hour, the man she loved, the father of her child, would come back to her.

He had made love to her. She was sure he hadn't planned to do it, but he had. He'd never slept with Phoebe. He had said he didn't love the other woman and equally important, he couldn't possibly need her the way he had needed Alexandra for the past year.

But he did not come and she had no choice but to contact him. She was furious with him, more hurt than she'd ever been in her life, but she carried his child and she had to tell him before he made the mistake of marrying another woman.

She refused to consider what she would do if the news of impending fatherhood had no effect on his marital plans.

The sound of the phone ringing beeped in her ear three times before he picked up. "Dimitri, here."

"It's Xandra."

She was met with unnerving silence.

"We need to talk."

More silence. "There is no more to say."

"You're wrong. There are things I must tell you." Did he notice how alike her words now to the ones he'd spoken to her two days ago?

"Can we not dismiss the postmortems?"

She sucked in air, but controlled the desire to scream like a fishwife at the insensitive tycoon dismissing her like yesterday's garbage. "No. We need to talk. *You owe this to me, Dimitri.*"

This time she didn't break the silence.

Finally she heard a heavy exhalation at the other end of the line. "Fine. Meet me at *Chez Renée* for lunch."

"I'd rather meet in the apartment." She did not want to tell him of his impending fatherhood and her true identity in a public setting.

"No."

She gritted her teeth, but didn't argue. "Fine." Maybe a public setting would be best after all. *He would hesitate to commit murder with witnesses,* she thought with black humor.

They set a time and hung up.

Dimitri cut the cell connection and turned to look out the large window in his Athens office. He had flown to Athens within hours of leaving the Paris apartment. He hadn't trusted himself to stay in France and not go back to her.

And that infuriated him.

His grandfather's life was at stake and Dimitri refused to allow an obsession with a woman deter him from his purpose. His parents had taught him all the lessons he needed to learn in that area. His father's obsessive need for his mother had resulted in years of volatile togetherness and ultimately both their deaths.

He could not allow a similar compulsive need for Xandra to affect the same result for his grandfather.

He'd been her first lover, but with a sensual nature like hers, he knew he would not be her last. There had even been times when he wondered if he were her only lover. There were areas of her life she kept hidden from him. She took trips abroad that were not modeling assignments, but that she refused to discuss with him.

He had told himself he was being foolish. She did not flirt or make meaningful eye contact with other men. She had always been gratifyingly hungry when they came together, but he'd never been able to dismiss the feeling she did not belong exclusively to him. If not sexually, than emotionally.

Which had led him to believe she would take their eventual but inevitable breakup with her usual cool sophistication, just as she took their many separations made necessary by her work or his. A memory of her tear-clogged voice the last time he'd called to say his stay in Greece had been prolonged rose up.

What if she had convinced herself she loved him? He shuddered at the thought. Love was an excuse women used to succumb to their passions. His mother had supposedly loved his father, but she'd also loved her tennis instructor and then the husband of a business acquaintance and finally the Italian ski instructor she'd run off with.

His mother had been a prime example of the treachery women perpetrated in the name of love. Dimitri preferred the frank exchange of sexual desire to protestations of a fleeting emotion that only caused pain in the end.

But Alexandra wanted to meet one more time. His curled fist settled against the windowsill.

He'd agreed because she was right...he did owe her.

They'd spent a year together and she had given him the gift of her innocence. She'd made little of it at the time, but his traditional Greek upbringing had planted it as a debt firmly in his mind. A debt he should not have repaid with such a soulless dismissal of their relationship.

He hadn't even given her a gift in parting. She deserved better than that. She had been his woman for a year. He would make sure she was set for the future.

He could only hope his control at their upcoming meeting exceeded that of the last one.

CHAPTER TWO

ALEXANDRA remained seated while she waited for Dimitri to weave his way between the small bistro tables and join her. She'd chosen to sit outside, hoping the late spring sunshine would imbue their encounter with some much needed optimism. Dimitri's aviator sunglasses hid his expression from her, but his mouth was set in a grim line that did not bode well for the meeting ahead.

She resisted the urge to rub her temples, giving away the anxiety she felt.

He pulled out a chair opposite her own and folded his tall frame into it. "Xandra."

What a cold greeting for the woman he had been living with for the past year. She pulled the cloak of sophistication she wore like a protective covering around her and inclined her head. "Dimitri."

He pulled off the aviators and tossed them on the table. His blue eyes revealed no more of his thoughts than the mirrored reflection of his glasses had. "Have you ordered?"

Why that question should cause pain to slice through her, she had no idea. Perhaps because it exemplified a new level of distance between the two of them. He had not asked how she was or how her morning had gone. Presumably those topics were no longer of concern to him.

"Yes. I ordered you a steak and salad."

"Fine. I presume you have a specific reason for insisting we meet." As if the dissolution of their year long relationship wasn't enough. "There is something I forgot to do at our last meeting as well." He grimaced. "It did not go as I expected."

She had thought she couldn't hurt more than she already did, but she had been wrong. Not go as he expected? They'd made love with desperate passion and then he'd ditched her. Which part hadn't he expected?

"There's something you need to know. Something I have to tell you before you…" She could not make herself say it.

His brow rose in query and he pulled a sheaf of papers from his briefcase. He laid them on the table and then placed a small box on top of them, a box obviously the size of a jewelry case. There was an attitude of finality in the action that cut the thread holding her composure.

"You can't marry her!" The words burst from Alexandra without thought. "She doesn't care about you. She couldn't and still accept your lifestyle for the past year."

Again that mocking black brow rose.

She answered the unspoken question. "You've been living with me." Surely no woman could tolerate such a circumstance and care even the least little bit for the man involved.

"I assure you, I have not publicized the fact."

She clenched her hand against her stomach, feeling as if she'd sustained a blow there.

He was right. He had been very careful to keep their relationship out of the media, no small feat when she was a fairly well known model in Europe and he was a billionaire. But those same billions along with her circumspect behavior had made it possible. She had her own reason for wanting to stay out of the international scandal rags.

Just as she'd had her reasons for keeping her identity as Alexandra Dupree a secret. Just as she had commitments that had forced her to put her job before her time with Dimitri. But those commitments no longer held top place in her priorities, not now that she was pregnant and he was talking about marrying another woman.

"Do you love her?" He'd implied he didn't, but she wanted facts. She needed assurances.

"Love is not something I think about."

That was telling her. She bit her lip, tasting blood before she realized what she was doing.

He swore and dipped his napkin in her glass of water before pressing it against the small wound, his expression furious. "Do not do this to yourself, Xandra. Our affair was bound to end. Perhaps that end is coming sooner than either of us expected or wanted, but it cannot be a complete shock to you."

She shook her head, unable to believe he thought she had spent the last year looking ahead to an end in their relationship. She had never allowed herself to imagine a future *with* him, either. In fact, she'd spent the last year pretty much refusing to think of the future at all.

"I love you." The words just slipped out.

"Damn it. Don't do this."

"Don't do what? Tell you the truth?"

"Try to manipulate me with such claims."

"I'm not trying to manipulate you."

Cynicism colored his features. "Then why have you said nothing of this great love for the past year?"

"I was afraid…"

His sarcastic laugh cut into her. "You were more sincere."

On one level, she understood his disbelief. She'd never spoken of love and he didn't know about Mama or Madeleine and the financial needs that had forced Alexandra to put him second to her modeling career. She might never have told him of her love either, but her pregnancy had forced her to reevaluate her life, a big chunk of which was her relationship with him.

Even understanding it, his scathing denial of her love still hurt. "You care about me. Don't try to deny it. Not after the way we have been the past twelve months, not after making love to me two days ago."

"I appreciate that having sex with you in the circumstances was wrong, but as I said I could not help myself."

Okay, so he hadn't agreed he cared about her, but such an admission from a guy like Dimitri Petronides wasn't something to dismiss lightly. He found her irresistible. Surely that must mean he had some feelings for her. "If it were only sex, you could have gotten that anywhere, including from your fiancée."

"A proper Greek girl does not give her innocence to a man before she marries."

Did he realize what he was saying? It was archaic. Prehistoric. "What does that make me? A tart?"

His broad shoulders tensed. "No. You are an independent, career-minded woman. I wanted you. You wanted me. We made no promises to one another. I never intended marriage and if you are honest with yourself you will admit you knew that."

"Why should I?" Maybe she hadn't thought ahead to marriage, but she sure as heck hadn't assumed they'd break up like this either. Not with him planning to marry someone else. "We had something incredibly special."

"We had great sex."

Her hands trembled and she put down the glass of

juice she had just lifted to her lips. "I can't believe you just said that."

"It is the truth."

"Your truth."

He shrugged. "My truth."

"Well, I have a truth I have to share with you as well."

"What is this truth?" he asked coolly.

It was hard, harder than she could ever have imagined to pluck up the courage to tell a man who had just informed her what she had mistaken for love had been nothing more than great sex that she carried his child. In the end only blunt honesty would do. "I'm pregnant."

For several seconds his expression did not change and then his eyes filled with pity. "Xandra, do not humiliate yourself this way. I will not leave you unprovided for."

He thought she was worried about the payoff gift? She glared at the pile of papers and jeweler's box near his right hand, wishing she could incinerate them with her eyes. "I'm carrying your child, Dimitri."

He groaned and rubbed between his eyes with his thumb and forefinger. "You've always been very forthright, very honest. Do not stoop to telling tales now. Surely you cannot believe it will change the outcome."

He thought she was lying? She felt hysterical laughter well up inside her. He thought she was lying now and had always been so forthright in the past. He *believed* she was Xandra Fortune, the French fashion model and orphan the world saw. And he *didn't* believe she was pregnant.

The irony almost choked her. "I am not lying."

His cynical smile galvanized her into action. She dug in her purse and grabbed the white stick that proved her pregnancy. She waved it in front of him. "One blue line means yes to a pregnancy."

She did not know exactly what reaction she had expected, but it was not the volatile, fury filled one she got.

He grabbed her wrist, lifting the hand with the pregnancy test, his body vibrating with palpable anger. "You dare to show this to me?"

What was wrong with him? "Yes, I dare. I won't let you ignore the reality of your baby just because you've decided it's time to marry another woman."

A nerve ticked in his jaw. "Do you think I am stupid? You cannot possibly be pregnant with *my* child."

"The condom broke, remember?" He should. He'd made enough of it at the time.

"That was before your period and we did not have sex again until two days ago." The grip on her wrist tightened painfully. "Tell me you are not pregnant. Tell me this—" he shook her hand "—is some kind of joke."

"You're hurting me," she whispered as tears clogged her throat and burned her eyes.

A flash went off and he let her go, throwing her arm from him with disgust. She watched out of the periphery of her vision as one of Dimitri's security men took off after the photographer. "It's not a lie. I am pregnant."

If anything, he seemed to swell with more anger. "It is not my child."

For a moment his words paralyzed her. How could he doubt it was his child? She'd never had another lover. He knew it. "It is."

His face contorted with revulsion. "All this time you have been haranguing me for planning to marry Phoebe, you have known you took another man to your bed. Who is it?"

His shouted question made her jump in fright. Dimitri never lost his cool. He hated scenes and putting on a public display was anathema to him.

"There is no other man."

"The evidence is not in your favor." His voice had dropped to freezing levels.

"I don't know how it can be, but it is."

"I had planned to be generous, give you the apartment. I thought you deserved it, but I'll be damned if I'm going to pay for your lover's lifestyle and support his bastard child. I am not that stupid." He grabbed the papers off the table, but tossed the box at her. "This should be a sufficiently memorable token for services rendered."

She shoved the box aside. "There is no other man!"

His face closed up and terror coursed through her. He did not believe her. "You can have the tests done."

He stood up. "Be assured I will demand them if you attempt to sue for any kind of support."

Alexandra gulped, trying to get enough air. Trying not to vomit, but the pain was so intense that she wasn't sure she could win the battle. Her arms were wrapped tightly around her middle and she still felt like she was going to fly apart into a thousand broken little pieces.

To have the gift of their child so brutally rejected hurt almost beyond bearing.

She whimpered.

Whipping her hand to her mouth, she blocked the sound with her fist. She did not want to let him see her weakness.

"You have twenty-four hours to vacate the apartment." He gave her one last sulfuric glare, spun on his heel and left.

Alexandra paced from one side of the living room to the other. She'd called Dimitri's cell phone at least a dozen times and gotten his message service every time. She'd left messages with the operator, at his Paris office, at his office in Athens, even with his grandfather's housekeeper.

Every message had said the same thing. *Please call.*

He hadn't. Not all day yesterday as she vacillated between tortured tears and blazing fury. Not through a sleepless night when she had tossed and turned in a bed too big for comfort without him in it. She'd tried to rest for the baby's sake, but every time she closed her eyes images of him telling her he planned to marry intruded, or worse…his expression of revulsion when she'd told him she was pregnant.

It was now close to one o'clock in the afternoon and she'd spent the last hour calling every contact number she had for him again. It hadn't done any good. She couldn't sit down. She was so strung out and edgy, she felt like she'd taken a couple of the diet pills some of her fellow models used to control their appetite.

One thought played itself over and over again in her brain. Dimitri believed she'd taken another lover. What kind of trust was that? He really did think she was some kind of slut.

The thought sent her to her knees only to hop up again at the sound of a key turning in the lock. She flew to the door. He'd come back. Relief surged through her in unstoppable waves. He'd realized how idiotic he'd been to believe she could make love to another man.

She wrenched the door open. "Dim—" Her voice

choked off mid word. It wasn't Dimitri at the door. "Who the hell are you?" she demanded in English before remembering where she was and repeating her question in French.

The stocky bald man pushed his way into the apartment, followed by an efficient looking woman and another man, this one lanky and sandy haired. The woman spoke. "I am Mr. Petronides's facilities manager. I am here to oversee your vacation of the apartment."

Alexandra barely made it to the bathroom before she lost the little bit of food she'd forced herself to eat that day.

When she came out, the brunette was directing the two men in the packing of Alexandra's things with an officious looking clipboard in one hand and a pen in the other. The facilities manager used her pen to point at a small Lladro figurine Dimitri had bought Alexandra when they were in Barcelona together.

The bald man picked up the statuette and began wrapping it in paper before putting it in one of the numerous boxes the moving team must have brought with them. Alexandra stood in appalled fascination as every item she could claim as her own was packed in a similarly efficient manner from the living room.

The last three days had been nightmarish, but this was beyond a nightmare. It was so horrifyingly real, she almost buckled from the pain of it.

"He sent you to evict me?" She asked the words in a bare whisper, but the other woman heard.

She turned to Alexandra, her face impassive. "I have been sent to facilitate your move, yes."

"Have you evicted many of his ex-lovers?" Alexandra asked.

The other woman's eyes twitched. "Your relationship

with Mr. Petronides is not my business. I am simply following through on my instructions."

"War criminals say the same thing in their defense."

Her mouth tightening, the brunette turned away without answering. Alexandra did not push it. Instead, she marched into the bedroom she had shared with Dimitri and started packing her clothes. She didn't want those men touching them. She already felt violated by their presence and the way they went through *her* home removing *her* things, removing traces of *her*.

Two hours later, the packing was done. Alexandra returned to the living room and surveyed the neatly piled boxes the two men were preparing to transport out of the apartment. Were they going to take them down to the lobby and leave them there? Out onto the street?

Suddenly emotions that had gone numb in the face of Dimitri's cruel ejection of her from his life, came back to life and Alexandra shouted, "Stop!" as the bald man went to pick up one of the boxes.

The man stopped.

"Some of the items you packed don't belong to me. You'll have to wait while I sort through the boxes and take them out."

"I had a very specific list from Mr. Petronides," the brunette began to say.

"I don't care." Alexandra stood to her full five feet, nine inches and glared the other woman down. "I'm not taking his property with me."

The movers must have read her determination on her face because they didn't attempt to dissuade her again. It took forty-five minutes, but in the end she had removed every single thing Dimitri had ever given her. She'd gone through her clothes as well, chucking sexy lingerie from her suitcases along with designer dresses...anything and everything he had bought.

When she was done, there was a pile of objects mixed with crumpled manila newsprint on the living room floor along with two stacks of neatly folded clothes.

"There's one more thing."

The brunette just nodded, her eyes registering some emotion after watching Alexandra's feverish attempt to purge her things of all items related to her ex-lover.

Alexandra picked up her purse and pulled out the white stick she'd replaced yesterday after the disastrous confrontation with Dimitri along with the jewelry case he'd left lying on the café table. She dropped them both on top of the lingerie pile. She stood up and grabbed the handle of her suitcase, slung the matching overnight case over her shoulder and exited the apartment.

Alexandra waited a week to hear from Dimitri, hoping time would calm him to the point of rationality. Seven days after she'd been evicted from their apartment, she read an article in the society column announcing his upcoming wedding to Phoebe Leonides. The girl looked about nineteen and as innocent as any virginal bride should be.

Alexandra checked out of the hotel she'd been staying in, arranged for her possessions to be shipped to the U.S., terminated her contract with her modeling agency, closed her Xandra Fortune checking account, canceled her credit cards under that name and bought a ticket back to the states in the name of Alexandra Dupree.

Xandra Fortune, fashion model and ex-lover of Greek billionaire, Dimitri Petronides, ceased to exist.

A little over two months later, Alexandra walked out of the prenatal clinic into the hot, sticky air of early autumn in New York City. She glanced down at the snapshot of her recent ultrasound. She'd put the videotape in her bag, but hadn't been able to tuck the photo away. She was enthralled with this proof of the baby growing in her womb. The baby she could not yet feel or even see in her only slightly thickened waistline.

It was a boy. A part of Dimitri Petronides she was free to love, someone who would return her love. Even weakened by constant morning sickness and exhausted from her pregnancy, she wanted to shout for joy.

Desperately wanting to share her news with someone, she flipped open her cell phone and dialed her sister's number. She got the answering machine and opted not to leave a message. She could tell Madeleine the news when she went home later. She considered and discarded the idea of calling her mother. Alexandra was not up to another dose of "You've brought shame to the family name."

Compulsion she could not deny had her dialing the number to the Paris apartment. There had been no news of Dimitri's wedding in the New York society pages. Fool that she was, she couldn't stop herself from looking and even more foolishly hoping. Had he come to his senses? Called off the wedding?

Perhaps the latter was too much to hope for, but surely after two months he would have had enough time to calm down and realize Alexandra would never have been unfaithful to him.

The phone rang several times and Alexandra remembered belatedly it would be the dinner hour over there. Perhaps he was out, or not in Paris at all. She let the phone continue to ring, knowing she didn't have the courage to call his cell. For some reason this was news she needed to tell him when he was in the apartment they had shared.

The other line picked up. "Hello?"

Alexandra almost dropped her phone. It was a woman's voice at the other end of the line. She forced her vocal chords to work, praying the unfamiliar voice was that of a new housekeeper and not Dimitri's newest woman. "Hello. Is Mr. Petronides available, please?"

"I'm sorry, he's out. This is Mrs. Petronides. Can I help you or would you like to leave a message?"

Mrs. Petronides. Alexandra stopped breathing. The bastard had gone through with it. He'd married another woman while Alexandra was pregnant with his child. Funny, until that very moment, she hadn't truly believed he would do it. And it was only in the absence of all hope that she realized how much she'd been living on the unspoken faith in a man who cared nothing for her and clearly never had.

"Are you there?"

"Yes."

"Did you want to leave a message for my husband?"

"No. I…" The words simply trailed into nothingness as the joy that had buoyed her up since discovering she carried Dimitri's son drained away.

"Who's calling please?" The young woman, Phoebe Leonides, no…Phoebe Petronides now, sounded impatient.

Because Alexandra was so emotionally devastated, she answered the other woman's question without thought. She couldn't think. Her brain had ceased to function. She gave the name an occupant of the Paris apartment would expect to hear. "Xandra Fortune."

"Miss Fortune, where are you? Dimitrius has been looking for you. He's desperate about the baby."

Dimitri had told his wife about her, about their baby? Alexandra pulled the phone from her ear and stared at it in her hand as if she didn't know how it had gotten there. She could hear the woman's voice, but not the words she was saying. She sounded frantic.

Alexandra cut the connection without putting the phone back to her ear.

CHAPTER THREE

DIMITRI took a sip of his neat whiskey and walked out onto the terrace of the New York high-rise apartment. It was empty, no doubt due to the chill in the air brought on by November's cooling temperatures.

He'd come late to the holiday party, at the insistence of a business acquaintance who'd told him the host was an investment banker he thought Dimitri should meet. For the past four months, Dimitri had had very little interest in making money. He'd had little interest in anything, but finding the mother of his child.

He was in New York because that was her last known whereabouts. She'd had her things shipped to a Manhattan receiving office and picked them up on the day of their arrival. One day before he had instigated a search for her. After that, there had been nothing. His investigators had been unable to find a single lead.

She'd canceled her contract with her modeling agency. She'd even closed her credit cards and checking account. No one had seen or heard from Xandra Fortune in three months.

Well, that was not strictly true. She'd called the Paris apartment four weeks ago and spoken to Phoebe. Xandra had hung up without saying why she'd called or answering Phoebe's questions about where she was. The call had been placed on an untraceable cell phone.

Dimitri still cursed whenever he thought of that ill-fated phone call. Would she have told him where she was if he had been there to answer the phone?

The sound of voices drifted out onto the almost deserted terrace and he asked himself why he'd bothered to come. He spun on his heel, intending to go when a woman caught his eye. She had her back to him. Long curling blond hair reached to the center of her back, a back that looked much too familiar. Then she moved, gripping the balcony railing and letting her head fall back as she took a deep breath of air.

"Xandra!"

She spun around to face him and his heart tightened in a painful knot, for although the woman had enough surface resemblance to Xandra to be her sister, she wasn't the model.

She smiled, even white teeth gleaming in the cool glow of the outdoor lighting. "Hello. I didn't realize anyone was out here."

"I came for the solitude," he admitted.

Her smile flashed again. "I know what you mean. I adore socializing, but once in a while the crush gets to me and I just need to breathe some air that's all my own."

He felt himself smiling for the first time in months. "Then I'll leave you to it."

She waved her hand. "There's no need. I don't mind sharing my little oasis of quiet. You said you knew Xandra?"

"Yes. I know her."

"She was an amazing model, wasn't she? She had just the right combination of innocence and passion to shoot her to supermodel status. It's too bad she refused to take any New York commissions."

"She prefers working in Europe."

Something odd passed across the woman's face. "Yes, I suppose she did."

"You keep talking about her in the past tense." Had Xandra given up modeling for motherhood?

"That's because Xandra Fortune is gone."

Everything inside him went still. "What do you mean gone?"

The blonde sighed. "According to my sister, Xandra Fortune is dead, if not buried six feet under."

The words had the effect of multiple body blows and he felt his knees begin to buckle. He reached out blindly for the balcony railing and it was only by sheer force of will that he remained standing. *"She's dead?"*

He tried to breathe, but his lungs refused to cooperate. He felt the whiskey glass in his hand break and the sharp pain of one jagged edge pressing into his hand.

"Oh, my word. Are you all right?" The woman's voice was filled with concern. "Wait right there. I'll get something for the cut and to clean up the glass."

He looked down at the blood beading against the dark skin of his hand and could not connect it to anything he felt because all he felt was numbness. Xandra was dead and his baby with her. That thought pounded through his consciousness with the power of an express train pushing away all other considerations.

It could have been minutes or hours later, but the woman returned armed with a first-aid kit and the maid behind her carrying a bowl of water and some small towels.

"Put those down on the table and close the door on your way out," the woman instructed the maid. She gave Dimitri a small smile. "I don't want an incident at the party. Hunter, my husband, doesn't like scenes."

"You said Xandra was dead." Perhaps he had misheard her.

"Yes." She bathed his hand and fixed a plaster over

the small cut with gentle efficiency. "I didn't mean to upset you. I forget that others don't know…" Her voice trailed off and he didn't press her to continue.

He didn't care if anyone else knew Xandra had died. "Was it…" He swallowed. "The baby?"

Her hands stilled in their task of putting the first-aid implements to rights. "How did you know about the baby?" Her light brown gaze pinned him and her charming air had transformed to one of suspicion.

"She told me."

"You're Dimitri Petronides?" The woman spit his name out of her mouth as if it were a foul tasting substance.

"Yes."

He didn't see the blow coming, but he felt it. Her hand landed against the side of his face with enough force to turn his head and make him stagger back a step.

"You filthy pig! I'd like to strangle you with my bare hands. How you have the gall to come here, to my home after the way you treated my sister."

"What the hell is going on out here?" Another man came storming out onto the terrace. A veritable blond giant. "What have you said to upset my wife?"

"Hunter!" The woman threw herself at her husband. "It's Dimitri Petronides. He's the one. You've got to get him out of here. If Allie sees him, she'll have a relapse. She's just started sleeping at night. Do something!"

None of the woman's words or actions had made sense since she'd told Dimitri Xandra was dead, but then how could anything make sense in the face of that devastating fact?

He turned to go, more than willing to abandon the scene.

* * *

Alexandra could hear her sister's voice raised in agitation from where she sat chatting with one of Hunter's many business associates in the penthouse's living room. She excused herself and stood up. Madeleine's voice had lowered to the point where Alexandra could not make out what her sister was saying, but the urgency was still there.

She walked through the dining room tastefully decorated in autumn colors for the Thanksgiving holiday and out onto the balcony. Madeleine was gripping Hunter's biceps and saying something about getting rid of someone. A bowl of water, tinged pink and a bloodied towel lay on the table to her right and the smell of spilled whiskey permeated the air. A small pile of broken glass lay winking in the outside lights near the outer wall of the terrace.

"Madeleine, are you all right, *chérie?*"

Madeleine whipped around, her expression horror stricken. She rushed to Alexandra and grabbed her wrist. "Come on, Allie." She started tugging.

Alexandra resisted simply because she didn't understand the urgency in her sister's voice and wanted to know the reason for it. She looked down the length of the balcony to see if she could discover the source of her sister's agitation and froze. Dimitri Petronides was heading in the opposite direction, toward the sliding glass doors leading into Hunter's study.

He stopped at the open doorway and turned. "I didn't mean to upset your wife," he said to Hunter in a voice unlike anything she had ever heard out of Dimitri's mouth.

His gaze flicked over the tableau she made with her sister pulling frantically against her arm.

His eyes appeared unfocused, as if he wasn't even seeing them. "I'll see myself out."

Then he was gone.

Again.

He'd walked away from her for the second time without a backward glance. It was no consolation that this time he would have been hard pressed to recognize her.

"I'm sorry, Allie. I don't know how he came to be here. Are you going to be all right?" Madeleine's voice buzzed in Alexandra's ears. "I slapped him." Her sister's words finally registered.

"You what?"

"I slapped him and I called him a pig."

Alexandra almost smiled. "He deserved it."

"Yes, he did."

"How did you know who he was?"

"I told him you were dead, I mean Xandra Fortune. Anyway, he asked if it was because of the baby and I just knew."

"You told him Xandra was dead?"

"Yes, she did, but it's not true is it? You're alive and I'd like to shake you both until your teeth rattle." Dimitri's fury filled voice sent Alexandra's nerves into overdrive.

Madeleine dropped Alexandra's wrist in shock. "Go away!" she shouted at Dimitri.

He towered over them, his skin an unnatural shade of gray, his eyes registering anger and a brief moment of vulnerability that disappeared before Alexandra could be certain of its existence. "I'm not going anywhere. In fact, I think it is you and your husband who need to go so Xandra and I may speak in private of affairs that do not concern you."

Madeleine opened her mouth to speak, but Alexandra

forestalled her. She pivoted her body so she faced Dimitri fully and fixed him with a bored stare. "My name is Alexandra Dupree and I'm sure you and I have nothing to discuss."

Since leaving her Xandra Fortune persona behind, she'd run into former colleagues and none of them had recognized her. She'd had her hair cut short and dyed back to the rather mousy-brown color she'd been born with. She'd ditched the green contact lenses and her body at five months pregnant in no way resembled the willow thinness of Xandra Fortune's trademark figure.

There was no reason she couldn't bluff this confrontation with Dimitri out. And a very good reason why she wanted to. She'd thought and thought about why he would tell his wife about her and the baby and the only logical solution she'd been able to come up with was that Dimitri had decided that though he no longer wanted his ex-lover, he did want their child.

Something dangerous flashed in Dimitri's indigo blue eyes. "Do not play games with me."

"I am not playing any games. If you do not believe me about who I am, I can show you identification. I've been Alexandra Dupree my whole life. I should know." She deliberately infused her voice with a New Orleans accent, one she hadn't spoken with since being sent to convent boarding school in France at the age of eight.

"Ten minutes ago I believed you to be dead."

"I can confirm without question that Xandra Fortune is indeed dead, but I am not and I am Alexandra Dupree."

He didn't even look disconcerted. "You may be Alexandra Dupree, but you are also Xandra Fortune and how you believe you could deny such truth to me, the man who knows you more intimately than any other, I cannot understand." His usual flawless English was heavily accented with Greek intonation.

"I assure you, you do not know me intimately at all." And that was the truth. If he had truly known her, he could never have suspected the baby had been fathered by someone else.

Terrible rage reflected in Dimitri's eyes before he leaned forward and swept her high against his chest, his arms as tight and inflexible as steel bands.

Madeleine shrieked, "Put her down!"

Hunter strode forward to grab Dimitri's shoulder.

Dimitri glared at him, his body tense with primitive masculine aggression. "Take your hand off me."

"I won't allow you to take my sister-in-law out of this apartment against her will."

The entire situation was unreal. Dimitrius Petronides doing something so uncool as to attempt to kidnap a pregnant woman from a party was beyond the scope of her imagination, much less believable reality.

Dimitri looked down at her, his blue gaze compelling agreement. "Tell him you want to come with me."

She glared back at him. "I don't."

Dimitri stiffened and Hunter became more menacing, but in his fury, Dimitri shrugged off Hunter's restraining hold as if it were nothing more than a wispy cobweb. He spun to face Hunter. "I'm not going to hurt her. She's mine. She's pregnant with my child and we're going to talk."

After that, neither Dimitri nor Hunter spoke for what seemed like several minutes, but was in all probability only seconds. Then something passed between the two men and much to Madeleine's dismay and Alexandra's irritation Hunter nodded.

"You can talk to her, but you'll have to do it here."

Alexandra tried to shove herself out of Dimitri's arms. "I'm not talking to him."

His hold tightened. "Be careful. If you fall, you could hurt the baby."

"What do you care about my baby?"

If possible, his expression turned grimmer. "I care."

Those two words scared her more than the thought of giving birth to a child. He was going to try to take her baby from her. She knew it. "I'm not giving you and your little Greek paragon wife my baby. I'm not!"

He shook his head. "Talk. Xandra. We need to talk."

"You didn't even believe the baby was yours at first," she said, giving up any hope at deceiving him about her identity.

Emotion passed across his chiseled features. "I do now."

"What changed your mind?" she demanded, ceasing her struggle against the increasing pressure of his hold.

He smelled like whiskey, expensive aftershave and sweat. Something had made Dimitri sweat. In fact, his hairline still showed evidence of moisture. The thought of losing his baby must have really destroyed him. She could almost feel sorry for him, but she refused to be so weak. He'd denied his paternity of their baby. He deserved what he got.

"I spoke to a doctor. He told me it was actually quite common for a woman to have one or even two menses after conceiving a child."

"So you believed some stranger over me. I'm impressed, Dimitri. It certainly shows where our relationship fit in the scheme of your life."

"He's not a stranger. He's a friend."

Who cared how well he knew the stupid doctor? "I'm not giving you my baby!" she reiterated while inside she cursed the doctor who had put her bond with her child at risk like this.

"If you don't put my sister down this instant and leave my home, I'm calling the police," Madeleine interrupted.

Eyes deadly with intent, Dimitri met Madeleine's gaze with his own inflexible one. "Go ahead." He turned to Hunter. "I'm not going anywhere without her."

Hunter sighed. "You can talk out here. We'll close off the doors to the house so you'll have some privacy."

Alexandra shuddered. She didn't want privacy with Dimitri. "If I have to talk to you, I'd rather do it somewhere public."

"You don't have to talk to him at all," Madeleine's angry voice interjected.

Hunter squeezed Madeleine's shoulder. "She's pregnant with his child, my love. They have to talk."

Her sister turned on her husband with murder in her eye. "I suppose that's some macho code all arrogant men try to live by, but I'm not standing by and watching him rip my sister into emotional shreds again. Don't you remember how she was when she got here?"

As much as she loved her sister and appreciated Madeleine's loyalty, Alexandra did not want Dimitri to know how much he had hurt her. Her pride would not take it. "Put me down. We can go to Casamir," she said, naming a French restaurant on B Avenue.

Dimitri and Madeleine said *no* at the same time. Alexandra opted to deal with her sister first. "Maddy, I want this settled."

Madeleine's eyes filled with tears. "I don't want you hurt again."

Alexandra shook her head, very certain of that if nothing else. "He can't hurt me anymore. I despise him."

Dimitri's body jerked.

She ignored the reaction and asked him, "Why can't we go to Casamir?"

"We tried to talk nicely in a public venue once and it did not work. Did you see the photos? They were all over the papers the week after my engagement to Phoebe was announced. *Wealthy Greek Tycoon Argues with Secret Pregnant Paramour*. My grandfather relapsed and had to have emergency by-pass surgery."

Alexandra stifled her urge to offer sympathy. Dimitri got nothing from her from this point forward. Nothing.

"Talk out here, Allie. You don't want your circumstances bandied about any more than Dimitri does. If pictures of you make it into the scandal rags here, your mother may not have a heart attack, but the hissy fit she'll throw won't be much of an improvement and it will all come down on your head."

Madeleine glared at her husband, but agreed. "Hunter's right. If you are going to talk to this swine it might as well be here where no sleazy journalists are waiting to quote an overheard conversation or take damaging pictures."

Dimitri's patience was wearing thin and Alexandra could feel his anger mounting. Some things, it seemed, had not changed. She could still read him like the other half of herself. She found the thought so disturbing, she buried it immediately.

"You're right. Mother is already prepared to disown me and make up some story about my early demise. We'll talk here."

She would have mistaken the breath Dimitri expelled as a sigh of relief, but she no longer believed he was capable of feeling enough vulnerability to be relieved.

With a few dire warnings to Dimitri and concerned

looks at Alexandra, Madeleine allowed Hunter to lead her from the terrace after turning on the small gas outdoor fireplace. The sound of metal sliding against metal indicated one set of doors closing. A minute of silent waiting and the second set of doors closed from the inside of the apartment. As the vertical blinds slid across the doorway and then turned to create a visual barrier against the rest of the party, Alexandra felt trapped.

She was alone with a man she used to love—a man she no longer trusted.

Dimitri didn't speak. He didn't move. He just stared at her and then at the football-size bump that indicated their baby living and growing beneath her heart. Tension arced between them and she became aware of the feel of his hard, muscular chest against her side.

"Put me down."

He seemed to snap out of a trance and his gaze shifted to hers. "Your eyes are golden. They used to be green."

"Color contacts."

"Even at night?"

"The lights were dim, or off."

"You cut your hair."

"Yes."

"It's darker."

She shrugged. He, of all people should know her natural hair color. He'd been the only one to see it in the last six years since she'd had her first bleach job and landed her first modeling contract.

"I like it."

That made her angry. He had no right to like anything about her anymore. He was a married man. "I don't care."

His eyes narrowed and his mouth set in a firm line.

She refused to cower before the signs of his anger.

"As fascinating as this discussion is, I thought you had more important issues you wanted to talk about."

He nodded. He gently lowered her into a wicker armchair before seating himself in its twin on the other side of a small wicker and glass table. Both were well away from the broken whiskey glass and first-aid supplies, but near the fireplace whose gas lit flames generated some heat.

Contrarily, she missed the warmth of his body as a slight autumn breeze caught the strands of her chin-length hair and lifted them to chilling effect. She shivered.

"You are cold. We should talk inside."

Where someone might hear? "No. It was just a breeze."

He shucked out of his coat and tucked it around her shoulders before she knew what was happening. She tried to shrug it off, but he held it in place by the lapels. "Do not be stubborn."

His nearness was doing something to her hard won emotional distance so she agreed in order to get him to back off. It didn't do a lot of good. The coat carried his scent and warmed from his body, it was like having his arms closed protectively around her. Stifling the image that thought provoked, she focused on getting down to business.

She smoothed her oversized, sage green cable knit sweater over the baby, reminding herself that possession was nine-tenths of the law and no one could deny that right now, she was the one in possession of their baby. "What is it exactly you think we have to talk about?" she asked, going on the offensive.

He looked her in the eye, his blue gaze dark with purpose. "I want my child."

CHAPTER FOUR

HE wanted her baby.

She had suspected it since her call to the Paris apartment, but hearing him say it was like being tossed into a black hole and having all the air sucked out of the universe at one time.

She put her hands protectively over her tummy as if by doing so she could somehow prevent him from carrying through on his monstrous plan. "You can't have him."

"You say *him*. Do you mean to say you know he is a boy?"

Should she lie? Would he fight any less ruthlessly for a daughter? The implacable expression on his face said not.

"Yes."

"How do you know?"

"I had an ultrasound at four months."

An expression of dawning understanding came over his hardened features. "That's why you called the apartment."

She refused to answer.

His hands fisted against the Italian suit wool covering his thighs. "You were going to tell me our baby was to be a boy." He sounded astonished by the fact.

Why shouldn't he be? He'd treated her like the lowest of the low, denied his paternity, ditched her to marry another woman and evicted her from their apartment like a bad tenant ninety days past lease. And she'd called to tell him the sex of their child. How stupidly sentimental could any one woman be?

An expression like grief passed over his face, though what he had to grieve about, she could not imagine. "And you spoke to Phoebe."

Why bother answering? He knew the details already.

"You refused to tell her where you were."

"Do you blame me?"

His jaw clenched. "Funnily enough. Yes. I can blame you. Phoebe begged you to tell her where you were and you refused. I've spent months of fruitless searching and hired no less than five world-class detective agencies, only to be told by all of them that Xandra Fortune ceased to exist."

"They were right."

"Yet, here you are."

"No. Here you see Alexandra Dupree. I will never be Xandra Fortune again." She would never allow herself to be vulnerable to the man she had loved as Xandra again, either.

"You told me you were an orphan."

She felt her mouth twist cynically. "No. That is what your agency told you when you had me investigated as a suitable candidate to be your lover. I just never denied it."

"You created an entire persona for yourself."

"Yes."

"You lied to me every day of our association."

Association? Was that anything like a relationship gone sour? "I did not lie to you."

"You let me call you Xandra."

"Many models use a working name."

"Only you lived a life completely separate from this

reality I now find in a New York apartment. That woman, Madeleine, she is your sister?"

"Yes. Hunter is her husband."

His brows rose in mockery. "I had figured that out."

She clenched her fists so she wouldn't hit him.

He laughed, but it was a sound without mirth. "Don't try it. Your sister already slapped me." He lifted his plastered hand as a silent indicator of that wound. "I'm in no mood to sustain further injury."

"Poor you," she jeered.

"Keep pushing it and my temper will override my patience."

Remembering the inimical fury he'd exhibited the day she told him of her pregnancy, she shivered. "I used to think you were such a cool guy, no scenes, no temper tantrums, all sleek sophisticated Greek male."

"Do not forget rich."

"I don't care about your filthy money. I never did."

"Yet it will be difficult for you to win against it, should you attempt to withhold my child from me."

Fear tried to take hold, but she refused to give into it. "You don't scare me. This isn't Greece. You can't take my baby away from me just because you're rich and male. United States family law is heavily balanced in the mother's favor." She'd looked into it as soon as she'd hit New York. She'd known even then that if Dimitri ever decided to claim her child, she would be facing difficulties ahead.

"Perhaps, but can you afford the constant legal battles? The draining expense of hiring top-notch lawyers to plead your case."

The picture he painted was a bleak one. "I'll do whatever it takes to keep my child."

"Anything?"

"Yes! Anything."

"Then come with your baby to my home."

That sent her to her feet in a hurry. "You arrogant toad! Do you honestly believe I would go anywhere with you after everything that has happened?"

Her stomach churned. Did he think she was such a dope that she would let him set her and their son up somewhere convenient while he lived happy families with Phoebe? Another ugly thought followed the last one. "I won't be your mistress," she hissed with enough venom to slay him.

He too shot out of his chair. "I'm not looking for a mistress."

"Good, because I won't be one. Not ever. I learned all I wanted to know about having uncommitted sex with a guy so primitive he should be in a museum. The next time I have sex with a man, I'm going to have a ring on my finger and an avowal of love to go with it!"

"Just who is this man?" he demanded in a near roar.

"I don't know, but when I find him, he won't be anything like you!"

"You think not?" Then he reached out and grabbed the lapels of his suit jacket again, yanking her to him. "I think this mythical man will be just like me because he will be me. No other man touches the mother of my child."

He'd said the words a breath above her lips and then closed the distance. And the electric current of desire was there, waiting, lurking in her deepest subconscious to come to the fore with the first touch of his mouth to hers.

She went under so fast, she didn't even have time to despise herself for her weakness. His mouth moved over hers with truly possessive passion and she responded like a woman deprived of physical intimacy for years.

Her hands locked around his neck, her body stretched to press itself to his and her mouth opened in serious invitation. He took it and deepened the kiss even as his hands caressed her back, pressing her closer to him, letting her feel his heat and his excitement. Blatant evidence of that excitement brought her to her senses and she shoved herself away from him so fast and so hard, she stumbled backward and fell flat on her bottom.

He was on his knees beside in her in a second. "You foolish woman! You could have hurt yourself. Are you trying to kill our son? Are you all right?" His hands were doing a hasty examination of her and her body was getting the wrong message entirely from those impersonal touches.

She slapped his hands away. "Stop it. I'm fine." Her bottom was sore, but she wasn't about to tell him that. "Babies are resilient. I'm not going to lose him from such a small fall." *Oh Lord, please let that be true.*

"You would take such a risk?" He glared at her. "What other risks have you taken with our child?"

If she'd had a gun, she would have shot him, or at least at him...to scare him a little and wipe that condescending look of censure off his face. "It's not my fault you acted like a lecher and kissed me. What was I supposed to do, tolerate it?"

He swelled with affronted pride. "You have never merely tolerated my kiss in your life."

She had no argument to that, so she didn't try making one. "Married men are not supposed to kiss women other than their wives," she said instead.

He shrugged. "I agree. Does this worry you?"

Was he for real? Of course it worried her. He was

married to Phoebe and he'd just soul-kissed Alexandra. "Am I crazy, or are you?" she asked, feeling helplessly bewildered.

His mouth twisted in a grimace. "I have been crazy since the first report from the private investigators trying to locate you. They had not a single lead and you had disappeared in one of the largest cities in the world."

He tucked the suit coat around her slender shoulders once again, then leaned down and lifted her in his arms. Was there something about imminent fatherhood that made the male of the species go all basic? She could remember only one other time he'd carried her during their year together and that had been one night she'd had a little too much champagne and fallen asleep in the car on the way home.

Yet, tonight, he'd picked her up like he owned her. Twice. "Please put me down, Dimitri." It was a sign of how vulnerable she felt that she made it a request instead of a demand.

Either way, he did not comply. "I do not think I should. You are too volatile right now."

She closed her eyes in frustration. "I'll control myself if you keep your hands and lips to yourself."

"I cannot promise this."

"Poor Phoebe. Does she know what an unfaithful letch she is married to?"

"Phoebe is married to a man of absolute honor," he replied, his voice laced with furious affront.

"You? Don't make me laugh," she scorned. A man with integrity did not marry one woman after impregnating another.

Dimitri sat down, keeping Alexandra pinned in his lap. His blue gaze scorched into hers. "You believe I am married to Phoebe? And you believe I have no honor?'' The last was said with escalating anger.

"I suppose you're going to try to tell me you're not married to your little Greek paragon."

"This is true. I am not."

Alexandra closed her eyes. She didn't know why, but she hadn't expected him to lie to her. She opened them again and stared into his deceitful face. "She told me she was your wife, so you can just forget about the smoothy deceptions."

"She would not have told you she was my wife." His voice was filled with such conviction that Alexandra thought back to the devastating phone call.

"She told me she was Mrs. Petronides."

"But then she told you she was married to my brother."

"What?"

"She told you she had wed my brother."

"She did no such thing!" But she could have. Alexandra remembered the voice still talking as she'd ended the call.

Dimitri wouldn't let her look away from him, his compelling eyes holding hers hostage. "She did."

"But..."

"She also pleaded with you to tell her where you were."

Alexandra remembered that part. "I wasn't about to have a heart-to-heart with your new wife."

"She is not my wife."

"Prove it."

In his shock at her demand, Dimitri's grip loosened and Alexandra extricated herself from his lap, this time much more carefully. "You say you are not married to Phoebe Petronides. Well, I don't trust you anymore,

Dimitri. If you want me to believe it, you'll have to bring me proof."

He shot to his feet again, all outraged male. "How dare you question my word?"

"You wouldn't believe how easy it is," she admitted.

That seemed to shake him. "I will get you the proof you require," he said angrily.

"Fine. Until then, I suggest you go."

"I am not letting you out of my sight again."

"What do you propose, setting up camp outside my sister's door and dogging my every footstep?"

"Count on it, but I have no desire to sleep in a hallway. You can come with me to my suite."

"No way. I'm not staying in a hotel room with you."

"There are two bedrooms, though there was a time you would not have required the other one."

She glared at his, to her mind, savagely insensitive reminder. "Forget it. I'm not going."

"Then I will stay here. It is a large apartment. I'm sure your sister has a spare room I could use."

She felt flummoxed. "You can't stay here. Madeleine would have a hissy fit. She hates you."

He shrugged his broad shoulders. "Speaking of hissy fits, your brother-in-law implied your mother would have one if you were featured in a scandalous article."

Alexandra couldn't prevent her eyes from rolling in exasperation. "Yes." She'd spent six years living as someone else to protect her mother's sense of family dignity. *Dupree women did not work.*

Only this generation of Dupree women would have been out on the street if one of them hadn't ignored the old money heritage and gotten a job to support the family. The cousin of a friend from school had offered her a modeling contract. She'd taken it with one proviso…she work anonymously under an assumed name. He'd gone one better and helped her create Xandra Fortune, French orphan turned fashion model.

Dimitri was speaking again. "She would be most upset to see an exposé interview with her daughter's discarded tycoon lover and rejected father of her child."

Her body didn't know whether to go faint or boil with fury at his implied threat and twisting of the facts. "I didn't discard you. You dumped me to marry Phoebe, the Greek *virgin* bride, or don't you remember?"

"I am not married to Phoebe."

"You don't have to have committed a murder to be guilty of a crime."

Instead of getting angrier, he smiled. "Are you saying you believe I did not marry her?"

"No!"

"You still require proof?"

"Yes."

"Then you'll have to convince your sister to give me a bed for the night because I'm not letting you out of my sight."

"And if I don't, you're going to make sure my family's name gets a good smearing in the tabloids, is that it?" she asked with all the derision at her disposal.

He didn't even flinch. "Yes."

"I despise you."

"Not hate?"

"No. I don't love you anymore, but I refuse to hate you. Part of you is in my child and I won't ever have my child believing there is anything about him I could hate." Her son deserved better than a mother eaten up by bitterness.

A look she could not decipher settled on Dimitri's

chiseled features. "That is commendable. Now, shall we talk to your sister about my accommodation?"

In the end, Alexandra decided it would be better to accompany Dimitri to his suite. The mere thought of trying to work out the current complications in her life with her younger sister breathing fire at Dimitri left her cold. Alexandra did not want Madeleine and Hunter forced into a position of enmity with a man of Dimitri's wealth and power because of her.

Going to Dimitri's suite was the only workable solution. It wasn't going to be all that bad, she decided. She didn't need to worry about Dimitri getting to her. She was well and truly over him. The kiss had just been physical reaction to memories and she wouldn't let it happen again.

All that was left between them was to determine how they would handle his role in her son's life.

If anyone had asked Alexandra two days ago the chances of her sitting down to breakfast with Dimitri in his hotel suite, she would have said nil. Nada. Zilch. Absolutely not one. Yet, here they sat. She pushed her eggs and fruit around the plate of breakfast room service had provided minutes earlier. He eyed her with calculating regard.

She knew what he saw. A positive hag. She hadn't been able to sleep again last night, not with the knowledge that Dimitri rested on the other side of the wall. Her eyes looked bruised while her complexion wore its usual sallow tint from her pregnancy. Most women finished with morning sickness at three to four months. Not Alexandra. She still woke up every day feeling like she had the flu and she was in her fifth month.

Her one consolation was Dimitri didn't look much

better. She'd been too overwrought to notice it the night before, but he'd lost weight and there were new lines around his eyes. His grandfather's illness coupled with the search for his unborn child must have taken their toll on the man usually untouched by human frailty.

"You need to stop playing with your food and eat it."

Her head snapped up. "Don't tell me what to do."

He leaned back in his chair on the other side of the small walnut table and smiled. "It appears someone needs to. I have always heard pregnant women glow. You look as if you've just come off a nine-day flu."

Stupid tears filled her eyes. She knew she wasn't the beautiful model he'd gone to great lengths to get in his bed any longer, but did he have to rub it in? She gritted her teeth and blinked her eyes, trying to rid them of their wet sheen.

She hated the emotional weakness she'd experienced since getting pregnant. "It's a good thing I'm not trying to make a living as a model any longer then, isn't it?"

He reached across the table, grabbing her hand before she had a chance to pull it away. "I did not say you are no longer beautiful, merely that you look unwell."

She jerked her hand out from under his as the warmth of his skin burned into her own. "I'm pregnant." It was fine for him to sit there looking a bit worse for the wear, but still sexy as sin and in sickeningly good health.

"Yes, but not happily so from the look of things."

"Are you trying to imply I don't want my baby?"

He exhaled an impatient breath. "I think the fact you are five months into an obviously difficult pregnancy is ample proof you want my child."

"I don't want *your* child. I want *this* baby."

His lips creased in a devilish grin. "Same thing."

Unwilling to agree on any point, but equally unwilling to deny the truth, she remained silent and took a bite of ripe melon, savoring its sweet and juicy freshness in her mouth. "I want this baby and I'm keeping him. Do you hear me?"

His mouth twisted. "Have I at any time implied that you should not?"

"You told me you wanted my son."

"You believe I am married to Phoebe, therefore I must want the baby without the mother?" His hands lifted in an expression of exasperation she knew well. "Do I have this right?"

She wasn't totally certain any longer, so she shrugged. He could make what he liked of it.

"Your opinion of me is very low," he said grimly, all humor gone from his countenance. "I should have the proof you need of Phoebe's marriage to Spiros within the hour."

She remained mute. She'd believe it when she saw it. It wasn't his brother Spiros who had announced his engagement to the young Greek heiress.

"I can see it is of no use attempting to talk with you until I have the documents."

"I don't want to talk to you at all," she admitted.

It was a useless sentiment. She was pregnant with his child. They would have to come to terms eventually, but those terms would not include her giving up her baby.

"Do not play the child."

She forced herself to eat a bite of her eggs. Their fluffy warmth tasted like sawdust on her tongue. She had believed she was even tempered before she met Dimitri.

"You said you are no longer modeling to support yourself."

She nodded, wary of where this was leading. She

didn't want to give away any more information than she had to.

"What are you doing now?"

"Maybe I'm just living off Hunter's largess." She knew the idea of another man supporting her while she was pregnant with his child would infuriate Dimitri.

Sure enough, his eyes narrowed. "Are you?"

"I'm living with them," she pointed out.

He just waited and when she remained silent, he sighed. "I already have five reputable detective agencies on my retainer. Now that I know the name you are living under, it should be a matter of a phone call or two to elicit the information."

"I'm working as a translator and interpreter for an agency that sends out temps."

His blue eyes narrowed and his jaw tightened. "You go out to work for strangers?" He made it sound like she was some sort of call girl or something.

"It's not that different from doing a modeling assignment."

"But then you knew the photographers, the other models."

She pushed her plate aside and took a sip of herbal tea. "What difference does it make?"

"You are pregnant and obviously ill." His gaze wandered over her with tactile force. "You should not be working."

If he didn't want Hunter supporting her, how did he expect her to live? "I have to support myself. I refuse to be my younger sister's charity case."

"Why have you not returned to your parents' home?"

A traditional Greek man who shared the loving rapport he had with his grandfather could never understand the complicated relationship she had with her mother. "I'm not welcome," was all she said.

"This cannot be. You are pregnant with their grandchild. Surely your parents desire to care for you at this time."

"My father died six years ago and my mother is only willing for me to return to New Orleans and the family home if I invent a fictitious husband who conveniently died recently or lives overseas. It's positively draconian, but that's the way she is. She refuses to even discuss the baby and hasn't come to visit Madeleine since I moved in."

His jaw set. "You refused to invent this pretend spouse?"

"Yes." She'd rather live without her mother's approval than continue pretending to be something and someone she wasn't.

"It will be a relief for her then that the real and in fact living father of your child will soon be your husband as well."

CHAPTER FIVE

"As jokes go, that's not a very good one."

He fixed her with an impenetrable stare. "I am not joking, *pethi mou*."

"Don't call me that. It's an endearment and I'm not dear to you which only makes it an insult."

He shoved his plate away from him in an uncharacteristic show of temper. "My marriage proposal is a joke and endearments an insult. Is there nothing I can do right with you?"

"You could leave me alone."

His blue eyes darkened to the color of the sky just before midnight. "This I will not do."

She forced another bite of melon down, its succulent juiciness lost on her. "I figured as much."

"Then why suggest it?"

"Wishful thinking?"

"Do not be facetious. This is a serious discussion we are having here."

"What exactly are we discussing? Your attempt at bigamy?"

His fist slammed down on the table, causing the dishes and plates to clatter alarmingly. "I am not married."

She eyed him warily, almost believing him. Maybe, deep down, she did believe him, but some imp in her wanted him to prove it, to see how it felt to have his word questioned on a claim that should be accepted without hesitation.

"So you said. Proof is to arrive within the hour, or

63

something like that..." She waved her hand in an airy gesture.

"Right," he gritted out between clenched teeth.

She really had to stop baiting him. "Let's say I believe you. Why would your brother marry your fiancée?"

"As I told you last night, your and my relationship came as a great shock to my family." Pain crossed his features. "The photographer did his homework and had chapter and verse on our year-long association. My brother was appalled on Phoebe's behalf. She'd been made to look a fool, something his perception of our family honor could not tolerate."

"So he married her? Wouldn't your intended marriage have been just as efficacious?"

"No. I was the philanderer, the one caught with my pants down in public so to speak."

She swallowed a smile at the imagery. Dimitri Petronides in such a vulnerable position was something she'd give a great deal to see. "I can't believe you agreed to let your fiancée marry your brother."

"He convinced her to elope with him. Her pride was saved. Our family honor was saved and now I am free to marry you."

He looked for all the world like he expected her to leap for joy and congratulate him on his good planning. She would have rather dumped his coffee in his lap. "Charming. You can marry your pregnant mistress now that the virginal bride-to-be has flown the coop. Thanks, but no thanks."

"Do you think our son will thank *you* for denying him his heritage, his Greek family, his role as my heir?"

"We don't have to be married for you to make our

son your heir or for you to be part of his life. You can have access."

"Of what good is this? You live an ocean away. How can I be his father with two continents and an ocean between us?"

"I don't know." She stood up wearily. She had to get ready to go to work. She had an assignment in two hour's time across town. "You'll have to forgive me for not having all the answers just yet. You ditched me three months ago, certain the baby I carried was not yours. I haven't been thinking in terms of parental sharing and visitation rights."

He stood as well. "Where are you going?"

"I have an assignment in a couple of hours. I'm going to get ready."

"I told you I am not allowing you out of my sight."

"Then come along," she offered sarcastically, "but I'm going to work."

She came to rue those flippantly uttered words. Dimitri insisted on doing just that. In addition, he refused to take a cab, but had his car called, along with his two bodyguards. It had been a while since she went out with security men in tow, a little over three months to be exact.

Dimitri refused to wait in the car while she did the short translation job for the group of French tourists. She walked beside the tour guide, translating the woman's rapid dialogue concerning the Empire State Building into French while Dimitri and his bodyguards brought up the rear of the line.

It would have been a comical sight if she wasn't so tired and stressed. By the time she slid into his car for the ride back to his hotel, she was disgustingly grateful she hadn't had to wait in line for a taxi. She didn't even have enough energy to enjoy looking at the city's Christmas decorations out the limousine's window. Commenting on her drooping appearance, he insisted on stopping for lunch at one of Manhattan's upscale Italian restaurants.

Alexandra walked back into the main room of the suite from her bedroom just as Dimitri was turning from the fax machine, several sheets of paper in his hand. She'd avoided him since their return by the simple expedient of taking a nap. For some reason, she'd slept better than she had in ages.

Dimitri waved the papers before her. "Proof."

"Proof?" She was still a little rummy from the nap and didn't know what he was talking about until she looked down and read the top sheet. "Oh."

She put out her hand for the sheaf of papers and he gave them to her. The first one was a marriage license. It was in Greek, but she was now almost as conversant in that language as she was in both English and French. She easily translated the names and the male listed was *Spiros* Petronides, not Dimitri.

The second one was a photo of Spiros and Phoebe in wedding regalia. Phoebe looked a little shell-shocked. Spiros looked arrogantly satisfied. Typical Petronides male.

The third was a letter from Spiros affirming Dimitri's account of the situation. This one was in English.

Alexandra took a deep breath, feeling an emotion she should not be feeling. Unadulterated relief. She told herself it was because she didn't have to worry about the complications of a stepmother being around the baby so early in life, but her heart mocked her. And that scared her to death.

"Why was she at our apartment?" She didn't notice her slip of the tongue until a look of approval settled over Dimitri's face. "I mean *your* apartment. I was evicted," she added for good measure, wiping the not fully formed smile off his face.

"I have had to take over the Athens office completely since Grandfather's first heart attack. Spiros and Phoebe moved to Paris so he could run the office there. I gave them the apartment as a wedding present."

"Is that something like conscience money? You felt guilty for embarrassing her with a public tiff with your discarded mistress, so you gave her the apartment you'd evicted me from?"

She should have kept her mouth shut. She really should have, but she couldn't seem to remember that when she was around him. His eyes snapped fury at her as he took one menacing step forward after another. She backed up, but eventually hit the wall between the main room and her bedroom.

"It was a joke," she said weakly.

"This is not."

Then his mouth closed over hers and she forgot he was only doing it to punish her. She forgot everything but how incredible it felt to be held so close to him, to taste him on her tongue, to be surrounded with his smell, his heat, his desire.

She worked her hands into the space between his jacket and his shirt, reveling in the feel of his muscles under her exploring fingers. He shuddered and she exulted in her power over this dominant Greek male. He pulled her to him, pressing their bodies as close as they could go without taking off their clothes. It wasn't close enough.

She started unbuttoning his shirt as he slid her sweater

up to expose the tight skin over her womb. His hand settled on it and he caressed her there, touching every square centimeter of the football-size lump. The baby moved and Dimitri stopped kissing her to stare down at his hand on her stomach in awe. The baby kicked right in the center of his palm and Dimitri's eyes slid shut, his breath stilling in his chest.

He let it out very slowly and met her eyes. "My son."

"Yes," she whispered, unable to deny such a poignant claim.

Triumph glowed in his indigo gaze before his mouth settled over hers again, this time with such gentleness she felt tears seep out of the corner of her eyes. He kissed her lips as if meeting them for the first time, while his hand continued to explore the new contours of her body.

His possessive touch coupled with the tenderness of his kiss completely undermined any resistance and she fell back into the kiss without a murmur.

She had his buttons undone and her fingers were circling his hardened male nipples when a shrill sound filtered through the passionate haze in her mind. She crashed back to reality with a bruising emotional bump. *What was she doing?*

She tore her mouth from his. "The phone."

His eyes were glazed with desire and his skin had that flushed look he got when they made love. He tried to catch her mouth again and she turned her head.

"The phone," she repeated as it rang again, its piercing jangle skating across her nerves.

He gently pulled the elasticized band of Alexandra's doeskin pants back to waist level before smoothing her caramel colored crocheted sweater back into place.

"This is not over," he said and then turned to answer the phone.

She walked to the other side of the suite, wanting to get as much distance between them as she could. She'd been so sure she was safe from her attraction to Dimitri, certain her feelings for him were dead. She might not love him anymore, but she wanted him and her pulsing body proved it.

"Yes, Grandfather." Dimitri went silent, apparently listening. "I remember." He cast Alexandra an assessing look. "It's being handled."

Why did she have the lowering suspicion the *it* being handled was her?

Dimitri made a few more remarks in Greek, asked his Grandfather about his health, listened silently, said goodbye and hung up. He turned to face her and she couldn't suppress a shiver. His eyes glowed like those of a predator with his prey firmly in his sights.

She stepped backward even though he hadn't made a move toward her. "That was a mistake."

He didn't ask what *that* was, he merely smiled. "I don't think so. It did not feel like a mistake to me *pethi mou.*"

"I'm not falling back into your bed, Dimitri."

"Are you certain of this?" he asked lazily.

"*Yes.*"

"We shall see."

"I think I'll order room service. I'm hungry." Her appetite had increased over the past couple of days. Maybe the awful morning sickness was finally passing.

"I have a better idea."

"What?" she asked, feeling wary.

"Let's go out."

"I don't know…" Being seen in public with a man

of Dimitri's wealth was always a risk for media exposure.

His eyes warmed with sensual lights. "We can stay here if you prefer."

"I'll get my jacket." A woman had to know how to weigh her options and the risk of staying in the suite with a sexually charged Dimitri far outweighed her concern about being caught in his company by the media.

The muted glow of candlelight lent entirely too intimate an aspect to Alexandra's dinner with Dimitri. He'd surprised her once again by taking her to one of the *see and be seen* restaurants so popular among the sophisticated New York social set. Dim lighting didn't stop recognition and surreptitious glances from one table to another.

Alexandra tried to concentrate on the food in front of her and ignore her compelling dinner companion. Dimitri had ordered a much larger meal for her than she usually ate and she had surprised herself by consuming almost all of it. The same thing had happened at lunch that afternoon. If nothing else, sparring with her ex-lover seemed to spur her appetite.

"Xandra—"

"My name is Alexandra," she said, before he could complete his sentence. "Xandra Fortune is dead."

Something passed across his face when she made that statement, but in the dim lighting she couldn't tell if it was pain or irritation. "You had no plans to go back to modeling after the baby was born?" he asked, conspicuously using the past tense for her plans, implying she had new ones.

"No."

He studied her like a man trying to decipher a complicated puzzle. "Why?"

"There were many reasons."

"Very cryptic." He smiled in a way that used to send her pulse to hyperspeed. "Tell me some of them."

She gave a mental shrug. Why not? This at least was better than arguing over custody rights and his insulting notion that now he believed her about the baby she should fall all over herself getting to the altar before he changed his mind.

"I want to spend more time with my baby than that type of career would allow and it would be too difficult to maintain two separate lives with a baby in tow. It was hard enough for me, but I think a life like that would be confusing and probably even frightening for a child."

He mulled that over much longer than she thought necessary. "Explain to me again why the Xandra Fortune image."

Had she explained it a first time? She couldn't remember. She knew she'd alluded to it. "My mother did not approve of my working. *Dupree women do not work*," she said in a fair imitation of her mother's soft Southern drawl. "But it was my choice of career that really upset her. The idea of her daughter traversing a catwalk in front of her peers or worse, doing swimsuit or lingerie ads sent her into hysterics."

"You chose to create a different persona rather than give up your desire to become a model?" he asked.

"I didn't have a choice. It was either pick up a career or see my mother dispossessed and my sister thrown out of boarding school for nonpayment of tuition."

"Explain this to me. Where was your father?"

"Dead."

"That is unfortunate. You have my belated condolences." The words were formal, but the emotion in his voice left her in no doubt to his sincerity.

"Thank you. He was a dear man, a fossil collector. Old bones interested him; business did not. Unbeknownst to the rest of us, the family had been living completely on credit for two years before he died."

"When did this happen?"

"Six years ago. I'd just graduated from my last year at Our Lady's Bower and thankfully the cousin of a school chum had shown some interest in my modeling for his magazine." She took another bite of her lobster fettuccine. It practically melted in her mouth.

"Our Lady's Bower sounds like a convent, or something."

"It is. Dupree girls have been French convent educated for the last six generations."

"No wonder it was so easy for you to adopt a French persona. Your accent is flawless, your gestures often gallic and your outlook quite European."

"Yes." She'd selected France for the debut of Xandra Fortune for those very reasons.

"Go on," Dimitri prompted.

She grimaced. "There's not much else to tell. Mother would have ignored the redundancy notices until the sheriff showed up to evict us from our home. Madeleine still had two years left at Our Lady's Bower and I couldn't bear for her to lose that stability after we'd all just lost Papa."

"So you went to work."

"Under an assumed name. I was trying to spare my mother's feelings. It didn't work."

"She could not reconcile herself to the thought of her daughter working?"

"No." She smiled ruefully. "I've always felt guilty,

that I had failed her, but I simply could not think what else to do. I hadn't gone to college yet. I was too young for most well paid career choices. Modeling looked like my only option. My friend's cousin helped me create Xandra Fortune. It was cloak and dagger stuff and he really got into it. He made sure the only people who knew about Alexandra Dupree's connection to Xandra Fortune were me, my family and him."

"So this man knew you were Alexandra Dupree, but I, your lover for a year did not." He sounded mortally offended.

"Got it in one. I didn't know about Phoebe, the patiently waiting bride-to-be, either. I guess we're even on that score." Her throat felt dry from all the talking and she took a long cool sip of water.

He didn't take the bait, surprising her. "Your mother's sensibilities are the reason you refused New York assignments."

"Yes. I never took an assignment in the States period. I was careful to avoid doing commercials for international products and as you know, I tried to stay out of the media limelight in my personal life."

"Yet, you were well-known in Europe."

"Yes, but only as a French model, not a supermodel. My biggest claim to fame was being your lover and you were careful to keep that fact under wraps."

"Not completely," he said enigmatically. "You did your family a great service and your mother should be proud of you."

His words warmed her, but Alexandra felt a burble of laughter well up and let it out. "*Proud of me?* Her scandalous *working* daughter who got pregnant without the benefit of matrimony? She hadn't forgiven me yet for not saving the family home. I'll be the black sheep of the family forever at the rate I'm going.'' She tried to hide the hurt that knowledge caused her. She didn't want Dimitri to see her weakness.

"Your mother lost her home?"

"My income as a model kept my mother in Chanel suits and provided a complete education for my sister. She graduated from Smith a month before she married Hunter last year." Pride in Madeleine's accomplishment tinged Alexandra's voice.

Then she sighed. "The money did not stretch far enough to keep up payments on a heavily mortgaged mansion and the staff necessary to run it. Mother was forced to sell and move into a converted apartment serviced by a daily maid. Although it's still in a socially acceptable New Orleans neighborhood, it is not the Dupree Mansion."

"And she blames you for this? Not your irresponsible father who left his wife and daughters in debt?"

She didn't take exception to Dimitri's view of her father. Dimitri was a responsible guy, someone who would never leave his family in the lurch. He couldn't comprehend a man who had absolutely no sense about money.

"Mama doesn't exactly blame me for losing the mansion, but she was furious when I wouldn't stop modeling after it was sold. She would have much preferred I married well rather than work to support her and Madeleine."

"But you did not wish to marry well?"

"I wanted to marry a man I loved, not a bank account."

"Then it should please you to marry me. If the words you spoke at *Chez Renée* were true, I can give you both."

"They were true then," so much so that parts of her heart were still cracked and bleeding after the abrupt way they'd broken up, "but I don't love you anymore."

"I refuse to believe a woman of such strong character could fall out of love at the first sign of adversity."

She was beginning to have a horrible suspicion he was right, but she wasn't about to feed his smug pride admitting it. "I wouldn't call you ejecting me from your life with the force of a rocket launcher so you could marry another woman the first sign of adversity."

"Yet I did not marry her."

"Because your brother beat you to the punch."

He sighed. "You are sure I would have married her otherwise?"

Why was he asking her that? Of course she was sure. He'd made his position very clear that last meeting in Paris. "Yes."

"If I told you I had already decided not to go through with the marriage, you would not believe me, hmm?"

Was he saying that? No. This was just another one of his subtle manipulations. "Don't tax your personal integrity making the claim. You're right. I wouldn't buy it."

"And yet I had hired a detective agency to find you within days of you leaving Paris."

"I waited for you to change your mind for a whole week, Dimitri. You didn't even call. I can believe you started to consider the consequences if I'd told the truth about the baby, but I don't think you were prepared to call off your wedding because of it. *I* didn't matter to you then, and I don't matter to you now. It's all about the baby and I'm not stupid enough to forget that."

His hand gripped his wine glass very tightly. The

same hand that still wore a bandage from the night he'd come to Madeleine and Hunter's party.

"How did you cut yourself? I never asked." Her mind had been on other things that night.

He carefully put his wine glass down, staring at it as if it held the answer to an important question. Then he looked up at her and she gasped.

His eyes held a torment that was haunting.

"When Madeleine told me you were dead, I crushed the glass in my hand."

CHAPTER SIX

DIMITRI'S statement hung in the air between them like a bomb that had not exploded, but still might.

"You were that upset at the prospect of losing your child?" She had not considered Dimitri's emotional involvement with their baby. Which wasn't all that surprising considering she'd seen him as an emotionless monster for the past three months.

His jaw tautened. "If it pleases you to believe so, yes."

"I'm sorry."

He inclined his head. "With your background, you should understand the importance of our child being raised in his home country of Greece and as a Petronides."

That was more like it. Dimitri wanted his son because family pride demanded he be raised Petronides. "I understand the importance of loving my baby for his own sake, not the sake of family pride. Whether he's raised a Dupree or Petronides, he will still be worthy of my love. Can you say the same?"

Dimitri's features took on the cast of the Iceman. "Apparently you do not believe me capable of any level of emotion, so why should I bother answering?"

She'd hurt him, wounded his sense of self and for some reason, she simply couldn't bear that. "I didn't mean—"

"Leave it. Do you want dessert?"

"No." She couldn't eat anything now.

"Then we will return to the suite. If we are to have yet another argument, we will do it in privacy."

The drive back to his hotel was a silent one. She felt guilty and kept telling herself she shouldn't, but the feeling remained. Just because Dimitri did not love her did not mean he was not capable of loving his son. She'd had no right to imply that it did.

She was still trying to work up to an apology when he let them both into the suite a half an hour later.

"Dimitri, I—"

"I said leave it." He rubbed his forehead. "I'm tired."

His admission of weakness stunned her.

His lips twisted wryly. "You think I cannot get exhausted like the next man? We all have our limits, *pethi mou*."

He hadn't in the twelve months she'd lived with him.

"I have not slept well for the three months I have searched for you," he further shocked her by admitting. "I believed once I found you, everything would fall into place. You would agree to marry me. We would be on the next plane to Greece so you could meet my grandfather. I believed I would have to assuage your anger, I did not expect to find a woman who hated me."

"I don't hate you," she averred, "I told you that."

"You do not wish to hate me for our child's sake. I understand this, but you do not want to marry me. You do not trust me. I am at a loss where to go from here. Just as you saw modeling as the only solution to your family's financial difficulties, I see marriage as the only workable solution to our situation."

It was her turn to sigh. "I know you do."

"And I am sexually frustrated." His laugh was harsh. "I don't like going without."

She didn't know if she could handle Dimitri in this strange mood. She was used to him taking charge, demanding. His admissions of weakness surprised her silly. "It hasn't been that long, surely?"

"I have not made love to another woman since the night I told you I was marrying Phoebe."

For a hopelessly oversexed male like Dimitri that was a lifetime. No wonder he wasn't himself. She didn't know why he had abstained, but something deep inside her was fiercely glad he had. "I see."

"I doubt it, but maybe you will someday." All tiredness disappeared from his expression to be replaced with predatory sensuality. "You could help me out."

She backed toward her bedroom. "I think I'll make an early night of it, t-take a shower, m-maybe read a book."

He'd already proven she couldn't resist him physically. She wasn't about to stick around and offer herself as the main course to end his months long sexual fast.

She took the image of his primitive smile with her as she closed the door to her bedroom. She pushed the lock in for good measure and took her first unhindered breath in five minutes. She couldn't let him make love to her again. She was too vulnerable to him and she needed to think. She wouldn't be able to do that with any sense of clarity while under the influence of his passionate nature.

Her eyes closed, Alexandra rinsed the lather from her hair, enjoying the feel of hot water cascading over her body from three different directions.

The luxury of the spa shower had even won out over a long soak in the oversized, jetted tub. Two showerheads shot warm showers of water toward her body from chest height while another sent down a gentle spray from above her head. She felt completely pampered in the glass and tile enclosure.

So pampered that she was almost able to push her chaotic thoughts away, but not quite. Somehow, she had to work things out with Dimitri. He had as much right to love their son as she did and more importantly, their child had a right to two loving parents if possible. Dimitri had made it clear such an eventuality was possible, *but he did not love her.*

Was it right though, for her to make her child pay the price for her own unfulfilled dreams? And their son would pay a price if she refused to marry Dimitri. He would be born outside the bonds of matrimony. For many that would not matter, but among his Greek family and future business associates, it would.

Her own mother might never accept him. While that made Alexandra furious, she knew there was little she could do to turn around a lifetime of conditioning. Her mother's belief system was as ingrained as a fossil in rock.

In his fossil research, her father had often been forced to leave rock sediment on one of his specimens because to remove it would be to destroy the fossil. She didn't want to destroy her mother. She didn't even want to upset her. Because despite her mother's irritating habit of seeing the world only from her own point of view, Alexandra loved her and wanted her to be happy.

Wishing she could brush her troubling thoughts away so easily, Alexandra swiped the water from her eyes and opened them…to blackness. She blinked, but no light penetrated the darkness surrounding her. Had there been a power outage? Didn't all the larger hotels have generators?

Suddenly the stream of water pulsing down on her head ceased. The two other showerheads kept going however, leaving her feeling disoriented. She fought down panic as she reached out to touch the tile of the wall for a sense of reference and touched bare flesh instead.

For an instant her brain could not take in the significance of the hair roughened, heated flesh under her agitated fingers. What...? Then, "Dimitri?" whispered because she couldn't force more volume from the frozen muscles in her throat.

"It is I." His voice surrounded her with more warmth than the steam from the hot water flowing over both their bodies.

"You shouldn't be here."

An arm wrapped around her waist and pulled her forward. "Should I not?" he asked against her shocked lips.

"No. I don't want this." Did she sound as unconvincing to him as she sounded to herself?

Knowing fingers brushed gently over nipples that had gone turgid and aching the moment she realized his naked body stood so close to her own. "Are you sure about that?"

"We need to talk," she tried again, while her body shook with the need to melt into his.

"No," he said with harsh emphasis. "We have talked enough. It gets us nowhere, but this..." He squeezed her nipple between thumb and forefinger and she could not stifle her moan. "This I can give you."

"Sex won't solve our problems. It's what started them

in the first place,'' she said, trying one last time to keep hold of her senses.

"*No.* It was not the sex. When we make love it is like a poem of rare beauty and beat. Words have brought this distance between us. My words. Your words. I will not let it continue. I cannot let it continue."

The urgency in his voice affected her as deeply as the emotive words and she felt tears burn the back of her throat. He was right. Their distance had been caused by words. Making love had never been anything but beautiful between them, even that last tempestuous time.

She couldn't stand the distance any longer either, but undoubtedly for a different reason. There in the steamy darkness, she accepted a truth her heart had been telling her all along. She was not over Dimitri Petronides. She would never be over him. The love she felt for him was too strong, too deeply imbedded in her.

Again it was the fossil in the rock, only this time she knew with absolute certainty that to try to rip the love she felt for him from her breast would destroy her completely.

She made a noise of need and longing. His arm tightened around her, bringing her body flush with his own. Familiar lips closed over hers in a kiss so passionate, she felt scorched by the heat of it. Dimitri nibbled impatiently at her bottom lip until she opened her mouth and then he was inside, laying claim to her softness and reminding her of the incredible physical bond they had once shared. A bond that rejection, distance and time had not been able to sever.

Hungry for the feel of him, she let her fingers trail over the musculature of his chest. His mouth broke from hers and she sensed his head falling back as his body shuddered. "Yes, *moro mou,* touch me. I need you to touch me."

She had no hesitation about obliging him. She'd tried to hide from it, but she'd missed him so much. She circled the hard little nubs of his nipples, making him grind his already pulsingly erect flesh against her stomach.

Memories of how that flesh felt filling her would have sent her to her knees, but for the almost bruising hold he had on her waist. Running her hands up his chest and over his shoulders, she got drunk on the ability to touch him once again. She leaned forward and took one nipple into her mouth. Gently she teased it with her teeth and small flicks on the very tip with her tongue. He was moving against her with almost uncontrolled desire and she loved it.

If nothing else, she knew that in this, he was hers… completely.

She started sucking on that same erotic bit of flesh and Dimitri made hoarse sounds of need from deep in his throat. Then his hands were on either side of her face, exerting light pressure to her head. She let go of his nipple with reluctance.

"I want it to be so good for you, you will never leave me again," he vowed with a fervency that was almost frightening.

He pushed against her shoulders until she was leaning against the slick wet tile wall at the back of the square shower cubicle. "Press your hands to the wall."

She did it because she couldn't seem to stop herself.

"Do not move them."

"Dimitri?"

"Trust me."

In this, he had never hurt her and she knew deep in her heart, he never would. "All right."

Masculine fingers traced her cheeks until one brushed her lips and pressed inside. She felt warmth flood her between her legs as she sucked on that hot finger sliding in and out of her mouth. He continued the light tracing of her skin with his other hand, brushing down over her collarbone to her left breast. He stopped there, exploring her new shape brought on by changes from her pregnancy.

It was fuller and more sensitive. He seemed to sense this and kept his touch feather light as he used all five fingers in a cone motion encircling her entire breast. He brought his hand toward himself, bringing his fingers together as he did so until they circled her distended peak. He squeezed lightly and then did the entire motion all over again, and again, and again until she felt feverish with the need for his mouth on it.

"Dimitri, please… Your mouth…"

He laughed huskily. "Not yet, hmm?" Then he pulled his hand from her mouth and gave the same treatment to her other breast until her head was thrashing back and forth against the wall in an agony of need.

"Please…" She could not articulate another word.

She didn't need to. He dropped to his knees in front of her and took one straining tip into his mouth. He started off suckling ever so softly, but soon increased the pressure until the pleasure was almost pain and she was crying out.

"More, please… Oh, Heavens… Stop! I can't bear it. No… Don't stop! Harder. Now, *Dimitri!* Now…" and she came with an explosion of color in the inky blackness of their sensual prison.

She sagged against the wall, but he wasn't done. He kissed a path down to her belly. If she thought his exploration earlier of their baby's current home had been erotic, it was nothing compared to the way he caressed every new curve, every bit of skin stretched tight over her womb with both fingers and lips that almost worshipped.

"Moro mou." *His baby.* He kissed the center of her distended tummy. *"Yineka mou."* *His woman.* Both his hands covered her skin in possessive declaration.

She was so lost in her sensual daze that she almost did not catch the significance of the words whispered against the taut wall of her stomach, but when they penetrated her brain she felt emotion course through her. Earlier he had called *her* his baby, but now he was acknowledging their son. And her, but in a very different way. He'd claimed her with an endearment he'd never used with her before. Words that both connoted her place in his life as his woman, but also laid claim to her as his wife.

"I will never let you go again."

She could not respond. What could she say? He acted as if her leaving his life had been voluntary and also that it had hurt him. She didn't know if she could believe him, but she didn't have time to dwell on it. His lips were traveling down her stomach until they found her most secret place. He kissed her there, a soft salute and then exerted pressure on the outside of her thighs to bring her legs together.

She was unprepared for the penetration of his tongue. He did not pull her legs apart again, but let his tongue slide between her slick folds of femininity. He stroked her sweetest spot with the tip of his tongue, going back and forth and then in circles, all the time keeping her legs together. She couldn't believe how incredible it felt to have her inner thighs touching and the swollen flesh of her womanhood pressed together and around the wet stimulation of his tongue.

She felt the sensations of pleasure begin to build to ecstasy once again. Tears ran down her cheeks to mix with the water on her skin from the still pulsing showerheads as she said his name over and over. His hands moved from their hold on her outer thighs to cupping the underside of her bottom and she pressed herself against his marauding mouth, unable to stop the wanton movement.

Then one of his fingers penetrated where she had not been touched in over four long months and she came apart, sobbing out her pleasure and his name. He didn't stop and she bucked against him, convulsing over and over again until she went limp and the impenetrable darkness was no longer responsible for the blackness before her eyes.

She came to on the king-size bed in Dimitri's room. He was toweling her dry with gentle movements. The bedside lamp was on, casting a gentle glow over his bronzed features.

He smiled down at her. "So you have decided to wake up."

"I fainted." She couldn't believe it.

"It happens sometimes, when the feelings are very, very intense."

A surge of purely possessive jealousy coursed through her and she stiffened, glaring up at him. "I suppose you've had lots of lovers faint in your arms."

He shook his head, all trace of smile gone. "Never, *yineka mou*. Only you. Only now."

"But..." How had he known?

He shrugged as if she'd asked the question aloud. "I am a man. It is something I have heard."

"Thank you." He had given her pleasure she'd never dreamed of, not even in his arms.

His blue eyes, the color of the midnight sky, bored into her. "It is I who thanks you. I have never experienced anything like the fire you give me when I touch you."

He laid the towel across her torso, giving the illusion of modesty and straightened to stand beside the bed.

"Dimitri?"

"I will leave you to sleep in privacy if that is your wish."

She stared at him, her heart pounding in her chest. "Don't you want me?"

He laughed and flicked a self-deprecating hand in the direction of his shaft. It stood proud and pulsatingly erect out from his body. "I want you more than my next breath, but I will not take what you do not wish to give."

She would have expected him to shore up his victory in the shower with a complete seduction. In fact, she was almost sure that had been his plan. She did not know what changed his mind, but only that it touched her deeply he had. He was giving her a choice, not trying to coerce her with their physical compatibility.

And in giving her that choice, he robbed her of her resolve. She wanted him, so much. The pleasure he had given her in the shower was beautiful, something she would never forget, but she needed to feel the connection of their bodies for it to be complete.

She tugged the towel from her body and dropped it on the floor beside the bed.

His face looked hewn from stone while a wild hope burned in his indigo eyes. "Alexandra?"

She put out her arms. "I want you."

He came to her in a rush of masculine possession,

covering her body completely with his own and entering her all in one incredible move. Then he went still. "This for me is a taste of Heaven on Earth."

Alexandra strove to breathe in the face of an indescribable pleasure she'd thought never to know again. His size was such that she was stretched and filled to capacity, but her earlier pleasure had made his swift penetration easy and smooth.

She too felt a need for stillness. She wanted to savor a sensation she thought lost to her. It felt different and at first she didn't understand why, but then she remembered. He hadn't donned a condom. He hadn't needed to. She was already pregnant with his baby. She loved the feel of naked flesh against naked flesh in such an intimate way.

She tipped her head and met his gaze.

He smiled. "In this, we are in one accord."

She couldn't help returning his smile. "Yes."

Then he started to move, sliding almost completely out before entering her again with torturing slowness. "We will not hurt our son?"

She shook her head vehemently. Her obstetrician had informed her she could continue conjugal relations right up until her son's birth as long as it remained comfortable for her. She hadn't appreciated the information at the time.

She groaned as he slid in again.

"Are you certain of this?"

She forced her mind to focus so she could tell him what the doctor had said. His look of shock was so funny, she came out of her passion glazed daze enough to tease him. "You are a man. This is something you are supposed to know."

Red scorched his well defined cheekbones. "This we do not discuss."

She giggled. "I bet you didn't know that there's a chemical in your fluid that helps me go into labor when the time comes, either." That had been another helpful tidbit she'd wanted to yell at her obstetrician for sharing. She'd thought she would be spending her pregnancy alone and the prospect of getting Dimitri's *help* in this way an impossible one.

The surprised expression turned to a smug one. "A Petronides knows his duty. I will be certain to provide you all the chemicals you need at the time."

She laughed, refusing to ruin the moment by reminding either of them that she was still unsure whether or not she wanted to be in a position to allow that. Both her laughter and her disturbing thoughts melted away as he began to move more aggressively. He rocked her body with his hands while he plunged in and out of her with passionate fervor.

Incredibly she felt a tightening sensation in her lower belly, telling her that her body was preparing for another explosion of pleasure. She grabbed his shoulders, holding on so tight with her fingers that her nails dug into his skin while their bodies rocked together toward a crescendo of satisfaction.

Just as she felt herself contracting around his hardened flesh, he went absolutely stiff above her and shouted out his release. For the first time in their relationship, she was allowed to feel every pulse as his warmth flooded her and she could not believe how that impacted her emotions. It felt more intimate than anything they had ever done.

It was as if he'd always held part of himself back from her, but now he willingly gave her that which had accidentally brought about the new life in her womb. She wanted to thank him again, but the moment was too profound for words.

Whatever became of their future, she would always have this moment.

CHAPTER SEVEN

DIMITRI rolled off her, but pulled her body close to his side as if he were afraid she was going to make a break for it.

She was almost too tired to breathe. She wasn't going anywhere. "I locked the door," she murmured on a yawn against the warmth of his chest.

"Yes."

"How did you get in?"

"Do you think I only know how to make money? I can pick a lock. My grandfather's security chief taught me when I was sixteen. He said every man should have the ability. I confess it has never been of use until now."

She laughed softly, picturing a younger Dimitri learning such a questionable skill. "Did your grandfather know?"

"It was his idea."

"You're having me on."

"No. Grandfather believes a man should be able to do things for himself, even if he has the money to pay someone else to do them."

She snuggled in closer. It felt so good. "No wonder you never balked at helping me with dinner. I always thought you were surprisingly domesticated for such a traditional Greek man, not to mention such a rich one."

"I enjoyed the simplicity of our life in Paris."

"Right. You threw a fit when I told you I didn't want a live-in housekeeper, cook and maid."

"It surprised me." He defended himself. "Most

women who worked as hard as you did would have been happy to leave the domestic chores to someone else."

"It kept me grounded. It would have been too easy to get wrapped up in the glitter and glitz surrounding the fashion industry." She sighed and kissed the hair roughened skin of his chest simply because she couldn't help herself. "I guess I didn't want to end up like my mother with my view of life and the world blinkered by the society surrounding me."

But like her mother, she'd willfully worn blinders in one area of her life...with him. She had refused to *consciously* acknowledge the transitory nature of their relationship, living only in the present. So, when he ended it—she had been devastated. She didn't want to think about that right now, maybe never again.

"Why the darkness?" she asked instead.

"I needed it to be only you and I. No more pain. No past. No present. No future. Just us."

She understood that. Allowing this area of their relationship to be tainted by the differences that plagued them would be like taking a color marker to the Mona Lisa.

They lay like that for a long time, his fingers brushing her side in an absentminded movement while her hand rested over his heart. It reminded her of their last time together and her words then. *A strong heart.*

"You said your grandfather had another heart attack? You never told me about the first one."

"It happened while I was in Greece that last time before you left Paris."

"Why didn't you tell me?"

"Why didn't you tell me who you really were?" he countered.

"I *was* Xandra Fortune in France."

"Yes, and you took periodic trips that were not modeling assignments and yet you would not tell me what they were. Presumably they were to return to your life as Alexandra Dupree."

"Yes," she admitted.

"I thought you had met someone else."

She sat up and stared down at him, his beautiful black hair tousled by her fingers, his naked body gleaming bronze above where the sheet rested across his hips. "You thought I was two-timing you?"

Chance would be a fine thing. If he had believed that about her, he would not have stayed. "I had never had another lover. Did you think that now I knew what sex was, I couldn't wait to try it with someone else?"

She wasn't prepared for the guilty stain across his cheeks.

"You did!" She didn't think about it, she just balled up her fist and smacked him right on the chest. Hard.

He grunted and caught her hand in his own. "I did not believe it. If I had, I would have ended our relationship."

Right. That sounded like him. "But you thought the baby was someone else's."

"Yes. I did hold this tormenting belief for a week. I have no excuse."

She glared at him. "No, you don't."

But inside she had to acknowledge her trips home could have looked suspicious to a lover as possessive as Dimitri. He'd hated the fact she had things in her life she refused to tell him about. She'd kept it that way to stop him from taking her over completely. She had loved him so much, she'd needed the defense mechanism of having a part of herself he did not know. Only when she returned to living that part of her life, she took the pain of his loss with her. The defense had not worked.

"My grandfather refused to have necessary by-pass surgery until I promised to set a date for my marriage with Phoebe. I was not ready to give you up, but I was not prepared to let him die, either."

She stared at him in disbelief. "You cannot be serious. You always told me what a great guy your grandfather was. How could he blackmail you like that into ditching me?"

"He did not know about you."

This new view of what had happened three months ago left her feeling disoriented. "But still..."

"He wanted an assurance I would do my duty by the Petronides name."

"And instead you got your mistress pregnant and yourself featured in a public fight with her."

He grimaced. "Yes."

"He'll be furious if you marry me."

He looked amused. "He will be thrilled to become a great-grandfather and he cannot help but be charmed by so lovely a new granddaughter."

"I'm not beautiful anymore. You said so."

He used the grip he had on her hand to tug her down to his chest. "I said you looked ill, not ugly, you foolish woman."

"But I don't have sultry green eyes now," she said, remembering what he used to say about them.

"Now you have eyes that change color with your mood. It is quite tantalizing."

"My hair is short and mouse brown."

He laughed and tousled the aforementioned hair. "It is sexy as sin and you know it. As for the color...how can you complain when it shines like liquid sand?"

"But I'm shaped like a pumpkin."

He used one knee to part her legs so she draped across him in intimate disarray. His male hardness pressed against her. He thrust upward. "Does this feel like I think you are ugly?"

What was the question? She couldn't remember; she was too busy melting into a puddle of desire on top of him. Silence reigned while he touched her in ways she'd forgotten and brought her body to the peak of pleasure over and over again. She didn't have the energy to start another discussion when they were done. She found herself slipping into sleep cuddled against his side, feeling more at peace than she had since discovering her pregnancy.

Warm security surrounded Alexandra and she didn't want to make the trip to full wakefulness. How many times had she had this dream since leaving Paris? She was back in Dimitri's bed, his arms wrapped around her like protective bands, their lower limbs entwined to make them two parts of one whole. It seemed so real, but she knew if she allowed her mind to continue its journey toward complete lucidity, the fantasy would disappear, leaving cold reality behind.

He shifted against her, rubbing his hairy leg between her smooth limbs and she rocketed to complete wakefulness. She opened her eyes to black curling hair over a bronze, muscled chest. *Dimitri*. Along with her sensory impressions, memories of the night before blasted her conscious mind.

They had made love. Many times. He had been afraid of hurting the baby, asking her every time if it would be all right and she had reassured him. Again and again. Because she had wanted him. The last time, he'd woken her around dawn and seduced her with a sensitivity that had touched all the way to her soul.

It was incomprehensible that the man who had treated her so tenderly the night before could be the same one who had walked away from her without a backward glance.

Only according to him, he *had* looked back and found her gone. His grandfather had refused life-saving surgery until Dimitri had set a wedding date with Phoebe. While the knowledge her eviction from his life had not been voluntary soothed some of her still lacerated emotions, it did not soothe them all.

Would his grandfather have made such a demand if Dimitri had told the older man about Alexandra and implied she had an important place in his life? The problem was, she had not had that place at the time. She had been a temporary lover to Dimitri, a mistress to an unmarried man.

Last night had not felt like the joining of a man and his temporary lover or mistress, though. It had felt almost sacred.

Knowing about his grandfather put a new perspective on the events four months ago, but the older man wasn't the reason Dimitri had denied paternity of their baby. As much as she didn't want to, she had to take some of the blame for that one. By withholding part of her life from him, she had set up fertile ground for distrust to grow.

In some ways, Dimitri had done the same to her. He hadn't told her about his grandfather's heart attack and when she asked about his family, he had been reticent. She knew things about his brother and his grandfather, but he'd always changed the subject when his parents came up. They hadn't died until he was ten, so it couldn't be because he had no memories of them. He'd never taken her to meet his family, never invited his brother to the apartment for a meal when the younger man was in Paris.

Now he wanted her to marry him. She shifted restlessly, at once both loving and hating the sense of security his warmth provided. What had changed? *The answer to that was obvious,* she derided herself. One, she was pregnant with a baby he now accepted he had fathered. For a Petronides male, that would change a lot. Hadn't she known that when she told him?

At the time she had hoped it would have the exact result it finally had: his desire to marry her. Now that desire felt like too little too late.

The second change was that his wife-to-be had married his brother. Dimitri had acted like the betrayal hadn't mattered to him, but even if his emotions had not been involved...his pride would have been. A quick marriage of his own would assuage some of the wounds his pride had sustained, particularly if it was to a woman who had adored him like she once had done.

She'd recognized last night that she still loved him, but she didn't *adore* him. Did that make her any less vulnerable?

"Have you figured it all out yet?" Dimitri asked from above her head.

She tilted back to look him in the face. "Figured what out?"

"Your life. My life. Our life together."

"What makes you so sure I was thinking about us? Or that I was thinking at all, for that matter?"

His smile was grim. "As much as you may want to deny it, I know you, *pethi mou*. You often spend your first waking moments lost in thought and what is of more importance to you at the moment than the future of the baby you carry?"

"You assume that future has to include you."

"You know it does. Married or not, lovers or enemies, whatever relationship you and I share, I will have a part in my son's life."

She didn't balk at the implacability in his voice. She hadn't meant to imply otherwise. Her wording had been unfortunate. "I didn't mean that. I will not withhold your child from you."

"No matter how much you despise me?" His voice was bleak and his face expressionless.

She stared at him. Could he honestly believe she despised him after the way she had responded to him last night? "I don't despise you."

"But you no longer love me."

To answer would require a lie, so she sidestepped. "Did you have plans for today?"

"Yes."

"Then, I guess we'd better get up."

He smiled wickedly down at her. "Not necessarily."

"But…"

"My plans today are to woo you. I think here," he said, indicating the bed, "is where I am at my best."

She didn't know what she would have said because at that precise moment, the phone rang. Giving her a last lascivious look that made her giggle despite her heavy thoughts, he turned to answer the bedside phone.

Was he really going to woo her? The thought was tantalizing. She remembered his two-month-long pursuit before he'd seduced her into bed and talked her into moving in with him. They had been heady days. Living with him had been pretty wonderful too, but a wooing…well, it sounded nice.

"Alexandra."

She looked up from her blind contemplation of his naked back. "Hmm?"

"The phone is for you. It is your sister."

Alexandra crawled across the bed and took the phone from Dimitri's outstretched hand. "Madeleine?"

"Yes. It's me. How are things going with you-know-who?" Madeleine sounded nervous.

"Don't ask."

"That bad, huh?"

Bad? No. More like foolish. Falling into bed with Dimitri the first time around hadn't been her smartest move, but doing it this time, when their future was unsettled and she was still dealing with the effects of his betrayal was outright stupidity. "We've got a lot to discuss, that's all."

"Did he show you proof he didn't marry that Greek girl?"

"Yes."

"That's good anyway. Hunter said he would. Maybe he's not a complete swine."

"Hunter or Dimitri?" she asked facetiously.

"Both," was her sister's surprising and emphatic reply.

"Is everything all right, *chérie?*"

"Well…"

"Madeleine…" she said in a voice she had used since childhood to encourage her sister to *fess up*.

"It's all Hunter's fault!"

Hunter, the man who went to any lengths to make her sister happy? Alexandra had a hard time believing he'd done anything to hurt Madeleine. "What's all his fault?"

"He had a business contact invite Dimitri to the party...on purpose!"

Pure shock traveled through Alexandra. *"What?"*

"He said he was worried about you. He didn't think you were adjusting to life without Dimitri very well and wanted to know if there was a chance for you two. Hunter made discreet inquiries and found out Dimitri had been searching for Xandra Fortune since a couple of days after you landed in New York. Remember that time he suggested you call Dimitri and try to work it out?"

She remembered. It had been a week after the ultrasound. "I told him I'd rather move in with Mama."

Madeleine laughed, albeit stiltedly. "He didn't know you thought Dimitri was married and he couldn't figure out why you wouldn't at least give the father of your baby one more chance."

"So he decided to take the choice out of my hands?" she asked, feeling both outraged and outclassed. Hunter had been right and she and Dimitri did need to work out their future, whatever that might be. Still... "Save me from arrogant men."

"I slept in the guest room," Madeleine said with a certain amount of satisfaction.

Evidently Hunter didn't know how to pick a lock.

"I'm sorry, Maddy. I don't want you and Hunter arguing because of me."

"He could have told me his plans. I might even have gone along if he told me Dimitri wasn't really married."

"Maddy!"

"Well, Hunter was right about one thing. You were wilting without Dimitri. You sound more alive this morning than you have in the past three months."

Alexandra didn't know how to respond to that bit of

truth, so she changed the subject. "Is that all you called about?"

"Actually, no..." She was back to sounding nervous.

What more could there be?

"Mother flew in on an early morning flight and she wanted to know where you were and I didn't want to tell her, but then Hunter came in. And just like a man, he didn't realize he'd be starting World War III and told her you were staying at a hotel with Dimitri. Mother fainted and I screamed at Hunter and now *he's* not speaking to *me*..." At this point Madeleine's voice broke.

"Oh, *chérie*. I don't want my problems to become yours."

Madeleine gave a watery laugh. "That's so like you. You took care of mother and me when Daddy died and tolerated Mama's disapproval. But when it comes time to lean on someone else, you feel guilty, for Heaven's sake!"

"I got myself into this mess. No one else should have to pay the price for my stupidity."

Dimitri stiffened beside her.

"Well, Mama's on her way over to get you out of it!"

She couldn't have heard right. "But..."

"She threatened to swoon again like some Victorian maiden, but the thing is, she looked pale as death...so I told her what hotel Dimitri was staying in and your room number."

Madeleine started crying and saying she was sorry over and over again. Her argument with Hunter and having their mother descend on her had clearly taken its toll.

"Calm down, Maddy. It will be fine. She's my

mother, of course I don't mind you telling her where I am," Alexandra said, lying through her teeth.

"But the newspapers. They're awful. I don't know how you're going to handle it."

Newspapers? "What are you talking about, Maddy?"

"You don't know?" Madeleine started crying again. "It's just terrible and after all you've been through already."

Knowing she wasn't going to get another coherent word out of her sister, Alexandra did her best to calm Madeleine before hanging up the phone. She turned to face Dimitri. "My mother is on her way over."

Dimitri's brow rose. "So I gathered."

"She's on the warpath, though Mother's version of warfare is quite genteel." That had never stopped Alexandra from feeling like she'd been through the meat grinder after one of her mother's lectures though.

"She is your mother. Her greatest concern is for your welfare," he said with absolute confidence.

She just laughed, although the sound was a hollow one. "Mama's highest priority is the dignity attached to the Dupree name. Appearance is everything and my staying in your suite doesn't look right no matter how you wrap it up and tie it with a pretty little bow."

He was silent for several seconds, his regard so intent, she felt heat rush into her cheeks. "What?" she finally demanded.

"I am shocked at my own naiveté. I believed the whole Xandra Fortune image. A French fashion model, an orphan, a woman of the world with a sophisticated outlook on life, a woman who had no sense of family responsibility because she'd never had one."

"And?" Honestly, some times talking to him was like going through a maze blindfolded and tipsy from too much wine. What was his point? And what did all this have to do with the impending visit from her mother?

He shook his head as if clearing it. "Many things did not fit the image if I had but looked at them."

"You were interested in an uncomplicated relationship with a worldly model. You saw what you wanted to see."

"This is true." He reached out and touched her cheek in an oddly affectionate gesture. "It is also true I saw what you wanted me to see, hmm?"

She couldn't deny it. She had considered telling him the truth of her background so many times, but self-protection had kept her silent. And then there had been the fear that he would lose interest in the real Alexandra Dupree. It had been a big enough shock that a man like Dimitri could find her Xandra Fortune persona desirable.

"Well, you know what they say… You don't usually know people as well as you think you do." She could admit now that both she and Dimitri were guilty of that truth.

"But you made it a point to prevent me from knowing you."

That wasn't strictly true. "You knew me, the woman. I only hid the trappings of my life as Alexandra Dupree."

"And gave me a false set of realities to replace them."

"In a way, you are a lot like my mother. You only see the surface. You only want the surface," she declared.

He tugged her into his arms and brushed his warm hand over the slope of her breast. Her nipple, still sensitive from their loving the night before, went erect immediately.

"It is true I like this surface." His smile was pure seduction, but then he went serious. "It is not all I desire, however. I want all of you and I will have all of you."

The possessive determination in the words made her shiver. She had the awful feeling he didn't just mean marriage. He wanted her mind and her emotions. It was there in his eyes and he would settle for nothing less.

"Madeleine said something about a newspaper, but wouldn't give me the details. I think you'd better look into it. Someone may have seen us together and is now speculating on who the billionaire's pregnant companion is."

He didn't look worried. "After we shower I will make a phone call."

She nodded and tried to pull away. "Mother's already left Madeleine's. She'll be here in less than thirty minutes unless she hits traffic. We need to get showered and dressed."

He stopped her from hopping out of bed. "Things have changed for us, have they not?"

"Because we had sex?"

He leaned down and kissed her on the tip of her nose. "Because we have once again established an area of our relationship that is nothing but beautiful."

"I won't let you seduce me into marriage," she said vehemently.

"Are you sure about that?" he asked, his wandering hands now wreaking havoc with her breathing.

She didn't answer and he laughed, pulling her from the bed toward the shower. "Come, we will bathe together and save time."

CHAPTER EIGHT

ALEXANDRA had been worried Dimitri would try to make love to her in the shower again, but he was as good as his word. They were dressed in record time and Dimitri was on the phone to his assistant when a gentle *rat-a-tat-tat* sounded on the door.

"Mother," she breathed.

Dimitri turned from the phone and gave her a sharp look. He cut the connection abruptly and crossed the room to open the door. Cecelia Dupree stood on the other side, looking fragile and quite lovely in her pale pink Moschino suit.

"You must be Xandra's mother," Dimitri said as he led Cecelia through the door.

Alexandra had to stifle a groan at his slip of the tongue. Her mother's face pinched and she swung on Alexandra, for once forgetting the social niceties. "So, this is what you do when you're living high as Xandra Fortune. Have you no sense of decorum at all? You're in New York now, where you are known as Alexandra Dupree. What do you think New Orleans society will say when they discover you've spent the night with some foreigner in his hotel room?" she asked in an outraged voice. "Think of your sister. The scandal could adversely affect Hunter's business dealings."

"I sincerely doubt Hunter's business associates care one way or the other about the behavior of Madeleine's pregnant sister, as for New Orleans society...I'm not taking out an ad in the paper. Why should anyone back home know?" Or care, she asked herself silently. Her mother lived in such a rarified milieu, she didn't know how ninety percent of the world thought and functioned.

"You are a Dupree," her mother said as if that should explain it all. "Yet, by the look of this," she said, waving a newspaper in Alexandra's face, "you have completely forgotten that fact. How could you allow this sort of information to become public knowledge?"

Alexandra put her hand out toward Cecelia. "May I see, Mama? The accused has a right to know the charges."

Cecelia flung the paper toward Alexandra with an absolutely surprising lack of restraint. When Alexandra saw the headline and pictures, she understood why. One picture was of her and Dimitri leaving the restaurant they'd had lunch in yesterday. The other was of her and Dimitri yelling at each other at *Chez Renée*. The headline read, "Greek Tycoon and Lover Reunite: Does Petronides Now Believe the Baby is His?"

With a sense of impending dread, Alexandra read the article. She was named as the famous French model Xandra Fortune *and* the *quiet living* Alexandra Dupree. The writer speculated as to the reason for her dual personas and the effect her pregnancy had had on Dimitri's scuffed plans to marry Phoebe Leonides. Dimitri's denial that he was the father was quoted, apparently having been overheard by the enterprising photographer or someone who'd been with him.

The writer went on to say it appeared Dimitri now accepted his role as father and ended the article with a pithy comment regarding a possible marriage between them.

Alexandra felt sick and she made a mad dash for the bathroom. When she finished retching, Dimitri was there with a cold wet washcloth for her face and a glass of water to rinse her mouth. When she was done, he swung her into his arms and carried her back into the main room of the suite. He set her gently on the cream colored sofa.

"I'm going to order some food, all right *moro mou?*"

She couldn't take it in. She couldn't even look at her mother, knowing how furious and disappointed in her Cecelia was bound to be. She'd spent years living two lives to protect her mother from embarrassment and possible scandal, only to have it all torn apart with one sleazy newspaper article. "Dimitri, they know... Everyone knows about us, about the baby, about Xandra Fortune."

He laid his finger against her lips. "Shh. All will be well. You must trust me. Now what do you want to eat?"

"Dry toast and maybe a little fruit."

He shook his head, his expression wry. "That is not sufficient sustenance for you and the baby. I will order your dry toast, fruit and some food besides, I think."

"Why ask me if you plan to do what you want anyway?" she asked petulantly, glad to focus on something less volatile and damaging than the newspaper article.

He chuckled. "Perhaps because I like to hear your voice?"

Her mother gave a most unladylike snort, reminding both Dimitri and Alexandra she was there.

Dimitri turned to Cecelia. "I understand your concern and will do everything in my power to mitigate it, but I will not allow you to harangue your daughter. She is in too fragile a state right now."

"How dare you?" her mother demanded.

"Can I order anything for you?" Dimitri asked, ignoring her mother's outraged question.

Apparently realizing when she was faced with a will stronger than her own, Cecelia subsided. She took a seat in one of the armchairs opposite the couch, her expression dour. "Tea might settle my nerves."

"Then I shall order you some without delay."

He went to the phone to do so, but kept his body toward them as if he were watching her mother to make sure she said nothing to upset Alexandra. His concern felt nice and Alexandra had to admit she was glad she wasn't alone to face her mother's recriminations. When he finished making the order, Dimitri returned to sit next to Alexandra on the smallish sofa. He took her hand and squeezed it reassuringly then turned the full force of his charm on her mother.

"Mrs. Dupree, allow me to introduce myself. I am Dimitri Petronides." His smile would have melted stone. He stood and leaned toward Cecelia, extending his hand. "It is an honor to meet the mother of the woman I intend to marry."

Alexandra sucked in air so fast she choked on it while her mother's "just sucked on a lemon" look turned to calculated charm in the space of a single heartbeat. Cecelia patted her perfectly coiffed ash-blond hair and smiled at Dimitri.

"Please, you must call me Cecelia. Marriage will be just the thing to alleviate the scandal. I'm so glad you'd already thought of it. Alexandra's been so impetuous these past six years and I declare the last three months have been the *worst*."

Alexandra gritted her teeth at her mother's digs. "I haven't agreed to marry him."

Cecelia dismissed Alexandra's words with a wave of

her hand. "Of course you will, dear. Now let's start making plans. It will have to be a quiet affair if there's any hope of avoiding more scandal."

Alexandra hadn't told her mother anything about Dimitri, including the details of their breakup. But she doubted it would have made any difference in the older woman's current outlook. In Cecelia Dupree's mind, babies came after marriage. Therefore, to preserve appearances, Alexandra had to be married.

"This isn't the Middle Ages, Mother. You cannot give my hand in marriage to a man without my permission." She turned her head to meet Dimitri's eyes. "And *you* can't *take* it."

"Alexandra, is that reporter correct? Is this man the father of your child?"

Alexandra's vocal chords froze. An affirmative answer would be her downfall with her mother.

"Yes," Dimitri said when Alexandra refused to.

"Then there can be no question that you will marry him."

"On the contrary." Alexandra didn't like the feeling of pressure emanating from both her mother and Dimitri. "I'm perfectly capable of having this baby alone. If that upsets you, I'm sorry."

She was proud of her little speech until her mother's eyes filled with tears. "Wasn't six years spent worried someone would discover my daughter's lifestyle enough a cross to bear? Now everyone *knows*." She sniffed and Alexandra felt a tug on her own emotions even though she suspected the tears were a tool as well used as her mother's Southern charm. "Now you balk at making things right. Think of the baby," was Cecelia last emotive appeal.

"You say lifestyle like my being a model was the

same as selling my favors to the highest bidder." Alexandra was more comfortable on the familiar ground of arguing her career choice rather than her current predicament.

Her mother shuddered. "How can you say such a thing? To even imply..." Clearly words failed her and two tears spilled over to trail down her powdered cheeks.

Alexandra felt the familiar sense of failure well up in her. "I'm sorry, Mother. I shouldn't have said it."

Her mother dabbed at her eyes with a perfectly white, lace trimmed handkerchief and simply shook her head in mute disapproval.

Knowing there would be nothing accomplished by sticking with the current subject, Alexandra asked, "What are you doing in New York, Mother?"

The paper with the damaging story had only come out that morning, not enough time for her mother to have made the trip from New Orleans unless she had already planned it.

Her mother sniffed and turned appealing eyes to Dimitri. "I'd come north to try and talk some sense into Alexandra, to mend fences before Christmas. A family should spend the holidays together, don't you think? But she's been so stubborn about her unfortunate circumstance, refusing to do anything practical to diminish the scandal. And here she is again, refusing to marry you. Is it any wonder I'm almost ill with my worries?"

"I do not consider the conception of my child an unfortunate circumstance," Dimitri replied in freezing tones. "I also fail to see why the fact your daughter modeled under the name of Xandra Fortune is such a tragedy for you. From what she has said, her work supported both you and your younger daughter for several years."

My, my. When Dimitri decided to defend someone, he came out with both guns blazing.

"But she didn't just model did she? She was your mistress, a tycoon's plaything," Cecelia said, quoting the article. "Now she is pregnant with your child. The Duprees have never had so much scandal attached to their name. What the nuns would think, I have no idea. Why, I'm terrified to send my monthly letter to Mother Superior for fear of letting something slip."

"Nuns?" Dimitri asked.

"The convent, remember?" Alexandra whispered.

"Ahh…those nuns."

Cecelia said, "Mother Superior didn't approve of the Xandra Fortune debacle any more than I did."

The unfairness of her mother's constant disapproval cracked something open in Alexandra. "My life as a model was hardly a debacle. Dimitri's right. It kept you in designer dresses and Madeleine in school. If I hadn't created Xandra Fortune, how would we all have lived? I can't see you getting a job."

Her mother gasped.

Someone knocked on the door. It turned out to be room service and Dimitri insisted Alexandra eat before the conversation was resumed. Her mother drank her tea with an expression of martyred stoicism.

When they were done and Dimitri had called to have the dishes removed, he resumed his seat beside Alexandra. Putting an arm around her waist, he met her mother's gaze. "Let me make a couple of things clear. One, I intend to marry your daughter. And two, it will not be some hole in the corner affair not befitting the bride of a Petronides."

He ignored both her and her mother's outraged gasps and stood.

"I'm glad you took the time to come by and see us," he said, taking her mother's arm and gently lifting her from the chair before he guided her to the door, "but as I'm sure you are aware, Alexandra and I have a great deal to do before the wedding. Perhaps we can get together this evening or tomorrow to discuss plans."

He continued talking as if he had both her and her mother's complete cooperation as he led Cecelia from the suite.

Dimitri called for his car and waited in the hotel lobby with Cecelia until it came. He shook his head watching Cecelia walk regally from the hotel. Running interference for Alexandra with her mother was going to take vigilance. Cecelia had tried to convince him again to consider a modest wedding by saying it would be cruel to Alexandra to make a media event of it when she had so obviously anticipated her wedding vows.

The car had not arrived one moment too soon.

Dimitri stepped into an empty elevator and pressed the button for his floor.

Would Alexandra be ashamed to marry him while she was so visibly pregnant? He thought back to what he had learned of her past. She'd been educated by nuns. Hell, maybe she would be embarrassed by a big wedding.

She had certainly been upset about the news clipping. He didn't want her upset and the part he had played in the breaking of the news story troubled him. He'd seen one of the paparazzi that often followed him outside the restaurant where they had eaten lunch. He hadn't said anything, had not sent his security man after the film—though as he'd learned in the past, that move was not always successful. His actions could be considered ruthless, but he thought of them as the acts of a desperate man.

She had to marry him.

For her own sake because she needed him.

For the baby's sake because he was a Petronides.

For Dimitri's sake because he needed her.

And for the sake of a promise he had made to his grandfather, a second promise when the first had been nullified.

He'd thought it would be easy once he found her. She'd obviously wanted marriage before she left Paris, but now she acted like the thought of it was worse than spending the rest of her life in Purgatory. No matter what she said to the contrary, it was obvious she now hated him. He mourned the warmth that used to shine from her eyes when she looked at him. The smile that had been just for him. Intimate. Special. He'd taken her for granted when he had her. He had ignored the underlying emotional commitment in their relationship.

He'd believed they had no hope of a future.

She'd been a career fashion model. It was lowering to admit, but he'd believed she had every intention of moving on when her career took off. He hadn't known about her family, hadn't realized she had no desire to be a supermodel. That ignorance had cost him three months of mental anguish wondering where she was and how she was faring with her pregnancy.

He'd never once considered she might terminate it…even when he'd gone to the apartment in Paris a week after she left and found her message for him on the floor of the living room.

She'd rejected everything he'd ever given her down to the sexy nightwear he'd bought her. His fists clenched at his sides when he thought of that neatly folded stack of silk and lace garments. He'd taken one look at the pregnancy test sitting on top and driven his fist through the wall. One look. That was all it had taken for him to realize she'd been telling him the truth. He hadn't understood how it could be true, but he had *known* it was.

He'd called the detective agency that very night, but it had still been too late. He'd lost her.

He'd spent three months tormenting himself with if-only scenarios. If only he had been thinking more clearly when his grandfather delivered his ultimatum, but Dimitri had been badly shaken and had gone into damage control mode. He would do anything to save his grandfather and he had done, hurting both himself and Alexandra in the process.

If only he had believed her about the baby from the beginning and told his grandfather then.

If only he had come back to the apartment sooner, but he hadn't been able to face its emptiness, the reality of what he had done to his woman. He hadn't been able to stay in Athens either, not after the announcement of his marriage to Phoebe had been made.

Everything had felt wrong about it. He'd seen the looks his brother gave Phoebe when he thought no one noticed. Dimitri could not miss the way Phoebe stood in fearful awe of him, but laughed in his brother's company. But most importantly—the look on Alexandra's face when he'd denied her haunted him.

He deserved her hatred, but he couldn't live with it. He had to convince her to marry him. He could not consider the alternative. She and the baby needed him even if she refused to admit it. *Theos* knew he needed her. Would she ever look at him with the warmth of affection in her beautiful eyes again?

* * *

Alexandra had picked up the paper her mother left behind and was rereading the article about her and Dimitri when he returned.

She looked up. "I can't believe they said all this. It's horrible. Conjecture about our relationship, your reasons for denying paternity. Where did all this come from?"

Dimitri shrugged. "The story ran for weeks in France and Greece, even some London papers picked it up. The press release your agency sent out saying you had retired from modeling and wanted to live a more anonymous life was all the more scintillating when news of your possible pregnancy got out. I'm surprised you didn't see any of the stories."

She'd avoided the European scandal rags after the announcement of his marriage to Phoebe. Alexandra hadn't wanted to see any pictures of the couple together. And of course, the stories hadn't made it to the States. They were about a French fashion model and a Greek tycoon, nothing of interest for American readers. At least not until the connection to her real identity was made.

"How did they make the connection?" she wondered aloud.

"I am, unfortunately, followed by a certain amount of paparazzi wherever I go. Once we were seen together, it was only a matter of time before one of them recognized you."

"But no one else had," she said helplessly.

"I find that inexplicable."

A wavery smile tilted her lips. "You certainly weren't fooled."

Remembered anger shimmered in his eyes. "No."

"You were so sure it was me and yet I must have looked very different to you," she mused.

"You are my woman. I would recognize you in the dark."

"You did," she said, helplessly remembering the passion they'd shared the night before.

His smile was predatory. "Yes."

"Sex isn't everything," she admonished him.

"But it is a start, is it not, *yineka mou?*" He resumed his seat beside her and placed his hand against her protruding belly. "And we have this precious child we share as well."

If only she could believe him, but she didn't trust him. Did he have an ulterior motive for the marriage? "You're afraid I won't give you access, aren't you? You think you'll have more say in our baby's life if we're married."

"I will, but that is not why I want to marry you."

"Then why?" she demanded.

"You once said we had something special. Perhaps I want that back again."

"Impossible."

"Nothing is impossible, Alexandra."

Believing he might come to love her was. "I don't know," she said, achingly aware her desires were at odds with her intellect. She wanted to marry him, but she was afraid doing so would only open her heart to more hurt.

"Your mother will be devastated if you refuse me."

Alexandra knew that all too well. "My mother's feelings do not dictate my life."

"You can say that after spending six years living a double life to protect her sensibilities?"

"Living as Xandra Fortune was infinitely preferable to the prospect of living as Alexandra Petronides." She didn't know why she'd said it. To wound him as he had once wounded her? Regardless, guilt assailed her the second the words left her.

His jaw tautened, his blue eyes flashing anger. "Think of our child. Life as a legitimate Petronides will be *infinitely preferable* to life as the bastard child of the black sheep of the Dupree family," he said, throwing her words back at her.

She flinched with the pain the words inflicted. "Don't use that word!"

His face registered regret and then determination. "I will never use it again in relation to our son, regardless of your decision, but I cannot say the same for others."

"I know." She felt tears fill her eyes and she tried to blink them away.

He cursed in Greek and pulled her against his chest. "Do not cry, *pethi mou*. I cannot stand it."

"Then it's a good thing you weren't around for the first month after I left Paris. I did nothing but cry," she said, hiccupping with her swallowed tears.

His arms tightened around her until she squeaked from the pressure. He loosened his grip immediately. "I did not intend to hurt you."

Was he talking about just now, or three months ago?

She looked at him. "Tell me about your parents, Dimitri. You never have."

His sensual lips thinned.

"How can you expect me to marry you when you won't share your family with me? I've never even met your grandfather or your brother."

"I will invite my brother to the wedding, unfortunately Grandfather cannot travel yet. You will meet him when we go to Greece."

"What do you mean, go to Greece?"

"It is where we will live."

"What if I want to live in New York?"

"Do you?" he asked with more patience than she expected.

She met his gaze and then looked away. "I don't want to raise our son in a big city," she admitted, knowing she was playing right into his hands.

"This is good." He gently tugged her face back around so she was caught in the compelling blue of his gaze. "The family home is on a small island off the coast near Athens. There is nothing on the island but the Petronides home and a fishing village. It will be a wonderful place for our son to grow up. I should know. I was raised there."

It sounded all too tempting.

CHAPTER NINE

"IF I marry you and you divorce me, you could keep my baby," she said, expressing her deepest fear.

He swore and stood. "You believe I would do this to you?"

She wanted to deny it. He looked so angry. "I don't know. I don't trust my instincts where you are concerned anymore."

"Marriage is forever. I would not do this." She could tell it infuriated him to have to say it. His pride was wounded and for some reason that made her feel bad. "This baby and the ones to come after will have both their mother and their father to raise them."

"You want more children?" The thought had never occurred to her.

"Yes. Do not tell me you only want this baby?" The thought clearly horrified him.

"No. I want at least two, but would really like four."

"Don't you think you had better marry me beforehand?"

"For the baby's sake?" she asked, wishing it could be different.

"For his sake yes, but also for your sake."

"You mean I won't have to work to support us both if I marry you?"

"You would not have to work regardless. From this point forward, you and the baby are my responsibility."

"Thank you." She knew he meant what he said. It

was written on the immovable features of his gorgeous face.

"You will be happier married to me than as a single parent," he asserted with inbred arrogance.

"You think so?"

"I know this."

"How can you be so certain?"

"Whatever you need to make you happy, I will give it to you."

Everything but his love, she thought sadly. But she would have his passion. Last night had proven that. She would have his support. He'd given her a taste of it this morning with her mother and it had been sweet. She would have his respect. If he did not respect her, he wouldn't be asking for marriage, she was sure of it.

"It would certainly relieve my mother's mind."

A calculating expression entered his eyes. "If you marry me, I will buy back the Dupree Mansion and staff it with servants for your mother's lifetime."

The sheer generosity of the offer stunned her. She understood his willingness to provide for her and the baby, but to take on responsibility for her mother as well was excessive and very, very endearing.

"Mama would love you forever."

"Yes." He frowned. "She does not want a big wedding. She believes you would be embarrassed. Is she right?"

"Embarrassed? To be marrying you?" she asked incredulously.

"To be married publicly when you are so obviously *enceinte*."

"I'm not ashamed of my baby." She wasn't comfortable with the fact he'd been conceived in a relationship rather than a marriage, but her son was precious to her all the same.

Dimitri's expression lightened. "I am very proud that you carry my child, *yineka mou*."

Alexandra pictured a traditional wedding, she and Dimitri decked out in formal white, her veil and train brushing the floor at least three feet behind her.

"Your eyes have gone soft and golden. Of what do you think, little one?"

She felt herself blushing, but decided to tell him. "I know it sounds really naff, but I always wanted to wear a traditional white wedding dress with a long train and oodles of lace in my veil." She sighed and touched her tummy. "But then I guess I would look pretty silly in white in my state."

He returned to the sofa and took her hand in his. "White is the sign of a pure heart. You would not look silly to me."

Her breath caught and she had to concentrate on getting her lungs to expand again. "I wouldn't?"

He leaned forward and she closed her eyes in preparation for his kiss. Why didn't she have more self-control with him? She felt a touch so light it almost wasn't there on both her eyelids, her cheeks and finally her lips. They parted of their own accord and the pressure increased.

He ended the kiss scant seconds later, leaving her feeling dazed.

That was nice.

He laughed and she realized she'd spoken aloud.

She smiled at him. "So you think I should wear white?"

"Yes."

"I'd like that."

"Does this mean you will marry me?"

Had there ever really been any doubt? Because she didn't want her pride stomped in the dust, she said, "It's the best thing for the baby."

His tender expression turned to stone and he stood up quickly from the sofa. "There are plans to be made. I want to be married a week from today."

"So quickly? What about my dress, the church—"

"I will take care of it."

She didn't argue. She supposed a billionaire could pull together a wedding on nothing notice. Money talked, or so they said. "I'm picking out my own dress."

He shrugged. "As you like."

He turned toward the phone, all signs of his loverlike countenance gone.

"Dimitri?"

He pivoted to face her. "Yes?"

"This is what you want?"

He laughed harshly. "I am getting what I deserve and can expect nothing more."

"But I thought you wanted to get married." Had she completely misread the situation? The one hope she clung to was the knowledge that he wanted her. Had last night satisfied that craving?

"I do." His eyes blazed certainty at her.

"But you seem unhappy now that I've said yes."

He came back and pulled her up and into his arms. "I am not unhappy, *pethi mou*. I am merely preoccupied with the details of the wedding now that you have agreed."

It made sense and she had no fears while his arms were around her. She yawned. "All right."

He turned her toward the bedroom and patted her bottom gently. "Take a nap. Pregnant ladies need their rest."

She went, feeling comforted. He'd pointed her in the direction of his bedroom. It was only later, while she hung on the verge of sleep that she realized he had once again sidestepped the issue of his parents.

Dimitri gripped the phone tightly without dialing. What had he expected, that she would say she was marrying him because she wanted to? At least she had agreed. He should not bemoan the fact it had been for the child's sake alone.

He would convince her to trust him again. He would show her that what they had had in Paris could be theirs again. The affection. The fun. The rapport. And once she saw that he would never dismiss her so cruelly again, she would once again glow in his presence.

At least he'd kept *this* promise to his grandfather.

"You are nervous, *yineka mou*. Why?"

Alexandra shifted the yards of fabric in her wedding dress's skirt an inch to the left on the limousine's seat. "There are going to be a lot people at the reception."

Which was an understatement. Dimitri had managed to invite an obscene number of wedding guests, all of whom would be staying for the reception...including Dimitri's brother, Spiros, and his wife Phoebe.

"You have modeled swimwear in front of a bigger crowd."

True. But the crowd had never included Dimitri's ex-fiancée and brother. "Does Spiros think I'm an awful tramp?"

Dimitri reeled as if she'd struck him and his eyes burned angry blue fire. "Why should you think this? Do you feel like this marriage has made you one?"

She wondered how Dimitri managed the Petronides

Corporation so effectively with his lousy communication skills. "Of course I don't feel like a tramp because I married you. It's just that your brother's read those awful articles. I'm sure he blames me for Phoebe's humiliation."

"My brother does not blame you."

She waved Dimitri's words aside. "Don't be ridiculous. Who else would he blame? I was the *other woman* even if I didn't know it. He had to marry Phoebe to save the family honor. I bet he hates me," she wailed.

Dimitri pulled her onto his lap, yards of white satin and all. He took her chin in his hand and forced her to look at him. "My brother does not blame you. He knows you were unaware of Phoebe's existence. He knows where the real blame lies. With me."

"But he's your brother. He's bound to forgive you." Look how many times she forgave Mama. "He's free to hate me." Dimitri laughed. He actually laughed and she wanted to sock him. "It's not funny. Your family's got no choice but to think you've married some kind of opportunist, five months pregnant with your baby and they've never met me."

"Spiros and my grandfather know this too is my fault. Do not worry, Alexandra. Spiros is content in his marriage and excited at the prospect of being an uncle. You made both things possible. He will adore you."

She would have continued her lament, but the limousine slid to a smooth stop and seconds later the door opened. Dimitri lifted her in his arms.

She squealed. "You're supposed to carry me over the threshold, not to the reception!"

He laughed, a true Dimitri laugh that she hadn't heard since before their breakup in Paris. "I can do both."

She wasn't about to spoil that smile, so she demurred.

He carried her all the way to the hotel ballroom where the reception was being held. A loud cheer went up when they came into the room and the next hour was spent accepting well wishes from their wedding guests.

Alexandra rested in one of the many Queen Anne style armchairs set in small groupings around the perimeter of the ballroom. Space had been left in the center of the floor for dancing. She was looking forward to being in Dimitri's arms.

"I guess he's not such a swine after all."

Alexandra smiled as her sister took the chair closest to her. "Hi, Maddy. Isn't this fabulous?" she asked, waving her hand to encompass the reception and its elegant guests. She was feeling incredibly happy for a woman who had just entered a marriage of convenience. It was all Dimitri's doing. "Can you believe the wedding?"

Madeleine grinned. "Believe it? I lived it. I was your matron of honor, after all. The horse drawn carriages were a very sweet touch. There were so many red and white poinsettias and that gorgeous Christmas greenery in the church, you couldn't see the pews."

"He did everything possible to make it special. He kept asking if there was anything else I wanted all week long, making sure my every fantasy of my wedding was fulfilled."

"And why should it not be?" Dimitri asked from behind her. He came to her side and rested his hand on the skin of her shoulder bared by the dropped shoulder neckline of her wedding dress. "You will only marry once. It should be the wedding of your dreams."

She tilted her head to smile up at him. "It has been."

He leaned down and kissed her softly on the lips. "I am glad, *yineka mou*. That was my only wish."

If she didn't know better, she'd say he sounded like a man in love. Even if he wasn't, he had to care about her a lot to have gone to so much trouble to see her happy.

"Making calf's eyes at each other again?" A man who could have been Dimitri's twin, but for his obvious younger age and dark brown eyes, slapped Dimitri on the back. "There will be plenty of time for that later."

Dimitri's hand on her shoulder tightened briefly in a reassuring gesture as if he could sense her unease.

"I do not make calf's eyes," he informed his brother.

Spiros smiled mockingly. "If you say so."

Phoebe, a beautiful woman with classic Greek features and an air of youthful innocence, laughed. "Do not tease your brother. A man is allowed to look pleased with his bride on his wedding day."

Remembering the picture she'd seen of Spiros and Phoebe's wedding day, Alexandra thought Phoebe must be intimately acquainted with the concept and said so.

Phoebe blushed sweetly while Spiros put his arm around her shoulder in a possessive manner. "This is true," he said.

Alexandra smiled. At least her pregnancy hadn't ruined their lives. They were obviously very happy to be married to each other. She couldn't help wondering what the Petronides family had been thinking to match a girl of Phoebe's gentle nature and obvious youth with an overwhelming man like Dimitri in the first place.

"It's not just reserved for the wedding day, you know. I'm still making calf's eyes at my wife," Hunter said as he joined the group, taking the chair closest to Madeleine.

Madeleine's air of complacent acceptance of such an accolade indicated whatever contretemps Alexandra's problems had caused in their marriage was well and truly over.

Alexandra looked up at Dimitri. She was not at all convinced he'd been looking at her with anything near the adoring glance her brother-in-law bestowed upon her sister. However, she was willing to tease him regardless. "So I can look forward to years of bovine expressions of affection?"

He stiffened with affront just as she'd expected him to do. "I am not a cow."

She smiled, feeling mischievous. "No indeed. If anything, you must be likened to a bull." She rubbed her protruding middle and felt their son move. "I would say that he is proof positive you are a male capable of breeding."

After a second of shocked silence, during which the entire group seemed to assimilate her rather risqué teasing, they all burst out laughing, including Dimitri. There were a few more teasing comments and Madeleine even went so far as to welcome Dimitri into the family which he thanked her for with grave appreciation rather than his usual arrogance.

After which, he leaned toward Alexandra and asked, "Are you ready to go?"

"We haven't danced yet." And she wanted to.

He smiled indulgently. "And we must do this to fulfill tradition, hmm?"

She nodded, loving the look of indulgence in his eyes. It made her feel cosseted.

He reached out his hand and led her to the middle of the ballroom floor, empty but for a few guests who stood in small groups chatting. Their presence on the dance floor was the orchestra's cue to move into a slow waltzing tune.

She and Dimitri took the traditional pose for a waltz, her train attached to her wrist making her feel like a nineteenth-century debutante at her comeout ball. Dimitri's dancing was divine and Alexandra lost herself in the pleasure of his arms and their bodies' movement to the music.

Other couples began to join them. Madeleine and Hunter. Phoebe and Spiros. Several guests she did not know by name.

She tilted her head to look into his eyes. "Thank you."

"For dancing with you?" he asked, a smile flirting with the edges of his lips.

"For all of this. The wedding. Keeping Mama calmed down over the last week. Charming Madeleine so she didn't think I was marrying an ogre. Buying the Dupree Mansion back for Mama. I guess I didn't think you were totally serious and yet you accomplished the purchase in less than a week. I'm stunned."

"I want you to be happy, *pethi mou*. I have told you this."

"Are all Petronides men willing to sacrifice for their wife's happiness?"

A shadow passed over his chiseled features, but was quickly gone. "All the Petronides males in my family, yes."

"That gives me a great deal of hope for the future, *mon cher*."

He stopped, stock-still in the middle of a turn.

"What's the matter?" she asked, anxiously. Had she stepped on his foot without realizing it?

"Say it again."

"What?" Then she knew. She hadn't called him by an endearment since he found her at Madeleine's. Even in the most passionate of their lovemaking, she had used only his name.

She could not deny him. He'd given her so much this week. She went up on tiptoes and still had to pull his head down so their lips could meet. *"Mon cher,"* she whispered against his lips before kissing him.

It was a kiss completely lacking in passion, a restoration of a bond that had been cruelly severed and left her bleeding. It had left its mark on Dimitri as well and now they saluted one another with a kiss of remembrance and renewal.

Three hours later, they were aboard Dimitri's private jet. She had changed into a comfortable, but chic honey gold, oversized, crocheted sweater and almond-colored wool stretch pants. Relaxed on the small couch in the plain's main cabin, she sipped on the glass of fruit juice Dimitri's personal flight attendant had given her.

"We should be taking off in less than half an hour," Dimitri informed her, walking into the main cabin from the cockpit after speaking to the pilot.

He had changed too and now wore tailored black slack trousers, a round-necked Armani sweater in gray over a black T-shirt. He lowered his long frame onto the sofa beside her, his outer thigh brushing her own sending the ever ready shivers down her limbs in anticipation of the next touch.

"How long will the flight to Athens take?" she asked, trying to tamp down the urge to slide her hands under his sweater and feel the well muscled contours of his chest.

He shrugged. "It depends. Perhaps eight hours."

"I'm glad I don't have to make the flight on a commercial airline. I don't think I could take it." So much sitting in one position would be painful to her back in her currently pregnant state.

His fingertips brushed her cheeks. "I would never expect you too." His hand fell away. "I did not ask if you were okay with changing doctors so late in your pregnancy."

"I can hardly have my New York doctor in Greece," she replied with a smile.

"So Madeleine said."

Her sister again. She bit back a grimace. "I'll be fine."

"I have arranged for you to be seen by an eminent obstetrician in Athens. He wants us to move to the Athens apartment for your last month."

"You've already spoken to him?" Why did that surprise her? This was his heir they were talking about after all.

"He comes highly recommended."

"I have no doubt," she said with some bemusement. So much for having to find a new doctor and arrange appointments for her last trimester.

"If you do not like him, we will find someone else."

Suddenly it struck her that Dimitri was worried about her reaction. She laid her hand over his. "I'll be fine. Really. Have you already arranged for my records to be transferred?"

"I had them faxed three days ago."

"Did I sign for that?" Between the marriage license, living Visa for Greece and other paperwork necessary for their wedding to take place, she didn't know what she had signed.

"Yes."

"Do you plan to be with me during delivery?"

"I would like this very much, but the final decision must be yours."

That surprised her. First that he wanted to be there. Dimitri wasn't exactly a New Man. And second that he would leave the choice to her. "I want you there."

"Then I will be. I believe there are classes we can take to help you through the delivery."

She stared at him, too shocked to speak this time.

"What is the matter? Do you not wish to take these classes? I had heard they were very beneficial for new mothers. I think you should consider attending them."

"I had always planned to do so," she choked out.

"You do not wish me to attend with you? Someone must be your coach. As your husband, I should fulfill the role." He was arguing with her like she'd denied him.

She hadn't. Didn't he realize how much she had wanted to share her pregnancy with the father of her baby? She'd dreamed of taking childbirth classes with Dimitri, but had known her fantasies were unattainable. Cold reality had been a life without him and the prospect of giving birth alone.

"I want you to be my labor coach. I want that more than anything." Then she burst into tears.

Dimitri looked like he'd just been hit by a truck. It would be funny, if she wasn't feeling so emotional.

"Alexandra, *yineka mou*, what is it?"

She shook her head and tried to stem the flow of tears, but the salty wetness kept up a steady flow down her cheeks.

"You must not upset yourself this way."

"I'm n-not upset," she sobbed.

"Come here." He took her glass from her hand and set it down, then pulled her into his arms and onto his lap. Just like in the limo. "Tell me what is making you cry." He sounded quite desperate.

"I wanted you to be there so many times. I would wake up and reach for you and only find an empty bed. The first time the baby really kicked, I wanted to call you, but I thought you were married. I m-missed you so much…"

His arms tightened around her and he whispered to her in Greek. The words were too low and quick for her to understand, but the soothing tone was not. She snuggled into his arms and cried out the frustration and pain of the last three months.

Her sobs eventually turned to small hiccups and he mopped up her face as if she were a child. She gave him a watery smile. "You'll be good with the baby."

He didn't respond to the joke. His eyes had darkened with unfathomable emotion. "You will never be without me again."

As vows went, that was a pretty comforting one. She nodded, accepting his words and the promise in his eyes.

CHAPTER TEN

HER tears were killing him. And she'd cried like this for a solid month after leaving Paris? The thought sent shards of pain slicing through him.

This was his woman. His wife. He had almost lost her. He would never let her go again. She had wanted him and he hadn't been there. He didn't want her to cry anymore. He wanted to look toward the future, for her to see things were going to be different.

He knew the truth now, who and what she was beyond the fashion model with an almost obsessive focus on her career. He understood that focus now. She'd been supporting her family, her mother now, but presumably Madeleine also until she had married Hunter. Alexandra hadn't been able to give up her career to travel with him because she had needed the money and she'd not wanted to take it from him.

His arms tightened around her of their own accord. She filled his arms so perfectly, their baby nestled between their bodies. Her tears were lessening, but had not stopped. He knew of only one way to completely overcome her outburst of emotion.

It was with the one thing he had not managed to kill between them with his actions three months ago. Passion.

Possessive pleasure coursed through him as he turned her face upward until he could cover her tear-drenched lips with his own. She belonged to him now, both legally and with the emotional ties of carrying his child. He did not have to seduce her into accepting his kisses. She tasted so sweet and her response was even sweeter. Her mouth opened under his on a small gasp and he deepened the kiss with one thought in mind.

He wanted to obliterate her sadness and replace it with pleasure in his arms.

He plundered her mouth, his own desire soon surging through him in unstoppable waves. She responded with all the generous eroticism that was in her nature, her hands coming up to cling to his shoulders, her mouth moving under his with enticing need. He wanted her under him, surrounding his sex, yielding her softness to the hardness that made him a man.

He needed to touch her. His hands were working their way under the hem of her sweater when a sound from the anterior of the cabin reminded him where they were. On his plane. Readying for takeoff. The flight attendant would be requesting them to buckle-up any moment now. The woman had probably already gotten an eyeful. He forced himself to pull back and gently set Alexandra from him.

She didn't understand at first and almost overcame his self-control trying to get back in his arms, but all at once she also seemed to realize what they were doing and where they were. Eyes gold with desire went round and wide while the pale perfection of her skin turned a rosy hue from embarrassment.

She primly straightened her sweater over the pants that clung to her sexy legs. "I forgot where we were."

He smiled. "I also."

She shot a sideways glance at the flight attendant who was pretending to be very busy in the galley.

"She's as discomforted as you are," he assured Alexandra.

"Is that meant to make me feel better like telling me a spider is more frightened of me than I am of it?" she asked, her blushing cheeks now almost fire engine red.

Unable to help himself, he reached out and cupped her nape. He needed to touch her in some way. "They are both the truth."

She cast another glance at the flight attendant, whose back was to them while she moved things around the galley in an obvious attempt to give them privacy. "I'm willing to buy the embarrassment thing, but not the spider theory."

He rubbed the delicate skin of her neck with his thumb. "After we have reached altitude, we can retire to the relative privacy of the bedroom."

That brought a smile, a very feminine, flirtatious smile. "You mean so I can get my sleep? Pregnant ladies need lots of rest, or so some domineering father-to-be has been telling me all week long."

He smiled at her reminder that she had not always taken his concern for her welfare with good grace. "I will assure you get your rest."

"Before or after?" she asked, her eyes sparkling with teasing lights he'd thought never to see again.

It *was* going to be all right. He would make it so. "After, most definitely after."

She gave an exaggerated sigh and clasped her hands, fluttering her eyelashes like a 1920's film star. "I can't wait."

The minx. "I'll make it worth your while," he promised, knowing that in this, he could satisfy her every desire.

"I'll see that you do."

Alexandra stood before Dimitri, divested of her travel clothes, her body throbbing with a desire he had fed until she was ready to scream for fulfillment. And that was before he undressed her. He was equally naked and his body's desire was apparent in the glorious size and rigidity of his erection.

His eyes were intent, appearing almost black in the dimmed lighting of the plane's bedroom. "You are so beautiful."

She felt the words clear to her toes and other nether regions that affected her breathing and her ability to stand. "I feel beautiful when you look at me like that, not like a misshapen woman with a football for a waistline."

"Misshapen?" His expression turned feral. "You are carrying my child. Your shape is the biggest turn-on imaginable. I get hard every time you turn sideways and I get a picture of the difference my son has made in your body."

She turned in silhouette, purposefully, provocatively and invitingly.

He accepted the invitation with all the speed of a jaguar going in for the kill. As prepared as she thought she was, she still squealed in the most embarrassing way when he swept her into his arms and then onto the bed in one heady rush.

He rolled onto his back and pulled her on top of him, spreading her legs so she was poised above his manhood, kissing him intimately. "You control how deep," was all he said.

And she did, sliding onto him centimeter by tantalizing centimeter. The feel of his hardness filling her so completely was incredible. She couldn't take all of him comfortably any longer, but he didn't push her or complain. He didn't seem disappointed at all if the look of intense ecstasy on his face was any indication.

While he allowed her to dictate the level of his penetration, he set the pace by holding her hips in an unshakable grip and moving her slowly and gently on his shaft. Her eyes slid shut as sensation crowded through her. How could she have survived months without this?

The answer was: she hadn't. She had spent that time living as half a person, hating him, missing him and wishing with all her heart things were different.

But now she was once again connected to the other half of herself and she celebrated the bliss that connection gave her. She forced her eyes open again. She wanted to see him, see the effect of their joining on *him*.

His eyes were slits, his face rock hard with passionate need. His grip on her hips was almost bruising, but she didn't complain. She needed to know she could push him to this place of no control. It gave her hope that his feelings for her were something more than guilt and responsibility, or even run-of-the-mill desire. There was nothing ordinary about the feelings they sparked in each other.

He increased the pace of their loving and she gasped as the pleasure increased as her insides began to tighten toward that ultimate satisfaction only he had ever given her. She couldn't support herself anymore and she whimpered, knowing she could not just collapse on top of him.

He seemed to understand her need because he rolled them both to the side, keeping their bodies intimately connected, pulling her thigh over his own. He took over the thrusting, holding her to him with a hand cupped possessively on her backside. Now that her hands were no longer occupied with holding her up, she could touch him. She brushed her fingers through the black silk of his chest hair and he shuddered.

She smiled, remembering what made him shudder even more and began to run light circles around his male nipples. When they were hard, she pinched them and his body bowed toward her in animalistic joy. She cried out as his body brushed hers in abandoned desire. The inner contractions started and she lost sense of time and place as her body convulsed in wave after wave of ecstatic delight.

His release was accompanied by a feral shout that left her eardrums ringing. The ecstasy of their union went on and on until they lay spent and sweating. He brushed his hand down her shoulder and her entire body contracted on another wave of pleasure. She moaned. It was too much.

He pulled her closer, until she was resting against him, shivering with intermittent aftershocks from their cataclysmic release. He soothed her with a hand on her back. "Shh. It's all right."

A sob welled up in her. "It's too much."

The calming motion of his hand did not stop. "No, *agapi mou,* it is so wonderful your body can barely stand it, but it is not too much."

Everything in her went still. Had he called her his love? Then reason asserted itself. After something as incredible as what they had just shared, any man would be forgiven for using such a tender term with his partner. It was just sex talk, but even so, it made her feel good and she hugged the endearment close to her heart.

She sighed and snuggled closer. "Relative privacy is right. If your crew didn't hear you shouting, they're deaf."

"I was not the only one making noise, hmm?"

She smiled against his chest. "I'm not answering."

Masculine laughter rumbled in his chest, vibrating through her. "I do not need this answer. I have ears to hear."

She didn't reply and they rested together in silence for several minutes before he shifted away from her. She murmured a protest, but he picked her up and carried her into the plane's small shower, where he proceeded to wash her so thoroughly she made a lot more noise and could not stand unaided when he was finished. He carried her back to bed and she fell asleep as he pulled her body snugly into his own.

She didn't know how long she slept, but when she woke, the lighting was no longer dimmed and Dimitri lay beside her watching her with an intent expression she could not decipher.

She smiled at him. "Hi. You're watching me."

"You are beautiful when you sleep."

Her smile turned wry. "Right. I bet my hair is sticking on end and I'm not wearing a speck of makeup."

A gentle finger traced the contours of her face. "You do not need makeup and your hair is very sexy."

She scooted into a sitting position. "I'm hungry."

He swung out of bed. "Stay where you are. I will order some food."

He pulled on a robe hanging in the miniscule closet and went into the main cabin. Which just went to show the difference between them. While she had modeled lingerie on the catwalks of Paris, she couldn't have faced the flight attendant in her bathrobe to save her life.

Dimitri was back fifteen minutes later carrying a tray laden with food. He laid it across her lap, dropped his robe and slid back into bed beside her. She ate a bowl of wild rice and mushroom soup, a crusty roll, and a brownie before sitting back against him, replete.

He pulled away from her long enough to set the tray on the floor. Settling back into their previous position, he laid his hand on the baby. Their son kicked and rolled, making both of them laugh. "He's very active in there, my son. He will be champion football player, that one."

"More like he'll keep us running with his antics."

"If he is anything like his mother, he will keep me on my toes until my hair turns gray."

She smiled at that and laid her hand over Dimitri's. "You know, you never did explain how you came to the conclusion the baby is yours."

"I told you about my friend."

"The doctor? Yes. I remember. That explains how, but not why. I mean just because you realized it was possible for you to be the father of my child, didn't mean you had to believe you were the father."

Dimitri exhaled a long breath. "I knew the truth long before I went to Nikos and asked him how it could be possible."

"Why?"

She felt his body go tense against her and she lifted her head off his chest to look into his eyes. They weren't revealing anything. "My mother and father died in an avalanche when I was ten years old."

"I know." It was the only thing he'd told her about his parents and one of the few things she knew about his family.

"My father was bringing her back from the ski lodge where she had been staying with her current lover."

"Current lover?"

Dimitri nodded, his head moving in a precise movement that was painful to watch. "She fell in love with daunting regularity, only one of those times was with my father."

She laid her hand over his heart and caressed the skin there in a comforting gesture. "Oh, Dimitri…"

He frowned as if her sympathy bothered him. It probably did. He was a very proud man.

"She had left before. There was even some question as to whether or not Spiros could claim the Petronides bloodline. My father insisted on having the tests done, my grandfather told me, not because he didn't love my brother but because he wanted to squelch the rumors. I believe he would have paid to have the tests doctored if they had come back negative. They did not."

"But if your mother was unfaithful, why did your father remain married to her?" She could not imagine a proud Petronides male doing so.

Dimitri's frown turned to a scowl. "He was obsessed with her. He too called this feeling love. Their marriage was volatile, their reunions dramatic but in the end her concept of love and his obsession killed them both."

No wonder Dimitri had such a jaundiced view of love. A depressing sense of hopelessness came over her. Would he ever allow himself that level of vulnerability after the example his parents had set him?

"It is not a pretty tale."

But it explained why he hadn't trusted her. He'd seen too much at an impressionable young age to take the fidelity of a woman for granted.

"We all have memories we would rather forget. Every family has its skeletons."

"Not according to your mother."

Alexandra smiled at his attempt at humor, but it was a small one. She didn't feel like laughing when she'd come face to face with Dimitri's reason for distrusting love. "Not all women are like your mother."

He shrugged. "Adultery is not such an uncommon thing."

"Is that why you were so sure I'd had a lover?"

He'd been waiting for her to betray him like his mother had done, because her betrayal had not only been against her husband. She'd done terrible emotional damage to her children as well.

The tension in him grew almost palpable. "It shames me, but yes."

"My unexplained trips must have played upon your fears."

"I was not afraid."

Right. "You don't like discussing your feelings, do you?" Why hadn't she caught on to that before?

"No, but you asked for a reason for my belief."

"Your mother's behavior explains why you didn't trust me. It does not explain what changed your mind."

"I realized you were not like her."

Hope erupted in her like Mount Vesuvius. If he already accepted she was nothing like his mother, he might eventually learn to trust her enough to let himself love her.

"I'm not," she reiterated for good measure. Then, because she was curious and couldn't help wanting to know, she asked, "When did you realize it?"

"When I returned to the apartment and found the pregnancy test on top of the lingerie."

"Oh." So, those final frantic moments in the apartment hadn't been wasted.

"There was a message in that, was there not?"

"Yes."

"You connected the pregnancy with our lovemaking."

He really did understand how her mind worked. "Did it make you remember what it had been like between us?" That was what she had intended.

"Yes." His expression was grim. "I knew you could not be that way with someone else. I still did not understand why you took trips you refused to explain to me, but I knew they were not to meet another man."

"Now you know."

"Now I know." His expression lightened and the hand on her shoulder ventured lower. "I know something else as well."

"Oh, what's that?" she asked breathlessly. That hand had found an already aching peak and gently tweaked it.

"There are things I would rather do with you than talk."

"I'm so surprised." She tried to sound mocking, but his touch was affecting her and her voice came out husky instead.

They spent a week in Athens, Dimitri insisting they have a honeymoon before he took her to the family home to meet his grandfather. It was a blissful seven days filled with touristy stuff and making love, lots and lots of making love.

Dimitri took her to see the obstetrician. She turned bright red and wanted to hide in a closet when Dimitri insisted on verifying her former obstetrician's advice about making love. He wasn't content until the doctor had done a full examination and Dimitri even requested an ultrasound to check the progress of the baby.

At four months, she hadn't been able to make out much on the ultrasound, but this time she didn't need the doctor to tell her where the baby's head and feet were. Nor did she need his interpretation to affirm the male sex of her child.

She pointed to the baby sucking its thumb in the womb and turned to share her delight with Dimitri. He was pale and his eyes had the dazed look of someone in serious shock.

"Mr. Petronides, are you all right?" the doctor asked.

"Dimitri?" she prompted when he didn't answer.

He turned to her, his eyes suspiciously bright. "That is my son. You nurture and protect him with your body. How can I ever thank you for this gift?"

She stared at him, nonplussed. She knew fatherhood had affected him strongly, but this was over the top...and she loved it. "No thanks necessary. He is my gift as well, *mon cher*."

Then Dimitri bent down and kissed her lips very gently as she lay on the examining table with the ultrasound gel making her tummy glisten.

The doctor looked on with tolerance. "You will be an indulgent papa I fear," he said.

Dimitri straightened to his full six foot, four inches and smiled. "Perhaps."

And Alexandra felt suffused with a glow of contentment.

That contentment lasted until Dimitri told her it was time for her to meet his grandfather.

"But what if he hates me?" she asked nervously. "He has every reason."

"Don't worry. He cannot help but adore you and he has no reason to hate you."

She would probably have been more confident of that concept if she were confident in Dimitri's adoration. But while he was overtly affectionate, complimentary and the charming companion she remembered, he never spoke words of love. He'd never called her his love again either. Not in Greek, not in English or even French which they slipped into frequently, it being the language they had originally used to communicate.

Love words never passed his lips…even in the height of passion.

CHAPTER ELEVEN

THEOPOLIS PETRONIDES did not look at all like a seventy-one-year-old man who had undergone heart by-pass surgery only a few months ago. Even leaning on a cane for support, he stood commandingly tall in the middle of the spacious Mediterranean-style room. His almost black eyes bore into Alexandra with disconcerting force from below steel-gray brows that matched the hair on his head.

"So this is my new granddaughter, heh?" He put his hand out commandingly. "Come here and greet your family, child."

Alexandra stepped forward with an assumed air of confidence, knowing to show her fear of his disapproval would be to lose his respect. She put her hands on his shoulders and reached up to kiss his cheek in greeting. He returned the salute with an approving smile before she stepped back.

"She doesn't look like her pictures," he said to Dimitri. Then he turned back to Alexandra. "I like you better this way. More natural. No fancy curls and dye jobs in your hair. My Sophia, she never used color on her hair." His gaze roamed over her face like he was taking inventory. "Eyes a nice hazel, not some impossible green. It suits you."

She bit back a smile at his blunt speaking. "Thank you. Dimitri thought maybe I was too ugly to support myself modeling any longer."

Both men spoke at once.

"I did not say—"

"What's the matter with my grandson?"

The smile broke through. "To be fair, I did look a fright from lack of sleep and morning sickness at the time."

Mr. Petronides beetled his brows at Dimitri. "Never tell a pregnant woman she looks a fright, even when her appearance would be enough to scare the goats from the hills. You will find yourself sleeping in the guest room and dealing with enough tears to sink a fishing boat, heh?"

"A little piece of wisdom Grandmother taught you?" Dimitri asked.

"My eyes. She taught me." He thumped his cane on the floor. "She asked me did I think she was fat? Of course she was fat. She was as round as a barrel and could barely walk. Your papa, he weighed ten pounds. She almost died. I said no more babies after that, I can tell you." Remembered fear clouded the old man's eyes for a moment. "I told her, yes I thought she'd gotten fat. She threw her dinner at me and then started in on the other dishes on the table. I said I was sorry and ended up with moussaka in my hair for my trouble. I ran for my life."

Dimitri's smile made Alexandra feel all gooey inside while she laughed at Mr. Petronides's story. "And she made you sleep in the guest room?"

He grinned and winked. "She locked our door."

"So you meekly found another bed for the night, hmm?" Dimitri asked mockingly.

Mr. Petronides laughed. "You are like me. Tell me what you would do if this lovely creature carrying my first great-grandson locked you out of her room." He waved his cane in Alexandra's direction.

Remembering a locked door and a very erotic shower, she smiled. No wonder Mr. Petronides had his security man teach Dimitri to pick a lock. For some reason that thought struck her as terribly funny and she started laughing so hard she was almost bent over double.

"So it's already happened, heh?"

Dimitri didn't answer, but took her firmly by the wrist and pulled her to a bright red armchair and almost pushed her into it. "The baby can't be getting enough oxygen with you laughing like a loon," he reproved her, but his eyes smiled and the corner of his mouth was engagingly tilted.

She took a deep breath and then another, finally managing to stop her mirth.

Mr. Petronides sat across from her, his face creased in a smile. "I did not have a smart grandfather to see to my education. I did not know how to pick a lock, so I threatened to kick in the door. She started crying so loud I could hear her through the thick wood." He rolled his eyes. "I climbed in through the window and took her by surprise, heh? It was a very satisfactory reunion."

Alexandra felt herself blush thinking of Dimitri's similar approach to the same problem.

He sat on the arm of her chair with his hand on her nape. "Are Spiros and Phoebe back in Paris?" he asked his grandfather.

"Yes. They came here first, though. Wanted to tell me what a wonderful new granddaughter I had."

Alexandra felt her cheeks heating again. She smiled at the older man. "I'm pleased they think so. I was worried they would resent me, but they were very kind as you have been."

Mr. Petronides waved his hand in an expansive Greek gesture. "It all worked out for the best, heh? I have both my grandsons married, a grandchild on the way and everyone is happy as a clam. Sophia could not have done a better job if she were alive to arrange it all,'' he said with obvious satisfaction. ''I think I must send prayers of thanks to the Good God above for so many gifts all at once to my family.''

His clear sincerity moved her deeply. She impulsively pushed herself out of the chair and crossed to give him another kiss on the cheek. ''Thank you. You are a very nice man.''

He waved her away, but his eyes revealed his pleasure in her words. ''Take her upstairs, Dimitrius. Pregnant ladies need their rest, heh?''

Which made her giggle again, being so close to what Dimitri said at least once a day since his return into her life. They were usually followed by his version of a nap, the resemblance to which was loosely based on the fact they went to bed.

Dimitri shook his head and swung her up against his chest. ''Come, *pethi mou.* I believe you need an afternoon nap.''

She went off into gales of laughter at that, but she choked back her amusement to protest. ''You can't carry me up the stairs. I'm too heavy.''

Dimitri's eyes glittered down at her. ''I won't be accused of implying you're fat. I learned my lesson from Grandfather's story.''

''Letting me walk on my own isn't making any sort of implication,'' she asserted.

He was already a third of the way up the stairs. ''It is after you said you were too heavy. Either you're implying you are fat or I am a wimp. I refuse to give credence to either.''

She subsided, secretly thrilled at his macho display of consideration.

He carried her into a bedroom so big that even the extra-long, king-size four-poster bed looked small in the middle of it. Two sets of side-by-side sliding glass doors looked out onto the wrap around terrace and the crystalline-blue sea beyond it and her gaze alighted there first.

"It's breathtaking, *mon cher*."

He let her slide down his body in a very suggestive manner and she turned from the incredible view to smile into his blue eyes. "A *nap* I think you said?"

"We must make sure you are properly tired," he informed her as he began working on the removal of her clothes.

Her gaze wandered around the room and was arrested by a familiar Lladro figurine on top of an antique chest of drawers. It was of a young girl in a garden. Dimitri had said the figure reminded him of Alexandra. The last time she'd seen it, it had been in a pile of paper wrapping on the floor of the living room in the Paris apartment.

She only had time to ponder the significance of it being here in Greece for a few moments before Dimitri's expert ministrations shut down her thinking processes entirely.

Alexandra pulled open yet another drawer in the antique bureau looking for her clothes. So far she had found a drawer full of Dimitri's socks, one full of silk boxers, another had the plain cotton t-shirts he liked to wear under sweaters or by themselves with jeans when he was relaxing at home. She closed the drawer and bent down to open the last one.

to midcalf. She loved the dress because it made her feel feminine even though she'd lost her waistline weeks ago.

She walked out of the dressing room to find Dimitri ready to go down in a dinner suit, silk shirt and understated tie.

Approval burned in his eyes when he looked at her. "I'm tempted to order dinner in our room tonight."

She gave him a severe look. "Don't you dare. I want to make a good impression on your grandfather."

"You already have, or couldn't you tell?"

"He's terribly nice."

Dimitri's dark brows rose. "When he wants to be."

"Well, I'm glad he wants to be nice to me."

"You are family."

She smiled, feeling warm inside. To be accepted simply because she was family and not because she did and said all the right things was a unique experience for her. She liked it.

Halfway through dinner, Dimitri was called from the table to take an international phone call.

Mr. Petronides winked at her. "Ah, the business, it intrudes, eh?"

She lifted her shoulders in a small, casual movement. "He must have a lot of catching up to do after all his time in New York and on our honeymoon."

"As you say." He beetled his brows at her in what was becoming a familiar gesture. "Tell me about your family."

So she did, telling him about Madeleine and Hunter, her mother and Dimitri's generosity in buying back the Dupree Mansion.

Mr. Petronides flicked his hand in a throw away gesture. "This is nothing to Dimitrius. Your mother is now his family. It is his responsibility to look after her."

Alexandra chewed her lip anxiously. "I did not marry your grandson so he would take over my financial responsibilities with my mother."

The old man laughed, long and richly. "Of course not, silly child. Had you wanted money from my grandson, you would never have left Paris."

She smiled with relief. "You're right. All I ever wanted was him. I didn't know about Phoebe," she added earnestly.

"*Ne.* Yes. I know."

"I'm sorry."

"For what are you sorry child?"

"Causing Dimitri to break his promise to you."

Mr. Petronides nodded his head knowingly. "You feel the weight of such things. I like this."

"Thank you." She wasn't all that fond of the guilt that plagued her, though.

"But I do not want you to feel badly my grandson could not keep a promise he made under the threat of my health." He sighed. "I should not have put such a pressure on him."

"He told me in Paris that his marriage to Phoebe had been expected for a long time," she said with a small spark of residual pain. She frowned. "You must have been very disappointed."

"*Disappointed?*" He looked startled, his dark eyes wide for a second of stunned silence. "I wanted the certainty of great-grandchildren and I have that now, heh?" he asked with a pointed look at her stomach, not quite hidden by the table.

She felt herself blushing...again. The Petronides men were not good for her composure.

He laughed again, this time with wholly masculine amusement. "Do not worry about Dimitrius breaking his promise to marry Phoebe. It all worked out for the best, heh? Phoebe is happier with Spiros, I think. She's a little afraid of Dimitri. I did not see this until after the betrothal was announced and they were here together."

It astounded her, but no one in Dimitri's family seemed bitter with her over the changes her pregnancy had wrought among them.

He took a sip of his wine. "And this grandson of mine, he kept his second promise, heh?"

"Second promise?"

"He married you just as he promised me he would." Dark eyes glittered with steely determination. "He gave my great-grandson the Petronides name. *Ne*, yes, I am a content man."

Shock congealed the smile on Alexandra's face. "He promised you he would marry me?"

Mr. Petronides nodded his gray head. "He is a man of his word, my grandson. His second promise more than negated his first," he said with pride. "Your son will be raised a Petronides. I could die tomorrow happy."

"Don't talk like that," she admonished even as her heart was breaking within her.

Dimitri had *promised* his grandfather he would marry her? He had *promised* to give their son the Petronides name?

"The young. They fear talk of death. I am old. I do not fear it, but I would like to teach my great-grandson to pick a lock before I go." He laughed at his own joke.

She forced her lips to smile. "I thought it was your security man who taught Dimitri?"

"He did, but I made him teach me too so I could

teach Spiros. Maybe Phoebe has a surprise to come one day, heh?"

Alexandra couldn't believe she could carry on a conversation with Dimitri's grandfather and pretend nothing was wrong while inside she felt like she was dying.

Dimitri had not married her because he wanted *her*. He hadn't even married her for the baby's sake. *He'd married her because he had made a promise to his grandfather.* His brother had prevented him from keeping the first promise, a huge blow to his Greek pride. However nothing, not even her angry rejection had been able to stop him from keeping the second one.

No wonder Dimitri had put up with so much from her. He had been determined to keep his oath to his grandfather, no matter what obstacles she put in his path. When she had refused to discuss the option of marriage, he had seduced her. He had charmed her mother and even used the repurchase of Dupree Mansion as an incentive to get her to marry him.

In the back of her mind, she'd thought all that effort must mean he cared, that he would have given up and accepted visitation if she didn't matter to him personally. Now she knew differently. He might not love her, but he loved his grandfather…enough to marry the mistress that hadn't been proper marriage material before.

How could she have forgotten that? Dimitri had dismissed the idea of a future with her out of hand. And gullible idiot that she was, she'd conveniently ignored that fact when he started talking marriage. For the first time since agreeing to marry Dimitri, she felt bile rise in the back of her throat.

She took a hasty sip of her fruit juice and prayed the nausea would go away.

"Are you all right, child? You look pale."

She looked down at her half-eaten dinner. "Just tired and maybe a little sick," she admitted. "Morning sickness did not go away after the first trimester like it's supposed to." But it had for a while.

Mr. Petronides nodded knowingly. "I remember. Do you want to lie down?"

Did she? She could hide from her misery upstairs, or end up wallowing in it. She really didn't want her own company right now. "I'd rather stay here with you."

"Ah, kindness to an old man."

"Not at all. I enjoy your company," she replied truthfully.

"Then tell me about this job you had. I have never met a fashion model."

She told him about her life as Xandra Fortune and ended up talking about how she had met Dimitri. Impossibly, she found herself laughing over memories of her life with Dimitri before she'd gotten pregnant.

She and Mr. Petronides had gone to the drawing room for coffee when Dimitri rejoined them. She was telling his grandfather about the first argument they'd ever had.

"I was doing a swimsuit cover. Dimitri came to the shoot on a whim."

"I came back a day early and surprised her," Dimitri inserted as he walked into the room.

Her head snapped around and she met his eyes briefly before her own gaze skated away. She didn't know how she managed it, but she didn't stand up and harangue him like a fishwife for once again withholding a crucial piece of information from her. For letting her believe he might be coming to love her when he'd been motivated by his personal sense of honor, not personal need.

Dimitri joined her on the brightly colored Mediterranean-style sofa. Her body tensed in response to his nearness. If only she could forget what he made her feel as easily as he conveniently forgot to tell her about his second promise.

She focused her attention on Mr. Petronides who was smiling benevolently at them. "He didn't like the suit I was wearing for the shoot and demanded I go to the trailer and take it off."

"So, being a reasonable woman and understanding the possessiveness of a traditional Greek male, you immediately changed, heh?" Mr. Petronides's eyes twinkled mockingly.

Dimitri snorted. "She threatened to take it off right there in front of everyone if I didn't shut up and go to the sidelines." He still sounded chagrined by her tactics.

She allowed herself a brief glance at him, but it hurt too much to make full frontal contact so she looked back at his grandfather. "It worked."

The older man roared with laughter and said something rapid to Dimitri in Greek that she didn't catch. Dimitri scowled.

She smiled. Anything that made him frown made her happy, or so she told herself.

"She has led you a merry chase, has she not, Dimitrius?"

Dimitri laid his arm across her shoulders. "Yes, but I have her now and I'm not letting go."

She wanted to cuddle into his side and kick him in the shin at the same time. Was she going crazy? She must be. And he was the one driving her there.

She jumped up. "I think I'll go to bed." She turned to Dimitri. "You needn't feel obligated to join me. I'm sure you and your grandfather have a great deal to catch up on." The words were stilted, but they were the best she could do.

Dimitri's eyes narrowed and he stood. "I will see you upstairs."

His grandfather stood as well, slowly coming to his feet, the expression on his face one of fatigue. It was the first time since she'd met him that he had shown a glimmer of the effects of his recent ill health. "Do not return downstairs for my sake, Dimitrius. Both the very old and the very young need their rest. I will find my bed."

She gave the old man a quick kiss on the cheek before turning to go upstairs.

Dimitri stayed behind a few moments saying goodnight to his grandfather, but caught up with her before she had reached the top of the stairs. She allowed him to take her hand, but when he reached for her later in bed she told him she was too tired to make love.

He'd married her because of a promise to a sick relative. For the first time she felt an unwelcome weight around her heart because of her pregnancy. If she hadn't gotten pregnant, Dimitri would have let her go without a second thought.

Even if Phoebe had still ended up married to Spiros, Dimitri wouldn't have gone looking for his discarded lover, Xandra Fortune.

Because his grandfather would not have extracted that second promise.

CHAPTER TWELVE

THE next morning Alexandra came to consciousness alone in the bed. She cuddled Dimitri's pillow, inhaling his scent, wishing his absence from their bed was not a physical ache in her heart. He had left for Athens two hours ago, but not before waking Alexandra with slow, tender caresses that had ended in such exquisite release she'd cried.

She'd gone to sleep determined not to make love with him. That determination hadn't lasted past his first drugging kiss around dawn. She rolled onto her back and stared at the ceiling. There were no answers to her predicament in the white plaster.

A knock on the door heralded the arrival of a maid with the breakfast Dimitri had ordered for her. She scooted into a sitting position and allowed the maid to lay the breakfast tray over her legs. An unexpected smile tilted her lips when she saw the dry toast, fruit, eggs and single slice of bacon. He'd teased her about her tendency to order the same meal for breakfast every morning. He'd said pregnant women were supposed to crave pickles and ice cream, not dry toast and bacon.

The food was accompanied by the awful tasting herbal tea she'd taken to drinking in the morning to settle her nausea. She ignored it, grateful the stomach upset that had plagued her the night before was gone. She refused to contemplate the possibility Dimitri's lovemaking had been more effective in making her feel better than all the herbal tea she'd drunk.

The maid opened the curtains letting in the bright Greek sun before leaving Alexandra to finish her breakfast alone.

She ate by rote, her thoughts casting back to the night before and then more recently to earlier that morning. She still tingled in places from her husband's possession. Remembered pleasure caused an unwelcome throbbing in her lower body. If he were here now, she'd be hard pressed not to beg him to make love to her.

Huffing out a sigh of frustration at her body's betrayal, she climbed out of bed. As she showered and dressed, she considered her situation pragmatically. What, after all, had changed? She'd known Dimitri didn't love her when she agreed to marry him.

But she hadn't known about the promise, her heart cried.

Did it matter?

Of course it mattered. It was humiliating to realize she'd been married for a reason totally unrelated to herself. She had her pride.

And it had been a cold companion for three long months in New York. She'd been miserable without him. She'd missed him like a wound in her soul every day they had been apart, even believing he had been married to another woman hadn't dulled the unwanted desire to be back in his arms.

She walked over to the dresser and picked up the Lladro statue. It was so delicate. She could remember with absolute clarity her sense of joy and wonder when he had bought it for her. She ran her forefinger along the figurine's head and the graceful lines of her dress. Then she lightly touched the kitten playing at the woman's feet.

Dimitri had saved this reminder of a happier time between them. He had saved her clothes. He had brought her things here, to the family home, obviously believing she would live here as well one day. Of course he had believed it. He knew about his promise to his grandfather, her mind insidiously reminded her.

But he hadn't had to save her things. She'd left them in an insulting pile on the floor, flouting his pride, condemning him with their presence and her absence.

She had a choice. She could fight the truth and make both Dimitri and herself miserable, or she could accept reality.

She and Dimitri would have the kind of marriage people in his world and her mother's world excelled at…a marriage of convenience. After all, she was no longer Xandra Fortune, the nobody model he slept with, but Alexandra Petronides, his wife and a woman with a background he could be proud of.

Sharp slashes of pain cut at her heart at the last thought. She'd spent her whole life being accepted for the trappings of who she was. Her own mother had withheld her love and approval for the six long years Alexandra had spent as Xandra Fortune. Cecelia had been effusive in her approval the week before the wedding though. She had been thrilled her daughter had landed such a catch in the marriage market.

And she'd positively gushed her appreciation for her oldest daughter when Dimitri repurchased the Dupree Mansion.

Alexandra thought of the empty years ahead being nothing more than the traditional Greek wife, an adjunct in Dimitri's life, not a major player. She determined then and there not to fall passively into that role. She'd married Dimitri as she'd said she would. Their son would be raised a Petronides.

Because she loved Dimitri, she would never leave him. But she wasn't going to play doormat. He'd said she could have anything she wanted to make her happy. What would he say if she told him she wanted to go back to modeling after the baby was born? What would he say if she said *that* would make her happy?

He said nothing.

Dimitri stared at her across the width of the bed, his blue eyes unreadable, his naked body erect and for once not showing the least signs of desire. Waves of something feral rolled off him and made her shiver.

"Do you have a problem with me returning to my career after the baby is born?"

His hands fisted at his sides and his jaw clenched. "In New York, you told me you didn't want to return to modeling."

She shrugged. "I didn't think I had a choice. The life of a single parent is difficult enough without pursuing a career as demanding as that of a model."

"You want to leave our son to be raised by a nanny?" Distaste tainted every word he bit out.

No. Damn it. That was not what she wanted. One of the things she'd been looking forward to after her marriage was the ability to stay home with her baby. She wanted to breastfeed. She wanted to be there for her baby's first word, his first step. What had her muddled thinking that morning led her to?

"I don't have to take every assignment. I can give up catwalks and commercials and concentrate on photo shoots."

"You can give up your job entirely." He glared at her. "You are my wife. *You have no need to work.*"

She gripped the sheet covering her until there was a

bunched up wad of polished cotton in her fist. "Are you saying you refuse to let me?"

He rubbed his eyes, looking as tired as he had that first day in New York. "Would you listen to me if I did?"

"I'm going to live my own life, if that's what you mean."

"When have you ever done anything else?" He climbed into bed and turned out the light before lying on his side facing away from her.

Evidently the discussion was over.

She scooted down and turned on her side, trying to get comfortable. She'd grown used to the security of Dimitri's arms around her while she slept. Now, the width of the king size bed divided them. She felt stupid tears burn the back of her eyes. She'd brought this on herself.

She didn't really want to go back to modeling. It had only ever been something she did to provide for her family. Something she *could* do with the resources at her disposal. Now, she'd threatened to return to it for nothing more than to anger Dimitri just because he didn't love her.

Okay…maybe not just to make him mad. A small part of her had hoped, against all evidence to the contrary, that he could accept her for what she was, not what he wanted her to be. She had thrown down the gauntlet of her career as a test, she realized now. A test that had failed spectacularly.

She had been looking for a way to assuage her feelings of rejection suffered as Xandra Fortune, his lover. Stupid. She'd only opened herself up for more of the same. Hot tears leaked out between her tightly shut eyelids and she sniffed, trying to swallow back the tears and pain.

Sudden heat engulfed her and she was surrounded by hard, masculine muscle. "Do not cry, *pethi mou*. I am an idiot. If you want to pursue your career, I will not stand in your way."

"Dimitri?"

"Who else?" he asked with lazy humor as he tucked her into the curve of his body.

That wasn't what she'd meant. "I knew it was you...I'm just surprised at what you are saying." She wished the lights were on so she could see his expression. Did he mean it?

"I am accustomed to getting my own way."

She gave a watery smile he couldn't see. "I know."

"I am sometimes arrogant."

She didn't answer, thinking silence more politic than speech.

"I hated the time your career took away from me before, but I must not be selfish. If it is what you need for happiness, I will not stand in your way."

Had he really hated to be away from her? "It won't embarrass you to have a model for a wife?" she probed.

"Why should it? I was not ashamed when you were my lover."

"That was different. You even said so."

"I said many things I learned to regret," he said heavily.

"Mama would have a hissy fit."

"I will deal with your mother. She thinks I am a god, I have returned to her the family home."

The remnants of Alexandra's tears turned to laughter. "You mean it?"

"Yes."

"Turn on the light," she pleaded.

"Why?"

"I want to see you."

He humored her and a second later the soft glow of the bedside lamp illuminated his chiseled features. Sincerity burned in his eyes.

"You really will support me returning to my Xandra Fortune career."

"No." His mouth set in a firm line.

She sucked in her breath on a wave of pain. She'd been mistaken. He couldn't accept the woman she'd been.

"You can model, but you are Alexandra Petronides. You will not deny me my place in your life."

The arrogant statement should have infuriated her, but instead it made her heart sing. Not only would he support her career as a model, but he had no desire to distance himself from it by her using a working name.

He didn't love her, but he did respect her. "I don't want to be a model," she admitted.

His expression turned to stone. "What?"

"I want to stay home with the baby."

"Then what the hell has this last half hour been about?" he demanded in a shout that hurt her eardrums.

"Don't raise your voice to me!"

His jaw clenched and she could just see him counting to ten. "Why did you tell me you wanted to be a model when you did not?" he asked, teeth gritted, eyes spitting frustrated anger.

"I needed to know."

"What did you need to know?"

"If you accepted the woman I was…the woman who became pregnant with your baby. When you asked me to marry you, I was living as Alexandra Dupree."

"They are the same woman. I have said this before."

But she hadn't taken it in, or maybe she hadn't believed him. "You tossed me out as Xandra Fortune."

"You thought if you went back to modeling and calling yourself this other name, I would do so again?" he asked, outrage lacing every syllable.

"No, of course not." But it all seemed muddled now. None of her thinking since discovering his second promise had been particularly clear. "I don't know."

He flopped back on his pillow and covered his eyes with his forearm. "You are never going to forget, are you?"

"What do you mean?" she asked anxiously.

"My stupidity. You will never trust me enough to let yourself love me again."

"You don't believe in love," she reminded him.

He moved his arm and she flinched at his bleak expression. "You do not know what I believe in, Alexandra."

"Why didn't you tell me about the second promise to your grandfather?" she asked in a whisper. She hadn't meant to ask, but now that the words were out, they could not be unsaid.

He sat up, his body vibrating with something she would not label defeat in a million years. "This is why you put me through hell tonight thinking you wanted to go back to a career that always came before me?"

"It didn't come before you."

"*Ohi? No? I can't come with you, I've got a photo shoot. I'll be gone for a week to do the commercial. We can't make love right now, I need to sleep so I won't look like a hag in the morning.*" He repeated excuses she'd given him in the past with cruel sarcasm. "Even our damned sex life was dictated by your career. Do not say you did not put it before me."

"I had to work, Dimitri. You know why now."

"But I did not then and you did not enlighten me."

"I couldn't."

"Why not? Why could you not tell me who you really were?"

"Because..."

"I will tell you why. You did not trust me. You gave me your body, but not your trust. Not your heart." His Greek accent had gotten very thick.

"That's not true! I loved you!"

He slammed out of bed and towered over it on the opposite side. "Such a love I can do without. You lied to me every day we were together."

She gasped in outrage. "I did not lie to you."

"You said you were Xandra Fortune."

"I was Xandra Fortune."

He sliced through the air with his hand. "What is the use? You rewrite history to suit your own purpose."

"I don't have to rewrite history to know you kicked me out of your life like a pile of garbage!" she screamed at him, shocked at her own loss of control.

His shoulders slumped, his face looked haggard. "It will always come back to this, will it not?" He turned away.

And suddenly she was out of bed, vibrating with rage suppressed for months while pain and despair held sway. "Don't you turn your back on me, you bastard!"

He spun around. "What did you call me?"

"Nothing worse than what you called me that day at *Chez Renée*," she accused.

"I called you nothing that day."

"You called me a whore!"

He looked shocked. "I did not say this."

"Yes you did. That damn jeweler's box said it for you!"

"I bought the bracelet before my grandfather's heart attack. I had meant it as a gift to express my affection...then in my jealousy it became something else."

So, it had been a bracelet. She'd never looked. "You expect me to believe that, after what you said that day?"

"No." He shook his head. "I do not expect you to believe anything I say. You did not trust me before I betrayed our love, how can you possibly trust me now?"

In the red mists of fury surrounding her, she doubted her hearing, but she could have sworn he'd said he'd betrayed their *love*. She shook her head, trying to clear it.

"As I thought." He stood there in silence for several seconds. "Is there anything more you wish to say?"

She slowly jerked her head to one side in a negative. She'd said enough.

He braced himself, as if for a blow and then nodded. "I cannot sleep here tonight next to a woman who hates me. I cannot hold you in my arms knowing you suffer my touch for the sake of our son."

She felt her heart contract like a vise had been clamped onto it and was being slowly tightened. "I don't hate you." As for suffering his touch, how could he think that?

His eyes said he did not believe her.

He went into the dressing room and came out wearing a robe. "I'll sleep next door in the guest room."

She wanted to beg him not to go, but her tongue would not form the words. His hand was on the door handle when she asked, "Why didn't you tell me about the second promise?"

"I knew you would believe I had only come after you to keep it. I needed you to believe I wanted you for myself." Then he opened the door and was gone.

I needed you to believe I wanted you for myself. You never trusted me. You lied to me. You hate me. Dimitri's words ran like an unending refrain through her head. *Such a love I can do without.*

Love. He had said he had betrayed their *love*. She knew it. While she'd been screaming her invective at him, he'd admitted he had loved her. Did he still love her? Could he after the way she'd rejected him over and over again since he found her in New York?

She still loved *him*.

She did love him, but she hadn't acted like it. Not when they'd been together in Paris and not since his resurgence in her life. She had withheld her secrets, herself and her trust. What kind of love was that?

The only kind of love she'd known—conditional and with limits. Her limits had been born of fear, but they had damaged Dimitri as much as her mother's limits had hurt her. Alexandra felt that knowledge clear to her soul. She had wanted to receive unconditional love, but she hadn't been willing to give it. Was it too late?

She went toward the dressing room with one purpose in mind. She flipped on the light and started sifting through her lingerie. There had to be something, then she remembered and started looking for white gossamer. Dimitri had bought it for her their second week together. It was a flowing nightgown with a princess cut and yards and yards of gossamer fabric that fell from the gathered waistline below her breasts. The wide straps accentuated the delicate curve of her shoulders and it had reminded her of a wedding dress...a see-through wedding dress.

It was one of the few gowns that would fit over her

pregnant stomach. She slipped it on, her mission firmly in her mind. To be on the safe side, she pulled a robe on over it as well. No telling who might be wandering around in the hall outside her door to witness her state of dress. Security cameras at the very least.

She sifted through her cosmetic bag until she found a hatpin she used to unstop clogged tubes of makeup. She walked over to Dimitri's dresser and pulled out the bottom drawer. The pregnancy test was still there. With it and the hatpin clutched firmly in her hands, she left the bedroom.

Dimitri had said he was going to be next door in the guestroom. The door to the room on the right of their bedroom suite stood open. The door to the left was closed. She walked toward it. She tried the handle. It turned in her hand and she breathed a sigh of relief. She hadn't had a grandfather with tremendous foresight see that she was taught how to pick a lock.

The hatpin was for effect.

She opened the door and stepped into the room. The bed was empty, she could see from the light spilling through the open doorway. There was no other light in the room. She didn't need light to know he was there, though. She could sense the presence of the other half of her soul as surely as she knew her feet were attached to her body though she couldn't see them.

He stood at the window, his hand gripping one of the heavy draperies. He'd shed the robe he had been wearing and the sculpted muscles of his virile body lured her with animal magnetism. She could never let this man go again.

"Go back to bed, Alexandra."

She dropped the dressing gown and took a step toward him. "Make me."

He tensed, but he did not turn around. "I am in no mood for further arguments. Spare us both more unpleasantness and leave me. Please."

CHAPTER THIRTEEN

IT WAS the "please" that did it.

She couldn't stand to hear her proud Greek husband pleading with her.

She flew across the room and landed against his back, her arms going around him like channel locks. She felt the baby move and kick. She was plastered so close to Dimitri, he had to have felt their son as well.

His entire body shuddered as if he'd been touched by a live electric wire.

She pressed her face into back, kissing him with feverish intensity. "I don't hate you. I love you," she whispered fiercely against his skin. "I'm sorry I've expressed my love so dismally you can't believe me. Love is supposed to be generous, but I've been too busy protecting myself."

He forcefully peeled her hands from his body and spun around. "Don't *yineka mou*. I cannot stand it. It is I who have hurt you. I who stupidly rejected your gift of a child, your gift of yourself. You have nothing to reproach yourself for."

"Don't I?" She shook her head and placed her hand over his mouth when he opened it to speak. "Please. Let me say this."

His lips moved against her palm in a kiss as gentle as the brush of angel's wings and he nodded.

She lowered her hand and stepped back from him. She met the blue depths of his gaze and held it. "I love my mother, but she's always doled out her approval and affection based on my performance as her daughter." Alexandra took a deep breath and let it out. "I learned early on that love was conditional, that it had limits and that it hurt."

He nodded as if he understood and considering his background, she had no doubt he did.

"So when I fell in love with you, I set limits on that love, impossible conditions you had no way of meeting. I didn't tell you the truth because I was afraid to. You were, you are, this incredible guy, Dimitri. You teased me about how my mom sees you as a god among men, but for me it's no joke. You're so much more than anything I ever believed I could have. More generous. More sexy. More wonderful. More man. More everything and I couldn't believe you wanted me."

She sucked in more air, trying to control her emotions, before going on. "It shocked me that you'd want Xandra Fortune, but I was sure you wouldn't want Alexandra Dupree, a convent educated girl from a conservative family that had lost all its money. And to be honest, I thought if I kept that part of myself from you, I could protect myself from you taking me over completely. There would still be that part of me left when you were gone."

At his look of dawning understanding, she nodded. "You were right in Paris. I did expect our relationship to end, though I didn't consciously acknowledge it at the time. By keeping the other part of my life from you, I was preparing to go on when it did. But it didn't work because as you've said more than once—I was both Xandra Fortune and Alexandra Dupree with you. I grieved your loss in my other life as surely as I would have grieved if I'd stayed in Paris."

"I wish you had stayed. I would have found you sooner."

She grimaced. "I didn't think you wanted to find me."

Devastating pain radiated from his eyes. "I know. This is my fault."

She didn't deny it. They each had their portion of blame for the disastrous end to their relationship.

"I should have told you where I was going on my trips. I made it easy for you to distrust me and when I told you about the baby, it was understandable you thought at first I might have had a lover."

"No! It was not!" The words exploded from him. "I let my mother's behavior color how I saw *you*. I had no reason to distrust you. You were so generous with me when we made love, so giving of yourself. I knew, I *knew* you could not have been that way with anyone else, but I was fighting a rearguard action against ending up as obsessed as my father had been. The feelings I had for you made me vulnerable. That was not acceptable, so I acted like the bastard you called me."

Tears clogged her throat. "No."

"Yes. My only excuse is that I was not thinking clearly. Worry for my grandfather, frustration over the promise he had extracted from me, it played hell with my thinking processes. The worst part was the desperation I felt at the thought of losing you. It horrified me and when I am afraid, I act. I lashed out at you and I lost you."

"I waited a week for you," she said helplessly. Not wanting him to feel worse than he already did, but wanting him to know she'd loved him enough to stay even after he had her evicted from the apartment. "I didn't leave until I saw the announcement of your engagement to Phoebe."

His eyes closed and his head went back, his jaw taut. "I knew I'd made the biggest mistake of my life when I let my grandfather put the announcement in the paper. It all hit me. How wrong everything was. How wrong everything would continue to be if I didn't get you back, but you were gone, *pethi mou.*"

There was a wealth of pain in those words.

"I'm sorry," she whispered.

"I could not find you," he said, as if she hadn't spoken, "I had my detectives looking everywhere, but you had disappeared as if you didn't even exist. When I slept, I had nightmares of you falling down a deep hole and vanishing forever."

His skin broke out in sweat at the memory.

She stepped forward and laid her hand against his heart. "Losing you hurt so much, I thought I was going to die."

He crushed her to him. "I'm sorry."

Two words sincerely spoken, words she had never heard him say in all the time they had known each other. And they healed wounds deep in her heart.

"I love you, *mon cher.*"

He kissed her with a passion that seared her soul. She was lost in the beauty of his kiss when he pulled away abruptly.

"Ouch."

She looked up, dazed. "What?"

"Something poked me."

She looked down at her left hand where the hatpin protruded from her tightly clutched fingers. She lifted her hand and opened it to reveal the two objects she held. "I think it was the hatpin."

"Hatpin?" he asked as if he didn't know what one was. Maybe he didn't. Not many women had them anymore, but her mother was old fashioned. She still carried starched hankies.

"Yes."

"You planned to wear a hat?"

She laughed softly. "No. It was to pick the lock."

"But I did not lock the door."

"I wanted to be prepared."

"You know how to pick a lock?" he asked, a smile tugging at his mouth.

She shook her head. "I wasn't going to let that stop me."

He laughed and pulled her back into his arms, this time with more caution. "Alexandra Petronides, you are my dearest treasure and I will love you forever."

She gulped back tears and pleaded, "Say it again."

He cupped her face between the solid warmth of his hands. "I love you whether you are the independent career woman, Xandra Fortune, the spitting kitten, Alexandra Dupree or any other persona you choose to take on. You are the wife of my heart."

"Show me, Dimitri."

And he did. Beautifully. Erotically. Thoroughly. Then he carried her back to their bed and showed her again. She fell asleep in his arms.

"So, what was the pregnancy test for, *agapi mou?*"

Dimitri had convinced Alexandra to redon the shimmery nightgown from the night before and she sat curled in his lap in a chair on their private terrace a little after sunrise.

"Just a minute. Let me show you." She jumped off his lap and went in search of the small white stick. She found it with the hatpin on the floor of the guestroom. She went back out onto the terrace and couldn't help smiling at the picture her husband presented in nothing but a pair of black silk boxers.

Her gown covered more of her body with fabric, but none of it with modesty and his eyes gleamed their appreciation at her as she approached him.

She knelt down on the tile by his knees and presented the pregnancy test to him. "I'm pregnant with your baby, Dimitri."

His eyes widened, then narrowed in understanding. "You are giving me a second chance."

"Love can erase the mistakes of the past."

Something profound moved across his features and he reached for the stick. "I can think of nothing greater in life than to have you carry my child."

They were the words she had wanted to hear so much five months ago and she smiled with a radiance she made no effort to hide. "I love you, *mon cher*."

She'd said it so many times over the past hours, the words should have lost their impact, but she knew they never would and the expression on his face told her he felt the same.

"I love you, Alexandra. Never leave me again."

"Never," she agreed fervently.

He leaned down and kissed her softly before lifting her back into his lap.

"I still feel bad about your grandfather," she admitted.

"Why should you feel this?"

"All those awful news stories. They must have devastated him."

Dimitri tilted her chin so they were looking into one another's eyes. "It was not the tabloid gossip that upset

Grandfather so badly he had another attack.'' Guilt chased across Dimitri's features. ''I am fully to blame.''

''But…''

''Grandfather didn't even see the news stories until after coming out of the hospital.''

''I don't understand.''

''I told my grandfather I couldn't marry Phoebe and then I told him why.''

''Because I was pregnant with your baby.''

He shook his head, his eyes warming her. ''Because I love you. He had the heart attack when he started yelling at me for being a fool after I admitted I'd evicted you from the apartment and could not find you.''

She couldn't take it in. ''You already knew you weren't going to marry Phoebe before the tabloids ran the gossip about us?''

''I knew I wasn't going to marry Phoebe the day you told me you were pregnant, but I was insane with unreasonable jealousy, angry at myself, angry at my grandfather. I went off the rails and didn't get back on them until I saw you standing next to your sister that first night in New York.''

''I don't know. You acted pretty derailed then too.''

''She told me you had died! Do you have any idea what that did to me?''

She was beginning to have an inkling. If he had loved her, and now she knew he had, such news would have been soul destroying. ''I'm sorry, Dimitri.'' She leaned forward and kissed him, wanting to heal the hurts of the past.

He kissed her back with enough passion to leave her gasping for breath a minute later.

''I don't know if I can ever forgive myself for what I did to you.''

Her eyes misted, but she smiled. "Please. You have to. I don't want to spend the rest of my life looking back. My present is glorious now that you are in it, now that I know you love me!"

"I saw the paparazzi outside the restaurant in New York and did nothing," he said with the air of a man who felt he had to admit everything.

She tried to figure out what he was saying. "Are you saying you wanted them to make the connection with my Xandra Fortune identity?"

He did his best to look humble, but it didn't come naturally. "I realize this was wrong."

"But you would do it again."

"I was desperate," he defended.

Dimitri desperate. Her heart just melted. "That's really sweet, *mon cher*."

"You are not angry with me?" he asked warily.

She snuggled closer, curling her fingers in his chest hair. "No. It's flattering to think of my Greek tycoon so desperate he stooped to nefarious means to win me," she said cheekily.

"I will never let you go again," he growled against her temple and then did something truly amazing with his tongue to her ear.

She shivered with the excitement only he could generate. "You're stuck with me for life, Dimitri Petronides."

"Count on it, *agapi mou*."

The baby kicked and they both laughed.

She rubbed the taut skin over the protruding little foot. "He approves."

"He's already brilliant," said the proud papa.

"Mmm…" she agreed, feeling contentment clear to her toes.

Dimitri shifted under her and she felt another protruding member, but this wasn't infantile at all.

"You look very sexy in that nightgown, even more sexy than you did when I first bought it."

"Over six months pregnant and you think I'm sexier than I was when we first met?" she mocked, secretly thrilled by the compliment.

He didn't smile at her joke. "Yes. Sexier. More beautiful. More everything because now you are mine and I know you are mine."

"For the rest of my life," she affirmed.

And then she set about showing him the kind of love she planned to give him for all that time: a passionate, unconditional, without limits kind of love.

Dimitri stood in the doorway of the Dupree Mansion nursery watching his wife tuck their small son into his cot. Little Theo, named after his great-grandfather, was nine months old. He had loved the excitement of Christmas, but had been ready for bed a good hour before Alexandra had been able to prize him from his fond grandmother's arms.

Cecelia had been in her element hosting Christmas for her family and Dimitri's besides in her New Orleans home. Alexandra had asked him to let her mother do it and as with so many things related to his wife's desires, he hadn't even considered saying no. She was the love of his life and he would do anything to make her happy.

He'd learned to appreciate the difference between that and the obsessive love his father had suffered from toward his mother. Alexandra had shown him by wanting only the best for him in return. It was a heady sensation.

Alexandra laid her hand on Theo's back and sang a soft French lullaby. Far from letting a nanny raise their son, she had insisted on seeing to all his needs, including midnight feedings, three-in-the-morning feedings and dawn wake-up calls to change Little Theo's nappy for the first few months. Dimitri hadn't minded. He liked getting up with Alexandra and watching his son nurse. It was a sight so beautiful, it transfixed him.

She was an amazing mother and an even more incredible wife. He thanked God daily for second chances.

She finally felt all was well with their son and turned to leave the nursery. She smiled up at him, her face soft with love. It was a look he would never take for granted again.

"He's out for the count."

Dimitri put his arm around her and drew her next door to their bedroom. "I have something for you."

"Dimitri." She drew his name out like it had six syllables. "You've already given me a mountain of gifts today. It's worse than last year."

He smiled in remembrance of their first Christmas together. They'd spent it with his grandfather in Greece. She'd cried when he gave her an eternity ring. He'd almost died from pleasure when she gave him his gift later that night...herself wrapped in a see-through red nightgown that had made her look like a very sexy, but pregnant elf.

Her eyes were soft with a love. "You're spoiling me."

"It is impossible to spoil perfection."

She shook her head. "I'm far from perfect."

She always said things like that, as if she wanted to remind him she was flawed and he always reminded her he would love her forever regardless. Which he did again and she smiled her contentment and love back at him.

They reached the bedroom and he pulled her to sit on

the edge of the antique four-poster. Then he pulled a small gift wrapped in red foil and topped with a tiny gold bow from his pocket. "Happy Christmas, *agapi mou.*"

With a smile on her beautiful lips, she carefully tore the paper from the white jeweler''s case.

She remembered it.

He could tell because just for a second, she looked uncertain and then her eyes glowed undying love at him. Her fingers trembled a little as she opened it, then she gasped.

He withdrew the bracelet from the box and attached it to her wrist. When he looked in her beautiful golden eyes, she was crying. "Are you all right, *yineka mou?*"

She nodded, but had to swallow before she spoke. "Is it the same bracelet?"

"Yes."

"If I had opened this, I would never have left Paris. It would have taken a crane to get me out of the apartment."

She understood. He breathed a sigh of relief. Finally this last ghost laid to rest.

The bracelet sparkled on her wrist, the intertwined hearts studded with diamonds glistening in the light.

It was not the parting gift of a man to his mistress. It was not even merely a gift of affection from one lover to another. The bracelet bespoke a deeper emotion than he had been willing to acknowledge or verbalize at the time, but she understood.

"You loved me then."

"I loved you from the morning after I made you mine. You smiled so sweetly, offering no recriminations to me for seducing you from your innocence."

"It took me a while to realize it," she said ruefully.

"I as well, but I will never forget it," he vowed.

"And you always keep your promises," she said, laughing like the teasing little torment she was, "just ask your grandfather."

"When they mean loving you, I do."

She went serious and looked at the bracelet again. "I wish I'd opened the box."

"I made you too angry to do so. I think I did it on purpose."

"Because you knew the message the bracelet would give me and you weren't ready to admit it then."

"I love you, *agapi mou*."

She accepted his words without reproach. "I love you, *mon cher*."

He pulled her into his arms. "Always."

She hugged him as if she would never let go and he knew she wouldn't. "Always."

And his mind spoke the words she did not say, but had proven over and over again she meant...love without limitations or conditions. His body spoke the message back to her and her smile was a benediction.

THE MARRIED MISTRESS

by

Kate Walker

Kate Walker was born in Nottinghamshire but as she grew up in Yorkshire she has always felt that her roots were there. She met her husband at university and she originally worked as a children's librarian, but after the birth of her son she returned to her old childhood love of writing. When she's not working, she divides her time between her family, their three cats, and her interests of embroidery, antiques, film and theatre, and, of course, reading.

You can visit Kate at http://www.kate-walker.com/

Don't miss Kate Walker's exciting new novel
The Greek Tycoon's Unwilling Wife
**out in November 2007 from
Mills & Boon® Modern™.**

To all my special friends in the Teahouse and Gonnabeez from the Queen Bee.

CHAPTER ONE

SARAH stepped back from the partly open door as smoothly and as silently as she could.

It wasn't easy. The thought of disturbing the occupants of the room, of making them realise that she was here, and that she had seen them, made her heart race and her head swim.

Beneath the bright red-gold hair, her face had lost colour, the brilliant emerald-green of her eyes standing out dramatically against the pallor of her cheeks.

She felt sick—sick with anger and betrayal—and she needed a minute or two to pull herself together before she faced the inevitable. She had to get downstairs again. Had to get away from the scene that had met her shocked eyes as she had first opened the door, taking with it that little peace of mind that just lately she had thought she had finally reached.

Peace of mind. Huh!

That was a laugh! she told herself as she reached the top of the stairs. Peace was something she hadn't known in a long, long time. Not true peace. Not the wonderful soul-rooted peace that came from knowing you were truly happy, deep, deep down. Truly happy and contented with your world. As she had been once, she'd thought, in a time that now seemed so long ago.

No, she wouldn't think of the past now. Couldn't think of it. She had to concentrate on the here and now. The past was what would destroy her ability to handle this.

'Sarah?'

Jason's voice: thick and rough with shock.

Sounds of the bed creaking. Of the thud of heavy masculine feet on the carpeted floor. He had heard her and was coming after her.

The man in the hallway heard the sounds too. Heard the voice—a very *male* voice that made his heart kick sharply and something like disgust twist painfully in his gut.

She had a man. *Here.* In this house they had once shared. Clearly she hadn't believed his threat to come back—and soon.

But not soon enough, it seemed. His sweet Sarah had been busy during his absence. She had found herself another man. Found him, and lost him too, if the haste with which the slim auburn-haired figure in the smart pale green shirt and darker pencil skirt was coming down the curving staircase was anything to go by.

Sarah was not happy. She was so unhappy that she didn't see him standing well back, where his black hair and dark leather jacket blended with the deep shadow of the door. And, that being so, it told its own story of just what she had discovered up in that first-floor bedroom.

The bedroom that had once been *theirs*.

It was a thought of dark rage, one that brought a red mist rising before his eyes, cutting off his vision completely, and destroying his ability to think rationally. To think at all.

'Sarah?' Jason called again, his voice thick with echoes of things she didn't even want to consider. 'That you?'

Jason sounded angry now, and before she could find a way to answer, or even make any sort of sound to indicate her presence, he had stumbled out onto the landing and was leaning over the banisters, staring down at her.

His longish fair hair was still ruffled, his cheeks distinctly flushed. But at least he had taken the opportunity to pull on a pair of jeans, even if his chest was still bare, as were his feet.

'So it is you? Didn't you hear me calling? Why the hell didn't you answer? What are you doing back this early?'

It was a technique she recognised only too well. A way of firing questions at an opponent in rapid succession, and so disorientating them that they didn't know which one to answer first. It meant he was rattled. Because he wasn't sure just how long she'd been there or whether she'd only stayed downstairs.

'I can come and go as I please, Jason. This is my house!'

My house, technically, the man in the shadows corrected in the privacy of his thoughts. The big London house had always been the property of the Nicolaides family. He had let her continue to live in it because it suited him that way, but she didn't *own* it. Even if she was still, technically, his wife.

But only technically, it seemed.

A moment ago he had been severely tempted to step forward, out of the concealing darkness, and confront the pair of them. But from the moment that the blond man had appeared on the landing outside the bedroom he had changed his mind. Watching and waiting seemed a much better idea. Because if ever he had seen evidence of an illicit assignation, a sexual romp unexpectedly disturbed, it was right there on that bastard's guilty-looking face. If he was any sort of judge, the other female involved was still right there in the room behind this Jason.

'Sarah, don't get so huffy about nothing!'

Jason was descending the stairs now, smoothing his hair back with a hurried hand, belatedly fastening his jeans as he came down.

'Nothing!'

The freezing note in Sarah's voice made the watcher grin sharply. He knew that tone well. Too well. Oh, yes, he'd been subjected to just that icy note of indignant reproof more than once. He was still mentally smarting from the impact of the last time.

'Nothing?'

'Well, OK, so I took a nap in your bed.'

Clearly the blond man thought he could bluff his way out of this.

'What's so terrible about that? We're going to be sharing it from now on anyway.'

'I haven't actually agreed to you moving in.' To anything, if the truth was told.

'No, you haven't said the words, but we both know it's only a matter of time.'

He sounded so sure of himself, Sarah thought, anger warring with hurt and betrayal and producing a highly explosive combination in her mind. So sure that it was obvious he believed she hadn't been upstairs; that she wasn't aware of what had been going on inside that bedroom.

He still thought that he could worm his way out of this. He truly believed that she was so simple, so gullible, that she would swallow everything he tossed at her. And what infuriated her most was the thought that, lonely and unhappy, she must have given him that impression.

'But we both know it was on the cards.'

'Jace? Jacey, baby...'

A third voice, a light, petulant, feminine voice, interrupted what Sarah had been about to say. And as Jason whirled, another violent expletive escaping his lips, the bedroom door opened and a small, curvaceous female sashayed out onto the landing. She was wrapped loosely in a deep red silky gown that Sarah recognised instantly. Made for her own slender height, it swamped the other woman's shorter frame and was too long for her on her legs, falling almost to the floor instead of mid-calf.

'Are you ever coming back?' she pouted, peering over

the banisters and down at where he stood, frozen to the spot in the hall. 'I'm missing—'

'Andrea, I told you to wait!' Jason cut in furiously. 'To stay where you were and—'

'I was bored!' the woman addressed as Andrea protested. 'I got tired of waiting for you to come back.'

'"Don't get so huffy about nothing"!' Sarah repeated bitterly. 'I wonder what your—*friend* feels about being described as *nothing*!'

Her outburst silenced Jason temporarily in the same moment that it drew Andrea's frowning gaze towards where the other woman stood in the hallway.

'And who are you?'

'Me?'

To her amazement, Sarah managed it with only a trace of a shake in her voice, though anyone who knew her would have recognised in the stiffness of her tone the struggle she was having to maintain control. The man who was listening to everything knew it only too well.

'I'm just the owner of this house—of the bed you've just got out of, the robe you're wearing...'

And Jason's girlfriend, she supposed she could have added, but the words stuck in her throat.

'The robe you're—almost wearing!'

She was tight-lipped against her emotions, stiff as a board.

The watcher in the shadows saw how the colour had ebbed from her cheeks, the muscles in her jaw clenching tight, and he was struck by a sudden and distinctly unwelcome attack of something close to compassion.

Dangerously close.

Compassion was a mistake with this woman—a bad mistake—because it left him vulnerable. Once he had given his heart completely and willingly to her and she had smashed it into pieces and tossed it back at him like so much rubbish. He wasn't likely to risk that happening again.

'So might I suggest that you go and get back into your own clothes and get yourself out of here? And take your cheating fancy man with you!'

'But Sarah—'

'Out!'

She might be able to hold herself together if he went *now*, she told herself. If he turned and walked out immediately, then she might be able to forget just how foolish she had been over the past couple of weeks. Foolish in that once again she had stumbled into a relationship that had been all wrong from the start.

It had been a relationship in which she had been looking for nothing but comfort and a hiding place, and that had led her to the mess she was in right now.

'Sarah—please. It meant nothing—honest! It was just a fling.'

'A *fling*? You were prepared to betray my trust—to risk our relationship—for something that didn't even *matter*! Nothing more than an itch you had to scratch!'

At least Damon had had the honour to really care for his 'bit on the side'. His mistress had been the woman he wanted as well, and *she* had only been the wife of convenience.

Jason's expression was every bit as hangdog and spuriously repentant as she had expected, and he had actually taken a step or two towards her, coming much closer. Too close.

'Oh, come on, Sarr! You have to understand.'

Another step forward, and this time his hand came out. He had almost reached her, almost touched her, and it was too much.

'No!'

Her own hands came up, knocking him away as her

nerve broke completely, and she whirled, unable to think of anything beyond getting away. She couldn't even bear to be in the same space as him any longer. She wanted only to be away and clear and free. Free to forget about Jason and all he had ever meant to her.

Free to think of the man who had once meant *everything*. Free to—

'Ooof!'

The cry of shock, confusion and near-panic escaped her on a violent expulsion of breath as she blundered, blind and disorientated, straight into an unexpectedly hard and solid mass that was where no mass should be. A hard and solid mass that blocked her path, barring the way.

A hard, solid and *warm* mass.

A hard, solid, warm, *living and breathing* form.

A form that was so intensely masculine, lean and hard and forceful, that it could only belong to a man. A tall, strong man, very much in the prime of life.

A man whose arms came out instinctively, folding round her immediately, supporting her, holding her when she swayed off balance and might have fallen. A man whose chest was wide and strong where it supported her head, her cheek resting against his immaculate white polo shirt. She could hear the heavy, regular thud of his heart, echoing the pulse of blood through her own veins. In her nostrils was the heady, sensually intoxicating mixture of clean skin, the subtle tang of some spicy cologne, and the purely individual aroma that was his alone.

A scent that Sarah knew as well as that of her own body. It was one that she recognised so instantly and so completely, not needing to see the man's face or hear a word spoken in his voice to confirm her immediate and horrified suspicion. Try as she might, she had no hope at all of denying the truth, or escaping from the forceful impact of it.

And if she had needed any further proof, then the instant

reaction that flared through her, burning away all other thoughts, all other hopes, provided it in the space of a heartbeat. It licked along every nerve path, obliterating any doubt even before it had a chance to form.

'Da...'

The single broken syllable was choked from her, impossible to hold back even though her voice didn't have the strength to complete the name.

Only one man had ever made her feel this way. Only one man had ever been able to stimulate her feelings and her senses so instantly and so furiously.

'Damon...' she whispered. 'Damon!'

Above her head she sensed rather than saw the sensual mouth break into a wide, wicked grin of pure triumph, and felt the faint rumble of amused laughter under her cheek. She knew without the shadow of a doubt that he was glorying in the fact that he had had such an impact on her, and at such speed, evoking the instant effect that she had been unable to hide.

Only the realisation that she had given him the weapon to use against her, putting it almost into his hands herself, kept her silent in mortification, and she had to grit her teeth against the flurry of angry rejection that nearly escaped her. Damon Nicolaides needed no encouragement at all to feel instantly and infinitely superior to any other human being. His head was already swollen wide enough, and he would only take her hurried protestations as an indication of exactly the opposite of what she said.

'Damon...' she tried again, aiming for a very different tone. 'Let me go this minute!'

Once more she felt the chuckle echo in his chest.

'You know you don't mean that, sweetheart.'

It was the first time in over six months that she had heard his voice, and the bitter-sweet sensation of its tug at her emotions, the memories it revived in the space of a heartbeat, almost undid her totally.

'Oh, but I do!'

Gathering together all that was left of her tattered strength, she twisted in his arms and flung back her head so that she could look up, straight into his dark, shuttered face.

And instantly regretted her action desperately.

If letting him feel her immediate response to his presence had been a mistake, then this was definitely error number two—and a far worse, potentially far more dangerous move than anything she had done yet.

Because as soon as she saw him, saw the dangerously handsome face, with the broad, defined cheekbones, the flashing dark eyes and the sensually warm mouth, it was as if he had never been away. In those few, shaken moments, the hundred and eighty days of his absence from her life slid away like so many seconds, and she was jolted back once more to the appalling, devastating moment in which she had learned the truth. When his own father had forced her to see how her love for this man was built not on the strong, sure foundations she had believed it to be, but instead on slippery, shifting sands that had slid away from under her feet, leaving her reeling and lost without any support.

'I do...' she tried again, only to hear the words disintegrate as soon as they hit the air, splintering into tiny pieces that had none of the emphasis she aimed for.

And none of the impact she needed, she admitted to herself as she looked into her husband's deep, dark eyes, and saw there only as much response to her protest as he might have shown if a fly had landed on the olive-toned skin of his arm and he had wafted it away idly with one hand. Instead his smile grew, becoming a broad, fiendish grin as he looked down at her.

'Hello, sweetheart,' he drawled in his softly accented tones. 'It's good to see you again.'

Before she could register just what the grin meant, before she had time to realise that she had also made mistake number three as well as one and two, the proud head had lowered swiftly and his mouth took hers in a searing kiss.

A kiss that swept away all pretence at resistance. One that slashed through her defences before she even had time to think about building them, sweeping them aside as a torrential flash-flood might deal with a few weakly rooted saplings it had found in its way, carrying them before it on its relentless, savage path.

Sarah was completely in the power of that storm force. Under attack from a bewildering, devastating array of emotions, she simply closed her eyes and went under, surrendering to the deepest, most elemental demand of all. That of total sensuality.

It was like the first kiss she had ever experienced and yet it was like no other she had ever known. It started hard and fierce and demanding, but instantly gentled as in spite of herself she opened up to him, her mouth softening under his, her lips parting, allowing the arrogantly knowing invasion of his tongue.

She was lost, drowning in sensation, losing all sense of substance, of strength, of reality. The ground was unsteady beneath her feet, the hallway in which she stood just a haze of blue, pale and dark, and the hum of the traffic outside, always present in any part of London, a blur of noise, the buzzing soundtrack to the frantic racing of her heart.

She wanted none of this, her mind screamed at her. Wanted nothing—and yet she wanted *everything*. She longed desperately for him to release her and in the same thought she prayed that he would hold on to her forever, never letting her go. Letting her go would mean that she was once more cast adrift into the emptiness of being alone,

'Hush, *agape mou*,' he reproved, infuriatingly more in control than she had ever been, so that she heard in his words a fake softness. A gentleness that he could never have meant but that he managed to communicate with total credibility. 'Leave this to me.'

'But—'

Again she tried to protest, and again she failed as once more he kissed her into submission, this time stealing her soul away with a stunningly enticing caress, one that made her senses swoon and her heart sing with rare delight.

'Leave this to me,' he had told her, his tone redolent with a supreme confidence that she would do exactly as he instructed.

And, weakly, she knew that she would. There was nothing else she could do. The ability to act, along with any hope she had of even thinking straight, had evaporated swiftly in the heat of her instant reaction to him. Just his very closeness, to be held so tightly in the warm strength of his arms, crushed up against the hard wall of his chest, had been bad enough, depriving her of the control, the restraint that she had believed she'd acquired in her time apart from him. But the sensations sparked off by those kisses had made everything infinitely worse, buzzing round in her head, fizzing through her body, until she was incapable of thought.

Those three very different kisses had revealed so perfectly the many sides of Damon's nature. In his make-up, the supremely gentle, irresistibly seductive blended so perfectly with the cruel, the almost brutal ruthlessness that was the opposite side of his personality. The negative to the positive, darkness as opposed to light. She had known them all in her short time with him, and at first she had believed that the gentle, enticing character had been the real man.

She had been very quickly—and very thoroughly—disillusioned. Life, and Damon's father, had stripped her of her rose-tinted spectacles with ruthless efficiency. And from then onwards she had never been able to look at him in the same way.

'You're *who*?' Jason demanded, the bluster in his voice showing how rattled he was.

'The name is Damon Nicolaides,' Damon tossed at him, clearly expecting, and getting, the instant start of response that always came with the recognition of his name.

'Nicolaides?' Jason's voice shook.

Everyone knew who Damon was. Everyone.

His wealth and his international, jet-setting life put his name and his photograph into the society pages. His relationships with models and actresses, his friendships with film producers and media moguls kept him in the celebrity magazines, where his stunningly masculine looks made a huge impact on every female reader from sixteen to seventy. His money and power meant that he frequently appeared in financial columns, and his ability to constantly acquire more of both made sure that his reputation was as huge as his business empire.

'*Damon* Nicolaides?'

He was clearly the last person Jason had expected to come up against in this particular situation. How the hell could *she* know *him*? The question was obviously in his thoughts, revealed in his stunned intonation.

'That's right.'

Sarah knew that tone of Damon's voice well—too well. Careful, polite, controlled—but only just.

It meant that Damon was right at the edge of his patience. That he would not take pushing any further or any harder. Not if the person he was talking to was wise and wanted to avoid a full-scale volcanic explosion.

'Jason...' she tried, only to feel her body given a small, rough shake of warning by the man who held her.

'Let me answer the questions, Sarah. It's simpler that way.'

'Simpler!' she couldn't help protesting. 'For who?'

'For everyone!'

The admonition that had been in the way he had shaken her was there again, more strongly this time, in the undercurrents in his voice, a note that sent a shiver down her spine in unnerved response.

This was the Damon she had seen in the past, when some member of his staff had angered him with a foolish mistake, or a journalist had proved too intrusive. It was the prelude to a much more savage outburst, one that made her shudder in fearful anticipation. She had only ever experienced that side of Damon briefly, but that had been enough. She never wanted to see it again.

'Everyone?'

Damon bent his dark head again until his sensual mouth was level with her ear, the warmth of his breath stirring the auburn tendrils of hair that lay against her cheek.

'Do you want me to get rid of him or not?'

Oh, yes, she wanted Jason out of here. Out of her house, and out of her life. And she wished he'd take Damon with him. But that, she knew, was not the slightest bit likely.

And so, grasping at what she could see was the only possible lesser of two evils, she clamped her lips tight shut on the furious protest that almost escaped her once more and forced herself to nod in silent acquiescence.

It was all that Damon needed. Satisfied that she had handed over control of the situation into his hands, he faced Jason again.

'Was there anything else you wanted to know?'

Everything, if she knew Jason, Sarah thought. But he contented himself with one question, his voice wobbling on a note of disbelief.

'You claim that you two are an item?'

'Not claim,' Damon retorted sharply. 'We are.'

As if to prove his point, he pulled her closer, one steel-hard arm coming round her to hold her just where he wanted her, staking his claim. One ear, one cheek was against his chest, muffling her hearing. But she caught Jason's dumbfounded response.

'And you agree with this, Sarry?'

Another silent nod was all she could manage. Just let Damon get rid of Jason, she prayed inwardly, and then she would get rid of Damon. If she could. Damon in one of these stubborn, determined moods was as immovable as a rock, and every bit as hard.

'So when did you two meet—and where?'

'The art gallery reception last night,' Damon stunned her by retorting immediately, and totally unexpectedly. 'You must have noticed that she didn't come home. Or perhaps not...'

The movement of his head told its own story. Sarah didn't even have to look to know that he had directed his black-eyed gaze across the room and up to where Jason's bedroom companion still lingered, watching everything, silently agog with curiosity.

So silently that Sarah had almost forgotten she was there.

'I'm sure you were otherwise engaged.'

Damon was fast losing patience now. The sordid little drama he had interrupted might have amused him for a while, but its appeal was strictly limited, and it was evaporating rapidly. He wanted Jason and his trollop out of the house as fast as possible. If they didn't move now then he couldn't guarantee that he would be able to keep a strict hold on his temper. And if it slipped from his control then he couldn't be answerable for the consequences. Things could get really messy.

And the worst part of it all was having to admit just what

was affecting him most. Which certainly wasn't this sleazy rat and his cheap little tart, that was for sure.

'I wasn't here last night! My name's Andrea, by the way.'

It was the other woman who spoke, and Sarah felt a shock of instant recognition at her tone, bringing with it the kick of some primitive reaction deep down inside her. Even fresh from another man's bed as she was, this Andrea had still responded to Damon's forcefully macho appearance with a predatory interest that put a husky purr of sensuality into her tone. Wriggling slightly in the iron-hard hold, Sarah could just peer upwards to where the voluptuous woman was leaning over the banisters, displaying an ample amount of what she clearly thought was enticing cleavage.

But Damon appeared far from enticed.

'You're here now,' he flung up at her. 'And I'd much prefer it if you weren't. So get some clothes on and get yourself and your lover out of here—fast! Or I won't be answerable for the consequences.'

Andrea pouted petulantly at his tone, but she read it well enough to know that he meant exactly what he said. Flouncing into the bedroom, she must have tossed on clothes at speed, pushed into action by the threat in Damon's tone, because it was only minutes before she reappeared, fully dressed in a tight white shirt and the miniest of miniskirts, the red satin robe slung carelessly over one arm. Clopping inelegantly down the stairs in white slingback stilettos, she marched over to the small group in the hall.

'I believe this is yours.'

She tossed the robe onto the floor at their feet, then turned to the still staring Jason and caught hold of his arm.

'C'mon, Jace,' she said. 'It's time we were out of here.'

'I should listen to the lady, *Jace*...' Damon laced both

the nickname and the word 'lady' with the stinging bite of acidic sarcasm. 'It *is* time you were going.'

'But—' Jason began, then looked straight into Damon's deep black eyes and clearly thought better of what he had been about to say.

'OK,' he muttered. 'I'm coming.'

But there was something in his voice that told Sarah he was not finished yet. That he had more to say—or do—before he left them in peace.

Instinctively she tensed in Damon's arms, waiting, wondering...

But whatever she had feared never came.

The slam of the door behind the departing pair was a sudden shock to her system, jarring every nerve in her tense body and making her head jerk upwards from its secure pillowing on Damon's hard chest.

'It's OK.'

Lazily he stilled her, soothed her with a stroking hand down over her hair, her shoulder, her arm.

'They've gone.' He looked down at her, grinned into her warily watchful green eyes. 'It's safe to come out now.'

'I wasn't scared!'

Desperately, Sarah tried to gather together some of the tattered strands of her shattered self-esteem so as to meet the smile in his eyes with some degree of composure. He looked too damn pleased with himself by half.

'I *wasn't*!' she repeated more emphatically, to answer the tormenting question that was clearly in his thoughts, lifting the corner of one jet-black eyebrow in mocking inquiry. 'I was simply—held prisoner by you.'

To emphasise the point she twisted in his still restraining arms, attempting to pull herself free. At first, for a heart-stopping moment, she thought he was going to resist, forcing her into either an ungainly and undignified struggle or a humiliating submission. But then, suddenly, he released her with an abruptness that had her swaying uncomfortably on unsteady feet, stubbornly refusing to reach out a hand and cling on to the strength of his arms for support.

The fact that he so obviously knew exactly what was going through her mind only added a hundredfold to her discomfiture. She hated the way that the gleam in his eyes brightened, the tiny quirk upwards at the corner of his lips revealing his amusement.

'So now you're free,' he drawled softly.

'Yes,' Sarah managed, adding because she felt she had to, 'Thank you.'

'My pleasure.'

He was bending as he spoke, reaching down to scoop up the red robe from where Andrea had tossed it moments before.

'This is yours, I believe.'

Sarah turned a glance of loathing on the inoffensive article that Damon held out to her. It was impossible not to notice the contrast between the strength of the blunt, strong, tanned fingers and the fine, slippery material that seemed totally insubstantial in the firm grasp. But the thought of touching either made her shiver inside.

Slowly she reached out, took hold of the crimson silk, then gave in to her inclinations and, crushing the garment mercilessly, she crumpled it into a ball and flung it with all her strength as far away from her as she could manage.

'I don't want it! Not after she's worn it! I couldn't bear to touch it again.'

Damon's dark eyes followed the bright sliver of material as it sailed through the air in a graceful arc and fell to the ground once more. Then his gaze swung back to Sarah's face, looking deep into her eyes.

'I'll buy you another.'

'No need—I...'

The words died away as she realised not just what he

had said but the implications behind it. Clearly Damon planned to stay around, for a while at least. And that was not something she was comfortable with. Certainly not after the scene he had just witnessed, and the interpretation he had obviously put on it. And, even worse, after the discovery that she had made about herself.

'I can get one myself. I earn a good salary at the art gallery; I can afford to buy myself a nightgown...'

She was speaking only to fill the silence, she knew. And to distract her own thoughts. There were too many things she didn't want to think about—didn't *dare* to think about—and for now it was so much easier to concentrate on the immediate present and what was happening in it.

After all, there was more than enough to face up to there. Sarah drew in her breath sharply and let it out again on a silent sigh. Jason might have gone—and Andrea. And quite frankly she was more than glad to see the back of both of them. But Damon was still here. And getting rid of him was a different prospect altogether.

Her shoulders, which had relaxed in the moments she had watched Jason and Andrea walk away, now tensed again. Her throat tightened so that she had to swallow hard to ease the dryness there, and her chin came up as defiance flared in the green depths of her eyes.

'What are you doing here, Damon?'

'I came to see you, of course, my darling...'

'That's not what I mean, and you know it!' Sarah put in hastily and sharply, terrified of hearing that emotive word 'wife' on his lips.

Once she had been proud and happy—*so* happy—to be his wife, even if for his own reasons Damon had insisted that, for a while at least, they told no one the truth. But now their brief, painful façade of a marriage was something she desperately wanted to forget. To obliterate from her mind, if she couldn't erase it from her past.

'I want to know why you're here—in London.'

'I have business in town. Important meetings.'

It was not the truth, at least not the full truth, Damon admitted to himself. But the truth wasn't something he was prepared to admit to. Not yet. Perhaps not ever at all.

He had had a meeting planned—one with Sarah to discuss their marriage, or what was left of it. The thoughts that had been in his mind as he'd arrived at the house such a short time before now came back to haunt him, mocking his gullible beliefs and the naïve hope that had been uppermost in his mind then.

He had given Sarah enough time to calm down, he had told himself. After six months of living on her own, stubbornly refusing to see him, returning every one of his letters unopened, surely she was now prepared to listen?

She *would* listen, he had told himself. No matter what he had to do to make her. He would talk—and she would listen. Somehow he would make her come back to Greece with him. To Mykonos. Where he would show her what he had done. And then...

He hadn't got any further than that.

'I see—business. Of course. What else?'

Sarah's voice was cold and tight. If he didn't know better, he'd have said she sounded disappointed. Which might have pleased him when he had first reached the house—when he'd still had hopes and illusions of a future. Before the appearance of Jason and his obvious familiarity with Sarah's bedroom had shattered those illusions.

'You know me, *ghineka mou*,' he shot back. 'Always busy, making deals, signing contracts.'

'Acquiring land?' Sarah returned with even more bite in her tone. Whatever disappointment she had been feeling a moment before, if disappointment was the right word, it was now totally submerged under the angry bitterness that blazed from her eyes. 'Built any nice extensions to your hotels lately, Damon?'

'Not since you left, my love,' he returned, his tone dripping saccharine-sweetness. 'And, as I recall, you never signed the papers agreeing to the one that I wanted.'

'No, I didn't, did I? That must have made things rather awkward for you.'

Damon's smile in reply to the barbed comment was grim, tight, totally without any warmth.

'No more awkward than they were already, *agape mou*. I told you then that your ownership of that land was not why I married you.'

'I know what you told me, husband, dear, but I also know what I believe.'

Let him think that what had driven them apart was the piece of land that the Nicolaides Corporation coveted most on all the island of Mykonos. That was the reason she had given him for leaving in the letter she had left behind, the one she had clung to when he had come after her in a towering rage, demanding that she return at once. That and the fact that she had grown tired of their marriage, bored with life on the small Cyclades island. And it was one she would far rather have him believe than the actual, the hatefully painful truth.

'Admit it, it was remarkably inconvenient for you that I discovered that the land my grandfather had left me was just the part of the island that you wanted. Especially when the old man had declared to your father's face that he would rather die than sign the land over to anyone from your family.'

Her grandfather had been half Greek on his mother's side. Through that line he had inherited the land on Mykonos. The land in question lay between two of the Nicolaides Corporation's smaller hotels, and it had been a long-held ambition of both Damon and his father to link the hotels into one spectacular resort by building across the empty space. But Alexander Meyerson's mother's family had had a long-running feud with the Nicolaides clan, one that he had held fast to in spite of the increasingly huge amounts offered in exchange for the tiny portion of the island he owned, much to Aristotle Nicolaides' increasing frustration.

So when Damon had learned that Sarah, as her grandfather's only heir, would now own the land on Mykonos, he had come looking for her.

And she, poor blindly besotted fool that she was, had made matters so much easier for him by falling head over heels madly in love.

'How you must have cursed those lawyers who wrote and let me know about my luck before you'd had time to get me to sign on any dotted lines.'

'It was certainly, as you said—inconvenient,' Damon growled, his stunning features setting into a dark frown. 'But it was not necessarily fatal. Or it need not have been if you had only stayed to talk things over with me, or come back...'

'Come back!' Sarah couldn't hold back the exclamation of shock and disgust that was pushed from her lips by his outrageous declaration. 'Come back to a marriage that had never been a real one right from the start? That was built on nothing but lies and deceit? A marriage that you had been determined not to let anyone know about because you were ashamed of it?'

'Not ashamed!' Damon flung at her. 'It just would have been...difficult to make our marriage public at that point.'

'I'll bet it would! Well, perhaps in the end I ought to thank you for that. After all, you spared me a lot of humiliation and the adverse publicity that I might have had to put up with if people had found out that we were married. Now all I have to do is wait for the legalities to be sorted out and we can be divorced as quietly as we were married. Excuse me.'

She tried to sweep past him, only to have to come to an awkward halt as he blocked her way, coming between her and her path across the hall.

'Where are you going?'

'Upstairs.'

'Why?'

'Is it any business of yours?'

'Humour me.'

Seeing the stubborn, unmoving set of his face, the taut line of his hard jaw, she sighed her exasperation, knowing only too well that he had no intention of letting her pass until she told him something.

'I want to go and strip the sheets off the bed that—that Jason and his fancy piece used!'

Distaste curled her lip, tasted bitter on her tongue.

'I have to put them in the wash immediately—though if I'm honest I'd prefer to burn the damn things!'

To her relief Damon sidestepped neatly, moving out of her way, but as she mounted the first of the stairs she realised that he was right there behind her, following close on her heels.

'I'll come with you.'

'No!'

But he totally ignored her protest and just kept on coming.

'Damon…'

She whirled on the stairs until she was facing him. Looking down into his handsome face, she saw the determination stamped hard on it, the unyielding set to his jaw.

'I don't need you!'

Just the thought of having this man, the man who had been her husband for such a brief time, follow her into her bedroom spoke of an intimacy that she was totally unwilling to allow herself to recall. I don't want you, she should have said. But the words had other, much more disturbing implications that meant her voice would not actually speak them with the conviction she needed.

'It'll be easier with two,' Damon returned, and just kept on coming so that she was obliged to skip backwards hastily up the stairs if she was not to have him collide with her.

'I've done it by myself many times...'

'I'm sure you have.'

Another step upwards necessitated another couple of hasty jumps back and away to avoid a crash.

'But I'm here now, so there's no reason for you to have to do it alone today.'

'Damon, it's *my* room!'

Exasperation, a touch of breathlessness from the undignified scramble up the staircase, and a shockingly sensitive awareness of the man below her put a betraying shake into her voice. The physical strength of his chest and shoulders was emphasised from this angle, the gleam of the sunlight on the dark waves of his hair made it shine like glossy silk, and the flash of white teeth as he grinned up at her was startling against the olive skin of his face.

'Sarah, it's *my* house!' he retorted, with an infuriatingly deliberate echo of her own tone, her own emphasis.

And what could she say in response to that? There was no answer she could give him. At least not one that he would accept, pay any heed to. It was his house, and that was the fact. She hadn't wanted to take anything from him, but she had desperately needed a roof over her head. And for all she knew Damon had already built on her disputed land. He was perfectly capable of ignoring any morality in the case and just going right ahead.

With inelegant haste she hurried up the remaining stairs

and arrived safely on the landing, facing him with determined defiance.

'You said I could live here!' she protested, and shivered as she saw a dark tide of change cross his face, shadowing his eyes.

'I said *you* could live here,' he acceded. 'Not you and sundry assorted hangers-on.'

Now was the time to tell him the truth, Sarah knew. The time to point out that, no matter how it had seemed, Jason had had neither her agreement nor her permission to be in the house. At least not in her bedroom, and certainly not in her bed.

So why did the words stick in her throat? Why could she not just fling them in his face and be done with it?

Because he had no right to interfere in her life. He had given up any rights to that when he had betrayed her trust and treated her as a thing, a chattel, something to be used for his own ends, not as a true wife of his heart.

Wife of his heart!

Hah! That was a joke. A very sick, very black sort of joke. One that slashed at her heart, her soul, like a rusty knife, reopening old wounds that had barely even begun to heal.

She had never really been Damon's wife, not in the truest sense of the word—not in *any* sense of the word, except perhaps the sexual one. She had been his wife in bed and nowhere else. He had wanted her physically. There was no way he could have hidden, or faked, the passionate desire he had felt for her. And that must have made the rest of his scheme so much easier for him to carry out.

The pain that came along with the rush of memory drove all thought of common sense from her mind and instead had her spitting at him in blind rage.

'And I suppose that you've been living a pure and celibate life for the last six months!'

He actually looked taken aback by her attack. It even silenced him, and she watched him withdraw into himself, shutters coming down behind the gleaming jet eyes, hiding his thoughts from her.

'Nothing to say, Damon? I thought not. Ever heard of the saying about pots calling kettles black?'

'I know the saying, yes. But I do not see its relevance to the current situation.'

He had the nerve to look innocent—and it was unnerving just how innocent he could appear, with his deep, dark eyes wide open in apparent ingenuousness.

For a brief second Sarah closed her own lids against the pain of memory. Against the hated recollection of the moment that Aristotle Nicolaides had revealed the truth about his son's relationship with Eugenia Stakis. About the marriage that had been planned for so long and that would unite the fortunes of the two Greek dynasties as well as the two lovers. In a moment, he had explained just why Damon had insisted that this pragmatic, purely business deal of a marriage should be kept secret from everyone.

But of course Damon didn't even know that his poor deceived wife had any knowledge of his machiavellian behaviour and so he still thought he could get away with pretending he was blameless.

'Of course you don't.'

Opening her eyes again, but carefully avoiding meeting any lying glance that Damon might send in her direction, she swung away, turning her attention to the rumpled bed before her.

'I didn't give Jason free run of my house!' she said abruptly, covering the savage bite of misery with a sudden rush into action as she snatched up a pillow and shook it roughly out of its pale gold case. 'And I certainly wouldn't even have given him a key if I'd known the use he was going to put it to.'

'But, as you've made only too plain, the way you've lived your life this past six months is no business of mine.'

Damon's voice had grown colder by the second. Now it sounded positively glacial, sending icy shivers sliding down Sarah's spine.

She managed some unintelligible murmur that he could take as agreement or not as he wished and dumped the denuded pillow on the floor, flinging the cotton case after it. It was as she reached for the crumpled sheet that a sudden recollection of how she had felt as she'd stood outside on the landing and heard the sound of Jason's voice attacked without warning, making her sway weakly, fingers clenching on the bedding until the knuckles showed white.

'Sarah?'

Damon must have been watching her every move because he stepped forward, reaching her before she had even realised herself that she was no longer steady on her feet.

'Sarah!' he said again, his voice rough with some emotion that she couldn't begin to name.

There was anger in there, but at who? And it was blended with a whole range of feelings that made her head whirl just trying to separate them.

But she was weak enough not to resist when he gathered her into his arms, held her close against him, her cheek resting on his shirt, one hand cradling the back of her head.

'Sarah, the bastard isn't worth it! Don't waste your tears on him.'

Tears?

Somehow Sarah edged a hand up to touch her face and find that Damon had spoken nothing less than the truth. Her skin was wet with tears that she had been unaware of letting escape, her eyelashes spiked into damply clinging clumps.

They were the tears that had been threatening ever since she had pushed open the bedroom door a crack and seen

Jason—the man who had said that all he wanted was to heal her broken heart—naked in bed with another woman. She would feel better if she could let them fall. If she could simply give in to her feelings and, abandoning all restraint, weep her heart out on Damon's supportive shoulder.

It was a dangerously tempting prospect and one she was having to struggle fiercely against, because if she did start crying then she knew the interpretation that Damon would put on it. The only interpretation that he believed was possible.

He would think that she was crying for Jason.

He would believe that the other man had callously broken her heart by being caught in her bed with his mistress in the middle of the afternoon.

He would curse him, call him every name under the sun, possibly even threaten vengeance on him. In fact, if she knew this husband of hers, estranged or not, he might actually try to take off after Jason and then she would have to hold him back, beg him to stay.

And if she did that then she knew it would destroy her.

There could never have been a good moment for Damon to reappear in her life, but this afternoon had to be the worst one possible.

At last she had thought that she was finally growing a new, protective skin over the wounds that this man had inflicted on her in their short marriage. Only this morning she had told herself that she was gradually starting to get her life back under her control again, get things in order, consider the prospect of beginning again without dissolving into total misery. She had a good job as PA to Rhys Morgan, an international art dealer and owner of a hugely prestigious gallery here in London. Jason seemed to have set himself to charming her out of the black depression into which she had fallen since her return from Greece. And, most important of all, the husband she had adored, and who had taken her love and used it for his own totally selfish ends, was thousands of miles away, on the Greek island he called home.

The only reason Jason had been in the house at all today was because she had been expecting an important delivery. The freezer in the kitchen had died with a spectacularly dramatic waste of food, and she had had to buy another. But when she had been asked to go in to the gallery to cover for a sick workmate, she'd thought she would have to cancel the delivery until Jason, who had recently been made redundant from his own job, had stepped in and offered to wait for it instead. They had been out on a couple of what he called dates but in her eyes they were little more than friends.

'I'm not doing anything important,' he'd said. 'Only checking the jobs pages—I can do that as easily at your place as I can at home.'

But then she had come home unexpectedly early, having been given the afternoon off by an unusually preoccupied Rhys, who had clearly wanted to be anywhere but in the office, and she had seen Jason's car parked outside as she had walked up the street towards the house. Some instinct had kept her silent as she opened the door, crossed the hall. A faint noise from the first floor, the sound of laughter—another woman's laughter—had drawn her to the stairs, and she had mounted them in silence.

'This is the life, Jace! I could really get to like this!' The woman's voice had floated out clearly to her as she reached the top, and set foot on the thick blue carpet of the landing.

'Well, don't get too comfortable, honey.' Jason's drawling, upper-class tones had been unmistakable. 'The prissy Ms Meyerson will be home by five—and you'll have to get your pretty little butt out of here well before then.'

'I wish I didn't have to! I don't like sharing you with her, Jacey. I really don't.'

'And I don't like wasting my time with her either, sweetie,' Jason had hastily assured her. 'But the lady is loaded! Look at this house for a start. It's huge, and in this part of London it must be worth a fortune! She has to be worth millions. And she's almost mine. She's already given me a key so that I can come and go as I please. Another couple of weeks and I'll have her eating out of my hand…'

And it was then that she had known. Known that whoever it was who had said that lightning didn't strike twice had been absolutely right.

Because even as she had listened to Jason and his witchy girlfriend planning to play on her emotions simply to use her, she had realised that she just didn't care. That in spite of her barely formed hopes, her dreams of starting again, Jason didn't mean a thing to her, and his greedy, grasping plans even less.

No, the shock that had ripped through her, shattering her composure and destroying all that hard-won peace of mind, was the realisation that it had all been just a delusion. That her hopes of a new life, of a new beginning, putting behind her the pain and the betrayal of the past, were built on the shaky foundations of self-deceit. She was no more 'over' Damon than she was capable of flying to the moon.

And if she had any room for doubt, any hope of being wrong, that hope had been totally destroyed in the moment that she had blundered into Damon's arms and into the feeling that she had come home.

She had fallen totally, blindly and irrevocably in love with Damon Nicolaides in the first seconds that she had ever seen him, and nothing that had happened had changed that. He had taken her heart prisoner and he still held it captive in his strong, powerful hands. All the dreaming of a future, of a new life, had been just a fantasy, one that had evaporated like mist before the sun at the first touch of reality.

The reality was that she loved Damon desperately and she always would, while he had never felt anything for her but the searing passion that had driven him to take her to his bed. And even that had been a complication he hadn't looked for, hadn't wanted in his campaign to use her to get what he wanted.

It was for that reason and that alone that she now wanted to weep. To try to wash away the savage pain in her heart under the rush of tears.

And of course she could do nothing of the sort for fear of betraying herself totally to the man who was responsible for that anguish in the first place.

note that asked, without any more words being needed, just what he thought he was doing.

What *did* he think he was doing?

What *was* he doing?

He was holding Sarah in the way that he had dreamed of, hungered for, over the past six months. He had her in his arms again and her hair was like silk under his cheek, her breath a warm whisper across his skin. When she spoke, her soft mouth came dangerously close to the strong muscle that corded his neck. If he moved—just an inch—then her lips would touch, would caress, would entice...

'Damon—please!'

It was the note of breathless protest on the words that told him how, unthinkingly, his hold on her had tightened, driving the air from her slender body, almost crushing the delicate bones of her ribcage.

'*Sighnomi*—I'm sorry...' he murmured, but he still couldn't let her go.

For a second he eased his hold on her, then almost immediately tightened it again, so fiercely that her head came up sharply, wide, startled green eyes looking up into his in an expression of shock.

'No, I'm not sorry,' he muttered, the words rough and thick. 'Do you know how long I've wanted this? Dreamed of it?'

The nights had been the worst. The nights when once he had lain awake, the pulsing throb of sexual satisfaction slowly, gradually ebbing from his satiated senses. He had never been able to sleep, because even when he had just experienced the wild, primal explosion of the fiercest climaxes he had ever known he had still been unable to surrender to the weary satisfaction that engulfed his body.

Instead he had always had to lie there; to prop his head up slightly on the pillow so that he could watch her drift

CHAPTER THREE

WHAT the hell was he doing? Damon asked himself furiously, suddenly convinced that he had made the worst move possible since he had come into this house.

Getting hold of Sarah like this had to have been the dumbest, the craziest, the most ill-judged thing he could have done. And he was regretting it savagely.

Or was he?

His thoughts might be screaming the need for caution, but in his senses it didn't *feel* like regret.

It had been bad enough when she had blundered into his grasp downstairs and he had let his arms close around her, holding her tight. He had known exactly what he was doing then. He'd been supremely conscious of Jason the rat standing there in the hallway beside them, watching every move. And those moves had been deliberately calculated for their maximum effect on the other man.

But they had had plenty of effect on him too. It had been impossible to hold this woman, to feel the satin warmth of her skin, inhale the sweet, clean scent of her body, and not react in the most primitively masculine way. Even now, his body still ached with the memory of the instant, savage hardening, the tightness that had twisted at his guts. The thought of how it had once been.

How easy it would once have been simply to fold her in his arms, lift her from the floor, carry her over to the bed. He could lower her to the mattress, come down beside her...

'Damon?'

There was a hesitation in Sarah's voice, a questioning

into sleep. And even just watching her had been a sensual act in itself.

His gaze had drifted from the high, smooth forehead, down over her softly closed eyelids, where the long, thick lashes lay like feathered crescents on the pale skin of her cheeks. He had traced the warm, sensual curve of her mouth, the sweet line of her jaw and chin, the length of her throat. And when his eyes had moved to the rich curves of her body, to the swell of her breasts and hips, still stained with the afterglow of their passion, then his body had hardened all over again, threatening to throw off the satiated sense of fulfilment in a second and start to clamour all over again for something more. For the renewal of the pleasure his senses had known; to climb once again to the peak of ecstasy that he had experienced during the night. He always ended up wanting her again with even more hunger than he had felt the very first time.

Theos! He felt that way now. His body was on fire; he had never felt so viciously hard, so brutally hungry. If she moved against him, it was blissful agony, making him grit his teeth hard against the groan of tortured response.

'Damon—you're hurting me.'

'Huh?'

Jolted from the fever of his memories, he looked down at her through passion-glazed eyes, struggling to focus. Her face was turned up towards his and her eyes were huge and emerald-brilliant against her pale skin.

'*Sighnomi...*' he began, then broke off violently. His hands clenched on her arms again, giving her a small, reproving shake.

'Maybe I want to hurt you—I want you to know how I feel. To understand what it's been like...'

'I do...I do...'

Kristos! Had he put those tears into her eyes? Had he made them spill out from under her lids until they soaked the fine skin of her cheeks? They didn't run down her face, but simply lay, like a soft sheen, glistening in the afternoon sunlight, a silent but eloquent reproach.

'Sarah!'

Her name escaped his lips like a sigh in the same moment that his proud, dark head bent, his mouth coming down, making her jump like a startled deer.

It was his gentleness that was shocking. It was so totally unexpected and so much at odds with the hard, heated pressure of the fiercely aroused body that was crushed so tightly against hers.

But his lips were soft and gentle, tenderly kissing away the tear stains from her face, pressing her eyelids shut and brushing the lingering salt drops from her lashes. And it seemed to Sarah that with them went her fury and distress, the need to fight seeping from her like air from a pricked balloon.

'Oh, Damon…'

Her breath caught in her throat, escaping on a small, choking cry, a sound of surrender. She subsided softly against him, feeling the need of his support, deeply grateful for his strength holding her when she couldn't stand alone.

Overwhelmed by all that she had just realised, she buried her face in his shirt, not knowing whether she needed to hide or simply to get much closer to him, burrowing into security like some small, vulnerable creature. She felt his mouth drift over her tumbled auburn hair, the warmth of his breath on the delicate curl of her outer ear. The clean, faintly musky scent of his skin tormented her with the memories it evoked, the heat of his body surrounding her like a protective cloak.

And with the memories came the awakening of need, the savage burn of hunger.

'Damon…'

Even in her own ears, the sound of his name had changed

totally. It was no longer the soft, submissive surrender, but a sharpened sound of longing, of demand. And as she spoke she drew in her breath on a sobbing gasp, turning her face to him once more.

'Damon, please—kiss me. Kiss me properly.'

'Kiss you—'

It was raw and thick, hopelessly roughened at the edges. 'Oh, lady...'

She didn't know who moved first, whether his dark head came down hard and fast or her own lifted to his as swiftly. She only knew that in the space of a swift, thudding heartbeat, their mouths had met and clashed and crushed so fiercely that she almost expected to see sparks fly up into the air from their joining.

All the loneliness, all the yearning, all the misery of the past six months was in that kiss. All the memory of the long, empty days and the cruel, bleak nights swelled up inside her, rose, and spilled out fiercely like red-hot lava erupting from a volcano and surging, wild and unstoppable, down the slopes of the mountain.

They snatched at each other's mouths, nipped, bit, came apart to draw in deep, ragged breaths, then rushed together again, unable to stay apart. It was like a fight for survival more than any sort of caress. Like a wild, primal mating ritual that had nothing of the civilised or of courtship in it, only raging need, uncontrollable craving, the desperation of having lost once and the terrible fear that it could happen all over again.

'I want you,' Damon muttered harshly against her mouth. 'Want you—want you...'

His command of language seeming to desert him, he broke into Greek, alternating the words of his native tongue with his suddenly roughened and disjointed English in a raw and incoherent litany of desire.

And Sarah could do nothing but nod again and again,

her own mouth only capable of forming the word 'yes', repeated with the gathering intensity of a growing thunder storm, a counterpoint to his harsh declaration.

'Yes, Damon, yes, yes, yes...'

This was all she would ever have of Damon, was the phrase that ran through Sarah's head. If she could only have today and this elemental, primitive passion that had flared between them, then she would take it and welcome it and enjoy it for as long as she was able.

No, *enjoy* was not the right word. It came nowhere close to describing this starving hunger, this aching, desperate need.

This feeling was as essential to her as each raw, painful breath she dragged into her burning lungs between each hungry kiss. Without it she could never live, only exist. And yet at the same time she felt each moment of contact, each desperate caress, as torment in her soul, ripping and shredding, increasing the emptiness in her heart in the same second that it appeased the hunger in her body.

'I want you too, Damon. I'm desperate for you... desperate...'

Her hands spoke for her when she could no longer string two coherent words together. Grabbing at the soft white cloth of his polo shirt, she wrenched it free of the waistband of his trousers, roughly pushing it aside so that her greedy hands could have free access to the bronzed skin she sought, her fingers almost scrabbling his clothing out of the way in her rush to touch him.

'Sarah—sweetheart—angel...'

There was a shaken, rough note of laughter threading through Damon's vain attempt at a protest, and the hands he brought up to try and catch at hers, to still them, or at the very least to slow their frantic, urgent movements, were as unsteady as his words.

'There's no need to rush—we have all day, the night...'

But even as he spoke, his own actions denied the muttered restraint, the urge to caution.

His movements mirroring Sarah's, he pushed her blouse up and away from her skirt. The ominous wrenching, tearing sound told of the fact that he had completely forgotten that hers was not a stretchy T-shirt, and a second later there were several soft thuds as broken buttons flipped away and bounced on the dressing table, the window sill, the floor.

'Forgive me...'

He sounded only vaguely apologetic. If anything, he was even more distracted than before, his attention on the few remaining fastenings that still needed undoing.

'I will buy you...*Theos*...'

The words died on his lips, and he froze into a sudden stillness. His silence tugged on her nerves, forcing her eyes to his face, to see the absorbed, intent expression there as he stared down at what his impatient movements had exposed.

The wrenched and torn shirt lay askew and gaping over her chest. Below the pale green material, the creamy flesh of her breasts was lifted up and forward by the pink satin and lace of her bra, openly displayed for his gaze to feast on.

'I had forgotten how lovely you were. Or, rather, I had remembered, but feared that my memory had played tricks on me. I told myself that you could not be so beautiful...'

Jet-black eyes, in which the golden flames of desire burned savagely, lifted and blazed into her hazy green ones. And Sarah felt her heart flip over inside her as she saw the hunger and the need he didn't trouble to disguise.

'But I was wrong...'

'You're—you're not so bad yourself.'

Sarah's tongue stumbled over the only words that would form in her mind.

'You're beautiful too. Quite beautiful, but...'

'But...' Damon echoed ominously, dark eyes narrowing swiftly, straight black brows drawing together in a frown at that impertinent and provocative 'but'.

'But you have too many clothes on.'

'Is that so?'

His quick, flashing grin was almost her undoing. The wide brilliance of it took her breath away, but there was something disturbingly triumphant in it that made her heart flutter in uncertainty.

'Well, that's easy to deal with.'

In one swift, efficient movement, he pulled the white polo shirt up and over his head, exposing the bronzed and muscled torso, shadowed with curling black hair, that lay beneath.

Sarah drew in her breath sharply then swallowed it down, her thoughts hazing swiftly. She half lifted her hand then dropped it to her side again, losing her nerve.

Standing there like that, half-naked, only inches away, he was pure sensual temptation. She wanted to touch, wanted desperately to feel the warm, satin texture of his skin under her fingertips, longed to trace the powerful lines of the straight shoulders, the muscles sheathing the strong bones, the broad ribcage. But she didn't dare. She felt like a child drawn to stick her fingers into a golden fire, yet knowing that she had been warned that to do so would bring devastation down on her head.

'Go ahead,' Damon murmured softly. He had caught the look on her face, the longing in her eyes. 'Go ahead and touch. I won't bite.'

Sarah closed her eyes against the temptation. But in the same moment she knew she was going to give in to it. She couldn't stop herself; couldn't resist it. *He* might not bite, but she couldn't help thinking that her own hunger, her own need would. She had been starved of the sight, the feel, the taste of him for six long months. And now she was presented with a feast that only a fool would resist.

Or was it just forbidden fruit like the tree in the Garden of Eden?

But she couldn't hold back all the same.

Slowly she reached out, still keeping her eyes closed. The moment that her fingertips made contact with hot, smooth skin it had the same startling, fizzing effect as making contact with a live electric current. She almost snatched them back, but then her eyes flew open, looking straight into the deep, opaque gaze of the man in front of her.

'Go on,' he encouraged huskily, his tone pure enticement. 'You know it's what we both want.'

Her throat was agonisingly dry; her lips felt as if they were cracking, they were so parched. She slicked her tongue over them in an attempt to ease the situation and saw from the faint flicker in the jet-dark stare that he was aware of the small betraying movement. But his gaze never faltered for a moment, holding her mesmerised so that she felt she had no will of her own, but was only capable of following his command.

'Touch me...'

'Yes...'

His will was hers anyway, she told herself, shrugging off the tiny pinpricks of doubt. What he wanted was what she wanted.

'Oh, yes...'

It came out on a long, slow sigh as her fingers trailed down the taut muscle cording his throat and along the hard, straight line of his shoulder. She watched his reaction intently, saw the tiny, involuntary jerk that he was unable to control, and a small, satisfied smile curved her lips.

'I'll touch—but only if you promise to do the same.'

Damon made a rough, raw sound deep in his throat as her hands drifted lower.

'You can be sure of that, lady,' he muttered hoarsely. 'Depend on it.'

He gave her free rein to wander where she would, standing still and unflinching under her caress. He swallowed hard when her teasing touch circled first one small, dark male nipple, then the other, making them tighten, harden instantly, his jaw clenching hard against a gasp of response. But a second later he had himself back under control again, though the pulse that beat at the base of his neck and his uneven, ragged breathing betrayed the amount of effort he was having to exert in order to remain that way.

'You're very—strong...' Sarah murmured, deliberately edging the last word with an emphasis that made its double meaning plain. 'Have you been working out?'

'Some.'

It rasped from a throat so raw that he sounded as if he hadn't used his voice in weeks.

He had had to do *something* to distract his mind from the fact that she had walked out on him with not even a backward glance, without a word of warning. He had come back from a business trip to find a bed that had been empty so long that the sheets were thoroughly chilled, and a note that was even colder, icy as the Arctic. The punishing physical routine he had set himself in the gym had helped to drain the burning energy from his body, leaving him drenched in sweat and limp with fatigue. It had filled hours in the day, but it had done little to ease the hungry longing that clawed at him in the night, keeping him wide awake and in restless torment from his thoughts and his memories.

It was in the darkness that images of her luscious body would come back to haunt him, hardening him in an instant, and refusing to ease the erotic hold they had on him. In the silence of the night he could almost feel her there beside him, hear the soft sound of her breathing. He could recall with agonising accuracy the warmth of her skin, the soft scent of her body, the tiny, wildly arousing murmurs she had made in her sleep as she shifted, stretching with a sensuousness that grabbed at his loins and twisted cruelly. No matter how he had shifted and adjusted his position on the luxurious bed, he had been unable to get comfortable, the hope of sleep just an unattainable fantasy.

'I—needed the exercise.'

'I like it...'

She more than liked it. He felt wonderful. He even smelt wonderful, the intensely personal scent of his skin intoxicating her senses in the way that no alcoholic drink, however potent, could ever manage. He felt leaner and harder and more powerful than ever before and it was strangely shocking to have such a fiercely masculine creature standing still and submissive under her lightest touch.

Almost submissive.

She couldn't deceive herself that he was actually under her control in any way. He was *letting* her do what she wanted with him right now because it suited him, and only for that reason. If he changed his mind, grew impatient, decided enough was enough, then she would stand as little chance against him as a buzzing fly that he would flick away with arrogant ease.

And it seemed that his patience was fraying, wearing thin.

Her ears, sharpened into acute sensitivity by the burning awareness of everything about him, caught the tiny hiss of a rawly indrawn breath as her wandering fingers drifted lower. She saw the quiver of his tanned flesh, the twitch of long, strong fingers and instinctively tensed in wary apprehension, green eyes locking with burning jet-black.

'Losing your nerve, darling?' he questioned huskily.

'Never...' she managed, though there was a disturbingly revealing tremble in the word.

His unwavering gaze challenged her to continue and, still

with her eyes fixed on his, she let her fingers move again, tracing soft, curving patterns over his skin, drifting across his chest, down—

'Enough!'

A hard hand snapped out, clamped over hers, stilling the teasing caresses in an instant.

'Enough,' he said again. 'It's my turn now.'

The hungry possessiveness in his tone turned her bones to water and she had to stumble backwards, sinking weakly onto the bed before she fell. The view she had from this position, of Damon's lean, muscled waist, the wide leather belt around his waist, the close-fitting jeans where the swollen force of his erection pushed at the taut fabric, did nothing at all to help her regain any sort of composure.

'Or, rather,' Damon went on, 'it's your turn.'

'My...?'

With an effort she dragged her gaze from the stretch of blue denim straight in front of her and looked up. And immediately wished she hadn't.

Standing above her like this, black eyes blazing down into hers, broad shoulders blocking out the light from the window, Damon seemed even bigger, stronger, more powerful, more *male*, than ever. And when his hands came down onto her shoulders it was all she could do not to flinch away in apprehension.

But all he did was to tug gently at the pale green linen of her shirt, flicking the collar with one contemptuous finger.

'Now you're the one who is wearing too many clothes. This will have to go.'

For all the softness in his words, it was clearly a command; one he intended to have obeyed. And Sarah didn't have the strength or the will to oppose him. Instead, she lifted her hands like someone in a dream, her eyes still fixed on his, and dealt unseeingly with the one remaining button which was all that held the blouse together at the neck. Then slowly, with a natural grace, she let the fine material drop, slithering down the length of her arms to lie in a soft, crumpled pool behind her on the bed.

Damon stayed as still as a marble statue, watching her through hooded eyes. She could feel the burn of his stare on her exposed skin; see the glitter of desire through the lush black lashes.

'Good...' he said at last, drawing in one long, deep breath and expelling it on a sigh, 'for a start... And what about the rest?'

The movement to reach the back fastening of her bra arched her spine, pushing her chest forward, making gold flames flare in the darkness of his gaze. But when she would have slipped the lacy straps down from her shoulders he moved suddenly, his hands coming out again to stop her.

'No—let me...'

Crouching down in front of her, he hooked his thumbs under the straps, sliding them down over her arms in a blatant caress that made her skin shiver at the promise of delight it held. He took his time about it, watching her for every long, enticing second, so that he couldn't have been unaware of the way that her eyes widened, and darkened, revealing her inner response to him.

But from the moment that the silky confection dropped away from her, letting her breasts tumble out into the hard heat of his waiting hands, everything changed. In the space of a thudding heartbeat, the atmosphere in the room became electrically charged, heavy with a dark sensuality that was primitive in its force.

'*Theos*...' Damon muttered, almost reverentially. 'You are so lovely...'

His hands closed over soft flesh, cupping, smoothing,

caressing, and Sarah moaned aloud at just the delight of his touch.

She had been starved of this. Hungered for it. And after so long an abstinence, the feeling of joy overwhelmed her. It rushed straight to her brain like the effects of some potent alcoholic spirit and she felt her head swim uncontrollably.

Heat coiled in the pit of her stomach, spiralled through her body, and she closed her eyes the better to experience the glorious sensations. Leaning back on her hands, she concentrated fiercely on what was happening to her, hearing the roughly muttered words in Greek in the same moments that she felt his mouth speaking them against her skin.

And then there was silence as the heat and softness of his lips closed over one nipple, his tongue circling it, arousing it, waking it to tight, yearning sensitivity. And only when it peaked in hungry demand did he take it fully into his mouth and suckle hard.

'Damon...'

The sound of his name was a swooning cry of surrender blended with an unspoken demand for more of the same. And yet when he moved his dark head to devote the same attention to the other breast, the erotic blend of stinging pleasure flooded so wildly through her that she felt she might actually lose consciousness from the joy of it.

'Damon...'

It was stronger now, harder, needier. And that need pushed her from simply taking, accepting the pleasure that he was giving her, into wanting to give, to return the delight she was experiencing, and reduce him to the same molten, mindless, abandoned state.

'Let me kiss you...'

Her hands clenched tight in the ebony silk of his hair, clutching at thick handfuls and pulling him upwards, forcing his head up towards hers.

'Kiss me,' she muttered fiercely, struggling to drown the

anguished protest of every fiercely awakened nerve at the abrupt cessation of the pleasure they had known under another, different, but equally drugging sort of delight.

The pressure of Damon's mouth against her own crushed her lips open, hot tongues tangling, two breaths mixing into one. And if it hadn't been for the support of his hands at the back of her head, holding her upright, she would have tumbled back onto the mattress behind her, falling under the hot, heavy weight of his strong body.

Damon went with her willingly, following her muttered demands with a sense of relief. His beleaguered body needed some moments to gather its resources, recover some degree of control. If he didn't then this lovemaking would be over before it began. As it was, he was more than tempted to simply fling her back onto the bed, force her skirt up, rip away the flimsy silk and lace barrier that came between him and the secret, female core of her, and bury himself deep and hard inside her welcoming body.

And that would be all he would be capable of doing. He knew that as soon as his flesh touched hers, in the seconds that the hot, slick sheath closed around him, he would be lost. He would come in a wild, uncontainable rush, all thought, all possibility of restraint leaving him in a split-second.

And so now he plundered her mouth instead of her body, seeking the moments needed to draw breath, get himself back in hand, so that he could make this into the experience it should be for both of them.

But she wasn't making it easy for him. In the same seconds that her mouth opened under his, inviting his intimate invasion, her hands started wandering, visiting all the most sensitive parts of his body, sparking off explosive reactions wherever they touched. He was kneeling astride her, his legs on either side of hers on the bed, the mattress giving under their joint weight. His chances of staying in control were reduced from low to impossible in between one breath and another, and when she fell back amongst the tangled bedclothes, still clutching at him, he had no choice but to go with her.

As they rolled together, twisting, turning so that he ended up as the one on his back, Sarah on top, he felt her hands move to his waist, tugging and pulling at the buckle of his belt.

'Sarah!'

Her name was pushed from him on a breath that combined laughter and protest, a tiny sense of desperation creeping in at the thought of how things had got so hot so fast.

He should be thinking—trying to think! This wasn't what he had planned on—or was it?

What *had* he planned on? He didn't know—couldn't remember—frankly, didn't care.

With a smothered half laugh, half groan of surrender, he gave up the attempt at using his mind and flung his arms open wide, stretching them out on the bed so that she could have free access to what was left of his clothing.

And froze as his left hand made contact with something cold and hard and metallic.

'What the hell…?'

It was partly hidden under the pillow, just a small section of chain sticking out across the sheet, and as he pulled on it he twisted his head to one side to see what it was.

A chain.

A thick, heavy-linked gold chain, with a circular St Christopher medal hanging from it.

A very *masculine* gold chain.

The sort of chain he could well imagine Jason the rat wearing.

And as he moved his head again he caught the heavy, musky aroma of some overly potent aftershave that was still clinging to the pillow covers. He recognised that scent immediately. It had been thick on the air downstairs—when Jason had come close as he walked past and out the door.

From being close to white heat, his blood cooled immediately, freezing in his veins. All trace of desire left him in a rush, to be replaced by a volatile mixture of cold fury, bitter betrayal and sheer blind frustration. Nausea grabbed at his stomach, making it twist violently.

'Damon?'

Sarah had noticed the change—how could she not? Her hands had stilled at his waist, the belt buckle lying open, and she lifted cloudily questioning eyes to his face.

'What?'

He didn't speak, couldn't speak. He could only lift his hand, the chain and medallion dangling from his fingers.

All colour leached from Sarah's face, leaving her ashen, tinged with a ghastly cast of green. The next moment she recoiled violently, almost throwing herself off the bed, scrambling inelegantly in her haste to get away.

Damon wasn't far behind her.

He felt sick. Sick, disgusted and damn well *used*. Twisting his long, lean body, he jackknifed off the other side of the bed to stand, blind black fury stamped on his face, glaring at her across the room.

'Whose is this?'

He didn't need to ask, of course. Didn't need his already certain suspicions confirming. But he had to ask—to say something, no matter what.

Sarah wouldn't meet his eyes. If he felt sick then she looked even worse.

'You—you know...'

'Answer me!'

Sarah couldn't find the strength to say a single thing. Bitterly conscious of her half-undressed state, the way that her hair was ruffled and tangled, the dishevelled condition of her skirt, she grabbed at the lilac towelling robe that lay over a chair and clutched it tight against her, gaining some morsel of strength at least from its protection.

'Whose...?' Damon repeated, ominous threat lacing every letter of the word.

'J-Jason's!'

He knew, damn him. He didn't need to ask!

But what he didn't know—and didn't trouble to ask—was that the only reason Jason's medallion had been in the bed was because the other man had been up here this afternoon—with Andrea. Never, ever with Sarah herself. Though that was the accusation that was etched savagely onto his face.

And his next words proved as much.

'Jason's,' he repeated, spitting the name out as if it was poison. 'Jason—your lover—'

'No!'

'No, not any more perhaps. Not since he spoiled things by playing away from home. Or, rather, *at* home...'

The grim humour in his tone, the glint of something demonic in his eyes threw her completely. How could he *laugh*?

But then Damon looked down at the rumpled, dishevelled bed, and all trace of humour, black or otherwise, vanished in the blink of an eye.

'How could you?'

It was low and savage, a brutal, slashing demand with danger in every word.

'How the bloody hell *could* you?'

'How could I what, Damon?'

Her lips felt so stiff and tight that they might as well have been made of wood for all the expression she could put into the cold little voice.

'How could I do—what?'

If he truly believed what she suspected then he was going

to have to say it. If he thought that she was capable of the appalling crime that had stamped that expression onto his stunning features, then he was going to have to accuse her of it to her face. She wasn't going to give him a chance to slide out of things later by claiming *I never said that*.

'Tell me.'

'You were actually prepared to make love to me in the bed that you normally share with your boyfriend!' he flung at her in pure 'you asked for it' tones. 'The sheets were barely cold—'

'From his assignation with *his* girlfriend!'

Her stomach lurched queasily at just the thought.

'So you thought you'd do what? Have your revenge with me in the same place that he'd betrayed you? What is it you call it? Tit for tat?'

'No! It wasn't anything like that!'

She felt so ill that she couldn't control her tongue in any way, letting it run away with her totally.

'And don't you dare call what just happened making love! We both know it wasn't anything like that!'

'We certainly do.'

After the hard incisiveness of his anger, the deliberately lazy drawl was viciously insulting.

'There was nothing of love in that. All you were after was a quick—'

A swift glance at her face had him cutting off the crude description abruptly.

'It was lust, nothing more.'

She'd known that all along; had been under no illusion from the start. But still it hurt so very much to hear him state his lack of feeling quite so openly and bluntly.

'But then we both knew that already.'

He had the nerve—the vicious nerve—to *smile*, directing the icy, humourless look straight into her clouded green eyes.

'Of course,' Sarah responded tightly, and he nodded his satisfaction. The smile faded, turning his mouth into a grim, hard line.

'At least we agree on something.'

Stooping, he snatched up his shirt from the floor and pulled it over his head. The brusque, decisive way he tucked it into the waistband of his jeans, pulling the belt tightly shut over the top, put a firm, cold stop to the passion that had flared so briefly and yet so wildly between them.

Not that he needed to bother, Sarah told herself miserably. She had never felt less passionate in all her life. Shaken and shivery after the desperate assault on her senses, the sudden, brutal halt to her arousal, she was distinctly unsteady on her feet. Her legs felt weak and hollow, lacking the strength to hold her upright. But she had to stay where she was. At least until Damon left.

She would rather die than have him see just how appalling she felt. So she tried to copy him by pulling on the robe she held, belting it so tightly round her waist that she pinched the skin underneath painfully.

'It was a mistake we should be glad we never made.'

'Absolutely.'

Damon's glare threatened to shrivel her right where she stood and bitterness and pain at his hypocrisy stabbed straight to her already wounded heart. The anguish pushed her into wild, unthinking words.

'Since when did you get so picky?'

'Picky?'

For a rare moment he frowned his incomprehension.

'I didn't put you down as the fastidious type!' Sarah elaborated cynically. The memory of Eugenia, beautiful, dark, exotic Eugenia, her looks so unlike Sarah's very Celtic pallor and red hair, gave her words an added bitter bite.

'I'm not just some sexual opportunist.'

'Of course not! You were just driven wild with passion for me!'

'So wild that I stupidly forgot what you are,' Damon muttered darkly.

'What I am...?'

Sarah froze in horror at his tone, looking into the carved coldness of his face, trying to read what was behind the black rejection in his eyes—and failing miserably.

'What *am* I, Damon?'

The look he flung at her said so plainly, You *know* what you are, that she almost thought she had heard the words spoken aloud, and she started in shocked surprise when he actually answered her as well.

'The sort of woman who will take a new man to bed when the door has barely closed on her last lover.'

'A new...'

Sarah swallowed hard but still the words seemed to gather in a tight knot in her throat.

'A new man!' she managed to croak. 'But you're not a new man, are you, Damon, darling? You're the past—over and done with. Nothing to me any more—or ever again.'

And right now she wished that it were true. At this moment she longed to be able to go back to the wonderful, if fleeting, days of peace she had known when she had thought that she was over Damon. That she had put their brief and unhappy marriage behind her and was ready to move on into the future.

But the truth was that she couldn't. And the volatile mixture of love and hatred that she felt was boiling up inside her, creating a violent volcano of emotion over which she had no control at all.

'Not quite the past, *agape mou*,' Damon tossed back with icy contempt. 'In the eyes of the law you're still tied to me; I'm still your husband.'

'And I wish you weren't! I wish I'd never set eyes on you; never been fool enough to say I'd marry you!'

'Nevertheless you are still my wife...'

'No, I'm not!'

That emotive word was just too much for her, driving her into desperate action. Whirling towards the bed, she snatched up the nearest thing to hand—one of the big, feather-stuffed pillows—and flung it straight at him with all the force she could muster.

'I'm not! I'm not! I'm *not*!'

Caught off guard, Damon didn't manage to protect himself from the first attack so that the pillow flew straight at him and hit him hard in the face, temporarily knocking him off balance. But he recovered with incredible speed, righting himself in time to catch both the second and third missile and drop them coolly to the floor.

'I'm not your wife—not any more! I'd rather be anything else than that! And I don't give a damn about the law either! All I want is for you to go—get out of here and leave me alone!'

'OK.' Damon was surprisingly agreeable, making her blink in stunned confusion at his easy acquiescence. 'I'll do that. I need to get my things from the car and bring them in anyway.'

'Get your...'

That was *not* what she had meant. And it was certainly not what she wanted!

'You're not staying here!'

'Oh, but I am, sweetheart,' he returned imperturbably. 'Where else would I stay?'

'Anywhere—a hotel...'

'Don't be silly, Sarah,' he chided almost gently. 'Why would I want to pay out good money for a hotel when I have the whole house at my disposal?'

'Because I live here!'

'But it's *my* house,' he reminded her, with a deadly emphasis on that 'my'. 'And, that being the case, I have every right to stay here whenever I choose. And there are another five bedrooms to choose from. It's not as if I'm suggesting that I share your bed.'

'Over my dead body! I do have some pride!'

Her defiant retort wiped the tolerant look from his face in a second, replacing it once again with the mask of cold black fury that made her quail inwardly in fearful distress.

'And so do I!' he snarled savagely. 'Which is why the first thing that I'm going to do when I get to my room is have a long, hot shower.'

He gave a faint, but definite shudder, a grimace of distaste crossing his strongly carved features.

'I don't know about you but I feel distinctly grubby.'

Then, just in case she hadn't quite got the point he was trying to make, he turned those deep ebony eyes on the bed once more before lifting them to look her straight in the face.

'I think it will take me quite a while to feel clean again.'

And while Sarah was still gasping in shock and horrified disbelief, unable to find a single word to throw at him, he turned on his heel and strode out of the room, letting the door slam shut emphatically behind him.

'Ohhhhh!'

With a scream of pure frustration, Sarah flung the last remaining pillow after him, needing to express her pain and anger in some physical way. She managed to retain what was left of her control only for as long as it took for the cushion to land against the wood with a soft, dull thud and tumble softly to the floor, but then all her strength left her. Throwing herself down onto the bed, she pummelled the mattress over and over again with her fists, wishing with all her heart that it was Damon's cold, uncaring face, the hard wall of his chest that was feeling the force of her blows.

'I hate him!' she muttered fiercely, timing each word to the pounding of her fists. 'I hate, hate, *hate* him!'

But even as she vented the words, willing herself to believe them, she knew that they were only in her mind. That her heart knew the truth.

And in that truth was the seed of real despair.

Because even now, even hating him for the foul insults he had tossed at her, for his hypocrisy in calling her undiscriminating, with the implication that he believed she was promiscuous, for the way he had seduced her quite callously and unfeelingly, she still couldn't deny the way she felt about him. She might detest him, but she also loved him desperately. He was as essential to her as the air she breathed, the beat of her heart, to keep her alive. And he always would be.

And as she admitted that to herself, the cleansing rush of anger waned, and in its place was a terrible sense of dread of what the future might hold.

How was she ever going to survive even the next few hours—never mind the possibility of *days*—with Damon actually living in the same house?

CHAPTER FOUR

It was a terrible struggle for Sarah to get out of bed the next morning.

Not because she had slept heavily. In fact she had hardly slept at all, but had spent most of the night lying wide awake and staring at the ceiling, wondering just what she was going to do. But by the time that dawn came around, and then each hour that passed after it, she was nowhere nearer to coming to any conclusions, and she was most definitely not ready to start the day.

Not with Damon living in the house and determined to stay there, no matter what she said or did.

Any foolish hopes she might have had that he had changed his mind, packed and left during the night, were cruelly dashed in the moments that she heard, dimly through the walls, the sound of his shower working. She was only able to listen to the murmur of the water for a few moments before the rush of memories it brought had her burying her head under the pillows to try and shut it out.

But even then cruel, painfully erotic images assailed her mind, forcing their way into her thoughts until she was gritting her teeth to hold back the cries of pain the recollections threatened to force from her.

Damon would be standing under the pounding water, his tall, powerful body slick and wet. His eyes would be closed, springing black hair plastered down onto his skull, emphasising the shape of the strong bones, the line of his jaw. His long, muscular legs would be planted slightly apart, bronzed skin startling against the white of the shower-stall floor, and his hands would be moving over his chest, spreading soap and foam over the wide ribcage, the narrow hips and down, down...

'No!' she moaned aloud, tossing restlessly as a flame of pure physical need shot through her, heating her blood in an instant. 'No, I mustn't think...'

But she couldn't *not* think, though the pain of her memories was almost more than she could bear.

In the early days of their marriage, Damon had rarely, if ever, showered alone. On the morning after they had shared his bed for the first time, he had woken before her and had silently padded his way on bare feet across the room to the *en suite* bathroom. Then, as now, the sound of the shower had woken Sarah and, unable to stay where she was, needing desperately to see this man who had come to mean so very much to her in such an amazingly short time, she had followed him, as if attached by a thread that had drawn tight and tugged her close.

He had already been in the shower, the steam from the water clouding the glass so that she could barely see him, and she had pulled open the door just a crack, meaning only to peep in. The faint touch of the cooler air had alerted Damon to her presence, making him turn. Sharply embarrassed by being caught acting like a peeping Tom in this way, Sarah had been about to hurry away, but, seeing her hotly pink face, the blush that washed her cheeks, Damon had laughed in good-humoured amusement.

'Good morning, little wife,' he had said softly. 'Couldn't you bear to be parted from me even for a second?'

And when she could only shake her head, too tongue-tied to be able to utter a word, he smiled a wide, triumphant, arrogantly satisfied grin.

'I like that,' he said, his voice thickening noticeably in the same moments that his body hardened, responded to her presence in a hotly aroused manner. 'I like that a lot.'

And he reached for her, opening the shower door to catch hold of her arm and pull her in under the water with him. Within seconds the fine silk of her nightdress was saturated, plastered against her body like a second skin, the water making it almost totally transparent.

For a brief time Damon contented himself with smoothing the wet material against the lines of her body, the heat of his palms adding to the warmth of the water cascading down on her. When her nipples peaked wantonly, pushing against his hands, he bent his proud head and suckled her hungrily through the soaking silk, sending stinging arrows of pleasure down right to the central core of her being. But very quickly this ceased to satisfy him and he tugged the delicate nightdress from her body, tossing it carelessly to the floor and trampling it underfoot as he pressed her up against the wall of the shower cubicle and pushed his hand down between her legs...

'No, no, *no*!' Sarah moaned again, flinging the pillow against the wall and tossing off the bedclothes, too hot, too jittery to stay still any longer.

She was out of bed and pacing restlessly around the room, struggling to get herself back under control, when she heard a new sound, that of a door closing, way down the long landing that separated them. Damon's footsteps followed it, moving closer, past her room then down the stairs into the body of the house.

He was up and about, then, and no doubt expecting that soon she too would make her way downstairs to start her day. She couldn't stay here and hide all morning. But she didn't know how she was going to face him either.

It took her a long time to force herself to get dressed. Going into the shower was an ordeal that brought hot tears to her eyes, reminding her as it did of the heated scenes she had been recalling only moments before. Not knowing whether it was herself, or Damon, or simply fate that she was furious with and hated most, she reached up and snapped the temperature control from warm to cold, gasping out loud in shock as the icy current pulsed down onto her exposed body.

Five seconds was all it took to drive the erotic memories from her mind. Shivering with cold, shaking all over, she turned the shower off again, and grabbed a towel, rubbing herself dry so roughly that her skin glowed pink from the friction.

But at least she felt more in control, cooler-headed as well as cooler-bodied. And, having pulled on a deep purple long-sleeved T-shirt together with a well-worn and distinctly baggy pair of jeans that had seen much, much better days, she felt stronger too, armoured both physically and mentally. A brisk, no-nonsense brush of her hair before fastening it into a tight pony-tail down her back completed her preparations—no need for fuss and fripperies like lipstick or mascara—and she was ready.

Head high, back straight, chin up, she marched down the stairs, ready to face any and every sort of sarcastic or caustic comment that Damon might decide to throw at her.

So it came as something of a shock when she stalked into the kitchen to find that Damon was not at all in the sort of mood she expected. Instead, he was lounging in a chair at the big oak dining table, long legs stretched out in front of him, his head buried in the financial section of one of the thick Saturday papers. He was even more casually dressed than she was, being still in a navy-blue silky robe, his legs and feet bare, and his strong jaw darkly shadowed with a night's growth of stubble. He might have showered that morning, but he certainly hadn't shaved or dressed.

'Good morning!'

She looked as if she was preparing for battle, or some other sort of terrible ordeal, Damon reflected, slanting a swift sidelong glance in Sarah's direction from under his eyelashes as she stood hesitating in the doorway. Aggression practically prickled all over her, sending out electrically charged sparks into the atmosphere so that it fizzled with tension.

And she'd clearly slept as badly as he had. There were blue-grey shadows under her amazing eyes and she had pulled her glorious hair back into a severe, ruthlessly controlled style. He knew that style of old. It declared quite clearly that she was not in the mood for any messing about. She was also, obviously, *not* dressed to kill.

'Morning,' he acknowledged easily, his attention apparently still on his paper, as she forced herself across the threshold and into the room.

What would she think if she knew the way that the print was blurring in front of his eyes, growing worse the harder he tried to focus on it? He could only pray that she wouldn't guess how much of a struggle he was having not to look at her, not to think of the glorious shape of her body beneath the baggy, unflattering clothes, the scent of her skin as it had surrounded him last night.

And didn't she realise that the dragged-back, schoolmistressy way she wore her hair was in fact a silent challenge to any man with red blood in his veins? It just made him want to pull off the constricting elasticated band that bound the red-gold locks into such confinement. To rip it off and release the tumbling silk of her hair so that it fell loose onto her shoulders. He longed to comb his fingers through its softness, feel it fall around his face, stroke across his chest...

No!

His hands clenched tighter on the sheets of paper he held and the figures in the report he was pretending to read danced before his eyes.

Damn it to hell, he must *not* think like that!

He had let such fantasies into his mind last night, and

look where that had got him! Tumbling into bed with her without a thought for the wisdom of his acts; the possible consequences.

Oh, face it, man, you didn't *think* at all!

Or at least if he had done then it had been with a far more basic part of his make-up than his intelligence! The part that was reacting only too visibly now, making him shift uncomfortably in his seat, crossing his legs in what he hoped was a casual manner, and drawing the concealing newspaper lower down so as to cover his lap.

Why the devil hadn't he taken the time to get dressed properly instead of just throwing on this far from covering robe, with only a pair of boxer shorts on underneath? He should have known that he wasn't in control of his sexual responses where Sarah was concerned. That his body was likely to betray him if she was near.

But he had slept so badly that when he'd finally given up on the attempt to get any rest he'd just forced himself under the shower and then shoved on the dressing gown, thinking only of hot, strong coffee, a much-needed shot of caffeine.

'There's coffee in the pot if you want some.' He tried to say it with a casualness he was very far from feeling.

'Oh—thanks…'

What else could she say? Having nerved herself for a fight, or at the very least some sort of confrontation, she was thoroughly thrown off balance by his relaxed, almost totally indifferent reaction to her appearance. After the appalling scene in her bedroom the evening before, she hadn't been able to force herself to go downstairs again, not even to get something to eat. Instead she had made up the bed with clean sheets and pillowcases, and stayed resolutely right where she was, watching mind-numbingly boring television programmes on the small portable set until well after midnight. It was only after she had finally heard Damon switching off all the lights and heading upstairs that she had even tried to settle to sleep.

So his calm nonchalance was the last thing she had expected, anticipating instead some challenge as to what she thought she was up to, or a taunt about her blatant cowardice in hiding away.

'Would—would you like some more?'

'Please.'

A hand appeared around the side of the paper, holding out a used, empty mug in her general direction, Damon not even looking up as he continued reading.

'Thanks,' he acknowledged briefly as she took it from him.

'No problem,' Sarah forced herself to mutter, struggling to resist the urge to fill the mug and then throw it and its contents straight at his uncaring head.

Which was so totally ridiculous when she considered it that she actually laughed out loud. All last night she had wished that Damon had never reappeared in her life. She had longed for him to be anywhere but here. And she had dreaded the prospect of the coming morning which would mean that she had to face him when she fully expected that he would subject her, if not to any physical harassment, at least to some sort of verbal assault that would make her want to curl up and die inside.

So why was she now so annoyed that he was actually ignoring her? Wasn't it really what she actively preferred? What she should feel most comfortable with? What would make her life a whole lot easier?

'What's so funny?'

Damon's question caught her unawares, making her hand clench so tightly on the coffeepot that it shook precariously in her grasp.

'What?'

The paper rustled as he finally lowered it to look straight

at her and, of course, with the perverse frame of mind she found herself in, she now would have preferred that he had done nothing of the sort.

'You laughed,' Damon explained mildly. 'I was wondering what had amused you.'

'Oh, just my thoughts.'

Sarah tried for airy carelessness and prayed that she had succeeded. She wasn't too sure, though, and the way that Damon's black eyes narrowed sharply warned her that she might actually have sounded revealingly uncomfortable.

'I—was thinking of something I saw on TV last night...' she invented rapidly, and was deeply thankful when he apparently seemed to believe her.

At least, he said nothing, but simply shrugged and went back to his paper, bringing it up before his face again as if as some sort of defence against her.

'It was a comedy programme,' she embroidered unnecessarily. 'A funny one.'

'Obviously.'

The dry comment made her realise how foolish she must be sounding and she forced her attention back on to preparing the coffee. For some strange reason the very simple task suddenly seemed to have acquired complications and difficulties that she had never encountered before. Impossibly, she couldn't decide whether to put milk in her mug first or the coffee, and instead found herself frozen into immobility as she dithered from one move to the other and back again.

'I take mine black.'

Unnervingly, Damon had sensed her hesitation, even though he hadn't lowered the paper again.

'Coffee—I take it black.'

'I know that!'

Tension made Sarah's voice tight and sharp so that she winced inwardly, just hearing it.

'I remember!' she added, struggling for calm. 'It's not *that* long ago.'

'No, it's not.'

The inflexion he put on the words twisted a knife in Sarah's heart, eliminating even the faint hint of amusement she had felt earlier. In an awkward, jerky movement she slammed the coffee-mug down on the table beside Damon's elbow, heedless of the way that some of the hot liquid slopped over the side and onto the table.

Then, purely for something to do and not because she was in any way really hungry, she opened one of the cupboards and pulled out the toaster, dumping it heavily on the worktop.

'Toast?' It was brusque to the point of rudeness, but it didn't even make Damon put down his paper.

'Please.'

He was regaining some degree of control over his wayward senses, thank God. Another minute and he might actually be able to look in her direction without making a total fool of himself.

Because he was determined he was not going down that road again. Yesterday he had let his libido get the better of him and had ended up feeling a total fool—and dirty into the bargain!

Inwardly, Damon shuddered at the mental image of himself rolling on the bed with Sarah—on the bed that she had been sharing with *Jason*, for God knew how long. That was not going to happen again!

But what *was* he going to do?

He'd come here to talk some sense into Sarah, to persuade her to give their marriage a second try. He had expected that it wouldn't be easy, that she would still be angry and distant because of the way they'd parted. What he hadn't expected to find was that she'd already moved another man in and was living with him.

Last night he'd vowed to himself that he wasn't going to stick around. That as soon as the day dawned he would repack the bag he had so recently unpacked and head back to Greece, shaking the dust of London and this house from his feet for good. But the lack of sleep and a need for coffee had delayed him and...

And—*face it, you fool!* he told himself furiously, recalling his body's instant reaction to Sarah's appearance in the doorway, the sound of her footsteps on the stairs.

Face facts!

He wasn't going to be able just to walk out and not look back, however much he had planned on it. Sarah Nicolaides, the former Sarah Meyerson, had him tangled up in her web of seduction, and no matter how hard he twisted and tugged, the sticky net was coiled tightly round him. So what was he going to do about it?

Of course after yesterday it was unlikely that Jason would be back, but he'd be happier if he thought that the other man was right out of the picture once and for all. If only he could think of some way that he could get Sarah to come back with him to Greece...

'One slice or two? Butter or margarine?'

Absorbed in his thoughts, he totally missed the tart edge to Sarah's voice.

'Two, please. And, yes, butter and...'

The faint thump of something hitting the back of the newspaper and then tumbling to the floor brought him up sharp, making him lower the defensive barrier and actually look at her properly for the first time. His puzzled frown was met by a brilliant emerald glare as Sarah turned a furious face to him.

'So what did your last slave die of?' she muttered angrily.

'Slave?'

Damon made a play of examining the newspaper where

whatever missile she had launched at it had struck before heading to the floor. There was a sticky, greasy patch—toast crumbs, butter and... He tested it gingerly with a finger.

'Lime marmalade! I haven't tasted that in ages.'

And that was something that Sarah knew only too well. In fact it was the marmalade that had been positively the last straw, driving her to rebel, to lose her temper and finally fling the toast she had prepared for him straight at the newspaper, desperate to bring him out from behind his protective shield.

'Well, yours is on the floor!' she snapped, pointing down at the slice of toast that lay, buttered side predictably downwards, at his feet. She found herself wanting desperately to provoke him. To put him into as spiky a mood as she found herself in.

'My, we are in a bad mood this morning.'

Infuriatingly, Damon seemed totally unprovoked. Instead he appeared mildly amused, a faint gleam of humour lighting in his deep eyes, incensing Sarah even further.

'What's the problem, did you—what is that strange saying you have? Did you wake up on the wrong side of the bed?'

'It's get *out* of bed on the wrong side!' Sarah flung at him through gritted teeth. 'As I'm sure you damn well know! Your English has always been just about perfect—so don't suddenly go all Greek on me! And no, I did *not* get out of bed on the wrong side!'

'Then what did happen? Oh...'

Abruptly his expression sobered, the teasing gleam fading from his eyes.

'I'm sorry. I understand. I was being insensitive.'

'You were?'

Sarah's head went back in shock at the sudden change in the man before her. Was she imagining things? Letting her mind deceive her into seeing things she wanted to find in his face? Or was that truly an expression of some sort of sympathy she could read there?

'Of course. You are missing Jason.'

'Missing—Jason!'

For a split-second, she actually couldn't think who he meant. But then memory came back in an unwanted rush.

'I'm doing no such thing! I was glad to see the back of him!'

Too late she realised, as she saw the softer light die from his eyes, just what she was making him think. He truly believed that Jason had been her lover. That she had at least shared her bed with someone that she cared for. Her total indifference to his departure, her casual dismissal of it could only make her look shallow at best and at the worst cheap.

But was that the worst?

Wouldn't in fact the worst of this be having Damon know the truth? The real facts of what she had been thinking and feeling which had made her react in the way she had?

Wouldn't it be far more difficult to have him know that in those few short moments since she had come into the kitchen she had somehow, unknowingly and unthinkingly, slipped into a once-familiar routine that she used to share with him?

It was as if the time in between, their painful separation, had never happened. During their brief marriage they had shared so many lazy breakfasts in just this way. In those early days, foolishly blind and besotted with her new husband, Sarah had been only too happy to pour him coffee, make him toast. And this morning she had slipped right back into that role, buttering his toast, reaching into the cupboard automatically for the lime marmalade because Damon had always loved it so much.

But she didn't want to remember those times. Didn't want Damon to think that she remembered them. Didn't want him to know that she still thought of herself as his wife in any way at all.

'Good riddance to bad rubbish!' she declared over-emphatically, waving her hand in a wild gesture to underline the point.

'Careful...'

But Damon's warning came just too late. Sarah's gesticulating arm caught her coffee-mug, knocking it to the floor, where it crashed noisily, shattering into fragments, the steaming liquid spreading everywhere.

'Let me...'

Before she could protest, Damon was out of his chair. He grabbed for a cloth in the same second that Sarah caught up a tea towel. Together they bent to the mess on the floor, reached to wipe it up. Then froze, eyes locking together.

Sarah drew in her breath on a long, deep sigh.

'Damon...'

She couldn't help it. She reached out a hand, just needing to touch him, to make contact. To somehow bridge the impossible divide that yawned there between them like a huge, gaping chasm.

'Please...'

For the space of a heartbeat it looked as if he might actually respond. But then he suddenly blinked hard, and she saw the change in his eyes with a terrible sense of dread.

They froze over like ice on a pond, black as pitch and hard as polished jet.

'I'll see to this,' was all he said, but the rejection and the callous coldness were there in his tone, if not actually in his words.

Big mistake, you fool! Damon reproved himself savagely. He had meant to keep his distance, had told himself that if he could just keep space between himself and Sarah then he would be able to get himself back under control. He didn't need the temptation of being close enough to smell the faint herbal scent of her shampoo, see the smudges of tiredness under those brilliant eyes. Already his heart had kicked into a heavier beat, making his pulse throb. If this was keeping his distance, then he was going to have to get a grip on himself and fast!

Would it always be like this? Sarah wondered miserably. Would she always be so desperately vulnerable to his closeness, to just the scent and the warmth of his body? When she had been in his arms last night it had felt so right, like coming home. But the truth was that she no longer belonged in Damon's arms, in Damon's life, if in fact she had ever done so. He had never loved her, never really wanted her. He had only ever married her as a financial move. A way of getting what he wanted easily.

She couldn't take it any more. Tossing down the cloth, she jumped to her feet in a rush, unable to bear Damon's closeness. It was impossible to guess what she felt most— regret or relief that he watched her go without protest or reaching out to hold her still.

'I'll make some fresh coffee.' Anything to distract herself, she thought, wrenching open the fridge door. 'Ah. No milk.'

She had used the last of it in the mugful that now was splattered across the floor where Damon was dealing with the mess with swift efficiency.

'Not to worry.' Did her assumed nonchalance sound as forced and fake to him as it did in her own ears? She prayed it didn't because it gave away far too much of her inner turmoil. 'There should have been a delivery by now...'

At least by going to the door she could gain herself some breathing space. A chance to still the racing judder of her heart, get her breathing back under control.

There was no sort of warning. No sound that might have given her an indication that things were not quite as usual. No shuffle of feet or murmur of voices that was not the normal routine of things on a sleepy Saturday morning, where no one stirred much except perhaps to walk the dog or stroll to buy a morning paper.

So Sarah fully expected to look out onto a silent, deserted street. She was totally unprepared for the chaos and tumult that assaulted her senses when she pulled open the door and stepped over the threshold.

CHAPTER FIVE

IT WAS the lights that affected her first.

The sudden, brilliant flashes, like lightning, but without any rumble of thunder to precede them.

And the strange, deafening sound of clicks and whirrs that she couldn't understand.

Flash! Click! Whirr! Flash! And then the calls began.

'Sarah! This way, darling!'

'Miss Meyerson—over here!'

'Sarah, can we just have a word?'

'What?'

She froze, halfway upright again from retrieving the full milk bottle from the step, stared, and blinked as another succession of brilliant flashes blinded her.

'So Sarah—is it true?'

'Have you really...?' The rest of the sentence was lost in a sudden flurry of movement as, somewhere beyond the blur that the light flashes had burned into her eyes, someone scuffled, jockeying for a better position, and was pushed forcibly out of the way.

'Sarah—give us a smile!'

'Who are you?'

Still blinking to clear her vision, she straightened fully, frowning her confusion. But at least the shapes before her were starting to be in some way recognisable—though what she saw made no sort of sense to her at all.

Photographers—hundreds of them, or so it seemed to her bewildered eyes. Rows of men and women, standing, kneeling—some of them had even brought stepladders so that they could get a better angle on things.

And other people, waving strangely fluffy things that she recognised vaguely as microphones she had seen in television interviews—and *film cameras*!

'Come on, darling—look this way...'

'Give us a smile, can't you? After all, he must be worth billions...'

'Who?' Sarah managed, but she was completely ignored.

'So where did you meet him?'

'How long's it been going on? Do you plan on making *an announcement* soon?'

'An announcement' was framed in such emphatic tones that it almost seemed to be written in the air in large italic letters.

'What sort of an announcement—about what?'

'Oh, come on, Sarah! Stop being cagey...'

It was impossible not to sense that the mood had changed, shifting from friendly to something else, something at the opposite end of the spectrum of emotions. Sarah began to feel uncomfortably, frighteningly, as if she was facing a possible lynch mob. They just didn't seem to appreciate that she really had no idea what they were doing there.

Clutching the milk bottle to her like some sort of hopelessly inadequate defensive shield, she blinked hard to try to clear her blurred gaze, focused as well as she could on a woman in the front row and tried to smile.

'Can you tell me what's going on?'

If she had thought she might have found an ally, she was swiftly disillusioned.

'Oh, come *on*, Sarah! Don't be coy! Your secret's out now. You and the Gorgeous Greek are public property. So how does it feel to be the latest love in the Divine Damon's life?'

Damon. The name struck home even if she didn't understand why.

Divine Damon. The Gorgeous Greek. She knew those phrases; she'd seen them in the newspapers often enough. She'd been aware of them even before she ever met Damon. The society pages, the gossip columns, the celebrity magazines, all fed happily on stories of the 'Gorgeous Greek' and his love life. And the reports had seemed to haunt her ever since she had run away from her travesty of a marriage. She couldn't open a newspaper or turn on the television without reading or hearing something about him.

She could have told them that they were all on the wrong track. That any woman Damon appeared with in public was only a cloak, a pretence, a piece of arm candy. He used his public amours to distract attention from the real thing—and it seemed it had worked because no one, not even Sarah herself, had ever suspected.

'But I'm not!' she protested, horrified at the realisation of what they thought. 'I mean—'

'Oh, stop messing around! We know—so where *is* he?'

'I'm here.'

The words came from behind her, cool and calm and pitched perfectly so that they sliced through the buzz of annoyance, falling clearly into the pool of questions and creating a sudden total hush of awareness. And in the same second a couple of hands came down onto Sarah's shoulders, apparently gentle, but in fact so forcefully controlling that they stilled her instinctive start of surprise and shock before it had time to form.

'So what did you want to know?'

The silence evaporated in a second, turning instead into a storm of flash bulbs exploding once again, of clicking, whirring cameras. The whole gaggle of reporters pushed forward, crowding round the steps so that Sarah automatically tried to back fearfully away, only to find her flight stopped by an even firmer pressure of Damon's hands on her shoulders, holding her where she was.

'You have five minutes.'

Later, Sarah was to wonder if it had really only been five minutes. To her it had seemed like a lifetime. A lifetime of noise and explosions and shouted questions she barely understood, let alone could answer.

She was vaguely aware of Damon speaking. Of him giving the same sort of responses—the lying responses—that he had fed to Jason only the night before. She struggled to understand the lift of laughter, the man-to-man intonation in his voice when he spoke of 'whirlwind romance' and being 'knocked off his feet'.

She even opened her mouth to protest loudly, but the sharp, painful squeeze Damon gave her shoulders warned her that he was aware of her thoughts and didn't want her to act on them.

She briefly thought about rebelling, but squashed down the idea of mutiny before it had time to even form fully. It was beginning to dawn on her just what was going on, though parts of it were totally incomprehensible to her.

Somehow the reporters had got hold of the idea that she and Damon were a couple. She had no idea where they had learned such nonsense, but they clearly thought they were on the trail of a very hot story indeed. What she couldn't understand at all was why Damon was going along with it. Why he didn't just tell them to go to hell and never come back again was beyond her.

'OK, that's enough now...'

Damon's voice held enough authority to quash even the murmurs of protest that began as he drew the interview to a close.

'I said five minutes; you've had nearly ten.'

To Sarah's intense relief the pens stilled; some of the notebooks actually closed. But then one of the photographers, more forward than the rest, pushed to the front of the crowd.

'How about a proper picture, Damon? Give her a kiss, can't you, man? It's what our readers want to see.'

'A kiss—no—' Sarah tried, but she didn't even manage to get the words out.

She had barely opened her mouth before Damon moved his hands, clamping them firmly at the tops of her arms, and whirling her round to face him.

As he was standing on the doorstep, just above her, the already forceful advantage of his height was given an extra edge of domination. But, with her face hidden from the cameras at least, Sarah was determined not to give in without a fight.

'Damon—no!'

'Damon, yes!' he interrupted rudely and emphatically, one hand coming under her chin and tilting her head up so that her raging green eyes met the impenetrable darkness of his black stare.

'Go with it, *agape mou*,' he told her bluntly. 'Give them what they want and they'll leave us in peace.'

'No way!' Sarah spluttered furiously. 'I'm not—'

The rest of her words vanished under the fierce pressure of Damon's hard mouth as it clamped down over her lips, cutting off what she had been about to say and silencing her with brutal effectiveness. His hands held her tightly, hard fingers digging into soft flesh so savagely that she was convinced he must be bruising the delicate skin, that she had no chance of escape, no chance to wrench her face away, no chance of any movement at all. She could only submit totally to the crushing, demanding kiss he pressed on her.

And the dreadful thing, the really shocking, scary fact, was that it excited her.

From the moment his cruel mouth touched hers she was lost. A sensual fever invaded her body, making her pulse throb, her heart race. A heated, blinding mist swirled in her head behind her closed eyes, obscuring any thought, and her lips opened up under his, welcoming the intimate invasion of his tongue, the erotic dance it created with her own.

She swayed into the hardness and heat of his body, too lost even to put her arms up around his neck for support. The strength of his hands kept her upright and she abandoned herself to them entirely.

Behind her back she was only dimly aware of a renewed furore of flashes and the sound of a hundred camera shutters clicking wildly. The reporters and photographers had vanished into a blur, only existing on the very outer limits of her perception. In her world, the one she was aware of, there was only Damon and herself and the blaze of hunger they had created between them. And she knew without a hope that she had totally lost her grip on reality and was falling, falling far and fast into a hell of her own making.

Because if he had caught her up in his arms right there and then, if he had put his dark head down to hers and whispered in her ear, if he had said, 'Come with me...come to bed right now, this minute. Come and let me make wild, passionate love to you all day long...' then she would have gone with him and taken only what he offered and not asked for anything more.

What the hell was he *doing*? The question was like a scream inside Damon's head.

What sort of damn fool was he? Would he ever learn?

But the truth was that he had never anticipated that a performance put on solely for display, for the delight of the cameramen, the perfect 'photo opportunity', would turn into *this*. Into something so deeply and stunningly intimate, so totally personal and private, that it was made for the secrecy of the bedroom, not a public display out in the open.

And if he felt bad then clearly Sarah was in an even

worse state. She was leaning against him as if all the strength had seeped out of her body and drained into the earth beneath her. Her eyes were closed and she seemed to be almost in a trance. She didn't look capable of thinking for herself so he was going to have to think for both of them.

'OK, gentlemen, that's enough.'

Gentlemen! That was a laugh! He knew this particular paparazzi pack only too well. Many of them he'd seen often before. And he knew what they were like. Give them the scent of a story—preferably one with all the vital elements of money, sex and glamour in any particular order—and they were hot on the trail with the intensity and concentration of a pack of foxhounds in full cry. Though in the case of one or two of them perhaps a pack of slavering wolves was a closer description.

And his presence here had thrown Sarah right into their jaws.

He was used to them. He'd lived with their intrusion into his privacy all his adult life and he'd learned how to handle it. He'd also learned that if you gave them something of what they wanted then they tended to shut up and go away far more quickly than if you seemed to have something to hide.

And so he'd given them what they were looking for. A kiss. But he had never thought for a moment that it would turn out quite the way it had. A quick peck on the lips, a brief, passing caress. No more.

He had been so damn wrong. And, with visions of the pictures that might appear in tomorrow's papers in his head, he was forced to wonder if this time he had miscalculated. Badly.

'We're going inside now…'

Damn it, Sarah—lift your head! Look like you're—if not

relaxed, then at least as if you're here, in the world! Not totally fazed out!

With an assumed casualness he tried to angle his arm around her waist. To support her in the same moment that he drew her close, hoping it would simply look like a gesture of affection. God alone knew what they would think if they saw her looking like this.

'You've got your pictures—and your story. There's nothing else for you here. So how about giving us some peace, guys?'

To his relief they seemed to agree. Certainly some of them nodded and shuffled as if about to move. A couple of cases even came out, ready to have the cameras put away.

'Say goodbye, darling... *Sarah*!'

Her head went back against his supporting arm; her face lifted to his. Her eyes were wide and dark and strangely unfocused. And in that moment another single, isolated camera flashed.

'Say *goodbye*!'

'G'bye.' She spoke like a dazed child or an automaton.

He couldn't get her inside quick enough, practically hustled her through the door, half lifting her over the threshold, kicking the door to behind him with a resounding thud.

'Sarah!'

With both hands under her armpits he gave her a swift, hard shake, concerned by the way that she seemed to hang like a limp rag doll.

'Sarah, what the hell happened to you out there?'

You happened, Sarah responded in the privacy of her own thoughts. Just like you happened in my life a year ago, exploding into it with the force of an atom bomb, blasting my world and my heart apart and leaving it impossible ever to build it back up again. You happened, damn you!

She tried to hate him. She desperately *wanted* to hate

him. It was safer and easier that way. But even as she tried to whip up anger from deep inside, she knew she was failing. That kiss had been her undoing and, having opened the lid of her own particular Pandora's box, she knew there was no way she could get it back on again.

'What the hell happened to *you*?' she managed, fighting to get herself back under control. 'What did you think you were doing out there?'

'Doing?'

He had the nerve to sound indignant, positively offended. And the brilliant black eyes sparked with warning anger.

'I *thought* I was helping you. Coming to your rescue.'

'My...'

Sarah could only shake her head in rejection and disbelief. But the violent movement had an unexpected benefit. It cleared her thoughts, focused her vision, and what she saw sent her temper rocketing up the Richter scale at the speed of light. He was still wearing only the navy silk robe. He hadn't even taken the time and trouble to put on any clothes before he had appeared on her doorstep.

'Coming to my *rescue*!' she repeated, injecting every ounce of scorn she could possibly drag up into the words. 'And how, precisely, did you feel you were doing that? I mean, look at you...'

A dramatic wave of her hand swept over him from the top of his crisp dark hair to the bare feet planted firmly on the tiled floor of the hall. He was leaning against the blue-painted wall, apparently totally indifferent to her tirade.

'You came out of my house dressed like *that*! Or perhaps I should say *un*dressed like that. You must have known what they were bound to think!'

She recognised the look that slid down over Damon's handsome face. She'd seen it many times before and it meant trouble. It was one part stubbornness, two parts pride—and injured pride at that—and a further quarter sheer bad temper. It was the emotional equivalent of the instructions on a particularly explosive firework—'Light the blue touch-paper and stand well back.' Instinctively she nerved herself for the coming outburst.

For once, Damon surprised her. If anything, his face hardened even further, taking on the icily still cast of a marble statue, eyes carefully blanked off. And when he spoke it was in a tone that was as deadly as it was low and soft, coming very close to the hiss of a striking snake.

'And that was what, exactly?'

Did she have to spell it out? As she looked into his unyielding glare, it seemed that she did.

'You're wearing a robe! N-nothing else. It must have looked as if you—as if we—had just got out of bed. And adding two and two together and getting five hundred, then they must have assumed that we had been sharing the *same*—'

'They'd decided that already.'

'And so—they what?'

'They'd decided that already. It was why they were here.' Damon levered himself away from the wall, turning and heading for the stairs. 'I should have thought that was obvious.'

'Not to me!'

How dared he dismiss her protests with a comment like that and then just walk away? Already she was only talking to his long, powerful back, and he was clearly intent on going upstairs without so much as another word.

'Damon! Why would they think that?'

He glanced back briefly over his shoulder, but didn't pause in his climb up the stairs.

'Because someone had told them it was what was happening.'

'Who?'

'Think about it, darling. It's pretty obvious really.'

Obvious? Not to her.

As Sarah stood at the bottom of the staircase, lost in thought and thoroughly confused, Damon disappeared from view. But then she heard him pause, turn...and a second later his dark head appeared over the edge of the banisters.

'Lover boy,' he declared succinctly before disappearing again in the direction of his bedroom.

'Lover boy?'

Sarah set off upstairs after him at a trot. She practically ran down the landing, pushing open Damon's door, not pausing to knock, and hurrying in without waiting for his reply.

'Do you mean Jason? Because I— Oh!'

Her breath caught in her throat, choking off any words, and for a second she could only stand and stare. Damon had discarded the robe, tossing it onto the bed, but hadn't yet had time to pull on any clothes. He stood in the centre of the room, naked except for a pair of jersey cotton boxer shorts that hugged the tight muscles of his buttocks, the bulge of his masculinity, exposing long, bronzed, powerful legs softly hazed with black hair. His torso was equally tanned, ridged with muscle, the width of shoulders and chest tapering to a narrow waist and lean hips without a spare ounce of flesh anywhere.

It was too late to look away. Both in the matter of time and emotionally. Damon had already seen her staring at him, unable to drag her eyes away from the sensual perfection of his body, and, besides, she knew that even if she closed her eyes, shutting off the view entirely, she would always see the image of him standing there stamped on the screen of her eyelids, impossible to erase.

'Seen enough?' Damon drawled, when she still couldn't speak, couldn't make herself look away. 'Or were you perhaps planning on taking advantage of me while I—?'

'I—I— No, of course not!'

Face burning fiercely red, she shook her head violently, taking several unsteady steps back, away from him.

'Of course not! I'm sorry—I shouldn't...'

The nonchalant shrug of the broad, straight shoulders dismissed her stumbling apology as totally unnecessary, a faintly mocking smile curving the sensual mouth.

'It's not as if you're seeing anything you haven't seen already. When we were husband and wife—'

'That was very different. And we aren't husband and wife now!'

'We are still, in the eyes of the law.'

'Well, not in my eyes!' Sarah flung at him, and saw the curve to his mouth flatten out completely, leaving it in just a cruel, narrow line.

'That much is only too obvious,' he returned flatly, squashing her totally.

'I wouldn't have minded...' he continued a moment later, while she was still struggling to find the mental strength to respond to him.

'Minded what?'

'If you'd decided to take advantage of me. In fact I think I would rather have liked it. And it would have made a pleasant change to be the one who did the rejecting rather than you.'

'I never...' Sarah began protestingly but then, belatedly, she recalled the letter she had left him when she had walked out on their marriage. The one in which, her anguished pride keeping her from admitting that she knew about Damon's relationship with Eugenia, she had claimed that she had found out about the land deal.

She couldn't—wouldn't—stay with someone who had lied to her, she'd declared. She was leaving and she never wanted to see him again.

'What makes you so sure it was Jason?'

Her gaze skittered away from his and the mockery she could see there.

Coward! He didn't actually say it, but it was there in the glint in his eyes, the cynical twist to his mouth. But he reached for his jeans, stepped into them as he answered her.

'It had his stamp on it. And you truly didn't think that he was just going to take his dismissal yesterday and not try to retaliate?'

'N-no.'

Sarah was thinking back, recalling the tension she had felt when Damon had told Jason to go, the fear that he would have just one final comeback at them both. And the rush of unexpected relief when he had turned and walked away instead.

'As soon as I saw those reporters out there, I knew Jason had to have a hand in it somewhere.' Damon zipped up his jeans with a decisive movement, crossed the room to open a drawer and took out a deep red polo shirt. 'He must have phoned them with an exclusive.'

'If you're so sure he was responsible then why did you come out?'

'You seemed to be having trouble.' The words were muffled as he pulled the shirt over his head, pushed his arms into the sleeves. 'I thought you needed help.'

Could she trust the tiny glow of warmth, the sense of being cherished that suddenly flooded through her? She *wanted* to feel that way, but wanting just wasn't enough.

'And when you kissed me?'

She hated having to say it, had to force the words past stiff, unwilling lips, but she could never live with herself if she didn't face the truth.

'Why did you do that?'

'Why?'

Damon had smoothed his shirt down, leaving it loose at

the waist, and now he picked up a brush from the top of the dressing table, swept it through his springing hair with a couple of swift, brusque strokes.

'I gave them what they wanted,' he declared, black eyes meeting green through the medium of the glass. 'They came to see a couple of lovers and that's what I gave them. It meant nothing; harmed no one.'

Harmed no one.

Each word was like a blow from an icy fist right into Sarah's wounded heart. Of course it would seem that it had harmed no one. There weren't any ugly, raw, gaping wounds on display as evidence of the cruel injuries he had inflicted on her. The damage was all on the inside, deep within her, where her spirit was bleeding to death from a thousand savage cuts.

She had put her whole being into that kiss on the doorstep. Damon had taken her mouth in a caress that seemed to draw her soul right out of her body, and she had kissed him back with everything that was within her. She had put her love on the line in that response and she wouldn't have cared if he had realised it.

And he had said with total carelessness that it had meant *nothing*.

'So it was all just a cynical publicity stunt? A public-relations exercise—giving the reporters and the photographers exactly what they wanted.'

What would she do if he said no? Damon wondered. Would she laugh in his face and call him the fool he knew he was? Or would she fling at him once more, as she had already done in no uncertain terms, the fact that in her opinion they were no longer husband and wife, that their marriage, such as it had been, was totally in the past, and she was more than ready to move on?

Tossing the brush back down onto the dressing table, he

turned to face her. She looked furious, high colour washing her cheeks, her eyes blazing like emeralds.

'Jason had clearly told them that you were my mistress and that was what they came here expecting to find. That was the story they wanted and that was what they got.'

'But it wasn't what *I* wanted!'

Sarah paced the room in evident exasperation, her hands coming up in a gesture expressive of her mood.

'I don't want to be known as your lover—your *mistress*! How could you ever think that? It's the last thing on earth I could want!'

'Apart from being my wife.'

The speaking look she flung him told him exactly what she felt about *that*. And this was the woman he had tried to protect! The woman he had foolishly wished he could find some way of keeping near!

He really was losing his mind.

'I know the Press,' he explained, enunciating his words coolly and calmly as if he was speaking to a difficult and bad-tempered child. 'If you look like you have something to hide then they're like terriers who can smell a rat. They never give up. And they'll use every dirty trick they can think of to find out what's really going on.'

'But nothing *is* going on! I've nothing to hide!'

'Oh, no?'

Sarah shook her head so fiercely that the band slid from her hair and the red-gold locks flew in a wild haze around her head.

'No!'

But even as she made the vehement declaration he could see that something had come into her mind, snagged her attention. She paused in her pacing, looked him straight in the eye for a moment and then shook her head, but less emphatically this time.

He could almost see the tiny seed of doubt take root in

her mind, leaching the colour from her face, clouding the bright green of her eyes.

'Nothing at all?'

'No...'

'Not even a certain day in June last year? A tiny church—'

'Stop it!'

'The words "I do"...'

'I told you to stop it!'

'The truth is, *ghineka mou*,' Damon said, throwing himself onto the bed and lounging back against the pillows, strong arms crossed firmly over his broad chest, long legs stretched out, 'it's way too late to stop it now. The time for backtracking was in those breathless moments just after the priest said "Speak now or forever hold your peace".'

'Stop it...' Sarah muttered, but in a very different tone.

If he had wanted to pick on a memory that had the most impact then he couldn't have been more successful. Somehow, subconsciously or knowingly, he had homed in on a moment that she still recalled so very vividly from the secret wedding ceremony they had gone through just over twelve months before.

They had only known each other a few sweet weeks. She had been so nervous, actually shaking with the shock of what she was doing. She still couldn't quite believe that this wonderful, amazing man, Damon Nicolaides, a man who could have his pick of all the world's beauties, who had them lining up outside his door, begging for his attention, had actually chosen *her*.

And so, when the priest had spoken the traditional words about knowing of any reason why the two should not be joined together in holy matrimony—'Speak now or forever hold your peace'—she had tensed in a form of panic. She had actually cast a surreptitious glance over one shoulder towards the back of the church as if in fear that someone might appear at the end of the short, stone-flagged aisle, and shout, Stop! Wait! This wedding can't go on!

She had never felt that any of it could be real. Men like Damon just didn't fall head over heels in love and marry quiet little nothings like her.

And the terrible, the foul, bitter irony was that her fears had all come true. Not at that moment, of course. The tense, scary seconds had passed, and she and Damon had taken their vows. They had exchanged rings and the traditional kiss, and they had walked out of there as Mr and Mrs Nicolaides, and it had all seemed as perfect as a fairy tale. But there was none of that fairy-tale happy-ever-after.

Because Damon had never truly loved her and had only married her to use her to get what he wanted.

And the death of all her dreams had caused her so much more pain by coming later, when she had known some of the happiness she had never believed could be hers.

'If we had denied Jason's story,' Damon went on, relentlessly ignoring her protest, 'the paparazzi would have thought there was no smoke without fire. They would have wanted to know why we were together at all, and they would have rooted around until they found something—and believe me, those guys don't give up easily.'

His dark eyes slanted a swift, assessing glance at Sarah's shaken face, seeing the faint shudder that shook her slender frame at just the thought.

'If you'd wanted them to find out about our marriage, then you couldn't have done anything that would have made it more certain they would be determined to ferret it out. They wouldn't have stopped looking until they found it. But with us apparently being so open about things...'

'And the cock-and-bull "swept off your feet with passion" story you fed them,' Sarah put in satirically.

To her astonishment Damon actually let his expression

lighten, breaking into a wide, devastating grin that made her bones turn to water, her legs weakening beneath her.

'But I sounded convincing, didn't I?' he shot back. 'Had them swallowing it—what is it you say?—line, hook...'

'Hook, line and sinker,' Sarah supplied automatically, admitting grudgingly that yes, he had been convincing.

So convincing that even she had almost believed him.

'But do you think it worked?' she asked sharply, needing desperately to distract herself from the tearing pain in her heart at the thought of how close she had come to being fooled by him. 'Do you think they're convinced enough that we're just lovers not to start investigating our pasts—digging up dirt...?'

The worst possible repercussion of that digging was only just beginning to dawn on her now.

She had hoped that after six months apart from Damon she could soon start divorce proceedings, that she could be free of him very quickly and very easily, and, above all, quietly. Those photographs would probably already spell the death of those hopes now.

If the marriage became public, the Press would have a field-day—even more than they had had already. And a divorce following soon after would only give them more scandal, and more column inches. Her private life wouldn't be private for a long, long time. Her head swam thickly at the thought.

One more reason to add to her list of why she hated Damon Nicolaides.

'Did they believe you?'

'I don't know.'

Damon shrugged in total indifference to the sharpness of her tone, stretching his arms up behind his head and leaning his dark head back on them in apparent relaxation.

'But there is one way that we could convince them.'

'There is? And what's that?'

If he had offered his hand, Sarah felt that she would have snapped it off in her eagerness to know.

'What do we do, Damon? How can we make sure?'

His eyes narrowed as he looked into her face and his change of expression set warning bells sounding even before he spoke.

'Well, it's quite simple really—but I don't think you're going to like it.'

'I don't care if I like it—I'll put up with it! It has to be worth it! What *is* it?'

Damon sighed, raked one strong hand through his hair, frowning thoughtfully. Then he apparently came to a decision and leaned forward, black eyes holding hers mesmerically.

'It's quite simple,' he said. 'We give them even more of what they want. We prove to them that you are my mistress.'

It was the last thing she had expected. Almost the last thing she wanted to hear.

'We—what?' she stumbled. 'We... How do we do that?'

'Easy.'

He grinned at her again, but it was a strange, cold, unamused grin.

'We just do one thing—we make it real.'

CHAPTER SIX

'YOU have got to be joking!'

Damon shook his head, his expression unsmiling now, polished jet eyes burning into hers.

'I couldn't be more serious,' he said in a tone that sent shivers running down her spine. 'I meant every word I said.'

He sounded serious too, Sarah reflected uneasily. In fact, he sounded absolutely convinced that this was the way out of their dilemma—but it *couldn't* be! How could making the reporters believe she was Damon's mistress do any good at all?

And 'make it real'?

'Would you care to explain?'

She was proud of the way the words came out. They sounded surprisingly balanced, calm even. No one would have guessed that deep inside her stomach was turning somersaults and her heart was racing in double-quick time just at the thought of Damon staying in the house another day—never mind the implications behind trying to pretend that she was his *mistress*!

'They think we're together as a couple so we give them us together as a couple.'

'You make it sound so simple.'

Perhaps it could *be* so simple, she told herself. After all, Damon was here now. The shock of his arrival last night had started to recede a little. While not actually growing accustomed to his presence in her life and in this house once more, she had at least started to adjust. They each had their own rooms and there was plenty of space in the house for them both to live almost separate lives.

And she had her job at the art gallery. And Damon had whatever business had brought him here in the first place.

'It could work! We could both be out all day, and in the evenings we don't even have to see each other.'

Which was not what Damon had in mind at all.

When he'd suggested this idea in the first place, it had been at the prompting of some inner impulse that he hadn't quite understood himself.

But then he had never been totally rational where Sarah Meyerson was concerned. From the first moment that he had met her it had been like plunging head first into an icy, freezing pool, the shock stunning his body and driving all hope of sensible thought from his head. His reasoning processes had been totally suspended and by the time they had started functioning again he had already been in way too deep and unable to find any sort of foothold or solid ground of common sense at all.

'You really don't think that would convince them?'

'So exactly what did you have in mind?'

She was looking as him as if he had just suggested that she drape herself in live, poisonous snakes or eat a couple of slugs. Had he really made such a mess of their marriage that she still couldn't forgive him? Or was the real truth, the one he didn't want to accept, the fact that she was a shallow, promiscuous little tart, one who really had grown as bored with the idea of one man for life as she had declared in the letter she'd left him?

One Sarah—the first—he had had high hopes of winning back. Of persuading her to forgive his mistakes, climb down from the very high horse on which anger had put her, and give their marriage a second try. The other, the Sarah that he had discovered to his shock and distaste on his arrival at the house—was it only last night?—was a different matter entirely.

She was someone he might want in his bed—but that was all. And *Kristos*, but he *wanted* her in it, underneath him, her flesh yielding to him, her mouth opening to him, making those soft little cries that escaped her as she became more and more aroused, closer and closer to her climax...

Theos!

With an abrupt, violent movement, he jackknifed off the bed, flexing his shoulders forcefully and pulling the dark red polo shirt down over his too-tight jeans as he struggled with the luridly erotic thoughts that were swamping his mind, drowning his thought processes.

'This isn't exactly the best place to discuss this,' he declared, marching to the door and flinging it open. 'We'd probably both be more comfortable downstairs.'

He'd be more comfortable anywhere that didn't revive the sort of memories that sent his libido into a sexual frenzy and stopped him from thinking clearly—from thinking at all.

The kitchen was no better. It held echoes of this morning and the way he had sat there, hidden behind the newspaper and wanting her with a desperation that bordered on insanity. Even to walk past the front door reminded him of the scene on the doorstep earlier and *that* kiss.

Hell, but he'd got it bad!

In the lounge, he paced the room again, too restless to sit still, knowing from the expression on her face that she was fast losing patience.

And her first words to him there confirmed as much.

'Well?' she demanded, perching on the arm of the big gold settee, facing him head on. 'Are you "comfortable" enough now? And are you going to explain just what you do mean? Because I warn you—'

'Simply living in the same house isn't going to convince

anyone,' Damon put in sharply. 'We've given the Press the story that we've just met—that we've fallen head over heels in love, and we're crazy about each other. We're going to have to stick with that story, otherwise they're going to sense something's up. And we're going to have to appear in public together. Make it look as if we really are lovers.'

'"Make it look as if we really are lovers"!'

Remembering the overwhelming heat of the kiss on the doorstep, Sarah hid the turmoil of her feelings behind a carefully assumed mask of satire.

'That sounds to me more like a blatant excuse for you to grope me in public, and I won't be able to do a thing about it.'

'You'd get to grope me too,' Damon tossed back. 'Will that make it easier?'

'Hardly!'

Just the thought sent her temperature spiralling, her pulse thudding painfully.

'No one's going to believe we're a couple if we don't look like we can't keep our hands off each other.'

'I am capable of some degree of restraint.'

Sarah tried for calm dignity and only succeeded in sounding stiffly cold and haughty.

'Well, you'd better lose it—or the whole idea's ruined from the start.'

The look Damon gave her as he spoke made it plain that he was making a special effort to bite back the retort that restraint had been the last thing she had shown when she was with him in the early days of their marriage. Then his teasing name for her had been *okulaki* or 'puppy dog' because she had always followed him so closely at his heels, her big eyes devotedly fixed on his face. Her stomach lurched queasily just to remember how blind and stupid she had been.

'And you'll need some time off work. Can you get it?'

'Some leave? Well, I could—but I'm not going to; I don't see why—'

'I'm only going to be here for one more day. Monday morning I leave for Paris.'

Paris. Just the name had the power to stop Sarah in her tracks. She had always longed to see the French capital and once long ago, in another lifetime, it seemed, Damon had promised that he would take her on a belated honeymoon there, once all the secrecy about their wedding was no longer necessary.

Except, of course, that they had never lasted that long.

'And that has what to do with me?'

Damon looked as if he couldn't believe that she had been stupid enough to need to ask the question.

'Well, you'll be coming with me, of course.'

'Oh, no, I won't!'

'You will if you want this story to work.'

Did she want it to work?

'I've decided that I don't think I do. It's all getting far too complicated and quite frankly it's not worth the effort.'

She let herself slide down onto the settee, and sprawled back against the cushions, trying to look as if she didn't give a damn about anything.

'I think we'd do better to forget the whole thing.'

She expected that he would argue with her and nerved herself for the onslaught of his forceful attempt to persuade her, but to her surprise it didn't come. Instead, Damon simply shrugged as if her decision was the last thing that mattered to him.

'That's your choice. But if you don't want to go with that you'll have to think of something to put in its place. Something else to tell them.'

'But I don't want to tell them anything!'

'Well, you're going to have to.'

Damon came and stood behind the chair opposite, strong

fingers resting on the cushioned back, the corded muscles in his arms tensing and tightening as he leaned forward.

'You're going to have to find some story to fob them off with.'

'I'll just say, No comment.'

Sarah adopted a bravado she didn't actually feel. She had been out of her depth with the horde of reporters who had surrounded her this morning and the thought of facing them again in any situation was not something she anticipated with any relish.

'And you think that will do the trick?'

'It will have to. I won't tell them anything and very soon they'll lose interest and pack up and go, and...'

Her voice trailed off as Damon shook his head, the firm, almost harsh set of his features draining what little confidence she had left right out of her.

'That lot out there won't "lose interest" if they get so much as a sniff of a story. And believe me, Jason must have already fed them quite a tale to get them here in the first place, so they won't get tired for a long while yet.'

'But I thought—'

'Think again.'

Suddenly he moved sharply, coming towards her and reaching out a hand. Before Sarah quite knew what was happening, he had caught hold of her arm, pulled her up from the couch with scant ceremony, and was propelling her across the room and towards the big bay window.

'Look,' was all he said.

It was all he needed to say. Sarah looked and what she saw made her blood run cold.

Not only had the reporters not moved, but the crowd appeared to have grown. The whole of the doorstep was sealed off; the pavement was blocked and people spilled out onto the road on all sides. Just looking at them brought back the memory of how it had felt to be surrounded, the noise, the pushing, the incessant questions that came so thick and fast she didn't have time to hear them properly, let alone think of an answer or speak it.

'What are they waiting for?'

'You.'

'But you're the celebrity! You're the one whose name is always in the gossip columns!'

'Which is why they're interested in you. They want to know how you met me, what you said, how you snared my interest—'

'But I didn't! I never snared anyone!'

In her concern Sarah completely forgot about caution. Pushing the voile curtain aside, she put her face close to the window, peering out at the crowd of reporters gathered outside her door.

'Sarah...' Damon's use of her name sounded a warning note.

But it came too late. Someone turned in her direction, spotted her, pointed. There was a shout and the next moment a fusillade of camera flashes exploded in unison, almost blinding her with their concerted brilliance so that she stepped back in fearful shock.

'Come away from there, you little fool!'

He grabbed her roughly, swung her round so that her back was to the window.

'Don't look at them!'

It was a command that brooked no sort of rebellion, not caring that he was the one who had told her to look in the first place. Even if Sarah had been capable of rebelling, she couldn't fight both Damon and the paparazzi. His contemptuous glare sizzled over her, scorching her skin, and she didn't know which was the greater problem, the man before her or the scandal-hungry pack of reporters outside.

'Don't you have any sense at all?' Damon raged, solving that problem in the space of a split-second. 'That lot would eat an innocent like you alive in less time than it takes to draw a breath. And the sort of thing you just did will only encourage them.'

'But you seem to think that encouraging them is just what I should do—that I should give them the story that they want.'

Behind her, she could hear the clamour of the interested crowd, and although she didn't dare to look back she knew that they were still watching the window, waiting for her to make a move.

'Oh, this is awful! Now I know just what it must feel like to be a wild creature trapped in a cage and have a horde of people standing outside the bars, staring in, studying everything you do.'

Damon's beautiful mouth twisted sharply.

'Join the club,' he returned cynically. 'It's what— Oh, hell...!'

'What?'

Half turning as he pushed past her, Sarah had a swift, blurred glimpse of a face that had suddenly appeared at the window and was pressed against the glass as hers had been, but from the outside peering in. Yet another flash bulb exploding made her jump violently just as she heard the sound of another ladder being thumped against the wall and heavy footsteps climbing to reach the sill.

'Damon!'

But he had already acted, pushing her away from the window and pulling the thick, heavy gold and black velvet curtains across the glass, blocking the light and cutting off the photographers' view.

'They won't be able to see in now,' he said on a note of grim satisfaction.

But Sarah was totally rattled now. For her that invasion of her privacy—her home—had been the last straw.

Desperate to get away from the mob at her door, she

hurried back into the room and sank down on the settee, burying her face in her hands.

'I hate this! I hate it! I can't take much more of it!'

'Still think you can get away with not telling them anything?'

He sounded so smug, so satisfied, that his question only added to Sarah's tension, incensing her wildly.

'I'm not going to tell them anything—but I think you should! After all, it was you that got me into this situation. If you hadn't been here then none of this would have happened. So why don't you do something about it?'

'Like what?'

'Well, how should I know? You set yourself up as the expert on these damn paparazzi, so you must know what to do. Surely there's something you can say!'

The silence that descended as her words died away was so deep, so disturbing that it drew every nerve in her body taut with tension. Damon remained silent and completely motionless for so long that it was scary and eventually, deeply reluctantly, Sarah couldn't take it any longer. She didn't want to look at him, was afraid of what she might see on his face, but she just had to.

She barely had time to take in his coldly blanked out expression, the bleak opacity of his eyes, before he suddenly snapped into action.

'All right!' he said, cold and crisp. 'I will.'

He was almost out of the door before she found her tongue again. Something in that ruthlessly determined 'I will' had set her teeth on edge, bringing with it a sensation of something icy cold and damp slithering slowly down her tautly held spine. She didn't know what he was up to but she was suddenly very, very suspicious that she wasn't going to like it.

'Wait!'

Had he even heard her? Would he stop?

Apprehensively she held her breath, then let it out again in a heavy, rushing sigh, as, just when she had become convinced that he wouldn't, Damon paused, turned on his heel and swung slowly round to face her.

'What?'

His eyes were still closed off from her, the gleaming black totally impenetrable, and no trace of emotion showing in their burning depths.

'Wh-what are you going to do?'

His sigh was a masterpiece. A blend of impatience, irritation and exasperation. With perhaps a little bit of contempt at the stupidity of the question thrown in for good measure.

'Exactly what you asked me to do. You wanted me to speak to them. That's what I'm doing.'

'But—but *what* are you going to say?'

Another of those terrible scathing looks scoured a protective layer of skin from her face, leaving her feeling intensely raw and vulnerable.

'Well, you don't want me to lie and claim that you're my mistress, so after the line we spun them this morning—and that kiss—I can see only one possible alternative.'

'And what's that?'

She didn't want to have to ask. She had the hopeless, fearful conviction that she wasn't going to like what he said in the least.

'The truth.'

'The...'

Twice Sarah opened her mouth to say the word and both times her voice failed her, fading away to an embarrassing, breaking croak that said nothing at all. With an effort she swallowed hard and tried again.

'The truth? What truth?'

'Isn't it obvious? I'm going to tell them that you're my

wife. That we married secretly a year ago. What else can I say?'

'*No!* Oh, no!'

Shock and horror pushed Sarah out of her chair, scrambling to her feet in an ungainly rush. Her legs were shaking so badly that she wasn't quite steady and had to reach out to grab at a nearby table for support.

'You can't do that!'

How could she bear to have everyone know that she had once loved him enough to marry him? That she had foolishly committed her life to his, had worn his ring, shared his bed, in the naïve, blind belief that he loved her? But it had all been a lie and if the world found out about her marriage then one day it would find out about the lie too. They would know how little he had loved her when Damon carelessly tossed her aside and married instead the woman he had always wanted—Eugenia.

And it would all be the worse for having been brought out in the open like this and used as fodder for the hungry gossip industry.

'I won't let you! I insist!'

'Insist all you like,' Damon returned imperturbably. 'We have to tell them something.'

But not this! Surely it would work against Damon's own best interests too, if their marriage became public knowledge. He had to be bluffing—or did he? Looking into his hard, set face, she couldn't be sure.

'So?' Damon pushed for an answer.

Her face was so pale that the skin was practically translucent, and she looked as if she'd just been told that her best friend had died, emerald eyes huge and bruised-looking above ashen cheeks.

Was it really so horrific to her to think that he might claim her as his? That the world might know they were not just lovers but also husband and wife, linked together legally as well as emotionally?

Hell—had she ever loved him at all? Once, at the beginning, he would have staked his life on the fact, but now he was forced to wonder. It was a road he didn't want to go down, one he'd been avoiding ever since she'd walked out on him.

She was angry over the land deal, he'd told himself. And she had every right to be. He'd messed up there. Badly. So he'd wait until she'd calmed down and then they could start trying to build bridges. But the longer he'd waited, the less likely it seemed that the land was the real reason she'd ended their marriage. Which left him with what?

With the boredom she'd claimed. And, of course, with Jason.

Jason.

The name twisted in his stomach, tying his nerves into knots. If he'd been asked, he would have sworn on his life that Sarah wasn't the type to leap into bed with just anyone, but he had barely been in the house for five minutes before evidence to the contrary had been thrown right in his face. Jason was clearly so well settled in the house that he even brought his bits on the side into the bedroom he and Sarah shared.

Which brought his unwilling mind right back up against the question of whether Sarah had ever loved him in the first place. Eugenia had unwillingly suggested a reason—that she had married him for his money—but, blinded by passion, he had refused to accept it. Now he was not so sure.

'All right, so maybe telling them we're married isn't the best plan.'

Suddenly the thought of going out there to the Press and declaring that he was married to Sarah lost all the false appeal it had had. They would love that story. The one about the supposedly sophisticated, worldly-wise tycoon who fell for the oldest trick in the book. Who lost his heart to a beautiful, innocent-looking face and a stunning body—and found himself married to a greedy, grasping gold-digger instead.

Though he supposed no one would blame him. They only had to look at her with her auburn hair tumbled around her face, the curvy body that even those appalling clothes couldn't disguise.

The way she was standing, leaning on the table, thrust her upper body forward, pushing her luscious breasts in sharp relief. And the curve of her tight backside against the worn denim was a temptation to any living, breathing man. If he wasn't very much mistaken, there was enough space in those loose jeans for him to slide his hands down inside both them and her panties, cup the peach-smooth softness of each buttock...

Oh, hell, no! He mustn't let his thoughts wander down that sexually distracting path. He had to think of Jason and the bastard's scheming that had got them into this mess.

'So what else is there? Any ideas?'

'Ideas!' Sarah scoffed, anger helping her regain just a little composure. 'You're supposed to be the ideas-man! The one who *knows how to handle the Press*! You should be the one coming up with suggestions.'

'I already did that,' Damon snarled. 'But you didn't like any of them.'

'And does that surprise you? I mean—look at what's happened as a result of the ''idea'' you came up with this morning!'

Remembering his idea, and that kiss, and the searing effect it had had on her, together with the devastation of knowing he had only done it for show, brought her up sharp, destroying the rush of confidence and bravado.

'I wish you had never kissed me!' she declared, choking on the bitter taste of a terrible sense of betrayal.

'So do I,' Damon tossed back darkly. 'You can't believe how much. But I did and we have to deal with that.'

To Sarah's intense relief he had at least turned back, his determined progress towards the door apparently abandoned for now. Standing in the doorway, he raked both hands through the midnight-darkness of his hair, frowning thoughtfully.

'How about this? If we go back to the original plan, let them think we're lovers, then I promise that whenever we go out—whenever you have to face them—I'll be right there, at your side, to see you through it. I'll answer all the questions, make sure you're harassed as little as possible. How does that sound?'

It sounded wonderful, Sarah had to admit. 'I'll be right there, at your side.' What more could she ask?

That he would be there because he loved her; not just because he'd been forced into it by circumstances and Jason's machinations. But that was the impossible dream, and one she had learned there was no point at all in hoping for.

'I don't know,' she said uncertainly.

How could she answer when her mind was threatening to split in two? Her thoughts were warring between horror at the idea of having to endure the reporters' attentions without him and fear of the pain she would have to endure at being with Damon and knowing that every smile, every touch, every gesture of affection that he made to her was a fake, a lie, an act put on purely for the public and to look good in the paparazzi's photographs.

Of course, her marriage had been like that: a lie from start to finish. But at least she hadn't known at the time. She had spent a few short months in blissful ignorance until the truth had been brought home to her with painful clarity.

'Hell, I'll even let you officially end it. You can dump me,' Damon went on, in the tone of someone making a major concession.

For him it probably *was* a huge surrender, Sarah admitted with a wry smile. Damon Nicolaides didn't get 'dumped' by the women in his life. He made all the running, called all the shots, deciding who he was dating and for how long. He was the one who said when a relationship had run its course and when he did there was no way back, no hope of appeal against the decision. He said goodbye and never looked back.

'We can stage some huge public row if you like—in a restaurant...at the theatre. And you can just storm out, declaring that you never want to see me again. And I can play the broken-hearted lover, lost without the woman I adore.'

He couldn't be serious. Sarah stared into his dark, handsome face, unable to accept what she was hearing.

'You'd do that for me?' she said in shocked and disbelieving tones.

'If it'll get us out of this fix.'

Suddenly a gleam of bleak amusement appeared in the depths of his eyes and his sensual mouth twisted into a wry smile.

'I'll even give you a ring that you can throw at me, just to make the perfect dramatic gesture.'

But that was just too much. The thought of throwing a ring in his face came far too close to the truth for any sort of comfort. Sarah couldn't meet the cynical humour in his gaze, couldn't raise so much as a flicker of a smile. She could never forget the agony of taking her wedding ring from her finger, knowing it was for the very last time— and forever.

Nothing in the world could induce her to go through anything like that ever again.

'I'll have to think about it,' she said flatly, her voice as dead as her heart.

Another of those exasperated sighs greeted her response and Damon shook his head impatiently.

'Then think about it!' he snapped. 'But don't take forever about it. We need to make some sort of decision and fast. Because unless you have enough provisions in for a week-long siege, pretty soon one or both of us is going to have to go out that door. And when we do, believe me, all hell is going to break loose.'

Sarah thought about it.

In fact, she thought about nothing else all afternoon. An afternoon in which the house was plunged into unnatural darkness by the way that the curtains on the ground floor were kept drawn shut, blotting out the sunshine.

As a result every room became gloomy and oppressively stuffy and uncomfortable. If she kept the windows closed she couldn't breathe, but the only time she opened one, even at the back of the house, she found that it brought the sounds of the Press pack, the shuffle of feet, the murmur of voices, the occasional almost conspiratorial laughter, right into the house. She couldn't get away from them and she couldn't settle to anything to distract her.

At least Damon had the decency to stay well out of her way. He shut himself up in his room with his laptop and spent the afternoon working, apparently, and infuriatingly, oblivious to the crowd outside.

By the time the afternoon began to turn into evening, Sarah still hadn't come to a decision. She would have to do so eventually, she knew, if only because once Monday morning came around she would be obliged to go to work—which, of course, meant going out through the door and facing the hunting pack outside. It made her shudder just to think of it. What could she say? And would they follow her right to the art gallery?

Oh, boy. Rhys would just *love* that!

She was crossing the hall on the way to the kitchen, struggling to ignore the small snowfall of notes pleading for 'exclusives' that lay on the doormat, when the rattle of the letterbox announced the arrival of the evening paper. Automatically Sarah caught it up and unfurled it from the roll the delivery boy had made.

One swift glance at the front page had her heading upstairs in a rush.

Damon glared at the small square screen before him and cursed out loud in savage Greek as he realised that once again he had pressed a succession of invalid keys, inputting totally the wrong data into a file. He would have to go back and start over *again*! And this should have been just a simple task.

Well, what did you expect? he reproached himself. Your mind's not on the job. In fact, it couldn't be further from it. All his thoughts and what little was left of his concentration were centred on the woman downstairs, and no matter how hard he tried he couldn't switch off from her.

It was her face he saw in the screen of his computer, superimposed on the spreadsheet he was supposed to be working on. Her perfume seemed to linger all around the house, hanging on the air wherever he walked. And it was her body he remembered, hot and hungry on top of his, when he walked past her bedroom on his way down to the kitchen to make yet another cup of coffee.

The sheets and the quilt had been stripped from the bed, dumped unceremoniously in the washing basket, but just the sight of the room itself, even with totally different bed coverings, was enough to make his blood race, hunger uncoiling, growing, demanding until he was ready to groan aloud with the frustration of it. He could still taste her skin on his lips, picture her luscious breasts naked and free and so, so close to his mouth...

'*Ohi, ohi!*' he muttered, shaking his head furiously in an attempt to clear it. 'No, no, no!'

He had to get himself under control—think of something else.

Think of Jason! Think of Sarah *with* Jason! Surely that—

The door banged open without warning and the subject of his thoughts marched into the room, rich-coloured hair flying with the speed of her stride, red flashes of colour scoring her high cheekbones.

'What the hell—?'

Jolted from his unwanted fantasies to be confronted by the reality of his dreams, Damon couldn't manage to find the self-discipline to put a curb on his tongue, his temper flaring in an instant.

'What are you doing here?' he demanded, glaring at her furiously. 'What do you want?'

Sarah glared right back at him, unconcerned by his anger; evidently she had other, more pressing matters on her mind.

'This "make it real" business,' she said sharply. 'What exactly is involved?'

'*Ti?*'

For a couple of unwelcome seconds, Damon couldn't remember a word of anything but his own language. But then something of the red haze cleared from his mind and he managed to get his thoughts to function once again.

'What? What the devil are you talking about?'

Sarah's breath hissed in between her clenched teeth in a sound of pure exasperation. But she clearly mentally counted to ten and managed to answer him with a greater degree of calm than he had shown to her.

'This idea that you had,' she explained with insulting care. 'The one about us pretending to be lovers to distract the flock of vultures outside. How far did you plan it to go? I mean—you didn't exactly mean that we should actually…'

Her gaze drifted over to his bed then back again to his stony face, the colour spreading wildly across her cheeks.

'That we would…'

Think of Jason. Sarah *and* Jason. Together.

'That we should sleep together? *Kristos*—no! That was the furthest thing from my mind!'

Liar! his conscience reproached him. Double-dyed liar. But perhaps it wasn't so very far from the truth—at least not now. The thought of Sarah and Jason together in the bed that he had very nearly shared with her had acted with the force and efficiency of a very cold, very hard shower. In fact, at the moment the idea of sleeping with her made him frankly nauseous.

'So it's strictly a *pretence*. A fake relationship?'

'Of course.'

He would have thought that his response would have made her feel better. That at least she would lose something of the tension that held her slim body stiffly taut, the anxious look in her eyes. But if anything she appeared worse, the flaring colour ebbing from her face, the emerald gaze cloudy and bruised-looking.

'An act put on to give the papers something to write about. Nothing more.'

He studied her face again through narrowed eyes, watching the play of emotions she was unable to hide. Uppermost in them was relief. And a certain amount of defiance.

'What is this, Sarah?' he demanded sharply. 'Why the questions? Are you thinking of going along with the original plan after all? Are you planning to come to Paris with me?'

She didn't speak but only nodded silently, unrolling the

curled newspaper she held and dropping it down onto the table in front of him.

He didn't have to look far to see what she wanted him to see. It was hard to miss.

The two photographs covered the top half of the front page. They had both been taken only that morning, on the front doorstep of this very house.

The first one was the kiss. The two of them tangled together, heads so close, arms around each other until it was impossible to tell where Damon ended and Sarah began. But the sensuality of the moment was there, sharply defined, unmistakable, raw and blatant in its power.

Seeing it, Damon closed his eyes for a brief second, muttering in thick Greek under his breath. But then he had to look at the other photo.

Himself and Sarah again. Of course.

But this one was of the moment when he had pulled Sarah close to him and her head had fallen back against his arm. *He* knew that she had been in shock at what he had done—the way he had kissed her. That the ordeal of being the centre of forceful media attention for the first time in her life had drained her of her emotional strength, left her dazed and bewildered.

But in the photograph it seemed as if she had eyes for no one but him. That she was looking up at him, with wide, stunned eyes, and an expression of total devotion on her face. And the way her body was pressed against his only underlined the blinding impact he seemed to have had on her.

The black banner headline above the pictures said it all.

'It Must Be Love!' it declared, a statement guaranteeing that no other possible interpretation would cross anyone's mind.

'Oh,' he said. It was all that he could manage.

'Yes—oh!' Sarah echoed flatly, no life, no feeling in

either her face or her tone. 'So does that answer your question? Yes, I am thinking of coming to Paris with you. In fact I'm more than thinking—I'm going to *have* to go with you now. I really don't think that I've got any choice.'

CHAPTER SEVEN

'DAMON, no!'

Sarah came to a determined halt in the middle of the huge, luxurious hotel room and turned to him in a fury, green eyes blazing, her delicate jaw set at a stubborn, rebellious tilt.

'I am *not* sleeping here! No way.'

A dramatic wave of her hand indicated the equally huge, luxurious bed that stood against the far wall, dominating the space between them and the wide plate-glass window that in the daylight would give a wonderful view of the River Seine and the rest of Paris, spread out below. But now, late in the night, all that could be seen were myriad gleaming lights of all sizes and colours, no sound of the traffic or the city's life reaching them in the high penthouse suite.

'You said we would have separate bedrooms! That we wouldn't sleep together! I'm not—'

'I said no such thing!' Damon interrupted harshly, striding in from the other room to stand beside her, a dark cloud of anger on his face. 'And why would I? We are supposed to be acting like *lovers*, for God's sake! So who's going to believe that story for a second if the first thing we do when we reach our hotel in one of the most romantic cities in the world is demand separate rooms? See sense, can't you?'

'I am seeing sense!' Sarah protested. 'At least the sort of sense I want to see. You did say we wouldn't sleep together…'

'Meaning that we wouldn't make love.'

'Well, if you meant only that we wouldn't *have sex*…'

Sarah amended the phrase with the deliberate bite of acid in her voice '...then you should have made it clearer—a lot clearer. Because when you said we wouldn't sleep together I took it as meaning exactly that. And, as I naturally assumed that the penthouse suite would have more than one bedroom in it, I didn't think there would be any problem. After all, we booked in here together; we came up to our suite together. No one would have had any idea of what went on in here once the doors closed behind us.'

'And what about the maid? When she came round to do the rooms in the morning—'

'I'm perfectly capable of making a bed! I could have tidied up after myself quite easily! And if I kept all my clothes and personal stuff in your bedroom, then no one would have been any the wiser. It wouldn't have been much trouble.'

'Well, now you won't have to go to any trouble at all. Because there is only one bedroom and one bed—and we're sharing both.'

'No!'

Sarah shook her head defiantly and then, as if that wasn't definite enough, she shook her hand too, for additional emphasis.

'You can sleep on the couch in the other room—or the floor.'

'No way.'

It was Damon's turn to shake his head.

'We're meant to be lovers. Lovers share a bed. We are sharing a bed—this bed. It's big enough.'

It was more than big enough, Sarah had to concede that. If a big bed was a king-sized one, then this would be fit for an emperor. But it wasn't the size that concerned her. It was the sheer *intimacy* of the situation. Even with heaven knew how many feet of mattress between them, she would still be in bed with Damon. And just the thought of it made her pulse rate skyrocket.

'I don't want this…'

'You've made that only too plain!' Damon growled. 'But to be honest, at this moment, I don't give a damn what you want! I'm tired and I want a decent night's sleep. Even if I was prepared to take the couch—which I'm not—it's way too small for someone of my height. So it's the bed or nothing.'

Glancing at him now, in the light, Sarah suddenly found that her conscience gave her an uncomfortable kick.

He *did* look tired, she admitted, and perhaps it wasn't surprising. She knew he hadn't slept much last night. It had been late, long after she'd gone to bed, that she'd finally heard him coming upstairs and she'd heard him moving around in his room at some point when she'd woken in the night. Then by the time she was up and dressed he was already in the kitchen, the laptop on the table in front of him, and had clearly been working for some time.

'You work too hard,' she said now. 'You ought to lighten up a bit.'

'My father's been ill. He's finally had to agree to handing over the reins of some of his companies to me.'

'I'll bet he didn't like that!' Sarah declared with feeling.

Aristotle Nicolaides was a totally unreformed, unmodernised Greek male. He clearly thought no one else could handle his businesses the way he wanted, not even his own son. And he had never liked the fact that Damon had brought one 'of that family' into his home. But at least the old man had been honest with her. Which was more than Damon had been.

Bitter memories surfaced, unsought and unwelcome, making her swing away from Damon and dump her handbag on the dresser before making a pretence at examining the wardrobe space, of which there was enough to provide clothes storage for a regiment.

'And how's Eugenia?'

She couldn't stop herself from asking it, though she could have bitten off her tongue as soon as the words were out of her mouth. The stunned silence behind her seemed to tell its own story, and feelings of misery and dread stabbed at her as she waited.

'Damon?' she asked again, letting the door swing shut so that she could see his reflection in the mirror. He was standing behind her, absolutely still, staring at her as if she had suddenly turned into a snake.

'Eugenia?' Even to speak the other woman's name seemed an effort for him. 'Why did you ask about her?'

Just what had made her suddenly bring Eugenia into the conversation? To call it a surprise would be a major understatement, Damon thought. It was almost as if she had somehow latched on to the concerns that had preoccupied him last night, the phone call he had received on his cellphone in the early hours of the morning.

'I just wondered about her.'

There was something wrong with Sarah's tone. Something he couldn't quite put his finger on or interpret properly. If he'd had a decent night's sleep then perhaps his head would be clearer, but, after spending the first night in London lying awake, fighting dreams of Sarah, last night had been no better. Genie's phone call had seen to that. And the throbbing headache he'd developed on the flight over didn't help.

'I didn't think you knew her all that well.'

He was trying to remember just how well Sarah had got on with Eugenia. Would they have confided in each other? Maybe shared secrets?

'You only met her once, as far as I remember.'

'So?'

It was definitely aggressive now, but for no reason he could think of. Just how had he stepped on her toes?

'I can still ask, can't I?'

'Of course.'

He had to tread carefully. If he said the wrong thing then it could cause all sorts of problems. If only he hadn't promised Genie!

'Eugenia's fine,' he said carefully. 'She had her twenty-third birthday party last week. She's grown up a lot these last few months—turned into a beautiful woman.'

'She always was—lovely.'

Sarah was prowling round the room, running her fingers over the polished wood surfaces, tracing the shape of a ceramic vase.

'And how's her father? He'd been ill too, hadn't he? A heart attack?'

'Yes. He was in hospital for a while but he's back home now.'

She'd moved around to the side of the bed, switching first one set of lights and then another on and off again as if testing that they were working. Then, losing interest, she picked up the remote control for the television and started pressing buttons. Her unsettled restlessness was getting on his nerves.

'He has to take things very easy, but— Do you *have* to do that?'

'*Sorry!*'

Sarah hastily clicked off the loud music video that had suddenly started blaring into the room and dropped the remote down onto a chair.

'No, I'm sorry,' Damon told her wearily. 'I'm not in the best of moods. I have a blinding headache—you don't happen to have anything that would help, do you?'

'There's some paracetamol in my bag.'

Sarah hunted through her handbag, then tossed him a silver-foil strip of tablets.

'You do look rough.'

'I didn't sleep too well last night.'

'Why's that? My gran always used to say that not being able to sleep was the sign of a guilty conscience.'

The comment sounded light enough, but there was an edge to it that had Damon stopping on his way to the *en suite* bathroom to fill a glass with water.

'And what would I have on my conscience?'

'How should I know?'

She had turned away from him and was unzipping the lid of her case, her tone perfectly casual, throwaway almost. But then she paused, glanced over her shoulder at him, the green eyes disturbingly intent. A second later she blinked, and the strange look vanished so completely that he was forced to wonder if in fact it had been a trick of the light. Certainly she now seemed purely interested in removing some shirts from her suitcase and placing them carefully in the top drawer of the dresser.

Hell, but he needed these tablets!

He had filled the glass with water and was swallowing the pills down when Sarah's voice drifted through to him again.

'Unless you have something you want to confess?'

'Should I have?'

Coming back into the bedroom so that he could at least see her face again, only to find that it gave him no clue at all as to what was on her mind, he frowned in irritated confusion.

'Is there a point you're trying to make here, Sarah?'

'Me? Not at all.'

It still sounded as if she was trying to needle him.

'Is this some sort of interrogation?'

The wide green eyes that turned his way were guileless and innocent.

'Only if you see it that way. We have a saying in England about "if the cap fits". That means—'

'I know damn well what it means!' Damon growled. 'My English *is* up to that! And if you've got something to say I wish you'd come right out with it. I don't have the energy or the inclination for mind games.'

'So your lack of sleep wasn't down to a guilty conscience?'

'It certainly wasn't! Unless you think I should feel sorry for a few deliberate lies I've told the reporters, in which case, tough—I think they deserve everything they get. Especially as they were told to protect your blushes.'

'I know they were—and I'm grateful.'

How the blazes did he do that? Sarah was forced to wonder. How did he manage to divert her purpose, deflect her attention away from a determination to see if he had any conscience at all where his affair with Eugenia was concerned, and turn it instead to an appreciation of how he had handled things today?

Because he hadn't put a foot wrong; she had to give him that. From the moment that they had stepped outside the front door to face the barrage of cameras and microphones, the deafening pandemonium of questions piled upon questions, with no pause in between, no chance to answer one before another butted in, Damon had been in control. He had answered the questions he could with a smile and an easy charm, sticking strictly to the story they had agreed on, the details they had worked out between them the night before.

And he had kept his promise to perfection.

'I promise that whenever we go out,' he had said, 'whenever you have to face them, I'll be right there, at your side to see you through it.'

Sarah couldn't fault him on that. Even before he had opened the door he had held out his hand to her, the strong, square-tipped fingers looking totally dependable, a perfect support. And she had put her own hand into it, feeling the warmth of those fingers close around her, their power enclosing her, their size completely dwarfing the frail slenderness of hers.

They had gone outside together, linked, sharing—a team. And Damon had been the stronger partner. Sarah had never had to speak once. Never had to do anything except be there with him, move when he moved, smile for the cameras in response to a gentle nudge from his elbow in her ribs.

And when the crush had become too intense, when she had started to feel surrounded, trapped, and the panic had started to clutch at her stomach, seeming to tie knots in her throat, he had sensed that too. He hadn't paused in his answer to a question, but an arm had come round her shoulder, warm and strong, drawing her close and into the protection of his lean body. There had been nowhere she could put her cheek but against his chest; nowhere her arms could have gone but round his waist. And when he'd moved forward, she had moved with him, steps in perfect unison, blinded by the camera flashes, but totally confident that he would get her to their car, and safety, and get her out of there.

He'd done just that. He'd promised to be at her side, and he'd never left it. He had stayed so close that when at last, having boarded his private plane and closed the door on all the fuss and attention, Damon had finally moved away to settle into his seat, Sarah had felt lost, strangely bereft, as if a part of her was missing.

The cruellest irony about the whole situation was that, now that she was officially his 'mistress' in the public eye, he was treating her with the open respect and affection that he should have accorded her while she was his wife. But while she had been his wife he had never even acknowledged the fact.

Still, he had looked after her wonderfully today. And she'd never actually thanked him for that.

'You were a great help today,' she said, wincing at the way the words sounded rather stiff and grudging.

She was still too uptight at the way he had blocked her questioning over Eugenia. Couldn't he see that she had been trying to give him the opportunity to talk—to confess—to explain if he wanted to? So had he really not understood what she was getting at? Or did he still not feel any trace of guilt at the way he had treated her, using her and her love for him callously for his own ends?

'I appreciated it.'

That wasn't any better, and clearly Damon thought so too, to judge by the way his black eyebrows drew together in a swift frown.

'No problem,' he returned, giving it a decidedly ambiguous intonation.

But at the same time he pressed two fingers of each hand against his temples, massaging hard, and Sarah's too-sensitive conscience gave her another unwanted tug.

'Headache no better?'

'Not yet. I'd probably feel better if I had something to eat. There's a room-service menu somewhere—why don't you take a look at it too, and see what you fancy?'

Was she being unduly suspicious, Sarah couldn't help wondering, or had he successfully managed to distract her totally from the points of dissension between them? She'd been sidetracked from her attempts to question him about Eugenia; the argument about the bed had been abandoned uncompleted; and now the business of selecting and ordering food would further distance those problems and move the conversation on to more practical matters.

But Damon did seem less than his normally robust self, she admitted. He looked weary and drawn, and there were shadows under those stunning black eyes that seemed to look vaguely cloudy, washed out, quite unlike their usual gleaming jet brilliance.

It would do no harm to call a truce for a time, while they ate at least. Besides, if she was honest with herself, she would welcome the time of peace after a fraught couple of days in which her life, the life she had begun to feel had reached a certain calm, had been turned on its head so that it was impossible to know any longer which way was up.

'When did you last take a break from work?' she asked when the food had been delivered, the waiter sent away with a more than generous tip, and they were seated at the small dining table, sharing a bottle of delicious red wine with their meal.

'Last year—May.' Damon's tone was brusque and she knew why.

May was when he had come to find her. When she had fallen desperately in love with him on sight. When all he had wanted was her signature on a document handing over the land on Mykonos for an extraordinary amount of money. And all she had wanted was him.

'And that was a working holiday,' she quipped, and knew from his face that the joke had fallen very badly flat indeed.

Damon sighed and stabbed his fork viciously into the steak on his plate.

'I didn't set out to get you to marry me.'

'I never thought you did. You wanted my inheritance. But you must have thought that the fates were truly smiling on you when you found you could get it cheaper by making me your wife!'

The sense of betrayal had a bite that burned like acid,

eating into wounds that had already been ripped open afresh since his reappearance in her life.

'What is it they say about the things Greeks value, hmm? Land first, money second—women a long way third? So was it worth it, Damon—five months of marriage to me in exchange for what your family had been after for generations?'

His smile was chilling, bleak as his eyes.

'I had anticipated that it would take much longer.'

Like his lifetime.

He'd thought he had finally found the woman for him: his partner. He had taken one look and known that he was lost. That his life would never be his own again. And *she* had got bored within six months!

The meal he was eating suddenly seemed to lose all appeal, taking on the flavour of well-chewed sawdust. Throwing down his fork, he pushed his chair back and got up from the table.

'Not hungry?'

Sarah's surprise grated badly. It carried too much of a reminder of the early days of their marriage, when she had teased him about the amount he could eat, claiming that she could never cook enough to fill him.

'No.'

He flung himself down onto the settee and dropped his head onto the back, staring moodily at the ceiling.

Six months seemed to be about Sarah's limit. She'd got bored with him in six months. Moved back to England. Six months later, another man—Jason...

'So where do you see yourself in six months' time?'

'What?'

He lifted his head again, turned to look at her where she still sat at the dining table. She looked frankly bewildered, as if the question was completely beyond her.

'It's a simple enough question. Where do you see yourself half a year from now? Not with Jason, obviously.'

'Of course not!'

Her faint shudder gave emphasis to the statement.

'Never with him!'

'Then with who? What about this guy who runs the art gallery? Morgan?'

'Rhys? No! He's a great guy but he has emotional complications of his own.'

Well, that put him in his place. He was an 'emotional complication'. And he'd be a fool to read anything into the 'emotional' bit.

Sarah got up from the table and came to sit in the chair opposite, bringing the two wine glasses with her.

'Here,' she said, holding one out to him. 'I think I should tell you about Jason. The truth about Jason.'

Damon's fingers clenched over the delicate stem of the glass until his knuckles showed white. He was frankly stunned that it didn't shatter under the pressure.

'I don't give a damn about Jason!'

Who was he trying to kid? The thought of her and Jason together had stuck in his throat like a stone ever since he had first seen the other man coming out of her bedroom. He'd never been able to get rid of the image and he'd tried. God help him, he'd tried!

'Well, I'm going to tell you whether you want to hear it or not.'

Sarah took a long swallow of her wine, and Damon was tempted to do exactly the same, to fortify himself for what was to come. But he had the unnerving feeling that he would find it impossible to swallow and he wasn't prepared to take the risk.

'He was never my lover. Not even really my boyfriend. We only had a couple of friendship dates. I asked him to be in my house to take in a delivery I was expecting.'

'Oh, yeah!'

Now he was truly glad that he hadn't drunk any wine! He would have choked on it for sure.

'I should have known you wouldn't believe me!'

Damon opened his mouth to retort that along with the saying about the cap fitting, the English also had one about pulling legs and bells. But even as he did so something totally inexplicable happened.

Looking deep into Sarah's eyes, seeing the way that their stunning emerald had turned to a deeper, softer, mossy green, he suddenly knew, totally without reason, that she was telling him the truth. Hastily he caught back the words he'd been about to speak, changing them rapidly and completely.

'OK, I believe you.'

It was Sarah's turn to freeze, the hand that held the glass she had raised to her mouth stilling instantly. Staring at him across the top of it, she blinked hard, swallowed.

'You…'

Her voice cracked, turned into an embarrassing croak.

'I believe you.'

'But why?'

'Why? I wasn't married to you for five months for nothing. I can tell when you're lying to me.'

He could tell?

Sarah's heart missed several beats, then skipped into double-quick time in order to catch up.

Damon *could tell when she was lying*? Desperately she thought back over the things she'd said to him, both in the last few days and when he had come after her, when she'd fled from Mykonos.

What *had* she said?

She decided to tough it out. Trying another sip of wine, she was relieved to find that at least it slipped down her throat without any problems.

'So when have I lied to you?' she challenged.

Damon placed his drink on the glass surface of the coffee-table with deliberate care. Then, leaning forward, confident black eyes locking with wary green, he began a list.

'When you claimed to "quite like" the taste of retsina when in fact you hated it. When you said you weren't scared of flying, that you'd travelled by plane before.'

He ticked off each item on the fingers of his left hand as he detailed them.

'When you said you loved the gold jewellery I bought you and in fact you preferred silver. When—'

'OK, OK! You've made your point!'

So he really did know. What *had* she said to him?

She'd said that she'd left because of the deception over the land. It was true—as far as it went. She'd said she hated him—and she had. At least at the time she'd said it. She'd said...

'And when you said you didn't mind the fact that I wanted to keep our wedding a secret for a while.'

'What?'

Sarah could actually feel the colour drain from her cheeks and she knew that her eyes were wide and staring. But she couldn't actually focus on his handsome features. They blurred and distorted before her as she struggled with the realisation that all the time she'd thought she'd convinced him, he had known otherwise.

It had hurt to know that she couldn't tell anyone about the wedding that had so delighted her, or wear the ring that she had been so proud to have on her finger. In the moment that Damon had put it there and the priest had pronounced them man and wife she had thought that she would faint away from the complete delight of it, her thoughts spinning in an ecstasy of joy. It had almost broken her heart to take it off and put it in her jewellery box until Damon said she could display it publicly.

'You said it was because of your father and my grandfather—some feud they'd had between them.'

'Between the families for generations. And because of the sort of publicity and scandal-hunger it would unleash on the part of the Press. The sort of thing you've just had a taste of in the past couple of days.'

That rang true. Thinking back over the intrusion into her life that she had had to endure since Jason had told them about Damon's presence in her house, Sarah could believe that trying to avoid it might actually have been a consideration.

'This feud between our families,' she said slowly, carefully. 'What was it about?'

'Oh, you know—the sort of things Greeks value.' Cynically Damon echoed her own words of just moments before. 'Land first, money second—women a long way third.'

Sarah winced inside, hearing the cruelty in his tone. She'd believed him with his story of the feud. Parts of it were true; she'd heard snippets of stories from her grandfather before he died. But now she knew that Damon had had a totally different motivation from the plausible explanation he had offered.

He hadn't wanted Eugenia Stakis and her father to know anything about his pragmatic and inconvenient marriage. Especially seeing as he'd planned to be rid of it as soon as he could and then marry the younger girl in order to add her fortune to his own.

Land first, money second—women a long way third.

'What a pity you didn't stick to the belief that our two families should remain sworn enemies,' she said rashly, pushed into unthinking speech by the savage slash of pain her thoughts brought. 'Then we would both have been happier.'

'You think so?'

'I know so!'

Belatedly recalling his claim that he would know when she was lying, she hastily lowered her eyes to stare down into her drink, swirling the rich red wine round and round in the bottom of the glass. But then a terrible thought struck her and her gaze swung up again, raw and agonised, to fix on his unreadable, withdrawn features.

'Unless of course you *were* sticking to the feud all the time! Is that it, Damon? Were you avenging your family's honour or something? Did you marry me only to gain the land and then plan to divorce me—walk out and leave me—?'

The words died abruptly as Damon's glass slammed down onto the coffee-table with a loud crash. And this time the fine crystal did break, splintering into many pieces, what was left of his wine spattering out and running over the table top like a pool of freshly spilled blood.

Damon barely spared it a glance. Instead the blazing fire of his eyes was fixed on Sarah's white and stricken face.

'If you think that, then you're out of your bloody mind,' he tossed at her, his voice never lifting above the quiet, conversational tone he had used before, but injected with a deadly intensity that rocked her back in her seat, flinching away into the chair.

'I...' she tried, but he swept on, totally ignoring her.

'And can I remind you that it was you and not me who walked out on our marriage? While I was away on business. You didn't even give me a chance to defend myself.'

'Oh, yes, and you'd have come crawling to me on bended knee, I suppose!' Sarah scorned, with the knowledge she was holding back, the fear that he might be able to know of that too, driving her to a point where she hardly cared what she said.

The temptation to throw it all in his face and have the whole truth out in the open was almost overwhelming, but some foolish touch of pride held her back. It was bad enough that he had deceived her over the land, that he had used her to his own ends that way. She couldn't bear it if he should find out that she knew about Eugenia too. That she was aware of just how total her humiliation at his hands had been.

'You'd have been begging me to forgive you—take you back?'

Damon's face had set so hard that it seemed to be carved from a single slab of granite. Even his eyes had gone dead, blank and opaque, so that she could read nothing in them. But at his right temple, in exactly the same spot where he had tried to rub away the ache earlier, a heavy pulse throbbed, revealing the savage fury he was fighting to keep under tight rein.

'Well, seeing as you weren't there to greet me, you never found out the answer, did you? And now you never will.'

He swung onto his feet in one lithe, furious movement, kicking the coffee-table and the devastation on its top out of his way as he headed for the door to the bedroom.

'Heaven help me, it's no wonder that my head aches! The only real surprise, *ghineka mou*...' He used the term of affection with a savage bite that took every last drop of warmth from it '...is that when you're around it never does anything else. You make me regret that I ever came to England—ever—'

'The feeling, *andhras mou*,' Sarah used the first two words of Greek she had ever wanted to learn—the words that meant 'my husband'—to equally deadly effect. 'The feeling is entirely mutual. You can't know how much I regret that you came back into my life.'

'Well, unfortunately I did—and, for my sins, we're both stuck with each other.'

Suddenly, shockingly, the harsh mask of cold fury split,

cracked, peeled away, and Sarah stared in total disbelief as he actually threw back his head and laughed.

But there was no warmth, no real amusement in his laughter. Instead it was so cold, so brutal, so hatefully cynical that it made her blood turn to ice in her veins.

'What a pity that we're locked away up here, out of the public eye. Otherwise, my sweet wife, this would have been the perfect opportunity for us to announce that break-up that we're both so eager for. More so now than ever before. But as, unfortunately for us both, we don't have the audience we need, I'm afraid that we're still stuck together.'

Roughly he rubbed the back of his hand across his eyes in a gesture that seemed to combine tiredness and frustration—but might just have been simply angry.

'I'm going to sleep,' he announced in a voice that made it plain he was not to be argued with. 'In the bed. And that point is not up for debate.'

Sarah didn't dare to argue. Instead she simply stayed where she was, sitting stiffly silent in the chair. With Damon in this mood, she knew she was risking being torn to pieces, verbally at least, if she so much as breathed in the wrong way or raised the slightest protest.

But that didn't mean she was happy about it.

When Damon stomped off into the bathroom and she heard the shower being switched on she allowed herself to relax enough to start thinking.

She could take the couch she had offered him earlier, but swift consideration showed her that in this at least Damon had been right. Stiffly elegant it might be, comfortable to sleep on it was not. And it was too small even for her slighter frame to have a chance of finding any comfort on it.

So it had to be the bed. Which, as Damon had already stated, was plenty big enough. If they could just keep to their respective sides, then there was no need at all for them even to touch.

'Of course!'

Inspiration struck suddenly, getting her to her feet in a rush. Hurrying through to the bedroom, she picked up three of the fat, fluffy pillows and laid them end to end down the centre of the bed as a soft, downy barricade separating left from right and—hopefully—preventing either herself or Damon from drifting across into the other's territory.

'There!'

She surveyed her handiwork with a degree of satisfaction and nodded approval. The barrier was probably more effective as a symbol than an actual deterrent, but at least it was there. And knowing that made her feel a whole lot better.

She had just finished when the bathroom door opened and Damon stalked out, making her heart skip several beats in reaction to just the sight of him.

He was naked apart from a towel knotted around his hips, the brilliant white material throwing the deep bronze of his skin into sharp relief. His black hair was still damp from the shower, and springing into the beginnings of curls, while on his lush black eyelashes tiny diamonds of water drops still sparkled.

As he surveyed the makeshift barrier she had created through narrowed eyes, his beautiful mouth quirked up sharply at one corner into something that might have been amusement. Or it might simply have been a response of total scorn.

'I get the message, *agape mou*.' He drawled the words laced with dark cynicism. 'But really you had no need. Believe me, you have never been safer from my unwanted attentions than you are tonight.'

Then, totally unselfconscious, he discarded the towel and slid in between the crisp linen sheets.

'Goodnight, wife!' he said, laying his head on the pillow and closing his eyes.

Sarah fled into the bathroom, where she spent an unduly long time washing and preparing for bed. Her tactics worked. By the time she emerged again Damon was sound asleep, his long body relaxed, his breathing deep and slow.

She fully expected to be unable to match him. Her nerves were strung so tightly after the events of the evening that she truly believed that she would be unable to relax and that sleep would be a long time coming.

She couldn't have been more wrong. From the moment that she curled up on her side of the bed, feeling the security of the pillow barrier snug against her back, a great wave of tiredness rolled over her, washing away her tension and sweeping her into an easy doze. From there it was just the space of a couple of seconds before she drifted into a deep, relaxed sleep that provided the oblivion she needed—at least for a time.

It was only later, in the early hours of the morning, that something unexpectedly startled her into wakefulness.

CHAPTER EIGHT

SARAH was dreaming.

Someone was trying to suffocate her. There was something big and soft and squashy pressed up against her nose and mouth so that she was finding it desperately difficult to breathe. She was struggling hard, so hard; clutching at it and trying to push it away.

But then suddenly she had a good grip on the thing. She could lift it, letting in precious air...

With a final effort she pushed it away completely, picking it up and throwing it right away from her.

But still she felt lost and afraid. She whimpered in her sleep, twisting and turning, until a gentle hand reached out and touched her arm gently.

'Sarah...' a voice said, soft and low.

And, responding purely on instinct, she stilled for a second, then rolled closer, coming into the comfort, the protective warmth of a strong pair of arms. Contentedly she nestled closer, her taut body relaxing, her breath coming easily again. And the arms encircled her and held her close. With a small sigh she drifted into peace again.

Damon had been woken by Sarah's thrashing about. She was crying in her sleep and seemed to be in the grip of a particularly bad nightmare. Suddenly she grabbed at one of the pillows she had placed as a barrier between them, picking it up and flinging it with all her might down to the bottom of the bed, where it slid softly onto the floor.

'Hey,' he said quietly. 'Sarah—relax. It's just a dream.'

Still with her eyes closed, she turned to him as if seeking comfort. And then, and even Damon couldn't have said whether it was to his delight or his horror, she suddenly moved towards him like a small, frightened creature seeking sanctuary. In her sleep, she totally ignored what was left of the pillow barrier. In fact she simply rolled right over it and into Damon's arms.

Reacting purely on instinct, he folded his arms tight around her slender body and drew her hard up against his own.

And instantly knew that he had made a terrible mistake.

'Theos!' he muttered, the sound raw and rough, low down in his throat. What *had* he done now?

Oh, why ask the question?

He knew what he'd done. He'd only acted on his most basic instincts, the instincts that had been clamouring for release from the moment he had first seen Sarah getting out of her car outside the London house a few days ago.

His overwhelming urge in that moment had been to grab her, hold her tight, kiss her until they were both senseless with need and longing. But of course he had had to resist the temptation, subdue the fierce, hungry need that simply being in the same space as Sarah whipped up in him.

The same fierce, hungry need that was eating away at him right now.

'Sarah?'

Her name was just a whisper. He didn't want to startle her, but he wanted her to wake, to realise where she was. Because if he did, then surely she would move immediately. She would want to break free from his arms, to move back over that ridiculous barrier and safely into the other side of the bed.

And he would be spared the torment of lying here next to her, with his body on fire.

But wasn't the truth that he didn't want to be spared?

Oh, hell!

Damon closed his eyes against the enticement of the

thought, then swiftly opened them again because unable to see only made matters worse. It left him far more sensitive to everything about the position he was in, so that he was totally unable to think of anything else but the feel of Sarah's soft form, curled up against his. The creamy silk nightdress she wore was long and modest, falling down to her ankles when she was standing. But in her sleep the fine silk had ridden up over her thighs and the long, slender legs were tangled intimately with his.

The nightdress was sleeveless, leaving her arms bare, and the delicate scent of her body, a tantalising mixture of clean, feminine skin and some flowery scented soap that she had used in the bathroom, drifted up to his nostrils, making him want to groan aloud with the delight of it. If he moved slightly, he could bury his face in the silk of her hair, feel the fine strands catching against the roughness of a night's growth of beard on his chin, and against his neck the sweet warmth of her breath was like a caress, gentle as the brush of a butterfly wing.

Sarah, *please* wake up!

Sarah! Please *don't* wake up!

Please don't wake up! Please stay...

His thoughts froze as she stirred, murmuring faintly. He heard her draw in a long, deep breath and then his heart stilled in shock as he felt the warm touch of her lips pressing a kiss against the corded muscles in his neck.

He tried to swallow hard but could find no moisture to ease the raw, painful dryness that made his throat ache.

Think about her and Jason. Sarah and Jason. It had worked once before. It had killed his desire stone-dead...

But it had no effect this time. She had told him that she and Jason had never been lovers and he believed her, damn it! He *believed* her.

Sarah stirred again and his mind went into shock as he felt her hands begin to move over his body. Still asleep, still with her eyes closed, she was exploring his torso with tentative, feather-light caresses, drifting her fingertips over the lines of muscle and bone, the width of shoulder, the ridges of his ribcage.

And all he could do was lie there and let it happen. If he moved now, if he reacted too sharply, he could startle her awake. And heaven alone knew what she would think if she woke to find herself right on the other side of her ridiculous barrier and with him holding both hands captive in his.

And with his body so heatedly excited.

Because he was aroused. Hotly, fiercely, brutally aroused. He was so hard that he hurt, not just with the ache of wanting, but also with the knowledge that if Sarah did wake up then she would immediately pull away. That after the confrontation they had had earlier that evening she would reject him totally, without a second's thought.

'Damon...'

Sarah had murmured in her sleep, and the sound of his name on her lips, here in the private, warm darkness of a bed as he had heard it so many times in the first glorious days of their marriage, clawed at something in his soul, leaving it raw and bleeding.

Dear God, but he *wanted* her so badly.

'Damon...'

Her hands had started wandering again, drifting down, over the indentation of his narrow waist, his hips...

Damon's breath hissed in sharply between his teeth in a sound of intolerable torment, of restraint perilously close to breaking as the soft fingers closed over the heat and hardness of his erection.

'*Sarah!*' he choked, unable to take any more.

The sound of his voice broke into the golden, blissful dream world in which Sarah had found herself.

She was dreaming about the early days of her marriage,

remembering how it had been when she was free to touch Damon each and any time she wanted. When she could let her hands rove over the warm satin of his skin, trace the corded lines of muscles, marvel at the hardness of bone. She had always loved to caress him, could never have enough of the feel of him.

And she didn't want to wake. Because even in her sleep she knew that this was a dream. Because now she could no longer touch Damon. He wouldn't allow her to come close to him, would brutally repulse any advances if she tried to make them. She had to stand back and look, and see the beauty of his lean, hard body, the wonderful rich colour of his skin, the beauty of those stunning black eyes—but she couldn't touch.

Never, ever touch again.

And so she wanted to stay safely cocooned in sleep, lingering in the dream world where reality had no place. Here she could not only look and see, but she could also caress to her heart's content.

'Damon...' she sighed.

'Sarah!'

The hoarse, husky-voiced cry jolted her awake, bringing her eyes open in a rush. For a second she couldn't see because of the shadows in the room, but then she blinked hard and found that she was staring up into the deep, dark, intent black eyes that she had just seen in her dreams.

But this time they were real. And so was the hard, warm body she was crushed up against. The strong, supportive shoulder on which her head lay. The heavy, thudding beat of his heart directly under her pillowed cheek.

The scent of his skin was in her nostrils, and her hand...

'Oh, dear God!' she muttered as she became aware of just exactly where her hand was lying.

And Damon said nothing but continued to look deep into

her face, as if searching her inner being for some vital, needed answer that only she could give him.

'I...' she tried, but her voice failed her, her throat drying painfully, the single syllable coming out on a fractured croak.

And she seemed to have lost any control over her body. Her hand refused to obey her, and even though her mind screamed at it to *move, move now*, it still lingered, paralysed in the most intimate caress imaginable, refusing to let go.

'Damon...'

She knew what had happened to her, though she could hardly believe it. In her sleep she had done what she would never, ever have done while awake. She had discarded the silly barrier she had set up and moved instinctively into his arms. And by doing so she had betrayed her deepest yearnings.

If only he would speak!

If only he would say something—preferably come out with one of his characteristic cynically sarcastic comments—then it would shatter the dream-like trance in which she still found herself held captive. It would drive away the last clinging threads of sleep and fantasy and wake her completely to reality.

But Damon said nothing. Instead, he lay there silently, holding her eyes with his own.

'Damon...' she tried again, with no more effect than before.

But then he moved. With a sense of shock and a terrible emptiness in the pit of her stomach, she felt his mouth drift over the tumbled auburn strands of her hair in the softest kiss imaginable. His mouth trailed down over her forehead, the tip of her nose, heartbreakingly briefly on her mouth.

And then he sighed, deep and raw.

'Yes or no?' he said, so softly yet with deadly intent.

His hands traced the slim lines of her throat, the fine bones of her shoulders, ran down her arms. Then he caught hold of both her hands and, lifting them to his mouth, he pressed warm, lingering kisses into each palm, then folded her fingers carefully over them.

'Yes or no?'

And Sarah knew that there was only one answer she could give him.

The empty space inside her had suddenly filled with a thousand fluttering butterflies, all desperately beating their wings against her ribs. And the warmth of those kisses was spreading through her body, heating her blood, making her pulse race, and the innermost core of her being throb with a hungry need.

Even if this was all he ever offered her, all he could give, she couldn't deny herself any more. She wanted him, needed him so desperately that there was no way she could say no, or turn away. All that was feminine in her was reaching out, responding to his very potent masculinity. She couldn't say no—it would kill her to do so.

'Yes...' she whispered, her voice cracking on the word. 'Damon—yes.'

She heard his rough sigh, the breath drawn in sharply and released in a rush, and then his mouth touched hers again. But this time the gentleness had gone. In its place was a beguiling, enticing sensuality, one that teased her lips open, had her mouth softening willingly, and seemed to draw her soul out of her body, rising to meet his.

'Damon...' she sighed against his lips.

And at the same time that his kisses made her head swim on a warm current of delight, his hands moved softly but surely over her body. Their heat and hardness smoothed the silk down her slender frame, stroking it against her skin until she didn't know where she ended and the fine material began. But when he reached the spot where the nightdress was pushed up, crumpled around her thighs, he paused, letting his fingers rest on the exposed flesh just for a moment before he began to trace slow, erotic patterns on her naked skin.

'Damon!'

Sarah's breath knotted in her throat so that she could only choke out his name, no other words forming in her thoughts.

'Damon, Damon, Damon...'

It was a litany of need, of yearning, of impatience, but he ignored the note of urging, allowing himself only a faint smile against her mouth, before he let his lips follow the same, teasing path that his hands had traced.

Sarah shifted restlessly on the bed, the hunger growing deep inside her, as he kissed his way along her jaw, down her throat, onto the soft skin at the top of her arms exposed by the sleeveless nightdress.

Beneath the creamy silk, her yearning nipples peaked, pushing against the delicate covering, and Sarah's heart kicked in raw shock as the wicked mouth closed over one hardened tip. With his tongue he encircled the straining bud, moistening the soft fabric until the pink of her skin showed through. Then, taking her nipple into his mouth, he suckled hard through the silk, sending wild electrical currents shafting through every nerve in her body, creating a pleasure so sharp, so primitive that it was dangerously close to pain.

'Oh, my...'

Sarah arched up from the mattress, pressing herself even closer to him, so that he could increase the pressure; take more of her into his tormenting mouth. She felt the faint graze of his teeth, blunted slightly by the delicate barrier, and gave a choking cry of delight that would not be held back.

Her nightdress seemed too hot, too restrictive. It came

between her and the heated satin touch of Damon's skin on hers, and her fingers scrabbled impatiently at the garment, struggling to rid herself of its clinging folds.

Damon understood at once, sensing her urgent need, and with one swift movement he pulled the nightdress up and off her restless form, replacing its soft covering with the warmth and hardness of his own body.

'Yes!'

It was a sound of pure joy, of satisfaction at the wonder of sensation that assailed her. But a moment later she stilled completely, shaken into almost total oblivion, when she felt the reality of Damon's mouth on her skin, his hands at her breasts. He cupped and held the soft weight, lifting them to his tormenting mouth once more, licking, nibbling, suckling until Sarah felt that her head would explode with trying to contain the tumult of sensations that was pounding at her brain.

The throb of her pulse was like the beat of a huge orchestra working towards the ending of some magnificent symphony, layering sound upon sound, building up to a crescendo like an explosion of fireworks, and she felt that her body just wasn't strong enough to contain it.

'Oh, please...' It was torn from her on a gasping cry. 'Damon, please...'

'Hush, *agape mou*,' he soothed her. 'I want this to be right for you.'

'It *is* right,' she muttered feverishly. 'How could it be anything but right? It's what I want. What I need.'

'I want you too. *Theos*, so much!'

His knowing, tantalising hands found the damp curls at the top of her thighs and he pressed his palm against her, holding her. Sarah's teeth dug into the fullness of her bottom lip so that she wouldn't moan aloud, but when one long finger touched on the sensitive bud at the centre of her desire she couldn't hold back from groaning his name into the mouth that had returned to kiss her senseless.

'Damon—I *want* you! I want you with me, in me. Deep inside me!'

'Yes... Oh, yes...'

It was just a raw mutter as one hair-roughened leg came between the slender length of hers, nudging them open to allow him access to the most feminine core of her. He slid between her thighs, hot and strong and so very, very aroused. Clearly as hungry for her as she was for him.

Sarah tossed her head impatiently on the softness of the pillow, her red-gold hair flying over her face, tangling into knots. Damon paused just for a second to tenderly brush the auburn strands away from her, easing the tiny tendrils that had stuck to her parched mouth.

Then, before she had time to think, he lifted his long body up, supporting himself on the strength of his arms, and thrust into her in one fierce, powerful movement.

'Sarah!'

Mixed in with Damon's gasp Sarah heard someone give a wild, keening cry of pleasure, and realised with a sense of shock that it was her own voice she had heard. But the next moment she was beyond thought, beyond speech, capable only of feeling as he moved within her, hard and strong, and only just in control.

She was already so far gone that she needed little to push her to the edge of her own restraint. She felt the forceful thrusts within her, the gathering vigour of his movement. She barely had time to snatch a much-needed breath before her body arched up to meet his, her head falling back, her hands clinging to the hard, sweat-slicked shoulders above her.

One more and she was pushed over and into a world of brilliant sensation where lights like a thousand shooting stars exploded around her and time and place ceased to exist. Where there was nothing but herself and Damon and the wonder of ecstasy that they had created between them.

'Damon!' she cried in an aftershock of delight. 'Oh, Damon!'

And, pushing her hands between their hot, damp bodies, she touched soft fingers to the point where they were joined, smiling against his mouth at his incoherently muttered response.

A ragged heartbeat later she heard Damon groan her name, looked into his eyes and saw the brilliant febrile glitter that burned there. And as she watched she saw his dark head thrown back, the flash of hot colour burning along the sharp line of each cheekbone, his throat corded and tense. In the wide ribcage she could see the heavy beat of his heart, see the rough, uneven breathing that raked through him.

And then he too reached the climax of sensation, taking her with him even higher, deeper, further, until she lost all knowledge of where and who she was and only felt.

Until at last, exhausted and replete, Damon collapsed across, her, dragging in raw breaths, struggling to ease the violent racing of his heart.

She held him, her own eyes closed, her body limp with satisfaction. One hand curled in his hair, twisting the night-dark strands around her fingers, the other stroked the length of his back, from shoulders down to buttocks, unable even now to get enough of the touch of him, unwilling to let him go.

But eventually he groaned, lifted his heavy head, and rolled to one side, releasing her from the pressure of his body. His arms came round her, gathering her close, and she felt his kiss on the top of her head, his face buried in her tangled hair, bright silky strands catching on the roughness of the night's growth of beard on his jaw.

'That is what it's about with me and you, my darling,'

he muttered, his voice rough and thick and filled with dark satisfaction. 'That is how it is, *agape mou*. How it always will be.'

And Sarah couldn't find it in herself to worry whether the husky-voiced terms of affection were true, if they were meant, or if they were just bedroom lies, pillow talk, needed to fill the silence of the time after such a violent explosion of passion.

If they were lies, they were sweet little lies, and she would be content with them, hold them close to her for now. Use them as a protection against the time when such lies might be all she had to comfort her.

Because she had no hope, no expectation that the passion that had flared between them so fiercely in the darkness of the night, the conflagration of desire that had burned them up, consuming them totally in its raging heat, was any sort of a new beginning. It had nothing of any promise in it, only the appeasing of a desperate hunger that wouldn't be controlled.

Damon had spoken no word of love, or a future together. He had been full of ardour and a primitive carnality that had driven them both beyond the bounds of control, but he had promised her nothing. Nothing but tonight, and with that she knew she would have to be content.

If tonight was all she would have, then tonight she would take and try to be happy with it. She would use it to garner memories, to hold them against the dark, cold, lonely days that must come soon. She knew they were, inevitably, just over the horizon, thankfully out of sight for now, but coming closer, ever closer with each second that ticked away far too swiftly for her liking.

Twice more Damon reached for her in the night, the first time before she would even have thought that either of them could have recovered. But already the hunger was growing deep inside and she responded with the same urgency, the same need as she had experienced before.

Eventually, they slept, but there was one more time, a time when it was Sarah herself who reached for Damon, who took him into her and sobbed out her delight just as the light slowly started to permeate the room. And she knew that for all the rest of her future, no matter where she was or what was happening to her, she would never be able to watch the sun rise, the dawn come up, without remembering this one special night when she had been with Damon in a hotel room in Paris.

Long, exhausted hours later, she finally struggled up from the drugging clouds of sleep into which she had tumbled to hear the sound of rushing water from the shower, and Damon whistling, slightly off-key, in the bathroom.

Hot tears stung at her eyes as the sound took her back to the brief, wonderful days of her marriage, when she had believed it was real. When she had thought that Damon loved her.

Every morning, just like this, she would lie in bed, worn out by the ardour and intensity of their lovemaking. She would hear Damon whistling or singing as he showered. And she would think that she had never been so happy.

But that happiness had been founded on a dream, an illusion. It had never truly existed; never been real.

She knew the truth now, and she would make herself accept it. Damon did not love her. He couldn't have done, or he would never have used her in the way he had, for whatever reasons.

A buzzing sound forced its way to her attention, distracting her from her unhappy thoughts. It was coming from the suite's sitting room, reaching her through the open door. It took a moment to register just what it was, but then she realised—Damon's cellphone.

'Damon! Phone!'

The sound of the shower and Damon's tuneless whistle continued unabated. He hadn't been able to hear her voice through the thickness of the door and the heavy pounding of the water.

'Damon!' she tried again. 'Damon—phone!'

Still no response. Another minute and it would be too late. Already she had thrown back the covers and was hurrying into the other room, reaching for the small silver phone on the table.

'Damon...'

But it was already too late. With the typical perversity of such things, as soon as she had it in her hand the ringing stopped. She had just enough time to glance at the screen, to try to register the name if not the number, before it went blank again. The caller had clearly given up and rung off.

But not before Sarah had seen the name and it had struck straight to her heart like a cruel knife.

Because the person ringing Damon had been none other than Eugenia Stakis. The woman his father had said he really wanted to marry.

CHAPTER NINE

DAMON knew that something was wrong as soon as he came out of the bathroom

He had left Sarah curled up in bed, dozing sweetly, while he took his shower, completely relaxed and totally naked. The woman who confronted him when he finally emerged was wide awake, out of bed, upright, obviously uptight, and very definitely dressed in one of the white towelling robes that the hotel provided for its guests' use.

And if he wanted any further evidence as to the mood she was in, then the very forceful way that the robe was gathered round her slender frame, belted to the point of her barely being able to breathe, and pulled close and tight at the neck so that not an inch of skin showed, would have given him the message loud and clear.

Not that he needed any such help. The look in her eyes, and the set of her mouth, pulled almost as tight as the belt on the robe, told him that. Something had happened in the short time that he'd been in the shower to swing her frame of mind from relaxed and contented to overwrought and totally on edge.

It was probably another report in the paper. They'd left most of the English Press behind when they flew out of London, but the French reporters had been there *en masse* when they had driven out of the airport, and they'd followed them to the hotel. The story of the Gorgeous Greek's new English mistress had spread far and wide, and everyone wanted a picture of her—preferably of the two of them together.

But until he knew for sure that that was the case, then discretion was definitely the better part of valour.

'You're up, then,' he said as casually as he could, rubbing at his still-damp hair with a white towel.

If the truth was told, he deeply regretted that she had ever got out of bed. He would much rather that she had stayed there, sleepily sensual and warm, with her glorious hair in a rich, red-gold tousled cloud around her fine-featured face, those amazing green eyes clouded partly by sleep and partly by sensual longing. Though if she had been in that state, he would have found it infinitely harder to leave her there, even though he knew he had to. He would much rather have slipped back between the sheets...

'Yes, I'm up.'

The words were clipped and curt, coming from a mouth that was tight-lipped and stiff.

'Any reason why I shouldn't be?'

Ouch! Someone or something had really riled her badly. She was *not* in a happy mood. Which was a pity, because after the night they had just shared she should, like him, have woken up with the feeling that all was well in her world. That it was a day for new beginnings, the resolution of differences, the clearing up of misunderstandings.

Not so, it seemed.

'It's just that I thought you were out for the count,' he replied, tossing the now damp towel onto a chair and crossing the room to where his case still stood against the wall.

He hadn't unpacked last night and so the clean clothes he needed were still folded away, something that piqued him slightly. If there was one thing he hated, it was suitcase-creased clothes. And he had an important meeting early this morning.

'You looked ready to sleep the morning away.'

'Another feather in your cap, I suppose?' Sarah snapped.

'*Ti ipate?*'

Damon paused in the process of shaking out his clothes, putting them on hangers to let some of the creases fall out.

'What do you mean?'

'You'd like to take the credit for wearing me out with your—sexual attentions, I suppose,' Sarah sniped. 'It would be an accolade for your stamina—a feather in your cap, we'd say. Or perhaps you'd prefer the phrase "a notch on your bedpost".'

'I most definitely would *not*!'

Damon still didn't know why she was goading him like this, but it was wearing his temper pretty thin. Already the cheerful, optimistic mood he'd woken up in was fraying badly at the edges.

'Just what is wrong with you this morning? This time you really have got out of bed on the wrong side.'

'I got out of bed on the side you left me on!' Sarah retorted obscurely, making him frown in puzzlement.

'And just what is that supposed to mean? I only went to the bathroom to shower!'

'And now you're dressing.'

She seemed to have jumped on to a totally different topic, with no logic at all in her behaviour.

'It is usual in the morning, *agape mou*.'

Never once in the past had he ever minded getting dressed—or undressed for that matter—in front of any woman, especially not Sarah. But somehow now, with her glaring daggers at him for her own private reasons, it was a distinctly uncomfortable feeling. And the way she had scowled at the term of endearment was decidedly disturbing. For the first time in his life he was glad when he had his underwear on, and pulled a shirt on over it.

'And I could hardly attend a meeting in the hotel's robe—delicious though it does look on you.'

Sarah ignored the blatant attempt at flirting, as he had suspected that she would.

'So you're going out.'

'I have an important meeting to go to. I did tell you that I had to work while I was here.'

'I know what you said, but that was before the news broke about—about us. I would have thought that you'd rather be out there flaunting your new mistress.'

'And I would have thought that you would much prefer to stay inside, away from all the publicity.'

'Great! So you finally bring me to Paris—only a year too late—and all I get to see are the inside of a hotel and the four walls of this suite! Wonderful!'

Oh, was this what it was all about? Was she sulking because she thought that he should take time off to be with her? Well, that he could deal with easily enough.

'I won't be working all day, Sarah,' he said, fastening shirt buttons with swift efficiency.

The attempt to be placatory was ruined by an edge to his voice that warned of the effort he was making to keep a grip on his temper. If she had deliberately set out to provoke, then she was certainly succeeding.

'The meeting finishes at noon. I'll come back here then and we'll go out together.'

He flashed her a cajoling smile, the sort that usually worked wonders on even the most bad-tempered woman.

'I'll show you all the sights—Notre Dame, the Eiffel Tower, everything. I promise.'

Would that appease her?

No response, damn it! No lightening of the sullen frown that had hovered ever since the moment he had first seen her. No answering smile putting a gleam into her eyes. Whatever was bugging her, she really had it bad.

'You don't have to bother—I'll manage by myself. I can find a street map and...'

'I really wouldn't advise that.'

'So what would you *advise* me to do? Sit quietly in here, in splendid isolation, twiddling my thumbs while waiting for my lord and master to come home?'

'You know what I mean, Sarah! If the paparazzi spot you they'll make your time hell. You won't have any peace and…'

As he zipped up his trousers and buckled the leather belt at his waist he realised that she had something in her hands. Something small and silver that she was tapping restlessly against one palm in a movement that spoke of severe irritation and a worrying inner tension.

'What's that?' he asked sharply.

The repetitive movement stopped abruptly, and Sarah flashed him a look of such mutinous defiance that for a second or two he was sure that she wasn't going to answer. But then she seemed to rethink and tossed something down onto the bed, where it bounced slightly on the sprung mattress then lay still, gleaming amongst the soft blue of the covers.

'My phone?'

It was the last thing he had expected, and he really couldn't understand what this had to do with anything.

'You had a call while you were in the shower.'

'You should have shouted for me.'

'I did—you didn't hear me.'

'Well, I'm sorry but…'

He was fastening his tie as he spoke, looking in the mirror. But his busy hands suddenly stilled as he saw her reflection in the glass, caught the look on her face.

It obviously wasn't just the fact that she had been woken by the phone, or yet that she hadn't been able to get him to hear.

'Is there a point to all this, Sarah? Because if there is,

I'd very much like to hear it. I really don't have time for this.'

'Of course not!' *Her* tone took the description 'tart' to a whole new dimension. 'You have your *meeting* to get to.'

That was just too much.

'Are you implying that there is no meeting—or that—?'

'I'm implying nothing. But there is something I want to say.'

With an exasperated sigh, Damon raked one hand roughly through the darkness of his hair, ruffling the locks he had only just brushed into shape.

'All right, Sarah.' He flung himself down into the nearest chair, and fixed his attention on her face. 'Spit it out. Whatever it is that's getting to you—stop dodging around it and get to the point.'

Well, she'd asked for it, Sarah reflected uncomfortably. But seeing him this way, with his arms folded across his broad chest and that disturbingly belligerent look on his face, she felt uneasy at actually broaching the subject.

She wished she could sit down. Her legs felt disturbingly shaky beneath her. But she much preferred to keep the advantage of height that being upright gave her. So she leaned her hips against the dressing table, supporting herself that way.

'You had a phone call,' she said carefully.

'You already said that. So what?'

'From Eugenia.'

His sudden start told her that she had his total attention. Unease and distress prickled over her skin as she saw the way his head came up, polished jet eyes opening wide for a moment then narrowing again thoughtfully. The phone call mattered. That much was obvious.

'What did she say?'

He had recovered slightly now, and his voice at least was well under control. If it hadn't been for that one, immediate reaction he might have convinced her that he was totally casual about the whole thing. But, agonisingly sensitive to everything about him, she had caught that initial tiny reaction and so was not so sure.

'I don't know. She rang off just as I picked it up. All I saw was her name.'

Had he relaxed—even just very slightly? She couldn't tell. His face was as impassive as if it had been carved from stone; his eyes carefully opaque.

'She'll ring back.'

'I'm sure she will. You must have had a dozen calls from her in the past few days.'

That brought his head up, ebony eyes narrowing sharply.

'How...?' he began, and just the tone he used pushed her into a nervy response.

'I—checked your call record.'

The silence that fell probably lasted no more than ten seconds, but it seemed that each of those seconds was measured out on Sarah's overstretched nerves. She felt as if someone was plucking at her heartstrings, playing out some ominous overture to a major explosion.

'Spying on me now, are you?'

The very pleasantness of the way he said it, the almost impossibly light intonation, the easy way he lolled in the chair, were all belied by a new and dangerous sharpening of his gaze, and ominous set to his jaw.

'N-no.'

'No? Then what would you call it, hmm? What is it when you invade someone's privacy, pry into their personal things—is that not spying?'

'Only if you have something to hide!'

'And do I? Have something to hide?'

'I don't know! You tell me!'

Oh, please, *please* tell me! If I have to know, tell me

now. Bring it all out in the open so that I know once and for all where I stand—or, rather, where I don't stand!

Please, Damon! Please don't keep pretending. Not after last night! Please tell me the truth. At least tell me to my face that Eugenia's the one for you. At least have the honesty, the honour to do that!

But Damon's face had closed up totally. His eyes were hooded and his mouth clamped so tightly shut that it was just a thin, cruel line.

Pushing himself out of his chair, he snatched his jacket from the hanger on the wardrobe door and shrugged it on. And in spite of herself Sarah couldn't help thinking how wonderful he looked. How stunningly handsome in the dark blue suit, the crisp white shirt and the sky-blue tie. He had the sort of devastating appeal that should carry a health warning. Certainly it was positively lethal to the shreds of the self-control she was desperately struggling to hang on to.

'I've nothing to say to you,' he stated icily, freezing every last hope she had had before it had fully time to form. 'Except goodbye.'

It was like a blow to the heart.

'What? Just like that? Good— But you said that I—'

'Goodbye until lunch time,' Damon elaborated, casting an impatient glance at his watch. 'I'm going to be late!'

'Then you—you're coming back?'

'I said I would! I promised I'd take you round Paris.'

But that was just too much. It raked up too many bitter memories of the promises he had made in the past. Promises that she now knew had been nothing but lies, or smokescreens to hide his real plans behind.

'It'll be too late.'

'Rubbish! We can see plenty of the city in an afternoon.'

'Not for that! I mean you're too late. A year too late!'

'Sarah, you're not making sense.'

A dark, dangerous frown drew Damon's black brows together over his glittering eyes.

'Just what *do* you want? Do you want me to come back at all?'

Did she? Her heart cried yes, she would put up with anything, endure the worst mental torment if she could only see him a little bit longer. Stay with him for just a short time more.

But rational common sense warned her that to break it *now* was the only way. That the longer she stayed with him now, the harder it was going to be to let him go. She was only prolonging the agony, making things so much worse for her. She had to let him go.

And yet deep inside she knew that she couldn't.

'Sarah?' It was a sound of pure exasperation.

Sarah hunched into the soft folds of the towelling robe, pushing her hands deep into her pockets as if she was cold. And the truth was that the ice that seemed to enclose her heart was freezing her from the inside outwards so that, in spite of the warmth of the day, she was shivering miserably.

'Sarah, what is this?' Damon was definitely impatient now. 'I would have thought that after last night...'

But that was just too much. That 'last night' was the trigger, the match that set a light to the barrel of emotional gunpowder deep in Sarah's heart.

'Last night!' she cried, whirling round to face him, her face a mask of anger to hide the bitter pain. 'Last night! *I* would have thought that after last night I would never want to see you again, and do you know why?'

'Why?'

It was cold, curt, totally emotionless.

'I'll tell you why. Last night was a mistake. In fact it was the worst mistake I've ever made in my life. Even worse than the day that I married you, and that was bad enough! I wish that I could go back and live my life again and make sure that they never happened. I don't think I've ever done anything I regret more!'

Her tirade faded away into the sort of stony silence that set all the tiny hairs on her skin quivering in fearful apprehension. She had to force herself to look up into Damon's face, and what she saw there dried her mouth in horror, making her legs shake weakly beneath her.

'"The worst mistake I've ever made in my life..."' he echoed savagely, sounding out each word with a terrible precision. 'Do you know, sweetheart, I couldn't agree more?'

And before the words could even register, before Sarah could focus clearly on what he'd said and exactly what he'd meant, he had turned on his heel and marched out of the room, letting the door slam to behind him.

And then she started feeling.

The first wave of emotion that swept over her was fury. Blind, red-haze-filling-the-mind, unthinking rage.

'Good!' she flung in the direction of the closed door, careless of the fact that there was no way Damon could hear her any more. 'Great! Perfect! So we both agree on something at last! It was a terrible mistake and one we hope never, ever to repeat!'

The silence when she finished speaking was deafening. A long, empty silence that seemed to reverberate around the room, pulsing in her ears. A long, final silence, when she realised that Damon really had gone and he wasn't coming back at least until lunch time—if then.

Maybe never.

A long, long, lonely silence when the implications of that thought finally set in.

And that was when the desperate feelings she had been trying to squash down finally broke free of her control and welled up inside her, totally overwhelming her. And, in a terrible mood of despair, she sank down onto the bed and gave in to the tears and the desolate fear that swamped her completely.

CHAPTER TEN

'SARAH! Hey, Sarah!'

Sarah stopped dead in the middle of the huge marble-floored foyer of the hotel and looked around her in confusion.

In the buzz of French voices and French language all around her, the English words stood out starkly. And the voice was the last one that she had expected to hear here, in Paris. It was a voice she associated with London and her job.

'Rhys?'

She stared at the tall, dark man striding across the foyer towards her, a smile of welcome on his face. Rhys Morgan was the last person she had expected to see in Paris. It was only just over twenty-four hours since she had phoned him to ask if she could take some unexpected leave, and he hadn't said anything about travelling anywhere himself.

But she was glad to see him. Glad to see anyone who could distract her from the trials of the day.

'Are you just coming in or going out?' Rhys asked after greeting her with a warm hug that did just a little to ease her unsettled, miserable feelings.

'Definitely staying in!' Sarah told him with a shudder. 'Have you seen the photographers outside?'

'Are they still waiting for you?'

Sarah could only nod silently. After her bout of weeping in the bedroom, she had finally gathered herself together enough to decide that she couldn't waste the entire day sitting around and moping. Besides, just supposing that Damon *should* come back to the room, it would do him good not to find her there, waiting for him. His ego was hugely over-developed as it was. He needed no extra encouragement to be totally impossible.

So she had forced herself into the shower, scrubbed herself clean in an attempt to get her spirits flowing as well as her circulation, and washed and conditioned her hair. It had worked, to a degree, and when she had finally emerged, with her hair blow-dried into a sleek, swinging mane, and dressed in a green and white striped shirt and toning slim pencil skirt, she had felt more like coping with a day exploring Paris, without Damon if necessary.

The determination had lasted as long as it had taken her to put one foot outside the door of the hotel. She had barely appeared on the pavement, under the red and gold awning that shielded the entrance from the weather, before the fusillade of camera flashes and the shouts of the reporters that she had come to dread had shattered the morning air.

'Yes, they're looking for me. This time they took just a couple of seconds to register the fact that Damon wasn't with me—so then of course they wanted to know why.'

The whole crowd of journalists and cameramen had surged forward so swiftly that she had been terrified she was going to be trampled underfoot. The uproar had destroyed her ability to think or act in her own defence, so that she had frozen to the spot, struggling desperately to think of answers to questions like:

'Have you had a row?'

'What is this? Trouble in Paradise, then?'

'Where is he...?'

'If the doorman hadn't acted quickly to get between me and them and get me inside, I don't think I would have got away,' she told Rhys now. 'I'm not going out there on my own again. It's not safe!'

'That's the price you pay for having a famous lover,' Rhys said wryly, the twist to his mouth and the bleak look in his eyes reminding Sarah that he had had his own experience of Press intrusion into his life when his marriage to a well-known actress had broken up publicly and with spectacular bitterness.

'So you understand.'

'I understand only too well. So, if you're trapped inside, how about having coffee with me—I could do with seeing a friendly face— Or are you expecting Damon?'

'Not for a while yet.'

Maybe not ever, a miserable little voice inside her head added. But she wouldn't let herself think about that, and she grabbed on to Rhys's suggestion as a welcome distraction.

'I'd love that...'

A short time later they were ensconced in the comfortable blue and gold lounge, a tray with a silver coffee pot and elegant bone-china cups and a plate of delicious-looking biscuits set before them. The room was impossible to see from either the street or the huge foyer and at last Sarah felt able to relax and think about something other than avoiding the scandal-hungry reporters.

'So now perhaps you can explain to me what *you're* doing here.'

'I'm looking for my daughter.'

Rhys's answer stunned her, making her put down her coffee-cup in shock.

'Your daughter! I didn't know you had one.'

Rhys's mouth twisted again.

'Neither did I until a few days ago. You remember that phone call I had on Saturday? It was to tell me that Amelie—my ex-wife—was dead. She'd always had a weak heart, and she never really took care of herself. Apparently it just gave out. But before she died, she admitted that her daughter—a child I didn't even know she had—was in fact mine.'

The shock of that discovery was etched on his face, deep in the blue, blue eyes.

'Oh, Rhys!'

Sarah leaned forward, reaching for Rhys's hand in sympathy, holding it tight.

'And where is the little girl—*your* little girl—now?'

'That's the problem. I don't know. Some cousin of Amelie's took her. I'm trying to track them down. That's why I'm here.'

'I do hope you find them. I really do.'

Impulsively she leaned forward and placed a soft kiss on Rhys's lean cheek. 'And you know that if there's anything I can do—anything—you only have to ask.'

'The same goes for me too,' her boss assured her. 'Look, you can tell me to butt out if you like, but is there something wrong, Sarah? You don't look happy, not like a woman newly in love should look. If there's a problem— you only have to call and I'll be there…'

'Oh, no, you won't!'

A male voice, deep and husky and subtly accented, broke into their conversation like the slash of a sword. And Sarah didn't have to look up to know who had spoken. But when she did, what she saw in his face made her heart quail inside.

'Damon…' She tried for a note of appeasement, to erase the black fury she could hear in his savage tones, but Damon swept on without giving her so much as a chance to explain.

'I don't know who the hell you are, and I don't care. You keep your hands off my lady—and your nose out of our affairs.'

Damon didn't know how long he'd been watching the pair of them. Too long. Long enough to have seen the intimacy in their total concentration on each other, the way that their bodies were positioned, turned towards each other, blatantly excluding anyone else in the room. And when Sarah had reached forward to take the guy's hand...

He hadn't been able to restrain himself any longer. He had pushed himself away from the wall where he'd been leaning and marched across the room to where they sat, rage like volcanic lava bubbling up from deep inside him.

'Damon, don't be silly...'

Silly! It was like a red rag to a bull. *Silly!*

He had been unable to stop thinking about her all morning. Ever since he had walked out of their room he hadn't been able to get her out of his mind. Memories of the infuriating way that she had provoked him, riling him to the point where he just couldn't take any more, had warred with the image he had of the way she had looked when he'd woken and found her fast asleep, curled up beside him, her head pillowed on his chest. And then when he'd finally walked out.

She hadn't known it, but he had seen her face in the mirror as he'd left, and he hadn't missed the bleak, lost and lonely expression that had crossed it, just for a second, as he'd turned away from her.

That expression had haunted his thoughts all morning.

It had come between him and the business deal he wanted to finalise. It had stopped him from thinking straight, prevented him from talking sense, until at last, having uncharacteristically lost the thread of his argument for the fourth time, he had finally given up.

'I don't have time for this!' he'd declared. 'I have something vitally important I have to attend to.'

And, leaving the finalisation of the deal to his second in command, he had left the boardroom, called for his car, and had the chauffeur drive hell for leather back to the hotel.

He had wasted long, precious minutes fighting his way through the crowd of reporters milling about outside the main entrance. Not in any sort of mood to smile and pose for pictures, he had given the paparazzi short shrift on his way in, pushing forward without a care for the way it looked, muttering 'No comment' and adding a few choice comments in very rude, very basic Greek at the way they were holding him up.

But at last he had made it indoors, heading straight for the fast elevator up to the penthouse suite where he had left Sarah that morning.

Only to find that she wasn't there.

His first thought was that she had left, running away without a backward glance as she had done six months before. He had actually hunted frantically for the carelessly written note that he fully expected to find, until it dawned on him to check that her clothes were still in the wardrobe, her cosmetics and toiletries in the bathroom.

When he'd found them, the relief had been so great that for a few moments he had had to sit down on the bed, dragging in deep, calming breaths in an effort to still the racing of his heart, get his mind back under some degree of control.

That was when he had come back downstairs. A few discreet enquiries at the reception desk had had him heading for the lounge, just in time to see Sarah reach out and take the hand of the man sitting opposite her.

The hand of the man who was the epitome of 'tall, dark and handsome', and who clearly held a potent fascination for her.

His jealousy had been like a red, buzzing haze in his mind, coming between him and rational thought. And when he saw Sarah—*his* Sarah—lean forward and kiss her male companion on the cheek, he had completely lost the vague grip he had been trying to keep on his temper.

'Sarah...' he said warningly, and his tone had the other man getting out of his seat. Damon had the unnerving experience of meeting him eye to eye. It was not something he was used to. And the stranger clearly had no intention of backing down.

'Is this guy bothering you, Sarah?'

'*This guy*' incensed Damon, especially as he had the very strong suspicion that the other man knew only too well just who he was, but was deliberately pretending not to.

'*This guy!* Do you know who—'

'No, really—he's—'

'I came back for you!'

He'd hit completely the wrong note. He knew it from the way that her face froze up, the spectacular eyes turning to chips of emerald ice between one heartbeat and the next.

'So you did,' she said coolly. 'But that doesn't explain your rudeness in barging in here like some uncouth yob while—'

'Damn you, Sarah, I came back for you and I find you with—with…'

'With Rhys,' she inserted calmly. 'With my boss.'

'With…with *who*?'

'With my boss,' she explained on a note of pained exasperation. 'This is Rhys Morgan, the man I work for.'

'Oh.'

It was all that Damon could manage.

'My apologies.' He forced himself to say it through gritted teeth, unable to smooth the stiffness out of his voice.

Rhys Morgan's nod of acknowledgement was equally distant, and he was watching closely, looking for any further wrong behaviour.

'I'll just be over here, Sarah,' he said quietly. 'I'll leave you and—'

'No!'

'Yes!'

Sarah's voice and Damon's clashed together, both speaking at the same time.

'No,' Sarah said again, more emphatically this time. 'Don't go anywhere, Rhys! Don't leave me alone with him.'

'Get the hell out of here,' Damon growled, only to be met with a total stonewalling expression, the Englishman refusing to budge.

'You heard what the lady said.'

'Yeah, I heard. But...'

'Damon,' Sarah inserted, getting to her feet too and forcing him to look her right in the face, 'I asked Rhys to stay and he's staying. Until you can speak to me like a human being, and get a grip on that stupid temper of yours—'

'I was jealous!' Damon flung at her, hating to admit it. 'OK, I know I was mad, but I was—'

'You were jealous!' Sarah echoed, total disbelief sounding on the last word.

'*Ne...*'

Damon ducked his head in a moment of severe embarrassment. Already their confrontation was attracting interest. The other hotel guests scattered around the room had stopped their conversations and were listening with various degrees of discretion. Some of them were openly, avidly staring.

'You were *jealous*!'

To his horror, Damon realised that Sarah wasn't just stunned. She was *furious*.

If the truth was told, he had never, ever seen her quite so angry before in his life. The green eyes blazed with golden fire, wild colour burned along the high, fine cheekbones, and even her nostrils flared as she struggled to breathe normally. And when his own startled gaze dropped to where her elegant hands hung at her sides, he was horrified to see how they were clenched into hard, tight fists, eloquently revealing the fierce struggle she was having for self-control.

'You were jealous!' she repeated yet again, giving every single word an emphasis that threatened to strip the skin from his body, flaying him alive. *'You...!'*

'Ne...'

He struggled to explain. He had been so sure that acknowledging he was jealous would sway her opinion round to his way of thinking. After all, damn it, admitting he was jealous was tantamount to saying he *cared*, wasn't it?

But Sarah didn't seem in the least bit convinced of that. On the contrary, she appeared even further apart from him than she had been upstairs, in their room. If that was possible.

'Sarah, I...' he began again, but she wouldn't let him finish.

'*You* were jealous!' she said yet again. 'You *dare* to be jealous of me! Of the way I was just sitting here—*talking* to Rhys! You have no right to be jealous! Do you hear me? No right at all! How *dare* you be jealous of me when all the time—right from the start—you were having an affair behind my back? When you...'

'An affair?' Damon pounced on the word like a tiger on its prey. 'What the devil are you talking about? An affair with who?'

'Oh, stop pretending, will you? Stop it!'

Sarah actually stamped her foot hard on the polished wooden floor, drawing even more eyes in the direction of their small group.

'You can't lie about it any more! I know! I've known all along. Your father told me! He said—'

'My father!'

Damon's thoughts whirled. Now he knew! Oh, yes, now he knew.

He should have realised that his father had had a hand—or, rather, a voice—in all this somewhere. Should have realised that the bitter old bigot would never have sat back and let the marriage that he hadn't wanted survive—or, rather, take place. Because, as far as Aristotle Nicolaides had been concerned, his son and Sarah Meyerson weren't yet married.

His son and the granddaughter of the man he had hated all his life. The granddaughter of the man who owned vital Nicolaides land and would never hand it over.

'My father!' he repeated on a dangerous note. 'And just *what* did my father tell you? Exactly what lies did he use? *Tell me*!'

'I— He—'

'No, on second thoughts,' Damon broke in savagely as Sarah struggled for words, 'don't tell me. At least, not here. We've provided a public spectacle for long enough. Come with me—let's get out of here and talk this over in private.'

'No.'

Sarah shook her head determinedly, russet hair flying wildly with the movement.

'No way! I'm not going anywhere with you ever again. I don't want to be somewhere *private*, and I don't want to talk to you any more! I want this over—over and done with. I—'

'Sarah!' Damon cut in on her in exasperation. 'Don't be stupid! Come with me...'

'No.'

She held out her hands before her, using them as a shield and a warning as he took a couple of hasty steps forward.

'Damon, I said no!'

'And I said yes!'

Beyond thinking straight, beyond any thought at all, he only knew he hated the look in her eyes. Couldn't bear to see her backing away from him like this.

'Sarah...'

He reached out in his turn, caught hold of her hands, gripping them tight.

'OK, that's enough!'

Rhys Morgan's cold, incisive tones sliced through the heated atmosphere like a blade of ice.

'Stop that right now, Nicolaides! I'll not stand by and let you treat Sarah this way. How can you claim her as your lover and—?'

'My *lover*!'

It was part laugh, partly a sound of total exasperation, part admission of defeat, and even Damon couldn't have said which one was uppermost. He only knew the feeling that he was fighting for his life—his emotional life at least.

'My lover!' he repeated ferociously, shaking his dark head almost as vehemently as Sarah had done. 'My *lover*! You don't get it, do you? You really don't know. Well, I'll tell you. Sarah isn't my lover—she isn't my mistress—never has been. She's my *wife*. The woman I married a year ago.'

'*Damon!*'

Sarah's cry of shock and disbelief fell into an atmosphere so thick that it was almost impossible to breathe.

And as Damon came slowly back to himself, as the red tide that had flooded his mind slowly ebbed, leaving his eyes capable of focusing once more, his brain able to function, he realised that the stunned silence was not just surrounding them.

It filled the whole room. And every single person present had abandoned any pretence at continuing with their normal morning and was staring straight at them, mouth agape and eyes wide with fascination.

'*Damon!*' Sarah repeated, on a very different note this time.

And as she did so there was the sound of movement, and a blinding flash as some opportunistic photographer who had somehow managed to con his way into the lounge under the pretence of being there as a guest stepped forward, pointed his camera in their direction and snapped the frozen tableau.

Oh, hell! Damon groaned inwardly. Oh, hell and damnation! He'd really done it now!

CHAPTER ELEVEN

SHE'S my wife.

Sarah couldn't believe she'd heard right. Had Damon really said what she thought he had—and out loud, in front of all these people?

One glance into the depths of those jet-black eyes soon told her the truth. He *had* said it. And clearly he was every bit as shocked as she was herself. More, in fact.

And no wonder. It had to be the last thing he should have said. The very last thing that he wanted anyone to know about. Because his whole aim had been to marry her, gain the land, and then divorce her without anyone—and preferably particularly without Eugenia—ever finding out.

He had realised what he had said too. And he was muttering a savage curse in violent Greek as someone stepped forward. The camera bulbs she had come to hate flashed and she flinched backwards, trying to bring her hand up before her face, only to remember that Damon had hold of them and was clearly not prepared to let them go.

'Is this true, Mr Nicolaides? Is it true, Sarah?'

The lone reporter was intent on making the most of his opportunity for an exclusive, asking questions as swiftly and determinedly as possible before the hotel management could get Security to come and throw him out.

'Are you *married*?'

But Damon didn't honour his question with an answer. He didn't spare him a glance. He didn't so much as blink. Instead his attention was fixed on Sarah, his burning gaze locked on to her shadowed green one.

'Sarah—darling—*ghineka mou*... We have to talk about this. Only talk. I won't hurt you. *Please* come with me.'

Sarah blinked hard in stunned confusion.

Please.

Had Damon truly said 'please' in that—that almost desperate way?

'I...'

'Sarah, no,' Rhys put in. 'Don't—'

'Sarah...' Damon cut across him. 'Trust me on this. Believe me...'

Believe me. It was as if the two words had created some sort of time slip so that she had gone backwards, back to the previous night, when she had been in the bedroom with Damon and she had told him the truth about Jason.

And he had believed her.

Illogically and irrationally and with just a leap of faith, he had believed her without question.

Just as she now believed him.

He wouldn't hurt her. At least not just now. Because hadn't all the hurting been done in the past? Hadn't he already done the worst he could?

'All right,' she said, never taking her eyes away from his. 'Let's talk.'

Damon allowed himself just one brief hint of a smile, then he twisted her hand in his so that he was holding it gently but firmly as he led her from the room and out into the foyer.

As he went, he pulled his cellphone from his pocket, flicked it open and spoke into it in rapid, authoritative Greek. He must have been calling his chauffeur because only a few moments later a sleek silver car drew up outside the hotel and Damon ushered her out to it, one arm at her waist.

He sensed her hesitation, the rising apprehension as the

crowd of paparazzi surged forward and the pressure of his hold increased, his grip tightening.

'Don't say a word—just walk...'

Whenever we go out, whenever you have to face them, I'll be right there, at your side, to see you through it.

And he was with her this time too. He drew her close, so that her face was against his chest, one hand protecting her from the intrusion of the cameras. The other arm around her waist guided her wavering footsteps forward and towards the car so that she didn't have to see for herself, simply follow where he led.

He wasted no time on smiles or answers to the hundreds of questions that bombarded them from all sides, but kept a strict, stony silence until they were in the car, with the door firmly shut, and edging away from the entrance as carefully as the crush would allow.

'Where...?'

Sarah's voice failed her on the question. But she didn't need to ask it because in that moment Damon leaned forward and addressed the driver, speaking in Greek. But there was one word that Sarah caught, and understood, making her stare at him in confusion and disbelief.

'*Aerodhromio!*' she echoed faintly. 'The airport! Damon, why...?'

'Trust me,' was all he said, once more looking deep into her face.

She had little choice. The car was rocketing through the traffic-filled streets; there was no way she could escape. She could do nothing physically but sit where she was and hope for some sort of explanation before too long.

But at least she could protest.

'Just what's going on? I want to know what's happening.'

'You will—I promise. Just bear with me... But first—

tell me who my father said I had as my mistress. Who was I supposed to be having an affair with?'

'I don't really have to say, do I? You know—there was only one person you really wanted to marry.'

A strange expression crossed Damon's face, one that made him look as if she had actually said something that he *wanted* to hear. That he had been expecting all the time.

'Eugenia?' he questioned sharply.

And when she nodded, his reaction was totally unexpected. He threw back his dark head and laughed. And the laughter seemed strangely real, his amusement genuine.

'Eugenia!' he declared in some satisfaction.

The next moment his hands were busy on his phone again, punching out numbers with an urgency that spoke of some desperate emergency.

'Eugenia?'

The sound of the Greek woman's name had Sarah sitting up stiffly, every muscle pulling tight. Her eyes turned to Damon again, clouding thickly with hurt. But he shook his head at her and continued with his conversation.

'Genie—speak English—it's important. I have Sarah here. Yes—Sarah…'

Pausing, he listened intently while Sarah clenched her hands tightly in her lap, nails digging into her palms. Her sharp teeth bit down hard onto her bottom lip, struggling to hold back the bitter reproaches she wanted to fling into his stunning face.

'That's exactly what's happened,' Damon continued. 'So I need your help. I'm going to pass her the phone, and I want you to talk to her.'

'*No!*' Sarah couldn't hold back the protest. 'No way!'

'*Yes,*' Damon insisted. 'Eugenia will talk and you will listen. Genie—I'm calling in that promise you made me. A little early, I know, but I need it now! I want you to tell

Sarah—tell my wife—exactly what you've been doing today.'

Without further conversation he pushed the phone at Sarah, who could only stare at it in blank confusion.

'Take it! Talk to her!'

What *was* he doing? 'My wife', he had said. *Tell my wife*...

And yet his father had been so insistent that Damon's true plan was to marry Eugenia. So why would he risk ruining that by admitting that he was already married?

'Take it!'

Sarah reached for the phone as gingerly as if it were a poisonous snake that might rear up and strike at any moment. With her eyes fixed on Damon's taut, intent face, she lifted it to her ear.

'Sarah?'

She recognised Eugenia's voice at once. The big surprise, the stunning, unbelievable fact, was that the other woman sounded—happy. She didn't seem in the least bit shocked or bewildered at the fact that Damon had announced he was married—to someone else. Instead, Eugenia seemed bubbling over with excitement, amusement, and delight.

'Yes...' she said cautiously.

'Did you hear what Damon said? I have to tell you what I've been doing today. But you have to promise me something. You must not tell my *papa*. Not till I get a chance to do so. You promise?'

'Yes...' Sarah said again, wondering just what was coming.

'Well, then—today I got married!'

It was the last thing she had expected. It was so stunning, so unbelievable, so totally confusing that she actually fell back in her seat at the sound of it.

'You...'

Her dazed eyes went to Damon, sitting darkly silent and watchful at her side, his face turned to hers, his concentration on her total.

'But Damon...' she tried, and heard Eugenia's laughter.

'Not to *Damon*, silly! Why would I want to marry him? He's like my big brother—nothing more. Oh, I know our fathers wanted the marriage—they wanted to merge our two families, the two fortunes! But it would have been purely a business deal, nothing more. And besides, Damon never wanted me. He hasn't wanted anyone since he set eyes on you.'

'He hasn't...'

It was just a raw croak, her throat so dry that she had to force the words out. And the look she saw in Damon's eyes only made matters so much worse. She had never seen such raw emotion in anyone's face, let alone this strong, capable man who had always seemed so much in control. Never seen such hunger, such need, such *fear*—a desperate, uneasy fear that she might not believe what he was trying to tell her.

'So what's the truth?' she whispered, directing her question at Damon, ignoring the fact that Eugenia was still at the other end of the phone connection.

It was weak with shock and confusion, just a tiny thread of sound almost drowned in the purr of the car's engine. But Damon caught it and something sparked in the darkness of his eyes as he answered.

'The truth is that Genie and I understood each other.'

His voice sounded bruised and flattened, but there was no hesitation in his speech, no unevenness or frailty in his words.

'We both wanted to marry someone our families wouldn't approve of. And we didn't want to marry each other. Genie was in a worse position because her father was so ill. She couldn't risk him finding out that she was in love with a Frenchman—Maurice—so I promised to help them.'

'He let my *papa* believe that we were thinking of marriage—covered for me when I saw Maurice...'

Eugenia had caught Damon's explanation and took up the story.

'I made him swear to me that he wouldn't tell anyone about my romance. That was before he met you. I never anticipated that he would be the one who got married first. I never thought he'd fall in love. He's been helping me meet Maurice in secret—even helped me arrange my marriage. And today I officially became Madame Maurice Messenguer....'

If Eugenia said anything more, Sarah didn't hear it. Her hand had started to shake terribly, so much so that she almost dropped the phone. Reaching forward, Damon took it from her gently. He murmured some words of thanks, said goodbye, switched it off.

And still Sarah hadn't moved. Still she sat there, white-faced, wide-eyed, staring at him. If only he knew what she was thinking. If only he could see what was in her mind!

'Sarah,' he said roughly, unevenly. 'Say something—please!'

Didn't she know she held his whole future in her hands? That she had the sort of absolute power that he had never, ever given to anyone else but her?

'Your father...'

The way she stumbled over the words made his heart lurch in hope, but he didn't dare to put any real hope in it. Not yet. He needed more before he knew that he was safe.

'Your father lied.'

'Yes.'

It was low and rough and husky. As he spoke the car swung round a corner rather wildly and Damon put out a hand to steady himself against the door, but his eyes never left her face.

'Yes—I'm so sorry, sweetheart—if I'd only known! He must have guessed—he must have seen that you were important. That you were a real threat to his plans to combine the two dynasties of Nicolaides and Stakis. I should never have left you alone with him.'

'And I should never have listened to him! Oh, *why* did I ever...?'

But Damon knew the answer to that one. He didn't want to admit it but he had put the weapon into his father's hands and he had only himself to blame if the old man had used it against him.

'The land,' he said simply, and saw her head go back in shock.

'Of course. The land.'

Aristotle Nicolaides was a canny old devil. He'd known that Damon had only come looking for her in the first place because he'd wanted that piece of land so desperately. He'd known that she would believe that, and so, naturally, she would think that everything else he said was true. Feeling desperately low already at the realisation that her inheritance meant more to Damon than she did herself, she had already been wounded and vulnerable, open to the final, the mortal blow.

She'd even challenged Damon about it and he'd admitted...

'The l-land!'

It was a very different sound now. A high-pitched, wavering cry of pain. And bitter, burning tears stung at her eyes.

'Oh, why...?'

Damon half reached out, then let his hands drop without touching her, in an oddly defeated gesture.

'I can explain that, darling,' he said very quietly. 'I swear on my life that it wasn't how you think. I came to see you to try and persuade you to part with the land, yes. But I took one look at you and fell in love. I lost my heart and I lost my head—my mind just wasn't functioning. I forgot all about the land and the reason I was there. All I wanted was you.'

He sighed deeply, despondently, raking one long hand through the crisp darkness of his hair.

'I just wanted to get you to marry me as quickly as possible. I thought that then I could explain everything. But I didn't dare to tell you the truth for fear that you'd turn your back on me—walk away...'

'As I did,' Sarah put in softly. 'When your father said...'

'And when you accused me of only coming to you for the land—I couldn't deny it. It was the truth after all.'

But not the whole truth, Sarah saw that now. Oh, if only she could have seen it at the start. But Aristotle Nicolaides had chosen his weapons well. He had studied her closely and he had seen that she was vulnerable. That the chink in her armour was that she didn't quite believe that someone like Damon could love her. Truly love her.

And he had used that fear with deadly intent.

But Damon understood. He truly understood just why she had been so vulnerable.

'I should never have kept our marriage secret.' Damon shook his head in despair at the mistakes of the past. 'If I'd come right out and said it...'

'I understand.'

Sarah's voice had a new strength, the strength that came from hope and joy and love.

'I understand that you were only trying to protect me. Keep me safe.'

'But instead I left you wide open to my father's scheming—to his lies.'

'But not any more—together we'll be more than a match for him. Damon...'

But her words were interrupted by the sudden stilling of the car, the sound of the brakes. Looking round, she realised that while they had been talking their journey had been completed. They were at the airport, and she didn't know why or where they were going.

'Damon?'

He had turned to her, pushing his hand into his pocket and pulling out...

'My passport! What are you doing with that? Damon, what—?'

'Sarah, *agape mou*, I have to ask you something. I need you to come with me. Not to ask questions, just to trust me and come with me now. I have something I need to show you. Something I want you to see. Will you come with me?'

Would she? Sarah didn't have to wait even to ask the question of herself. The answer was there in her mind, fully formed and totally confident. After all, hadn't she made it when she had left the hotel and come with him? When she had put her trust in him then?

'I'll go with you to the ends of the earth if that's what you ask of me!'

'Oh, Sarah!'

Her name was a choking sound of delight. Of total happiness. And his face lit up as if the sun had just risen behind his eyes, making their darkness warm and glow.

'Do you know that I adore you? That you are my life?'

'I know,' Sarah whispered. 'Because I feel the same.'

The flight he took her on passed in a haze of delight. Damon's private jet was fitted out with every luxury imaginable—including a huge and marvellously comfortable double bed. And as soon as the plane had left the runway, and had levelled out at the altitude for flight, Damon took her hand and led her to that bed, where he made love to her so thoroughly and so wonderfully that she felt as if she had no need of the jet, that she was capable of flying high up in the clouds all by herself, lifted and carried on the wings of pure joy and the ecstasy of love.

'But where *are* we going?' she demanded when, some hours later, they had landed and, all the formalities behind them, Damon had hurried her to a waiting helicopter. Taking the controls himself, he piloted them up into the air once more and out over a sea so bright and so brilliant a blue that she knew it could only be the ocean around the island of Mykonos. Damon's home.

'Be patient,' he shouted over the noise of the whirring blades. 'Wait and see!'

And with that she had to be content until at last he turned the helicopter in a wide circle, bringing it down onto a large expanse of land—a stretch of the island that ran down to the edge of the sea, with a perfect strip of gleaming sandy beach between the earth and the water.

'Recognise it?' he asked when, with the engine turned off, they climbed out of the helicopter and stared around. Damon caught hold of her hand and gripped tightly. 'Do you know where you are?'

'Recognise...'

Sarah couldn't make her voice work properly—or her thoughts. She did know where she was, or she thought she did. But the last time she had been here, the only time she had been here, it hadn't looked like this.

'Damon—is—is some of this my grandfather's land?'

'Yes—but it's not your grandfather's land any more. It's yours.'

'Mine—no, it can't be! My land was never this big—this is huge! It's...'

Something dawned on her, making her head spin in shock.

'Damon—where are the hotels? *Your* hotels? What happened?'

'I had them pulled down,' he told her. 'Knocked to the ground—and every last bit of them taken away.'

'But why?' She was stunned with the craziness, the extravagance of the gesture. 'What made you do that?'

'You did—or, rather, my need to prove to you that this land didn't matter—that if I couldn't have you I didn't want any of it. My father always wanted this land to link the two hotels—from the moment I met you I didn't give a damn about that. So I bought the land off him, knocked down the hotels and—here…'

His hand went to his inner jacket pocket, pulling out a sheaf of papers.

'These are for you.'

Through the welling tears Sarah struggled to read the documents, incapable of taking in what they said in spite of the fact that they were written in English.

'What? Damon—I don't understand!'

His smile was wide and brilliant as the hot Greek sun blazing in the cloudless sky.

'Don't you see, my darling? This land is yours. All of it. Every last centimetre of it. Those are the deeds to it—all signed and sealed and totally legal. That's why I came to you in London—I wanted to bring you here and give it to you. I wanted you to know that it was yours—all yours—whether you were my wife or not. And then I was going to beg you to come back to me. I wanted you to be sure that I love you for you and not for anything you own…'

'But I know that now!'

Sarah cut off his words, flinging herself into his arms and kissing him with all the love that was bursting out of her heart, all the joy that made her soul sing.

'Oh, Damon, my love. You don't have to do this—you don't need to—I love you and I believe you and I'd trust you with my life. All that unhappiness, it's all behind us. It's in the past. The future's ours and it's wonderful and clear and bright.'

Her words were kissed away in their turn, and she was gathered into Damon's arms and crushed against him, the strength of his hold and the passion in the way he took her mouth making promises for that future that no words could ever express.

And after she had dragged in a much-needed breath, when at last she could speak, Sarah lifted her head and looked around her at the beautiful spot in which they stood, the land that had once been a cause of such dissension but now was like a symbol of the two of them together. The end of the feud. The two families united and at peace.

'Is this really mine?' she said thoughtfully. 'To do with exactly as I please?'

There was no hesitation in Damon's response. It came swift and clear, and filled with total conviction.

'It's really yours, *ghineka mou*. Totally yours.'

'Good. Then in that case...'

She smiled up into his glowing eyes, the perfect happiness in her heart showing clearly in her face.

'What I'd really like is to build a house here. A wonderful, big, happy family house. The sort of place where we can settle down and raise our family and live together for the rest of our lives. So what—*andhras mou*—what do you think of that as a plan?'

'It sounds wonderful,' Damon assured her deeply. 'Perfect. In fact it was just what I was hoping for too. Especially that "for the rest of our lives". Because I can't think of anything that I would rather do with the rest of my days than spend them with you, having you by my side, making love to you each day and making you as happy as I possibly can.'

And, gathering her up into his arms, he took her lips once more in a kiss that sealed the promise forever.

HIS TROPHY MISTRESS

by

Daphne Clair

Daphne Clair lives in subtropical New Zealand, with her Dutch-born husband. They have five children. At eight years old she embarked on her first novel, about taming a tiger. This epic never reached a publisher, but metamorphosed male tigers still prowl the pages of her romances, of which she has written over thirty for Mills & Boon, and over fifty all told. Her other writing includes non-fiction, poetry and short stories, and she has won literary prizes in New Zealand and America.

CHAPTER ONE

THE bride and groom proceeded triumphantly down the aisle to the door of the church. Behind them Paige Camden, chief bridal attendant, kept her own smile in place and one eye on the five-year-old flower girl who seemed in danger of walking on the bride's white satin train.

Paige bent to place a restraining hand on the child's shoulder. As she straightened, casting an idle look at the nearer pews, her hazel eyes met a glittering jewel-green gaze that jerked her shoulders back and instantly eliminated her smile.

What the hell was Jager Jeffries doing at her sister's wedding?

And still as stunningly handsome as ever. Those astonishing eyes under well-defined brows contrasted with naturally olive skin; the stubborn masculine mouth and proud warrior's nose hinted at an unknown connection to some Maori ancestor.

The dark, luxuriantly waving hair was somewhat tamed by a surely expensive cut. An even more expensive suit hugged broad shoulders, tapered hips and long, muscular legs, its perfect fit and exquisite tailoring proclaiming how far the mature thirty-one-year-old had come from the wild young tearaway Paige had once known. And loved—with a passion so intense it was inevitably self-destructive, burning up in its own heat until only gray, dusty ashes remained.

"Paige?" The best man's hand was on her arm. "Are you okay?" he murmured, bending toward her.

The bridal party had forged ahead and guests were pressing from behind.

"Yes," Paige lied, resurrecting the smile. "I just stood on my dress, that's all."

She wrenched her gaze away from the piercing green one, unnecessarily shook out the violet floor-length skirt of her dress and stumbled forward, glad of the best man's supporting arm.

They reached the steps and the sunshine pouring out of a clear late-winter Auckland sky. A photographer motioned them into place beside the happy couple.

Paige kept the smile all through the photo session, and was still wearing it when they arrived at the crowded reception and she took her assigned place at the main table.

By that time her jaw was aching and her nerves humming like fine, overtensioned wires. When the best man poured her a glass of ruby-red wine she grabbed it with a shaking hand and downed half of it before she realized she'd spilled a drop on her satin gown.

Surreptitiously she dipped a corner of a linen table napkin into the crystal glass of iced water before her and dabbed at the stain. The wine color faded, and she rubbed the spreading watermark with the dry part of the napkin. At least at a distance it would be less noticeable than the wine.

She fixed a glazed stare on the table before her, telling herself it was imagination that she could feel Jager's gaze on her, that the hot prickling of sensation that assailed her skin was a by-product of long-buried memories that seeing him again had brought to the surface.

The succulent chicken and crisp salads on her plate might have been old rope and grass. She scarcely managed half a dozen mouthfuls, trusting the wine to stop them sticking in her throat.

Somehow she replied to her neighbors' efforts at conversation, and raised her glass and applauded the speeches at the right moments. And finally, despite her limited vision without her glasses, was unable to resist the urge to sweep her gaze about the red-carpeted, white-pillared reception lounge with its gilded decor and lavish floral arrangements, and find out if Jager really was there.

He was.

He sat at one of the nearer tables, leaning back in his half-turned chair and looking infuriatingly relaxed. As if he'd been waiting for her to find him, he lifted his glass to her in a mocking little gesture and drank, his eyes holding hers. Although the people around him were just a blur to Paige, and he was slightly out of focus, she felt the full force of his eyes.

Her hand tightened around her own glass, but she didn't return the silent toast, instead staring at him accusingly. *How dare you!* her eyes demanded. *How dare you turn up at Maddie's wedding and ruin the day for me?*

He must have been invited. Not by Maddie—her

sister would never have done that to her. So the invitation had come from Glen Provost, Maddie's new husband, or his family. How did he know Glen? Was Maddie aware of the connection, whatever it was? Why hadn't she warned Paige?

Jager replaced his glass on the white cloth. His long fingers twirled the fragile glass stem, and the corners of his mouth lifted in a faint smile while he continued to hold Paige's eyes.

Who was staring back at him, she realized, like a rabbit at a snake.

For the second time that day she dragged her gaze from him. She could feel the increased beat of her heart against the low-cut, fitted bodice of her dress, that seemed too tight. Drawing in a deep breath, she saw the best man's newly aroused interest in her bosom, his eyes first lingering, then in surprise flicking up to her face.

Not nearly as interesting, she mentally told him with grimly cynical humor. Her face would never be her fortune, not that she needed one, since she and Maddie were her father's only heirs.

There was nothing particularly wrong with ordinary hazel-green eyes, an unremarkable no-nonsense nose and a clear but hardly milk-and-roses complexion. They just didn't add up to the kind of eye-catching, man-snaring feminine prettiness that blessed her younger sister.

Maddie's eyes were blue and wide, her mouth a classic full-lipped bow, her nose cutely retroussé. And her hair was a tumble of blond natural curls that Paige would have killed for if she hadn't been so fond of her sister.

After years of trying to make hers curl, or fluff up, or even stay pinned in a style of any sort, Paige had despaired of persuading it to do anything but hang straight and fine, *au naturel*. Now she kept it neatly and boringly cropped to just below her ears, brushed it briskly to a satiny sheen every night, and after unsuccessfully experimenting with bleaches and rinses, allowed it to retain its own unexciting nut-brown color.

Long ago she had decided against competing with Maddie or any other pretty girl. Paige was plain and there was no point in pretending otherwise. She could just be thankful that she wasn't downright ugly, and that her figure as well as her face was passable, even if neither was likely to launch any ships. In fact her measurements were the same as her sister's, but Maddie had always seemed more rounded and ultra-feminine, perhaps because she was three inches shorter than Paige's five-eight.

Maddie had never had to worry that she was turning into a giraffe at age twelve. Their mother had never advised Maddie that makeup couldn't work miracles, and that discreetly enhancing her best features would be more effective than drawing attention to her face by using too much.

As the newlyweds cut the cake, Paige's mother put an elegantly slim, diamond-ringed hand on her waist and hissed in her ear, "What's Jager Jeffries doing here? Did you know he was coming?"

"No I didn't," Paige answered, scarcely moving her lips. "And I have no idea."

Margaret Camden's precisely reddened lips tightened. The blue eyes she had bequeathed to her younger daughter glittered with annoyance as she shook a head of artfully lightened curls. "I can't *believe* that Glen's family knows him!"

When the cake-cutting was completed and the bride and groom began circulating among the guests, Paige handed out wedding cake but stayed well away from the table where Jager sat, allowing the flower girl to deal with it. After returning the empty tray to the kitchen she retrieved her small makeup kit from her mother's handbag and crossed the carpeted lobby to the ladies' room.

She touched up the minimal color on her lips, checked that the subtle beige shadow on her eyelids was intact and the mascara that tipped her lashes hadn't run, and put on her large, rimless spectacles. Now that the photographs and the formal part of the wedding were over there was no reason she shouldn't wear them. It would have been nice to have contact lenses for occasions like this but, after painfully trying them several times in the past, Paige had accepted she was one of those people who just couldn't tolerate them.

Coming back into the lobby, she wished she had left the glasses in her bag. Because Jager stood only a few feet from the door, and without the slight, comforting vagueness that her impaired natural vision had imparted, he was very clearly, very solidly, in her way.

She knew, with a sense of inevitability, that he was waiting for her. That he'd followed her. A shimmer of pleased anticipation passed over her, and she firmly repressed it.

For a second or two neither of them moved. Paige searched Jager's face for some clue to his emotions, his intentions, but apart from the brilliance of his eyes he was giving nothing away.

Deciding to take the initiative, she ordered her lips to a smile—she'd had plenty of practice at that today—and said brightly, "Hello, Jager. This is a surprise! I didn't know you knew Glen."

"I don't," he answered, and at her flicker of surprise added, "not very well. It's a long story."

Which she didn't want to hear. "I'm sure it's an interesting one," she said, "but it will have to wait for another time."

Trying to look busy and purposeful, she attempted to pass him, but he reached out, closing his fingers around her arm. Her heart tripped over itself and her skin tingled.

"When?" His voice was low and gritty.

Something hot and disturbing happened in her midriff and began to spread throughout her body. Dismayed and disoriented by the force of it, she took a moment to make sure her voice was steady. "When what?"

"When can I see you?"

Warily she pulled away, and he let go. "Why do you want to see me?"

Thick black lashes momentarily hid his eyes. Then he looked away from her as if trying to distance himself. She saw the faint widening of his nostrils when he took a breath before looking back at her, his gaze curiously speculative. "To catch up," he said abruptly. "For old times' sake."

Two women and a man came out of the reception room, chatting and laughing as they headed for the rest rooms. Jager cast them an impatient glance and shifted so they could pass, his gaze homing in again on Paige.

"That's hardly necessary," she said.

"Necessary?" He pushed his hands into his pockets, looking down at her under half-closed lids from his six feet two inches. Dropping his voice to the deep purr that had always made her toes curl, he said, "It isn't necessary...but I'm curious. Aren't you?"

Intensely. But also cautious. Getting involved with Jager again was the last thing she needed right now. Ever. "No," she said baldly.

More people were trickling out of the lounge, some going outside, one group pausing to talk a few feet away. Jager ignored them. "Come on," he chided. "I thought your family was all keen on being tremendously civilized."

"Leave my family out of this!"

"Gladly." His beautiful lips curled.

She couldn't raise her voice here, but it trembled with anger. "I can't imagine why you'd want to talk—all we ever did at the end was argue."

Some spark of emotion lit his eyes, and a complicated expression crossed his face. "Not *all*," he reminded her. "There was always a way to end the argument." His lazy, explicit look invited her to remember...

Paige's lips compressed. Sweet, sweet memories—they had tormented her for years. "You said you wanted to talk!"

His head cocked, his expression becoming bland in the extreme. "Have I suggested anything else?"

He hadn't—not verbally. Paige felt wrong-footed, stuck for an answer.

Lights flickered on around them. In the big room the three-piece band her parents had hired struck up the wedding waltz.

"I have to go back," Paige said. "They're dancing."

Jager stood aside but she knew he was right behind her as she returned to the lounge.

The center of the floor had been cleared and Maddie and Glen were circling alone. A number of people had congregated near the doorway. Without pushing and causing a stir, Paige couldn't get through.

The music paused, and the Master of Ceremonies urged everyone onto the floor. Both sets of parents took up the invitation then, followed by several more couples.

The crowd at the door began to part, and Paige moved forward to skirt the edge of the dance floor.

An arm curved around her waist, urged her onto the polished boards.

"I can't..." she protested, but already her feet were following Jager's lead. "The best man...he'll be looking for me."

"He can find someone else," Jager said ruthlessly.

He took the makeup bag from her hand and dropped it onto the nearest table. "Dance with me, Paige."

He wasn't really giving her any choice unless she was to make a scene. He pulled her close, his other hand closing over hers and folding it against his chest. He'd opened his jacket and through the fine fabric of his white shirt she could feel the warmth of his skin, the faint beat of his heart. His scent enveloped her, familiar and strange at the same time.

A long time ago she had tried to teach him the proper steps that she'd learned at her exclusive girls' school, but he'd grinned and just held her and swayed to the music, scarcely moving his feet. Holding her close, body to body. Close enough for him to lay his cheek against her hair. Close enough to kiss.

Paige's eyes drifted shut. Memories washed over her and for just a few minutes she let them. She didn't speak and neither did Jager. She just breathed him in, his warmth, his personal male aroma, and remembered how it had been when they were young and in love, when she had believed they could overcome her parents' opposition, the differences in their backgrounds, lack of money, their own inexperience of life. Anything, so long as they had each other.

And of course like most young love it had come to nothing, all their dreams shattered into sharp, hurtful pieces against the cold, hard reality of the adult world.

She made a small sound—half sigh, half laugh—that should have been drowned by the music, and the chatter all around them, but Jager drew back a couple of inches and looked down at her. "What?" he queried.

A wry smile on her mouth, she said, "Nothing."

He continued to look at her, his gaze unreadable. "Nothing," he repeated. A gleam entered his half-closed eyes. "O-oh yeah?" For a moment his white teeth showed in a brief, blinding smile. Then his head went back and he laughed, a deeper, richer sound than she remembered from the days when he'd been scarcely more than a boy, but retaining the same uninhibited enjoyment.

Something caught at her throat, hot and thick, and an answering joyousness sang in her blood, a powerful echo of long-buried emotions.

Then he actually executed a few dance steps, quite expertly, taking her with him, holding her tight as she instinctively followed. She felt the power of his muscles as his thighs brushed against hers before he stopped, swinging her slightly off balance so she had to cling to his shoulder to stay upright.

They remained in an embrace that shut out everyone, everything. The laughter had left his face and he looked somber, the strong jaw clenched so that his beautiful mouth became uncompromising, his cheekbones more prominent. In the dark centers of his eyes Paige saw her own upturned face, and she was dimly aware that his hand had tightened on hers to the point of pain. Other sensations overrode the tiny hurt. Her breathing was shallow and quick, her throat tight, her body licked by a slow, languorous fire.

"Paige," he said, almost wonderingly, as if he'd just realized who it was he held.

Her lips parted hesitantly. His name hovered on them, then escaped like a sigh.

And another voice—her mother's, sharp and anxious—broke the moment. "Paige!"

She blinked at the interruption, instinctively trying to pull away from Jager, but he wasn't giving an inch.

Her mother stood within her father's arm. Henry appeared uncomfortable and annoyed, while his wife looked militant. "Blake is looking for you," she told Paige. "This should be his dance."

Blake? For a moment Paige's memory balked. The best man. "I didn't see him." She had seen no one but Jager since he'd swept her onto the dance floor. She looked up at him. "I'd better..." Again she tried to move away.

She recognized the quick jut of his jaw, the "don't push me" look in his eyes. But then he loosened his hold, dropping his hand from her tingling fingers although he still retained his grip on her waist, and allowed her to turn to her parents. Looking at them, he said politely, "How are you Mrs. Camden...Mr. Camden?"

Henry Camden nodded stiffly. Margaret said crisply, "We're well, Jager, and Paige...as you can see, she's fine." She paused, giving her daughter a covertly anxious glance before turning to him again. "We didn't expect to see you here."

"It was kind of a last-minute invitation."

"Really?" The chilly reply didn't encourage elaboration and he didn't offer it.

Henry's mature male rumble was directed at Jager. "I hear you've been doing very well for yourself."

Margaret looked at her husband in surprise. It was evidently the first she'd heard of it.

Jager said, "You do?"

"A bit of a highflier these days."

"I get by."

Henry gave a bark of reluctant laughter. "More than that, I'd say."

"Would you?"

Margaret demanded, "What are you talking about, Henry?"

Instead of explaining, Henry looked around them and said, "We're holding up the traffic here. If we're going to talk, we should move."

But the music stopped then, and other couples began walking off the floor.

Margaret shifted her gaze to Jager and said pointedly, "Paige has certain duties as her sister's attendant."

Jager inclined his head, and lifted both hands away from Paige. "I haven't balled and chained her." His eyes challenged her. His voice low, he asked, "Do you want to leave me, Paige?"

Echoes of the past rose, hauntingly. Had he meant to arouse them? "I do have things to do." She hated the apologetic note in her voice. Trying to sound more assertive she said, "It's been nice seeing you again, Jager."

Her mother looked relieved and approving. Jager merely lifted one dark brow a fraction and grinned at Paige. A tight, feral grin that both teased and promised, telling her she couldn't dismiss him so easily and it amused him that she'd even tried.

A shiver of apprehension spiraled about her spine. Jager had changed in the intervening years. Formidably self-assured instead of cocky and defensive, he carried a distinctly unsettling aura of sexual potency that had little to do with the height and good looks bequeathed by his unknown ancestors, and everything to do with how he saw himself as a man. The raw, brash, quicksilver sexuality had been replaced by tempered steel under the polished surface of a new sophistication. Which made him all the more dangerous if, as she suspected, he had learned to use it as a weapon.

Well, she had changed too, Paige told herself as she left his side to hunt down either her sister or the best man. She was no longer in thrall to teenage hormones and romantic fantasies. There was more to love than the seductive siren call of sex, more to life than falling head over heels into lust and expecting it to overcome all obstacles.

Paige no longer trusted feelings alone in her relationships. Having learned her lesson the hard way, she had determined a long time back that for the rest of her life her head would be the ruler of her heart.

She spied Maddie's veil enveloping blond curls, and joined her sister, smiling at the people who had engaged the bridal couple in talk. Maddie slid a glance at her and gracefully extricated them both, heading for the room set aside for the newlyweds to change in later.

Closing the door, Maddie turned. "Are you all right? I'm sorry, Peg." The childhood nickname slipped out. "I had no idea Jager would turn up. It's the most incredible coincidence—you wouldn't believe it!"

"Coincidence? Wasn't he invited?"

"Glen invited him. He didn't know...well, I've never mentioned Jager's actual name to him, so how could he? The thing is, Jager's kind of a long-lost relation."

"Of Glen's?"

Maddie nodded. "They're half brothers."

Paige's mouth fell open. Her thoughts whirled, and the one dazzling, golden one that surfaced and burst out into words was, "Jager found his family!"

Maddie was giving her a peculiar look.

Slowly the implications sank in. Paige gulped, swallowed and made a connection. "Glen's mother...?"

Her sister's white-veiled head shook vehemently. "His father...and some girl he knew before he got engaged to Glen's mother. Mrs. Provost doesn't know yet...with the wedding and everything it's not a good time for extra family stress. Mr. Provost asked the boys to keep it quiet until he gets around to telling her, but Glen wanted his new brother here for his wedding day. They've only met once or twice but they hit it off from the start, he said."

Glen was an only child; Paige could imagine he'd have been intrigued at the advent of an unknown sibling. "How long ago?" It must be recent.

"A few weeks, I think. Glen only told me today. I had no idea until then, and I couldn't get you alone before...I still haven't said anything to him about you and Jager." Maddie twisted her hands together. "Has it ruined the day for you?"

"Of course not!" It had been a stressful occasion

anyway, fraught with old pain and regrets, but she'd weathered it for Maddie's sake, and she would weather this too. No guilt and worry about Paige should be allowed to cloud Maddie's happy day. "Both of us have put our youthful indiscretion far, far behind us. It's quite fun," she lied gaily, "seeing him again, catching up on things."

His phrase, she realized, as Maddie looked doubtful, then relieved. "I guess it was all over years ago," Maddie said hopefully. "Are you sure you're okay with this?"

There wasn't much she—or anyone—could do about it. "I'm fine, stop worrying, Mad. Hadn't we better get back? Your husband will think you've left him already."

"Never!" Maddie turned to the mirrored dressing table and the makeup container sitting on it. "My husband," she repeated dreamily, fishing in the miniature hatbox and bringing out a lipstick. "Fancy me being an old married woman!" She began expertly applying the lipstick.

"Hardly old," Paige argued. Maddie was twenty-five to her own twenty-nine. "But old enough to know what you're doing, I guess. Which is more than I can say for my first venture into matrimony."

In the mirror, Maddie threw her a sympathetic look, shook out a tissue and blotted her lips. Gorgeous lips, Paige noted abstractly. Pink perfection. Glen was a lucky man. Her sister was as sweet as she was pretty, without a malicious bone in her body.

Scrunching the tissue, Maddie said, "It wasn't even

a proper wedding, was it? I mean, it hardly counts, really.''

"No." Paige's voice was perfectly steady. "It doesn't count at all."

CHAPTER TWO

JAGER didn't approach her again, but while Paige dutifully danced with the best man and then others, she was continually aware of him, leaning against a wall with arms folded or prowling the periphery of the room, exchanging a few words here and there with other guests, and for several minutes talking with Glen and Maddie.

When the bride and groom left, Paige kept her hands at her sides as Maddie tossed her bouquet into the crowd of well-wishers, allowing an excited young girl to catch it.

She was looking forward to slipping away now her duties were over. She couldn't have turned down Maddie's tentative request to attend her, hedged about with anxious assurances that Maddie would understand if she didn't want to. But now she felt drained and tired, with an incipient headache beating at her temples.

She sought out her mother and said quietly, "Do you mind if I go on home now? I'm not needed anymore."

"Of course, dear." Margaret searched her face. "Your father and I have to stay until everyone's gone, but I'm sure Blake would drive you…" Margaret looked around for the best man.

"No, give me my purse and I'll call a taxi. There's a phone in the lobby."

"Well...if you're sure."

"Yes. I'll see you in the morning." Paige leaned down and kissed her mother's cheek. "It was a lovely wedding."

"Yes, wasn't it?" Margaret glowed. At least this time she'd launched a daughter into matrimony in style.

In the lobby Paige found a card pinned above the phone with the number of a taxi company printed on it, and was dialing the final digit when a lean, strong hand came over her shoulder and pressed down the bar, leaving the dial tone humming in her ear.

"You don't need them," Jager's voice said. "I'll take you home."

Her hand tightened on the receiver. She didn't turn. "Thank you," she said, "but I'd prefer a cab."

"Why? My car's right outside."

Why? She couldn't think of an answer that didn't sound either unnecessarily rude or like an overreaction.

He lifted his hand and gently removed the receiver from her grasp, replacing it in the cradle. Belatedly she said, "I wouldn't want to take you out of your way..."

He didn't even bother to reply to that, already steering her toward the doors that swished open at their approach. "Where are you staying?"

"With my parents." She waited for some caustic remark, but all he said was, "The car's over here."

It was long and shiny, a dark navy-blue, she guessed, though it was difficult to tell at night.

The interior was spacious and the upholstery was real, soft leather.

Unless he was living beyond his means Jager had come up in the world. Her father had said something about him apparently doing well.

He slid into the seat beside her and buckled up his safety belt. When he turned the key in the ignition she scarcely heard the engine start, but they were soon gliding out of the car park.

"So," he said, "you came home for your sister's wedding. Last I heard you were living in New York."

"Yes." Paige shifted uneasily in the leather seat. "And you…? What are you doing now?"

He spared her a glance. "I run a telecommunications business, providing systems for industry."

"Is it a big business?"

"Big enough." He shrugged. "We're expanding all the time, increasing staff numbers."

"It sounds…interesting."

"It's challenging. New technologies are being invented and refined all the time. We have to stay a jump ahead, deciding which innovations are a flash in the pan and which will become industry standards."

"It sounds risky?"

"I've built a solid enough base that we can afford the odd risk. So far I haven't been wrong."

"You must be proud of yourself."

He seemed to ponder that. "Pride is what goes before a fall, isn't it?"

"Are you afraid of falling?"

He laughed, with that new, somehow disturbing male confidence. "Not anymore. Are you?"

She looked away from him, not answering.

He gave her a second or two, then said quite soberly, "I learned a long time ago, no matter how hard the fall, I can survive. And I never make the same mistake twice."

"It seems like a sound philosophy." She'd survived too. And she had no intention of scaling any heights again with him.

He said, "I heard you got married in America."

"Yes."

"Did your parents approve?"

"Yes, actually." They had come to the wedding, given their blessing.

"But you're alone now."

She didn't want his sympathy. Even less did she want to bare her feelings to him, of all people. To take the conversation away from herself she asked, "Are you married?"

The first question that had come to mind, but immediately she regretted asking. It could lead to a minefield.

"Like I said," he replied, "I never make the same mistake twice."

"Marriage isn't always a mistake," she said.

It left him an opening, she realized, and was thankful that he didn't take it. He gunned the motor and the car leaped forward before he lifted his foot slightly and the engine settled back into its subdued growl. When he spoke again his voice was remote and cool. "I suppose you can't wait to get back to…America."

Evasively she answered, "I'll be spending some time with my family."

"How much time…days, weeks?" He paused. "Months?"

"I'm not sure."

He flashed a glance at her. "He must be pretty accommodating…your husband."

Her thoughts skittering, she realized Jager didn't know…

Why should he? Her mouth dried, and her throat ached. She stared through the windscreen with wide-open eyes until they stung and she had to blink. "My husband—"

She didn't see the other car until it was right in front of them—it seemed to have come from nowhere, the headlights blinding, so close that her voice broke off in a choked scream and she raised her arms before her face, knowing that despite Jager's frantic wrench at the wheel, accompanied by a sharp, shocking expletive, there was no way he could avoid a collision.

A horrified sense of inevitability mixed with cold, stark terror, and the awareness that maybe this was how—and when—she was going to die.

With Jager, said a clear inner voice, and the thought carried with it both tearing grief and a strange, fleeting sensation of gladness.

The heavy thump and screech of metal on metal filled her ears and the impact jolted her against the seat belt. She was vaguely aware of the windscreen, glimpsed between her shielding arms, going white and opaque, then it disappeared and the two cars, locked together, slid across the road in a slow, agonizing waltz until they came to a jarring halt against a building.

Daring to lower her arms, Paige heard Jager's voice, seemingly somewhere in the far distance. "Paige—*Paige!* Are you all right?"

His hand gripped her shoulder, and by the light of a street lamp she saw his face, a deathly color, with dark thin trickles of moisture running from his forehead, his cheeks and his eyes blazing.

"You're bleeding," she said, raising an unsteady hand to touch one of the small rivulets, wanting suddenly to cry. She couldn't bear the thought of him being disfigured.

"Never mind that," he said impatiently. "Are you hurt?" His hands slid from her shoulders down her arms, and he swore vehemently. "You're bleeding too."

She was, from several tiny glass nicks on her bare forearms. "It's nothing." She moved her legs, found them whole and unhurt. "I'm all right. Are you?"

"Nothing broken."

In the background someone was yelling. Car doors slammed and then a face peered into the space left by the broken windscreen. "The police and ambulance are on their way," said a male voice. "Anyone hurt in there?"

"We're okay," Jager answered. "Can you get the passenger door open? My side's too badly damaged."

* * *

Ambulance staff checked them both and told them they were lucky, but to contact an emergency medical service if they experienced delayed symptoms.

The other driver, miraculously walking, though groggy and with a broken arm, was taken to hospital. While the police were noncommittal when they breath-tested Jager and took statements from both him and Paige, it was fairly obvious the injured man had been drinking.

Within half an hour the cars had been dragged away and the police offered to take Paige and Jager home.

Jager gave them Paige's parents' address and climbed into the car beside her. He handed her purse to her and she realized he'd retrieved it from the wreckage.

When the car drew up outside the house he got out and helped her to the pavement, and said to the driver, "Thanks a lot. We appreciate the lift."

He had his arm around her and was urging her to the gateway as the police car pulled away from the kerb.

"Don't you want them to take you home?" she said. "You don't need to come in with me."

"It doesn't look like your parents are in yet. I'm not leaving you alone."

The garden lights were on—they were on an automatic timer—but the house was in darkness.

When she drew out the key Jager took it from her and opened the door, closing it behind them as he accompanied her into the wide entryway. He found the light switch and she said, "The burglar alarm. You have to press that yellow button on the key-tag."

He found it and then handed the key on its electronic tag back to her. She felt a trickle of moisture on her forehead and lifted a hand to find the source, wincing as her fingers encountered something sharp. She stared at the tiny droplet of blood on her finger. "I've got glass in my hair."

Jager had regained some of his normal color, but his eyes were darkened in the center, the irises now more gray than green, his mouth tight as he surveyed her. "We need a bathroom," he said, "to clean up."

There was one off her room, shared with the bedroom that had been her sister's when they both lived at home. "Come upstairs," she offered. It was the least she could do.

Jager's face was streaked with blood too, and there were red spots on his shirt. His hair was ruffled out of its sleek styling, speckled with sparkling fragments of glass.

He followed her up the wide marble staircase, carpeted in the middle so that their footsteps were silent.

The door to her room was open. Paige swiftly crossed to the bathroom, switching on the light. White and merciless, it shone on shiny decorative tiles and a glass-enclosed shower, bold gold-plated taps and big fluffy towels.

She took a towel and facecloth from a pile on a shelf, handing a set to Jager. "You'd better wash your face."

While he did so she opened one of the mirrored

cupboards, grimacing at her pale reflection, with a smear of blood across the forehead.

As Jager dried himself she turned with a comb in her hand, holding it out to him. "Wait. I'll get something to catch the glass." If they used one of the towels the slivers would be caught in the pile.

In the bedroom she removed a pillowcase, leaving the covers rumpled, and hurried back to spread it on the bathroom floor. "Now you can comb the glass out of your hair."

"You first." He reached out, lifted her spectacles from her nose and placed them on the marble counter. Before she could protest his hand curled around her nape, warm and compelling.

"I can do my own."

"You can't see it," he replied calmly. "Bend forward a bit, honey. You don't want glass down your cleavage."

The casual endearment had caught her unawares, sending a soft warmth through her. Afraid he'd read the heat in her cheeks, and maybe something in her eyes that she didn't want him to see, she bowed her head.

His fingers slid gently through her hair from nape to crown, followed by the stroke of the comb. Fragments of glass made a tiny pattering on the pillowcase. He combed carefully though the fine strands, then gave a muttered exclamation, and she felt a prickle of pain.

"This might hurt," he said tersely. She held her breath, and bit her lip against a sudden sting.

"There." He dropped a bloodied sliver on the pillowcase. "It was embedded, but I think I've got it all. Don't move."

He grabbed a facecloth and ran cold water on it, then she felt the coolness pressed to the place where the glass had pierced the skin. "It's bleeding a bit," he said, "but it wasn't deep."

"You're bleeding more than I am." He'd taken the full force of the shattered windscreen, too busy fighting for both their lives to even try to protect himself as she had done.

"It's nothing. Just a few nicks." He lifted the cloth. "That's better. Do you have some disinfectant?"

"Not necessary." She lifted her head. "I'm fine, really."

"Really." He sounded as if he didn't believe her. His free hand caught her chin, a frown of concentration on his brow. "You didn't get any in your face."

"No." She stepped back, but now he took her hand, and led her to the wide basin. "We haven't finished yet." He put in the plug and turned on a tap with one hand, still holding her in a firm grip with the other.

"Look, I—"

"Shh," he admonished. "Hold still."

He gently wiped the remaining blood from her forehead and bathed her arms, washing away the red streaks, leaving only tiny puncture wounds. "You were lucky," he said. "We both were."

The water had turned pale pink and he let it out, reached for one of the towels and patted her skin dry. "You'll want to change." He was eyeing her ruined dress—streaked with blood, and torn where she'd caught it on something as they were helped out of the car.

Paige recalled worrying about the wine stain, seemingly aeons ago, and thought how little it mattered. They might both have been killed.

She shivered, remembering the horrible, stark fear of those few moments when the world seemed about to end for her. And for Jager.

His hands closed over her arms. "It's all right. You're all right."

"I know." But her voice was unsteady and she couldn't stop trembling. She supposed shock was setting in.

Jager drew her toward him, but then he stopped and cursed under his breath, looking down at his bloodied clothes. "Can you get out of that dress by yourself?" he asked her.

Paige nodded jerkily. But she didn't move, and the tremors that racked her were getting worse.

"Here." He turned her, and she felt the zipper at the back of the ruined dress being opened, all the way to the end of her spine. Then the dress was lifted away from her shoulders and it slithered to her feet, leaving her in a mauve half-cup bra, matching bikini briefs and a pair of lace-topped stockings that were snagged and laddered.

"Step out of it," Jager said.

Like an automaton she obeyed, lifting one foot from the tangled satin of the dress. Her shoe caught in the folds and she lost her balance, kicking off the other shoe in an effort to regain it.

Jager's hands closed about her arms, swung her around to face him, and her hand momentarily flattened against his chest.

Her startled eyes met his, and her trembling abruptly stopped.

The particles of glass caught in the blackness of his hair sparkled like a scattering of diamonds, and his eyes had the sheen of polished jade. The flawless male skin was marked by small wounds, one trickling a thin line of blood onto his cheekbone.

Unconsciously Paige touched her tongue to her upper lip, bringing Jager's gaze to her mouth. Another tremor shook her body, and his head jerked up a fraction. His hands tightened but he kept the few inches space between them. "Have you got something warm to put on?" he asked her, his voice low and rough.

Paige blinked, nodded.

"Then go and do it," he ordered. "I'll clean up in here." He gave her a little push. "Go on."

She did, dragging a thick terry-cloth robe from her wardrobe. When Jager pulled the bathroom door wide and entered the bedroom she was tying the sash at her waist, clumsily because her hands were shaking. Her torn stockings lay on the bed.

The light no longer picked up glints from his hair. He must have combed out the glass. And he'd taken off his jacket—and his shirt. To wash out the bloodstains, she supposed. "I tossed the glass in the waste bin," he said. "And the pillowcase into the clothes basket. What do you want to do with this?" He had her dress in his hands.

"Leave it." She was trying to be calm and controlled, but little shivers kept attacking her in waves. Despite the heavy toweling wrap she felt cold. Her gaze went to the dress in his hands. "I'll have to throw it out."

A faint, knowing contempt touched his mouth, and she said defensively, "It's ruined." It might be a waste but the dress was beyond repair.

He looked down at the crushed and stained fabric. "Pity. You looked marvelous in it."

He began folding it, clumsy but careful.

She had never looked *marvelous* in anything. She'd looked good in it, Paige knew—as good as she ever would. But it was silly to feel a pleased glow at the compliment.

The shiny fabric slipped in his hands, his attempt at folding coming to grief.

"It doesn't matter," Paige said, unaccountably irritated. "Give it to me."

She crossed to him and took the dress from him and into the bathroom, where she shoved the thing willy-nilly into the rubbish container in the corner, slamming the lid back on.

Jager's shirt was spread across the heated towel rail, damp in patches. She couldn't see his jacket, and supposed he'd hung it on the hook behind the door.

When she turned he was standing in the doorway, watching her.

Defensively she folded her arms across herself as she made her way back into the bedroom. Jager stood aside but as she passed him she caught a whiff of his skin-scent, bringing back unbearably powerful, poignant memories. Warm nights and a warm bed, and

Jager's warm raw-silk nakedness under her hands, against her own heated skin...

Hurriedly she moved away from him, and turned to find him looking at the ruined stockings lying on the bed, but then he lifted his eyes and they seemed to be searching for something in hers.

She should look away. Instead she found her gaze wandering to his mouth, a mouth made for temptation, for seduction. A mouth that could wreak magic on a woman's body. And his broad chest, a masculine perfection where her hands had once roamed at will, where she'd lain her cheek against his heart after making love. Her eyes reached the discreet silver buckle of the belt that snugged his dark trousers to his slim waist, and her heartbeat quickened.

She didn't have her glasses on, she reminded herself. Any flaws would be mercifully invisible to her. No man could possibly look as good as Jager did right now.

"Enjoying yourself?"

His voice brought her back with a start to what she was doing.

She tried to brazen it out. "Just checking. I would have thought you'd at least have bruises."

He flexed his right shoulder and shifted his leg, apparently testing. "I may have, tomorrow." He grimaced.

"You *were* hurt! Why didn't you tell the ambulance officers?"

"It's nothing. They gave me a pretty thorough going-over."

"They're not doctors."

"I'm fine." He swung the arm to show her. "See?"

Unconvinced, but conscious of how much worse it might have been, she shivered again. "You might have been killed."

"So might you." He looked grim suddenly. "You're still cold. Maybe you should have a warm shower and get into bed."

"With you here?"

"I won't join you—unless I'm invited."

"You're not invited!"

He folded his arms across that splendid chest, and looked regretful. "I thought not. But don't let me stop you." As she hesitated, he said, "This is no time to be prudish, Paige. It'll be at least fifteen minutes before my shirt is dry. You might as well use the time—unless you'd rather spend it talking to me."

No, she wouldn't...would she? Paige plumped for the lesser evil. "All right," she mumbled, and made for the bathroom.

The shower felt good. Wincing at the tender spot where Jager had dug glass from her scalp, she washed her hair. Five minutes with the hair dryer left it shining and soft, and she put her undies into the clothes basket and pulled the terry gown back on, because she hadn't thought to bring anything else into the bathroom with her.

She fingered Jager's shirt and lifted it from the towel rail, switched on the hair dryer again to play it over the remaining dampness, then returned to the bedroom with the shirt in her hand. "It's dry," she told him.

"Thanks." He'd been lounging on the bed, his head propped on the pillows. The sight gave her a start; he looked so much at home, as if he belonged there.

He stood up and stretched out his hand for the shirt, but then, as if he couldn't help it, his hand bypassed the shirt and touched her hair, stroked its newly washed sleekness, and his thumb traced the outline of her ear.

Paige's heart stopped. She forgot to breathe. Couldn't speak. Her eyelids fell of their own accord, before she jerked them open. "What are you doing?"

His hand had come to a stop, a hank of her hair trapped in his fist. "Where's your husband?" His voice was deep and indistinct, and his jewel-eyes glittered into hers. "Damn him, why isn't he here looking after you?"

The unexpected question widened her eyes, and her lips parted on a caught breath. Obscure anger shook her. "I'm a grown woman, Jager. I don't need a man to *look after* me." Never mind that Jager had done just that tonight, very competently, for which until this moment she'd been grateful. "And as for my husband," she added huskily, and took a deep breath, "he...Aidan's..."

"Not here," Jager said harshly. And then his other arm came around her body, crushing her against him, and his mouth on hers smothered the words she was trying to say, sent her thoughts spinning into deep space and made her forget everything except his kiss.

CHAPTER THREE

IT WAS a kiss that took her breath, her heart, her soul. She couldn't think, couldn't move, except to lift her arms and cling, as if she were drowning in the wine-dark sea of desire and he was her only hope of survival.

The blood running through her veins sang his name, her skin was licked by fire, her limbs turned to liquid flame. The taste of him was an intoxication, the hard length of his body against hers a ravishment.

She opened her mouth to him and he took swift advantage of the invitation, making the kiss deeper, unashamedly sensual, a merciless invasion of her senses.

His hand pushed aside the front of her robe and settled on her breast, his thumb and forefinger finding the budding center, making her moan with ecstasy and arch herself against him, triumphant when she recognized the thrust of his arousal pressing at the apex of her thighs.

She brought one hand down to his bared chest in imitation of his caress, reveling in the heat and slight dampness of his skin against her palm, once as familiar to her as her own body.

Then his mouth left hers and his arms lowered, lifting her. She gasped, clutching at his shoulders, and his lips closed over her breast. With an inarticulate cry of pleasure, she let her head fall back. Dizzy and disoriented, she was wholly given over to sensation.

She hardly realized he had swung them round until his mouth momentarily left her and they fell together onto the bed. Before she'd drawn breath he impatiently untied the belt of her robe and bared her body to his hot, questing gaze. She stared back at him boldly as his hands traversed her from neck to knee, rediscovering the shape of her breasts, her hips, her thighs. There was color on his lean cheekbones, and his fingers were unsteady, his eyes heavy-lidded and glowing with desire. That look had always filled her with wonder—wonder that *she* could do this to him. That he wanted her so much.

One hand slipped between her thighs, and the other left her to undo his belt. He stroked her softly until she was wild with need, then stood for a few seconds to shuck the remainder of his clothing and sheath himself. Watching, she was briefly thankful that he'd thought of it, then he was beside her, taking her again into his arms, answering her frantic, silent plea to let her take him in, to experience the whole of him, and at last, without equivocation or delay, filling her with himself, driving her to the pinnacle and beyond, to that nameless place where past and present and future didn't exist, but only the blinding, transcendental moment.

While the world drifted back into focus Paige resisted opening her eyes. Her cheek rested on Jager's shoulder, and her legs were still tangled with his, his arm warm around her.

He moved, and she held her breath, afraid he would

leave, but he only settled closer, enfolding her again. He kissed her closed eyelids, then feathered more tiny kisses along her cheek, and down her neck to her shoulder. She smiled, and he kissed her lips, long and tenderly, with an underlying hint of passion. Against her mouth, he murmured, "Tissues?"

Paige gave a little laugh, and reached without looking for the drawer of the bedside table.

Eventually she had to open her eyes. Jager was on his way to the bathroom, giving her a heart stopping view of his naked back, but in minutes he returned. She said sleepily, "Turn off the light."

He detoured to do it, then came back to her, drawing her again into his arms and pulling a sheet over them both. "That was to dream of," he said. "But too damn quick."

His palm spanning her belly, he teased her navel with his thumb, while his lips wandered along her shoulder, nuzzling and nibbling. Her eyelids fluttered down, and a deliciously lethargic pleasure rippled all the way to her toes. As Jager's hands and his mouth pleasured and tantalized, she moved her body subtly under his ministrations, allowing him better access there, hinting that some attention would be appreciated here.

He had always been good at this, she thought, a hint of sadness penetrating the dreamy aura he was creating. A silent tear trembled at the corner of her eye and coursed into her hair.

Jager found the salty track with his lips, and murmured, "What? Crying?"

"No," she denied, not wanting to think about what

had been or what might have been, or what might still be. She turned her head and met his lips with hers, aligned her body with his, thrust her knee between his thighs, to blot out the thoughts, the memories.

Jager responded with a surge of passion, and when she opened herself to him again and welcomed him with a sigh of satisfaction, he came to her as deeply and completely as before, but until the moment when he shuddered uncontrollably against her, a muffled sound tearing from his throat, there was gentleness in him this time, a tender concern in his touch.

Afterward he didn't leave her side, holding her close in his arms until she drifted into an exhausted, velvety sleep. Her last thought was that he'd be gone by morning, and her heart gave a small throbbing ache at the prospect.

When she woke a weak morning sun was streaming though the window. Jager, fully dressed but without tie or jacket, leaned on the window frame, watching her.

"Oh, God!" She closed her eyes again, hoping he was a figment of her imagination. Or perhaps she was still dreaming.

"I didn't think I looked that bad," he said.

Paige opened her eyes again. He was fingering his chin, his eyes both wary and amused. He'd shaved, and his hair was damp and sleek. He must have used her bathroom, borrowed a razor, and she hadn't heard a thing. "You've been here all night?" she said.

A dark brow rose. "You don't remember? I'm disappointed. Shall I tell you what we did?"

"I know what we did!" Foolishly, she felt her cheeks burn. "I thought you'd leave before...now."

"You mean before your parents find out I'm here."

Paige clamped her lips. It was what she'd meant. No point in restating the obvious.

Vaguely she recalled hearing a car, the sounds of her parents' return, but she wasn't sure when. She'd been too engrossed in Jager, in the pleasure he was giving her, to even care.

She felt at a distinct disadvantage, lying naked in bed while he stood there patently at ease, his arms loosely folded. Clutching at the sheet for modesty, she sat up and looked around for something to put on.

Jager moved, a little awkwardly, stooping to pick up the toweling robe from the floor. "Is this what you want?"

"Thank you." She had to drop the sheet to take it and pull it on, and he didn't turn away.

Kicking away the bedclothes, she swung her feet to the floor, belting the robe. When she stood up he was close by, only a foot or two from the bed, his hands now thrust into the pockets of his trousers. "You should have told me if you wanted me to leave," he said.

"Would you have?"

"What the lady wants, the lady gets." The mockery in his voice reminded her that last night she'd wanted *him*—desperately, recklessly. Without any thought of consequences and repercussions.

Well, this was what she'd got. She looked at the clock. She could hear sounds of stirring in the house. There was little hope of spiriting Jager out without being seen. Being caught trying would be more embarrassing than fronting up about his presence.

Maybe reading her thoughts, he said, "I could climb out the window, but the neighbors might notice."

Paige said stiffly, "If you wait until I'm dressed, we'll go downstairs and I'll explain we were involved in an accident and you were slightly injured so...as my sister's room was free, you stayed overnight."

Momentarily his jaw tightened. "And I'm supposed to go along with that?"

Her gaze fell away as she said, "I hope you will."

"I don't suppose they'll swallow it." He paused. "Will they tell your husband? Will *you?*"

Her eyes swung back to him, wide with shock.

"What sort of man is he?" Jager queried harshly. "If he hurts you..." His hands clenched into fists, and his expression turned dangerous.

Paige took a moment to orient herself. "Do you think I'd have slept with you if...?" Stopping short, she swallowed and took a deep, sustaining breath. "You have no idea," she said, gathering dignity to herself like a shield, "what you're talking about. My husband died six months ago."

For once she saw Jager rocked off balance. His expression went totally blank, his cheeks almost colorless. The firm, stubborn chin jerked up as if he'd been hit, and his body seemed to go rigid.

Before he could pull himself together, she'd marched across the carpet into the bathroom, locking the door behind her.

* * *

When she came out Jager had recovered his equilibrium, although he looked a trifle paler than usual. His eyes were shuttered, with the watchful, not-giving-anything-away look that he'd worn for much of the previous day. He had taken up a stance near the door to the passageway, his back to the frame, hands in his pockets.

"Why didn't you tell me before?" he asked her.

Paige was opening a drawer to pull out undies. "I was trying to when we crashed. When I realized you didn't know." She went to the built-in wardrobe and opened the double doors. They made an effective screen as she blindly reached for a pair of jeans and hauled them on.

"You didn't say anything last night...here."

Paige found a sweater and pulled it over her head. What was she supposed to have done? Paused in the middle of that mind-blowing lovemaking and said, *By the way, did you know my husband died?*

She adjusted the sweater over her hips. "The subject didn't come up."

Stepping out of the screening doors, she closed them with a snap. When she went to the dressing table she could see Jager behind her and to one side. She picked up a hairbrush and flicked it cursorily over her hair. Last night she'd omitted the customary fifty strokes, but with him watching she wasn't inclined to make up for it now.

"We might as well go down," she said, replacing the brush.

"And get it over with?"

Paige shrugged, on her way to the door.

His hand on the knob, Jager said, "I should say I'm sorry about your husband."

That was an odd way of putting it, but he looked sober, even genuinely sympathetic. She nodded. "Thank you."

For a long moment he stood just looking at her, his gaze probing and perhaps puzzled. Then he opened the door and waited for her to precede him.

Their appearing together in the breakfast room caused a distinct shock to her parents, but on the face of it they seemed to accept Paige's explanation. At the mention of an accident her mother was more concerned with any likely injuries than where—or how— Jager had spent the night. She peered at Paige's face anxiously. "You might have been scarred!"

"I'm not," Paige pointed out. "We were lucky."

She invited Jager to sit at the table, and offered him toast and coffee. Her mother, after a minute or two, switched to hostess mode and asked if he'd like bacon and eggs.

"No, thanks," he answered. "Coffee and toast is fine."

Her father turned to Jager. "You hurt your leg?" he asked gruffly.

Jager had come down behind Paige and she hadn't noticed anything wrong. She looked at him. Was it an act to back up her story?

"Nothing's broken," Jager answered her father, just as he'd told her. "I'm a bit stiff after last night." He glanced at Paige, and she looked hastily away. "I seem to have muscles I never knew about."

"What about you, Paige?" Henry asked. "Perhaps we should take you to a doctor just in case."

"I'm all right. The impact was mostly on the driver's side."

Jager had made sure of that, turning the wheel as far as he could before the other car hit. Startled by the thought, she looked at him. "Were you trying to save me?"

He looked back at her for a moment, then shrugged. "I was trying to save us both. Instinct took over."

An instinct that put him directly into the path of an oncoming car? Paige curled her hand around the cup of coffee she'd poured for herself. He'd have done it for anyone, she guessed. Any woman, at least. A natural male reaction maybe, latent even in twenty-first century man.

"I'm grateful anyway."

Her mother said, "I'm sure we all are."

Jager's mouth twitched at the corners as he turned to Margaret. "Thank you, but I don't need gratitude, Mrs. Camden." His tone, although perfectly courteous, implied he didn't need anything—not from her nor her husband. "And Paige has already shown hers." His eyes sought her apprehensive gaze and he continued smoothly, "She patched up my wounds, such as they were, and insisted I stay the night."

Margaret's eyes too went to her daughter. Paige avoided her gaze, reaching for marmalade that she didn't need. "The cuts looked worse than they were," she said. "I'll wash the things from the bathroom later. And the sheets from Maddie's room." She didn't want her mother or the cleaning woman who would come tomorrow noticing that Maddie's bed hadn't been slept in. And she'd certainly be washing the sheets from her own bed.

Paige had little appetite, and Jager ate quickly and sparingly before pushing back his chair. After thanking Margaret he said, "I'll collect my things from...upstairs and be on my way."

Paige rose too, noticing that he winced as he stood up, his grip on the chair back turning his knuckles momentarily white.

He was limping as they left the room, and he gripped the banister all the way up the stairs.

In the bathroom he picked up his jacket and tie, then came back to her room. "Thanks," he said, "for everything."

"I could borrow a car and run you home."

He seemed to be trying to read her expression before shaking his head. "I'll call a cab."

"If you like."

They were standing feet apart, and it seemed he was as tongue-tied as she.

Then he moved, came close and lifted her chin with his big, capable hand. "What was it about—last night—Paige? For you?"

Paige struggled for words. It had been unexpected, out of character and, in the light of day, inappropriate.

But fantastic, an inner voice reminded her.

Trying to ignore that, she said huskily, "I don't know. I suppose...reaction to the accident." She'd heard danger was an aphrodisiac, but had always found the theory difficult to believe. Maybe there was something in it after all." "And," she added, determined not to flinch from the truth, "it's some time since I...since I had sex."

His eyes narrowed, so that she couldn't read their expression. "Since you were widowed?"

The brutal question stiffened her spine, and she stepped back, away from his light grasp. "Yes," she said harshly. "If you must know." Surely he didn't think she made a habit of one-night stands?

"And before that," Jager's voice was soft, "did your husband fulfill your needs?"

"Yes!" she shot at him, and then firmly clamped her mouth. She wouldn't discuss Aidan with him. And her sexual needs were her own business.

His mouth too had tightened, to an ominous line. What did he want, a confession that he was king in the bedroom? He wouldn't get it from her.

"So," he said, "where do we go from here?"

Be strong, she exhorted herself. We've been down that road once and it only leads to heartache. Heartache and emptiness. "We're not going anywhere, Jager. Last night was...nice..."

"Nice!"

"...but it doesn't mean we have any kind of...relationship."

"We have a relationship," he argued, "whether you like it or not. Whether your family likes it or not."

"Had," she insisted. "Past tense."

"You know that's not true!"

Rallying herself, she argued, "It's true for me. I've

moved on, and I don't want to go back. Whatever we had in the beginning didn't last long, did it?"

"It might have if—"

Paige said sharply, "Better not to go there, surely. We'll only start fighting again, and I don't want that."

"Neither do I."

"Then leave it, Jager...please? Last night...maybe it was a mistake, but let's not spoil the memory by parting in anger."

He looked belligerent and frustrated, but finally nodded curtly. "All right. You've made your point. You won't object to one goodbye kiss?"

Without giving her a chance to do so, he crossed the space between them and took her shoulders in his hands, bending his head to part her lips with his mouth.

Paige tried to remain unmoved, but the persuasion of his mouth moving across hers softened her resistance, and although she somehow kept her hands clenched at her sides her mouth gave him back kiss for kiss.

Then she was free. Jager gave her a hard look, nodded briefly as if satisfied, and turned to limp to the door.

Trailing after him, she felt uneasy despite his apparent capitulation, and there was a hollow feeling in her midriff that threatened to turn into panic.

She had done the right thing, she assured herself when his cab had collected him. There was no future for her with Jager. Once bitten was enough.

Turning her mind to practicalities, she hurried upstairs and stripped the beds in both bedrooms, bundled up the sheets with the used towels and cloths from the bathroom and took them down to the laundry.

Her mother found her sprinkling washing powder into the machine. "Paige? What on *earth* were you thinking of? I'd have thought you'd have more sense than to let that young man drive you home. And as for inviting him to stay...! I suppose he'd been drinking."

An emotion familiar from long ago made Paige clench her teeth. Busying herself with the control panel she said, "He offered me a ride and it seemed silly to refuse. The accident wasn't his fault, Mother. I suppose he'd have had a glass or two of wine at the reception, but he was under the limit when the police tested him. And he probably saved my life—or at least saved me from being injured."

"You're defending him again," Margaret accused shrilly. "Just as you always did."

"I'm trying to be fair." Jager didn't need her to defend him—he never had. She'd expended a lot of energy doing it nevertheless, and alienated herself from her family. She didn't want that to happen again. "Don't worry, I won't be seeing him anymore."

Relief flooded Margaret's face. "I'm so glad to hear that, darling!" She stepped forward to put her arms around her daughter. "He was never suitable for you, you know that."

"Yes," Paige said dully. "I know."

She did know. Her parents had been right all along, so why did the words make her feel like a traitor?

* * *

The following day while she was helping her mother pack some wedding presents that had been sent to the house, ready for the honeymooners' return, the phone rang and the cleaning woman called her.

Picking up in the spacious foyer, she wished she'd chosen a less public extension when Jager's voice answered her brief hello with a simple, spine-tingling, "Paige."

Her breath momentarily stopped. She found herself looking about furtively for anyone within earshot, but the cleaning woman had disappeared and her mother was still busy with wrappers and boxes in another room. "What do you want?"

For a second he didn't reply. When he did there was a subtle change in his tone. "That's a leading question."

"It wasn't meant to be." Remembering his limp yesterday, she said, "Are you all right?"

"Yes. What about you?"

"Perfectly. Is that why you rang?"

"Not the only reason. What are you doing tonight?"

"Nothing—I mean, nothing that involves you."

He gave a short laugh. "That's blunt."

"I'm sorry."

"Are you? Then why cut off your nose to spite your face—or is it to keep the peace with your family?"

"I don't think there's any point in raking over old...embers."

"They were more than embers the other night."

Paige bit her lip as a warm tide of remembrance

washed over her. "It didn't mean anything—if we hadn't both been reacting to the shock of nearly being killed it would never have happened."

"Not then, maybe..."

"Not ever. And it will never happen again."

"If I were a betting man..."

She knew she'd made a mistake. Jager could never resist a challenge. "Jager," she said, closing her eyes tightly. "Don't. It's only six months since I lost my husband. Maddie's wedding was a bit of a strain, then with the accident coming on top of it...I guess I wasn't thinking straight."

"And now you're regretting it." His voice had hardened.

Obviously he didn't share her regret. "It didn't mean anything! So please, leave it at that."

"What if I can't?"

"It takes two," she argued. "And I hope you'll respect my feelings."

"I respect your feelings," he said. "Why don't you?"

"What do you mean?"

"Think about it," he advised dryly, "and let me know when you've sorted them out."

She heard the gentle click in her ear with a mixture of anger and relief. Let him know when she'd sorted out her feelings? Hell would freeze while he waited.

When she had allowed Jager to believe she would be returning to America, Paige had been less than frank. She had come home prepared to review her future and start a new chapter in her life. And grateful for the support of her family.

By the time Maddie and Glen returned from their honeymoon, Paige had a job doing graphic design in a large printing firm, and she'd bought a cottage perched on the edge of the inner harbor. The back of the house gave a view of the water through native trees growing on a steep slope.

"Mother thinks you're nuts," Maddie told her candidly the first time she and Glen visited, finding Paige scraping flaky paint from a window frame. "She expected you to get a place in the city. Something low maintenance and—well, not like this."

"So did I, really."

She had only looked at this place because of its location. When the estate agent told her he had an old cottage on a neglected section with native bush and a sea boundary, she'd envisaged demolishing it and putting up a new home to her own design, but something about the shabby, sleepy-looking cottage appealed to her, and impulsively she'd decided instead to rescue it.

Glen surveyed the tired paint and sagging porch. "It'll take more than a lick of paint to fix this up."

Reluctantly Paige put down the scraper. "Can I make you two a cuppa?"

Inside, Glen looked around the small, dark living room and scuffed his toe on its worn carpet. "I bet there's kauri under that. Or rimu, maybe."

There probably was. Most old houses had native timber on the floors.

"They come up beautifully with modern finishes," he added.

"Glen's a frustrated handyman," Maddie told her. "He wanted us to buy an old villa and fix it up, but living in the middle of renovations would drive me crazy. We have friends who've been 'doing up' for years!"

"This will be a big job for one woman," Glen commented. "You're not planning to do everything yourself are you, Paige?"

"It's already been rewired and reroofed. I'll hire professionals to fix cupboards in the kitchen and renovate the bathroom. But I hope to do a lot."

"I'm a dab hand with a paintbrush," Glen said.

Maddie rolled her eyes. "For heaven's sake, Paige, take pity on the poor guy and let him help you."

Laughing, Paige said, "I'll take all the help I can get." Glen's attitude was refreshing after her father's frowning comment that she should have asked his advice before being talked into a lemon by a slick real estate agent, and her mother's scarcely concealed horror.

"There!" Maddie kissed Glen lightly. "You're hired."

He grinned down at her, hooking an arm around her waist to kiss her back. Paige looked on with a pang of envy. She was glad Maddie had found someone who obviously adored her and was committed to sharing their future. But in comparison her own future looked bleak and lonely.

"By the way," Maddie said, breaking reluctantly away, "we're having a dinner party Saturday night for the families, mine and Glen's. You're invited, of course."

Of course she was, and of course she had to go. It wasn't until the day before the party that Maddie told her Jager would be there too. "Glen took it for granted that his family includes Jager now. His mother is being awfully good since she found out. She told Jager he's welcome in their home anytime. You will still come, won't you? Only I thought I should warn you, when I realized what Glen had done."

"Are you going to warn Mother and Dad too?"

Maddie groaned. "I suppose I should. I hope this party isn't going to be a disaster!"

"It won't. Mother will turn on her best manners, and Dad will follow her lead."

And as for her, Paige resolved, she would do her utmost to ensure that Maddie's first postwedding party went as smoothly as possible.

When Paige arrived at Maddie and Glen's third-floor apartment in the central city, Jager was already there, looking relaxed and urbane with a shot glass in his hand and talking to Glen's parents.

Maddie ushered Paige in and Jager got up, crossing the thick deep blue carpet to kiss her cheek. "Paige," he said, "how are you?"

Even that light touch sent a tingle right to her toes. Without quite meeting his eyes, she said she was fine, thank you, and how was his injured leg?

"No problems. I told you it was only bruised."

Glen asked her what she'd like to drink, and somehow she found herself seated next to Jager on one of the three leather couches arranged in a U shape. The room was a picture of understated modern elegance. Glen was a junior partner in his father's law firm, and Maddie worked for an advertising company. Their family connections ensured they had no need to be upwardly mobile, nor, despite Glen's yen to be a handyman, any need to do their own decorating.

Glen's mother said, "You two know each other?"

While Paige was wondering how much her sister had told Glen, Jager said, "We knew each other very well at one time." He glanced at Paige. "It's not exactly a secret. As a matter of fact, we were married."

Mrs. Provost's mouth opened in surprise. "Married?"

Paige said, "It was a long time ago. We were very young and...it didn't last long."

Mr. Provost raised his eyebrows and shook his head. "New Zealand is such a small country, but...well. Quite a coincidence."

Glen handed Paige a glass that she accepted gratefully, glad to have something to concentrate on. His mother said, "Did you know this, Glen?"

He cast an apologetic look at Paige. "Maddie told me."

Paige took a gulp of the wine he'd given her. "As Jager says, it's no secret."

"I'm glad to see you can still be friends," Mrs. Provost said warmly. "I do think it's sad when two people who've found they made a mistake can hardly be civil to each other."

"So do I," Jager agreed.

Friendship had never entered into the equation, Paige thought, looking back. Their feelings had been too raw and white-hot for anything so tepid as that. And their marriage had ended in recrimination and bitterness. They'd been hurting too much to entertain any possibility of remaining friends.

Her eyes met Jager's and she searched for some clue to his emotions. If he cared about his newfound brother as she certainly cared about her sister, they would have to come to some kind of accommodation. This wouldn't be the last time they'd find themselves involved in a family occasion.

As Paige had predicted, her parents accepted Jager's presence with a show of equanimity. After the meal her father was deep in conversation with him while her mother talked with Maddie and Mrs. Provost.

Glen was picking up emptied coffee cups and offering refills, and Paige went to help. "Thanks, Paige," he said as she followed him to the kitchen, where the counter was filled with dinner dishes and cooking utensils roughly piled together. "We'll stack the dishwasher later." He balanced cups and saucers precariously on top of one of the piles.

"I'll stack it," Paige offered. "You go back to your guests."

She had made some headway and was bending over the machine to slot a plate into one of the last spaces left when she heard someone come in.

Straightening, she said, "Nearly there," and turned, expecting to see Glen or Maddie.

Jager stood in the doorway, holding a couple of empty wine bottles and some used glasses. "Maddie wondered where you'd got to," he told her. "Lawrence and Paula are leaving."

"You call your father by his first name?"

"It seems a bit late to be calling him Dad."

"I'm glad you found him," she said. "It must be…" She faltered, unable to imagine how it would be to find a father you had never known. "What about your mother?"

"She's dead."

"Oh, Jager…I'm sorry."

He shrugged. "Don't waste your sympathy. I never knew her."

"I always thought that was sad. For both of you."

"It was her choice. Are you going to come and say goodbye?"

She went ahead of him back to the living room.

Her parents had decided to leave too, and after a decent interval and another cup of coffee Paige said she must be going.

Jager echoed her, and they rode down together to the ground floor. When the elevator doors swished apart he followed her into the lobby and opened the outer door for her.

"I'll walk you to your car," he said.

He accompanied her in silence, but as she unlocked the door of her new little hatchback he said, "We need to talk, Paige."

With the key in her hand, she straightened. "We talked tonight."

The conversation had flowed remarkably easily

considering the possible tensions in the room. Jager had easily discussed the news of the day, business and politics with incisive, well-thought-out opinions, and made the others laugh a couple of times with his understated but razorlike humor.

Even her mother's perfect but lukewarm courtesy warmed and shifted to reluctant graciousness when he'd shown an appreciation of one of her favorite composers. And Paige had enjoyed lightly sparring with him over their differing views of a recent hit film.

He said impatiently, "You know what I meant—we need to talk about…this."

His hand was under her chin, and he crowded her against the car as he turned her and brought his lips down on hers, compelling and insistent.

She managed to resist the temptation to kiss him back, not fighting him but staying rigid in his arms.

He lifted his head but didn't move away.

Her voice husky, Paige said, "That isn't talking, either."

Jager gave a short, breathy laugh. His hands left her and he placed them on the roof of the car, trapping her in the circle of his arms. "It's a start."

"No," she said, suddenly angry. "It isn't a start of anything. It's a leftover—from something that finished long ago."

"Finished?"

"Finished. Finito. Over. Dead."

"And what about the night of your sister's wedding? Was that a leftover? It didn't feel dead to me."

"That was an aberration, a stupid impulse that

should never have happened. *Would* never have happened if it hadn't been for the accident.''

"Okay, if you need an excuse, go ahead. It doesn't change anything. That night you wanted me as much as I wanted you, for whatever reason you care to cook up."

"You don't understand!"

"The hell I don't! You can't stand the thought that you slept with me six months after your husband died, so you need something to blame it on—you weren't yourself, you were in shock, you didn't know what you were doing. But don't try to make me swallow your theories, honey. We both wanted it, we both enjoyed it.'' His hard voice dropped to a seductive murmur. "And I promise you'll enjoy it next time…and the next, and the next. Once you can bring yourself to admit that you still want me."

Paige was trembling. He couldn't have made it more clear that he had no interest in her as anything other than a sex object, and that he was convinced she felt the same about him. "You arrogant…sod!" Even in anger she couldn't bring herself to call him a bastard, knowing what she did about his parentage. "Try this for an excuse, then! My husband was *killed* in a car crash!"

CHAPTER FOUR

JAGER glared at her for several seconds, assimilating that. His throat moved before he said hoarsely, "I didn't know."

"Well now you do," she said. "So maybe you can begin to see why I was so shaken up that night. Why I would have done anything to help me forget..."

"With anyone?" he queried harshly.

Chewing on her lip, she looked away.

At last he moved, dropping his hands and taking a step back.

Paige looked down at the key in her hand. She turned to open the door, and Jager leaned forward and did it for her.

"I'll see you again," he said, making her pause.

"I suppose so."

"Count on it."

About to climb into the car, she turned her head to him. "Jager—for Maddie's sake, and Glen's, can't we be friends?"

"Can't friends be lovers?"

That was how it had been with her and Aidan. Friends, then lovers, then husband and wife. But not with Jager. "Friends can become lovers," she conceded, "but—"

"I suppose it's too much to hope that's a promise."

"It isn't a promise! I wasn't talking about us."

"I thought that was exactly what we were doing."

He wouldn't give up easily. He'd always been tenacious and clever. Presumably that had got him where he was today, a successful, dynamic young businessman, with few signs of the rough edges that had so grated on her parents when he was younger, and made them anxious for their daughter's welfare.

Closing her eyes, she said, "I'm tired, Jager. I don't want to fight."

"No one's fighting," he said. "Except maybe you. Does it count that you're fighting yourself?" His hand touched her arm. "Good night, Paige."

She didn't answer, getting into the driver's seat and settling herself without looking at him again, even when he closed the door and let her drive away.

Glen had promised to be at the cottage the following weekend, when Paige intended to start painting the exterior, but she was surprised to see Maddie hop out of the car too.

When the rear door opened and Jager uncoiled his long legs and stood up, she felt her heart lurch and her welcoming smile falter.

Maddie's eyes were anxious as she approached her sister, with a cloth-covered basket in her hands. "I made some muffins for the workers. Jager called in when we were leaving, and Glen brought him along to help. Do you mind?"

Glen said, "You told us you'd use all the help you could get."

Jager was looking at the cottage, his gaze going from the new roof to the shabby walls. As Maddie finished her breathless speech he brought his eyes to Paige and lifted his brows in silent inquiry.

"I don't mind," she said mechanically. Annoyingly, she was conscious of the shabbiness of her stained jeans and faded, baggy T-shirt. Maddie, in stretch-fit pants and scoop-necked blue silk-knit top, with a matching blue ribbon in her hair, looked fresh and sparkling and quite delicious. And Jager's beige slacks and white open-necked shirt didn't remotely resemble work clothes.

Glen, dressed for action in old shorts and a disreputable T-shirt, rummaged in the back of the car and tossed a gray bundle to his half brother. "Here, Jay."

The bundle unraveled into a pair of workmanlike overalls as Jager caught it. Maddie was moving toward the kitchen, Glen inspecting the walls, and Jager paused in front of Paige. "If you want me to leave," he said quietly, "say the word. I'll square it with Glen."

"There's no need." She couldn't avoid him forever without making things awkward for her sister. "It's good of you to help."

His gaze returned briefly to the cottage. "You've taken on quite a task here."

"It keeps me occupied, which is what I need." Sanding back paint and filling holes and gaps was therapy. The physical work sent her to bed ready to sleep, instead of tossing restlessly as she had in her parents' house.

She saw curiosity in his eyes followed by comprehension, and then a strangely wooden expression settled on his face.

Glen turned to them and called, "Right, where shall we start?"

Jager and Glen painted the exterior walls, and Maddie helped Paige color the window frames. The morning went quickly, and the sun made the paint dry fast and brought the men out in a sweat.

Glen ripped off his shirt and wiped his forehead with it. "I could do with a swim."

Unzipping the overalls, Jager said, "The sea's right at the bottom of Paige's garden."

Glen grinned. "Yeah."

"You don't have swimming togs," Maddie objected.

"Who needs them?" Glen looked at Jager, who dropped the overalls to reveal a pair of snug black briefs. Paige hadn't realized he wasn't wearing his clothes.

Glen said, "What's it like down there, Paige?"

"There's a little shingly beach and some flat rocks. The water's deep enough to swim quite close to the shore, and it's usually calm."

Glen looked at Jager, who nodded. Paige said, "I'll get you some towels."

"You're not coming?" Jager queried when she handed him one.

She shook her head. "Maddie and I will have lunch ready when you come back."

The men came back with their wet underwear plastered to them and the towels slung around their necks. Maddie made a show of being impressed by Glen's state of undress, running a hand over his bare chest and cooing at him. Jager, the black briefs clinging to his hips, gave Paige a blatant come-on look which she ignored, although she couldn't help a smile twitching the corner of her mouth before she turned away.

When the men had dressed the four of them sat on the little porch eating sandwiches and the scones, Maddie and Glen shoulder to shoulder on the bottom step, Paige and Jager facing each other with their backs against the corner posts at the top, their legs carefully not touching.

A neighbor walking his dog waved at them as he passed. Paige waved back. She felt happier than she had for ages.

Jager shoved back a lock of damp hair and swallowed a bite of his sandwich. "D'you know him?"

"He lives just down the street."

"Alone?"

"I don't know. He walks the dog every day and we say hello. People are friendly round here."

"How many of them know you're living alone?"

She stared at him. "No idea. I haven't broadcast the fact."

"You'll need a burglar alarm. Have you done anything about that?"

"I'm not sure I want one." She almost laughed. "Dad said that too." It was so rarely the two of them agreed on anything.

"He was right."

Paige wet a thumb and raised it. "Chalk that up."

"It's no joke," Jager said. "I know a good firm. I'll get them to send someone round to give you a quote."

"I can get my own quotes, thanks."

"*Paige—*" He seemed about to say something sharp, but pulled himself up. Moderating his tone to mildness, he said, "Let me do this. It's only a quote. No obligation."

Paige inspected the filling in her sandwich, giving herself time. No harm, she supposed, in agreeing. "All right." She shrugged. "Thanks for the offer."

They worked until dark and then stopped for a meal that the two women scraped together from what was in the kitchen, and sat for a while in lazy companionship, sipping coffee. Jager hadn't talked very much but the other two made up for that. Paige was conscious of his gaze brushing her, producing a physical reaction, a light feathering across her skin, but they'd hardly spoken to each other all day.

Glen suggested another swim. "And why don't you girls come too?"

Maddie shook her head. "Paige said it's deep, and in the dark...? No thanks."

"Got a torch, Paige?" Glen asked.

She rummaged in the kitchen drawers and handed it to him.

"What about you?" he asked her, and when she shook her head he said, "Still afraid of deep waters, Paige?"

It would be silly and childish to rise to such a blatant dare. "I'm not in the mood."

After they'd gone Maddie said, "Do you really think you can make something of this place?"

"You wait." Paige started picking up coffee cups. "It'll be as good as new. Better. Thanks for letting

Glen help." She pecked Maddie's cheek in passing. "He's been great. You too. I didn't expect you to turn up."

"And Jager."

"And Jager," Paige agreed.

Maddie followed her into the half-renovated kitchen. "Isn't it funny the way things turn out? I mean, me being sort of related to Jager."

"It's a small world."

"I suppose Aidan *was* more your type, really. Mum and Dad's type, anyway…"

"My type too," Paige said firmly, starting to rinse cups. "Aidan and I understood each other. I was lucky to find him."

"He was one of the nicest men I've ever met," Maddie said warmly, finding a tea towel. "A lot like Glen."

Paige gave her sister an affectionate smile. "Yes."

"Not that I don't like Jager. But he's…different. Harder. I was a bit worried when I found out he's Glen's half brother."

"About me?"

"About Glen." Maddie looked at her apologetically. "You too, of course. But Glen was so pleased to have found a brother, keen to get close, make Jager feel like one of the family, and Jager…well, he was kind of aloof at first, as if he was weighing us all up. I wasn't sure if he really liked any of us—even Glen or his father. I wondered if he had some kind of hidden agenda, but maybe he just needed time to get used to the idea that he had a family."

"Jager's never been really close to anyone," Paige said. She knew exactly what Maddie meant.

"Not even you, when you were married?" Maddie's eyes widened.

"I thought he was but...some people are not good at relationships."

"With his background, not surprising. Is that why you broke up?"

"It wasn't all his fault," Paige said hastily. "We were both too young for that kind of commitment. And too different."

Maddie nodded. "Is it okay for him to come again tomorrow? If you don't want him just say. I'll talk to Glen. I was a bit wild that he brought him along without asking you, but—" a frown creased the perfect skin between her fine brows "—I guess it seemed a good idea to him."

"Sure it's okay." Glen was doing her a favor and if he wanted Jager along, it shouldn't hurt her to accommodate his wishes.

They finished the dishes and Paige showed Maddie what she intended to do with the interior of the house.

"Well, better you than me, but I expect you'll work wonders," Maddie said. "That's one thing you inherited from Mum, an eye for design and color. I'm hopeless with anything like that. Wouldn't know where to start. Clothes, now...that's different!" She yawned. "The men are taking a long time. There's a torch in the car. Why don't we go down and hurry them up."

The path was short but rough. Paige went ahead with the torch, emerging at the bottom from the manuka and tree ferns onto crushed shells and tiny pebbles mixed with soft dark sand. The water lapped in low ripples along the narrow shoreline, and across the harbor Auckland was a glowing blur of city lights with the illuminated Sky Tower rising above the others. A pale half-moon cast a sheen on the glassy blackness of the sea.

The men were still in the water, making muted silver splashes. Maddie called to them, and after a quick sweep of the torch, picking up their glistening faces and arms, Paige switched off the light.

Glen said, "Come in, Mad. It's great."

Maddie laughed. "You're nuts. Both of you. Anyway, I don't have anything to put on."

Glen said patiently, "It's dark, love. No need to put on anything. We didn't."

"You're skinny-dipping?"

"Why not? We're the only ones here."

"It's cold—"

"Not that cold, and once you're in it warms up. Live a little dangerously. I'll look after you, promise."

After a few more seconds of hesitation Maddie pulled the pale knitted top over her head and said nervously to Paige, "Do you think I could swim in my undies?"

"Everything will cling when you come out with them wet," Paige warned. "If you're worried about your modesty you'd be better off nude."

"Oh. I suppose you're right."

A louder splash carried to shore, and Paige

glimpsed the line of an arm raised in a crawl. Jager, she guessed, because Glen was still trying to coax his wife into the water.

"I'm coming," Maddie called bravely, and waded in, squealing before she plunged in and swam to Glen's side.

They exchanged some laughing murmurs, and Paige sat on the cool sand and waited.

She couldn't see Jager anymore. Or hear him, she realized. Her eyes hunted the dark water. "Where's Jager?" she called sharply.

"Over there," Glen called back, but she couldn't see him clearly enough to know where he meant. "I think."

He *thought?* How long was it since she'd seen that arm, apparently heading out into the harbor?

She switched on the torch again, to sweep the beam over the sea. It found Maddie and Glen, their arms around each other, and Maddie squealed again in laughing protest.

"Sorry." Paige stood up and moved the beam across the inky surface. Where was he? She crunched forward over the shingle until the cold water seeping into her canvas shoes brought her up with a small shock.

Instinctively she retreated a step, then put down the torch and began tearing off her clothes. Blind panic fluttered in her throat.

She was down to her bra and briefs when Jager's voice nearby said, "Decided to join us?"

Paige jumped, and swallowed a scream. "Where were you?" she said, swinging toward the voice, seeing a large glistening shape against paler rocks at the water's edge. "Have you been there all the time?"

"All what time? I was in the water until half a minute ago. You're going in?"

He didn't know she'd been looking for him. That she'd had some mad idea of diving in and rescuing him. Maybe he'd been underwater when she'd missed him. She remembered he'd always been able to hold his breath for long periods beneath the surface. "Yes," she said, trying to sound nonchalant. "Just a short dip."

Paige could scarcely make him out in the darkness. So it followed he couldn't see her, either. Quickly she dispensed with her bra and panties and waded in, getting under the water as soon as she could.

She breast-stroked parallel to the shore, a little further out than the other two, who were playing around like a couple of dolphins—or a couple in love. As Paige and Jager had once done, chasing and splashing each other, then falling silent as they glided near, touched, even kissed until the water closed over their heads and they had to surface...

Paige turned on her back and looked up at the pale stars that competed with the city lights. She'd been floating for a few minutes when Jager's voice close by interrupted her reverie. "Paige?"

"What?" She turned over, treading water.

"Just checking you're okay. I couldn't see you."

Paige almost laughed. Him too? "I'm getting out."

She started back to the shore, and found him beside her, matching stroke for stroke.

They splashed to the shingly sand together, and Jager said, "Where's the torch?"

She didn't remember exactly. "Over here, I think." Heading off blindly, she stumbled over a smooth rock embedded in the sand, and found herself on her knees.

Jager dropped beside her. "Are you all right?" One of his hands brushed her water-slicked breast. "Sorry," he muttered, as she drew in a startled breath. His hand found her arm and closed on wet, slippery skin.

Paige could scarcely breathe. She was suddenly hotly conscious of her nakedness—and his. And of the delicious tingling where he'd touched her. She pulled away, repudiating her feelings. "I'm not hurt," she said. "I need my clothes."

"Stay there, I'll find them."

He left her and found the torch, hunted down her crumpled clothes and turned off the light before giving them to her along with a towel.

"Thanks." She dried off, scrambled into her clothes, and was thankful when the other two came out of the water, arms still around each other, and with much muffled laughter got dressed.

On the way back Maddie and Glen took one of the lights and led the way, walking hand in hand. He turned his head to kiss the top of hers.

Paige shone the other torch on the path for herself and Jager. A trickle of water ran coldly down her neck to the neckline of her T-shirt. Her hair still hung in wet rat's tails. Maddie had tied hers into a topknot before going into the water and somehow kept it almost totally dry.

Paige sighed, and Jager said, "Something the matter?"

"I'm a bit tired." Her T-shirt was clammy because her hasty drying had been less than thorough. She was conscious of Jager beside her. They weren't even touching, yet she was sure she could feel the warmth emanating from him, and smell the scent of his skin mingled with the salty tang of seawater. To take her mind off it she said, "You and Glen have done wonders. It was rather a cheek for him to rope you in."

For an instant she saw his smile flash, a glimpse of white teeth. "Thanks for not sending me away."

He had surprised her with his offer to go. "Would you have gone?" Perhaps he'd counted on her unwillingness to upset her sister. Maybe it had been a bluff.

"Whatever you wanted," he said smoothly. Which told her nothing. "I'd like to come back tomorrow."

Paige shrugged, trying to convey supreme indifference. "A tiger for punishment," she said lightly. "Please yourself."

After they'd gone she had a quick shower and went to bed in the spare room. When she closed her eyes she could see against the darkness the outline of Jager's masculine form, naked as he had been on the little beach, more clearly than she had in reality. She felt again the brush of his hand against her, and her body yearned for him.

She turned on her back and opened her eyes, trying to dispel the tormenting images. Deliberately she conjured up a mental picture of Aidan. Gentle Aidan, who had been sweet and funny and had helped mend her wounded heart, who had taught her that the wound wasn't mortal after all. Aidan, who deserved at least a proper period of mourning.

But thinking about him only made her sad, and when her lids drifted down again and she slipped into sleep, it was to dream erotically of Jager.

By Sunday evening the cottage walls gleamed a warm pinkish cream, the trims a dark dusky rose.

Jager's promised contact visited Paige on Monday with brochures and advice on security, leaving her with a couple of quotes. Afterward Jager phoned to check the man had been and said, "You won't mess around on this, will you? You need something in place as soon as possible."

"It's a quiet neighborhood," she protested.

"Women have been attacked in quiet neighborhoods," Jager said. "Get it done, Paige."

"You're not my keeper!"

"I want to be sure you're safe."

She was an independent woman, Paige reminded herself, who could fend quite well for herself. Yet his concern lit a warm glow in her heart, as if he'd put strong, protective arms around her. And it was decidedly galling to realize that she liked it.

CHAPTER FIVE

AS THE renovations progressed it seemed tacitly taken for granted that Jager as well as Glen was involved in the makeover. Paige almost became used to his presence alongside his half brother.

They helped lift the old carpets and the layers of even older cracked lino that a preliminary investigation had shown underneath. Taking a short break, Glen ran a hand through his thick brown hair, rubbed at it and grimaced. "I could do with a shower."

Paige knew how he felt. The dust and grime of years had worked its way through the carpet fibers. Even Jager was grime-streaked, his hair dusty. She probably looked as though she needed a shower too.

"Feel free to use the bathroom," she said, sitting back to rub black dust from her glasses on a corner of her shirt. "Although it isn't very glamorous at the moment." They'd ripped up the flooring in there too, and everything was covered in fine, gritty debris. "Or you could swim."

Bending back to the job in hand, Glen said, "A swim would take too long. Let's finish this sucker."

Jager looked over at Paige. "Why don't you go and clean up, and leave the rest to us?"

She shook her head. This was her project and although grateful for the help she wouldn't sit back and let them do it for her.

Maddie was as fresh as ever. She'd been wonderful at providing sustenance for the others and fetching and carrying, but drew the line at going down on her hands and knees and getting physical. When the old carpets and pieces of flooring had been shoved into the hired bin at the gate, she told Paige, "You'd better sleep over at our place. Your bed's under all that furniture the men shifted."

They'd moved everything movable into one room to clear the other floors.

"There wasn't much." Jager looked at her questioningly. "You don't seem to have a lot."

"I didn't want the place cluttered up with furniture while I was renovating."

It would have been sensible, Paige supposed, to have the floors finished before she moved in, but once the cottage was hers she'd been impatient to start living in it, making plans for its restoration.

"You must have had furniture and things in America," Jager observed.

"There didn't seem much point in transporting it all that way." It had been hard but she'd sold or given away almost everything she and Aidan had owned, keeping only a few pictures and some knickknacks for their sentimental value.

"You just left it?" He paused. "Yes, I suppose you would. Cutting your losses."

Even Glen looked a bit disconcerted. Maddie glanced from Jager to Paige. "You must be exhausted," she said to her sister. "Let's get you over to our place and find you a bed."

Sliding between cool sheets an hour later, Paige

consciously tried to relax. Despite the men's help with the physical labor her muscles ached. And something else ached—something in the region of her heart.

Her dreams were filled with images of Jager—Jager accusing and angry, his green eyes hard as glass, saying something she couldn't hear. Jager wielding a paint brush, laughing. And then Jager walking toward her, taking her in his arms, bearing her down on a shingly midnight beach that in the way of dreams became a soft, rocking bed, a black satin sea on which they miraculously floated as they made passionate, sweet love until they sank into the water and a dark oblivion.

The morning was still new when Maddie came into her room. "Did you sleep well?"

"I slept okay," Paige said. Her sister looked blooming. She hadn't had to rely on dreams.

Maddie seemed to want to say something more, and finally decided to take the plunge. "It's a bit soon to be bringing it up, but you're young to be a widow, Paige. And it would be nice if…"

"I'm sure it would, from your point of view," Paige said crisply. And Glen's, maybe. A nice neat equation. "It won't work, though. Didn't before and can't now."

Maddie pouted but didn't press the point.

Paige brushed away the remnants of her dreams, banishing them to the ether. "I'd better get up."

When Paige had patiently removed stubborn rusted carpet tacks and ensured there were no protruding nails or splintered boards, she hired a professional to sand the floors, which turned out to be kauri as Glen had predicted.

During the long Easter break he and Jager helped apply polyurethane to protect and bring out the grain of the wood, and while each coat dried they all tackled the overgrown shrubs and vines in the neglected garden. Even Maddie donned gardening gloves to pull weeds and reveal long-forgotten plant treasures, while the men chainsawed a tree whose rotting trunk endangered the new roof.

Paige stayed at Maddie and Glen's apartment to escape the fumes while the floors dried.

"That's that," Glen said, as he cleaned the last of the brushes. "Another twenty-four hours and then we can move the furniture from the bedroom and do that floor."

"I can manage that one room on my own," Paige said. "I owe you all. Dinner's on me. Where shall we go?"

"I'm not fit to go anywhere!" Maddie objected, although there was hardly a spot on her pink cotton top and stretch jeans.

Glen flexed his shoulders and yawned. "Why don't we just head back to our place and see what we can scratch up?"

In the end they decided on pizzas that Paige insisted she would pay for. And this time, back at the apartment, Jager joined them.

Glen poured wine to go with the pizzas, and they ate in the kitchen, crowding around the small table. Maddie and Glen were in high spirits, Glen plying Paige with far more wine than she was accustomed to. She felt relaxed and warm and well-fed, and the happy glow that surrounded her sister and brother-in-law affected her too.

Jager lounged in a chair, one thumb tucked into the waistband of his jeans, a faint smile on his mouth and lazy lids concealing his eyes. He seemed to be watching his half brother with almost clinical fascination, and for a moment Paige felt as if a cold draught had entered the room. He switched his gaze to Maddie, who was getting giggly.

Maddie's eyes were bright, her cheeks flushed like a rose. She smiled a trifle muzzily when she found Jager looking at her. That smile would have melted stone, and Paige was relieved to see him smile back, his expression softening.

Glen leaned across and poured more wine into Jager's glass, emptying the bottle. "I'll fetch another one," he announced.

"Not for me," Jager protested. "I have to drive home."

"Get a taxi or stay here," Glen said. "Plenty of couches to choose from." He opened a fresh bottle and Jager didn't protest at his glass being filled to the top.

Things became hazy after that. At some stage they shifted to the living room, more wine appeared and Glen put on some music. He and Maddie danced a little, their arms wrapped around each other, and then Maddie yawned and announced she was going to bed.

She walked uncertainly toward the door, tripped on something invisible and said, "Oops!"

Glen swooped to steady her. "Come on, love," he

said. "One foot after the other." Looking back, he said, "You two will be okay if I don't come back?"

Sitting opposite Paige, one arm resting on the back of a couch, Jager raised his glass. "Sure. Good night."

Paige was nursing half a glass of wine. She put it down on a side table, and got up to turn off the music.

Into the resultant silence Jager said, "Spoilsport."

She turned to him. "Did you want it on?"

"Only if you're going to dance with me." His eyes sent her a brazen invitation.

Paige shook her head. The room swayed, and she said, "I doubt if I'm capable. What do you suppose is in that wine?"

"I think we're probably suffering from the effects of fumes from stuff we put on the floor, combined with alcohol."

"You too?" She eyed him doubtfully. He looked the same as always—unruffled, handsome, contained.

"Put it this way—I'm not driving home." He downed the rest of the liquid in his glass. "I don't suppose you'd like to share the spare bed with me?"

"I'm slightly under the weather," she said, "but not that much."

Jager laughed. "I guess I'd better call a cab."

He didn't move, and neither did she. They were almost at opposite ends of the room, and yet Paige felt as if a golden cobweb was being spun about them, binding them.

She shook herself, a physical movement to bring her back to reality.

"What was that for?" Jager got up from the couch and came toward her, his feet soundless on the carpet.

"Keeping myself awake," she said. "It's been a tiring few days."

"Don't work yourself too hard. I'll help Glen shift things out of the bedroom tomorrow night."

"You've been awfully helpful. Thank you."

"I wanted to do it."

"Why?"

"You think I have an ulterior motive?"

"Don't you always?"

He laughed. "Below the belt, Paige. And untrue."

"Is it?" she asked wistfully. "I don't know."

He frowned at her. "Have you the faintest idea what you're talking about? Because I don't."

"Maybe not, maybe it's the wine." She had just begun to grasp at a thought but it eluded her. Somehow it seemed important and yet she couldn't put it into words. "Did you ever really love me?"

His eyes darkened, and his face became a mask. The words hung in the air between them. She despised herself for uttering them. But the question had been lurking in her subconscious for years. Right back to the very first time he'd told her he loved her, and she'd wanted so much to believe it that she'd pushed aside her instinctive doubt and decided to ride the dream.

"What do you think?" he said, turning the question back at her. "My God, if you have to ask me…"

"Did you?" she said. "Or did you think you were marrying my father's money?" It was too late to retract, and suddenly she desperately needed an answer.

He looked as though he would rather kill her. She blinked at the ferocity in his stare, in his voice when at last he spoke, the tone shockingly at odds with the words.

"I thought the world revolved around you," he said. "That the moon and stars would disappear into black, endless night if you left me. When that happened, I thought I'd die. The sun would never shine again and nothing in the wide world could ever make things right. You were the center of my soul and the thing that kept my heart beating, you gave me a reason for taking every breath. Does that sound like love?"

Paige was dizzy. She couldn't speak. Her lips parted, but while she was trying to fumble words to her tongue he laughed, making her cringe. "I was wrong, of course," he said almost conversationally. "The world didn't stop and I went on breathing, and eating and walking around. Everything continued just as before, until one day I realized how little it had all mattered, really."

How little *she* had mattered? Paige swallowed a lump of unreasonable hurt.

He went on, "One more broken heart doesn't stop the world. One woman had let me down—but there were plenty of other women around, once I stopped nursing my wounds and feeling sorry for myself."

"You didn't marry any of them!" she blurted, stung by a shaft of unwarranted jealousy.

"Like I said, I don't make the same mistake twice."

"Neither do I."

He was silent for a moment. "So you don't want another wedding ring from me?"

Immediately she repudiated that. "Good God, no! Didn't we make enough of a mess of it the first time?"

His laughter this time signaled genuine amusement. "At least we agree on that." He gave her a long, considering look. "But the sex was great. It still is...judging by the night of Maddie's wedding."

Paige wasn't sure what was causing the hollowed feeling in her midriff. Any relationship involving sex was out of the question. She tilted her head in defiance. "I don't want a wedding ring," she said, "and I won't sleep with you, either."

"Impasse," he drawled, looking as though he couldn't take it seriously.

Uneasy, she tried to hide it, refusing to look away from the glinting green eyes. "Are you going to call that cab?"

He didn't move immediately, but then with a faint shrug he crossed to the telephone on the wall and dialed. "Don't let me keep you up," he said as he turned after hanging up. "I'll wait for it outside."

Paige nodded. "Good night, then."

"Good night." He started to make for the door, then swerved and fetched up in front of her again. Not touching her with his hands, he bent and brushed a kiss against her mouth. "Sweet dreams."

She stood rock-still, her hands unconsciously clenched at her sides as he let himself out.

The following evening the men moved the furniture and laid the first coat of polish on the bedroom floor.

Maddie and Glen left but Jager lingered by the open door. He said, "What's the next step, Paige?"

She chose to take him literally. "Stripping the walls ready for hanging new papers, painting skirtings."

"Need help with that?"

"Not really. I'm in no hurry and it gives me something to do."

He frowned at her. "Why so desperate?"

"Desperate?"

"To fill every waking moment." He reached out and took one of her hands, ignoring her surprised resistance. Turning it in his, he studied her palm. It was roughened from working on the garden and in the house, and she had tiny blisters on the pads below her fingers. "Why are you doing this to yourself?" he asked.

Paige pulled away. "I'm enjoying finding what's hidden away under those layers of paint and paper. Once all that's stripped off this place will be beautiful, the way it was when it was first lived in by people who loved and cared for it."

"Loved it? How do you know that?"

"Laugh if you like, but I sense it was a home where people were secure and happy."

"I'm not laughing." He was looking at her curiously. "Were you secure and happy—before your husband died?"

Paige blinked at him, disconcerted at the change of subject. "Yes. Very happy."

He searched her face as if he wanted to catch her out in a lie. But it wasn't a lie, and she stared fearlessly back at him. Finally he gave a curt nod. "I'm glad."

He looked around them. "Do you think a house can give that back to you?"

"I think it's what I need right now."

"But not all you need."

She agreed cautiously. "I need my family too. My job. Friends."

"Is that enough?"

"For now."

"It isn't much." He sounded almost contemptuous.

"It's a lot. Plenty of people don't have those things."

"True." A corner of his mouth turned down.

Paige bit her lip. He wasn't reminding her, but when they'd met he'd been unemployed, friendless in a strange city, and had no one. She said, "I don't mean to reopen old wounds."

He smiled tightly. "They don't hurt anymore."

"You found your family—your father."

"He found me. I wasn't looking."

That was a surprise. "I thought you must have..."

"Changed my mind?" He shook his head. "I don't need him."

That's what he'd said when he'd told her that his father was some spoiled rich kid who had got a teenage girl pregnant and then scarpered. His name didn't even appear on Jager's birth certificate. Now he added, with the same note of indifference verging on contempt, "If he's discovered some need to salve his conscience after all this time, it's no skin off my nose."

"Don't you feel anything for him?"

Hands in his pockets, he regarded her. "Should I?"

"He's your father, and I know it's late in the day, but if he went to the trouble of finding you, he must have some sense of...responsibility."

Jager laughed. "I'm responsible for myself. Always have been. That's not going to change."

"How did he find you?" Paige moved to the couch and sat down.

After a moment Jager followed, sitting half facing her on the other end, one arm draped along the back. "He hired a detective. The guy found the aunt up north who cared for me after my mother walked out on me."

Paige recalled the insouciance hiding an underlying bitterness with which he'd first told her that when he was only a few months old his mother dumped him with an aunt who had several children of her own, while she traveled from the small country town of his birth to the city. She'd send the aunt a little money now and then, but she never came back, never sent for him. And after a while the money stopped.

When he was five the aunt had packed his belongings into a bag and told him a nice lady was coming to take him to a new mum and dad. He hadn't understood what it meant. "I guess she'd had enough," he said when Paige asked why. "She hadn't asked to be saddled with an extra kid, she had enough on her hands with her own family, and I was probably a brat even then."

He'd been hardly more than a baby, Paige had thought indignantly. The first foster home lasted until the couple started a family of their own. When the new baby arrived they asked the department to take Jager away.

"That was mean!" she'd exclaimed when he told her.

"They never promised to keep me forever." He shrugged. "It wasn't their fault I was too young to understand the concept of temporary foster care."

She'd sensed his hurt at the third rejection in his then short life. No wonder his next foster parents had found him difficult to deal with and finally given up. As did several others.

By the time the department found a successful placement for him, he had lost the will for a real relationship with anyone, keeping his emotions guarded behind a wall of indifference.

Not that he'd ever said so. Paige had deduced a lot of what she knew about him from offhand, unguarded remarks rather than heart-to-heart confessional talks. Jager had never been big on verbal communication.

He'd been smart enough, she gathered, to see for himself eventually that making trouble didn't get him anywhere. And that no one could look after him as well as he could himself.

Following skirmishes with teachers and a couple of minor brushes with the law as a teenager, involving underage drinking, illegal drag races and a couple of street fights, he'd left school and found a temporary job on a fishing trawler.

A couple more jobs followed before he'd gone south.

"To find your mother?" Paige had asked him.

He laughed. "Why?" he demanded derisively. "She doesn't want me turning up on her doorstep. And I wouldn't cross the street to give her the time of day."

Work in the city wasn't easy to find, and when he walked into a charity shop looking for secondhand clothing to replenish his meager wardrobe he'd had no job and no prospects.

Paige, in school uniform and with her shoulder-length hair in two neat pigtails, was serving behind the counter as she did twice a week. Her school catered to Auckland's elite who could afford to pay its substantial fees, but the staff tried to instil a social conscience into their pupils. When an appeal was made for the girls to consider helping out at the nearby shop after school, she put up her hand.

Most of the volunteers were elderly, but the clientele varied from university students buying funky retro outfits to young parents saving on clothing that their children would grow out of within months, and older people obviously down on their luck.

Paige's mother had wrinkled her nose at the idea. "Ugh! Dealing with other people's used clothes and discarded pots and pans—you don't know where they've been!"

"They're cleaned before they go on sale," Paige assured her.

"Still..." Margaret shuddered delicately, but hadn't vetoed the idea. She herself was involved in a couple of charities, although her activities were confined to committee work and fund-raising.

Paige was fascinated by the people she met at the

shop. And never more so than by the lean, darkly handsome young man who walked in one day and made for the racks of men's clothing.

Earlier she'd noticed him peering into the window with an air of indecision, but when her glance collided with his he'd moved away.

She'd glimpsed black, slightly unkempt hair falling across a tanned forehead, a flash of startling green eyes under brooding black brows, making her blink behind her round, steel-rimmed glasses. His hands had been thrust into the front pockets of disreputable tight jeans.

Then she'd forgotten about him while she packed secondhand crockery, embroidered sheets, cooking utensils into a box for an excited young couple setting up house. "See ya," the man said, hefting the box into his arms.

The girl, her face aglow, added, "We need *lots* more stuff for our place! We'll be back."

Paige smiled after them. One day she might be like them, in love and looking forward to a future with someone special, like the people in the secondhand romance novels that were among the most popular items in the shop, and which she sometimes took home to read.

An older staff member asked her to retrieve a large vase from the top shelf. Perched on a stepladder to hand the item down to the well-dressed, bargain-hunting matron who coveted it, Paige saw the young man again, just inside the doorway.

As she climbed down he cast a comprehensive gaze

around the cramped shop before strolling toward the menswear section.

After steering a young family to a basket of swimwear, Paige deftly rescued a pile of odd saucers from the toddler's inquisitive fingers, and presented him with a box of colored wooden cubes to keep him occupied while she helped an elderly customer compare price tags.

Back behind the counter, she saw the dark-haired young man looking through the clothing section.

Covertly she watched him push aside several hangers, pull a couple of shirts from the rail, put one back and go to the suits and trousers.

Paige walked over to him. "Can I help?"

He gave her the full force of those green eyes, reminding her of a cornered big cat, wary and ready to pounce if threatened.

Apparently deciding she was no threat, he flashed her a killer smile, and later she wondered if she'd fallen in love with him right there and then. It was enough to make any woman go weak at the knees. And Paige, young and inexperienced at sixteen but a woman all the same, was no exception.

"D'you think these'll fit me?" he asked her, holding out front-pleated dark plum pants, and then glancing down at the shabby but clean jeans he was wearing.

She looked down too, and blushed as she realized where she was staring. "Don't they have a size on them?" Assuming the most businesslike manner she could muster, she took the pants from him and inspected the faded label. "I think these are a thirty-four."

"I don't know what size I am," he told her, "but the ones I'm wearing are too small."

She could see that. They hugged him as if they'd been poured on, and the hems showed his ankles. "What size are they?"

"Dunno." He looked across his shoulder, then turned his back to her. "Have a look?"

The jeans weren't the only garment that was too small. His threadbare white T-shirt clung to his broad shoulders and outlined the muscles of his back all the way to the waistband of the jeans.

Hesitantly she slid a thumb into the band of the jeans and tried to peek at the label inside. He smelled of soap and faintly of male sweat. Surprisingly, she didn't find it offensive.

"I can't see it," she said. Her cheek brushed against his warm, hard back and she jerked hastily away.

His hand went to the front of the jeans and she heard the snap open, the zip slide down a little. "Try now."

This time she kept a few inches distance between them, and gingerly turned the band. "Thirty-two," she informed him, trying to sound brisk and as if she wasn't feeling odd little hot shivers down her spine. "Why don't you try these on? There's a fitting room at the back of the shop."

He turned, and she sternly kept her gaze away from the unfastened front snap, the tantalizing inch or so of opening. "Do you think I need to?"

"It's the only way to tell for sure."

"I guess." He held up the shirt he'd picked out. Gray and hardly worn. It could almost have passed for new, but was half the price. "What do you think of this?"

What did *she* think? Paige blinked at him from behind her glasses. "I think you'll look terrific in it." He'd have looked terrific in anything. Didn't he know that?

"Really?" The killer smile reappeared.

"Really." She tried to sound firm and knowledgeable, like a real salesperson. "Why don't you try this with it?"

She turned to the shelves, remembering a waistcoat she'd unpacked last week. The front was green silk with self-stripes, the back velvet, and she'd thought at the time how elegant it looked. It would show up his unusual eyes.

He looked at it dubiously, obviously a bit taken aback. "That?"

"This." She draped it over his arm. "It might have been made for you."

He laughed. "If you think that, I'll try it."

He was doing it to humor her, and she thought he had no intention of buying it.

But when he came out of the cubbyhole with its spotted wall mirror and tired orange curtain he placed all three items on the counter. "Okay," he said. "But the waistcoat will cost me a meal."

Not sure if he was joking, she looked anxiously at him, and saw he was smiling again. "For all three," she said primly, "I'll give you a discount." She knocked fifty cents off the price, and later surreptitiously made it up out of her pocket money.

The following week she was crouched awkwardly in the small shop window, arranging some china that had just arrived, when she looked up and found him staring in at her.

She dropped a cup and had to scramble to rescue it before replacing it on the display stand. When she emerged from the window and made to negotiate the tricky deep step from the raised window to the floor, he was standing there, holding out his hand for her to grasp.

She took it, and he steadied her as she reached the floor. Somehow he was holding both her hands, looking down at her, and she pulled them away, feeling a bit breathless. "Thank you."

"Did I give you a fright?" he asked.

"It's all right. I hadn't realized anyone was there."

"Is that your job—the window display?"

"Part of it." She was more nimble than the older ones and enjoyed the task. It gave her a buzz when her display lured someone into the shop.

The new jeans he wore looked good on him, and so did the maroon T-shirt tucked into them. They fitted snugly, without the strained look that suggested he'd grown out of those he'd been wearing last time. No matter what he wore, he had to be the sexiest real-live man she'd ever seen, easily beating into oblivion the pop star pinups on her bedroom wall.

"Can I help you?" she asked him, as she would any customer, but instead of warm and welcoming it came out starchy, almost prissy.

He grinned as if he thought it amusing. "You already have," he said.

"Really?"

"Guess you don't remember, but you sold me some stuff last week—clothes."

As if she'd forget! Paige thought. Didn't he know how stunning he was? She nodded. "I remember."

"I wanted to thank you," he said. "I wore them to a job interview, and...well, I got the job."

"Oh, that's cool!" She broke into a smile. "What kind of job?"

He was looking at her strangely, as if she'd just given him a small shock. Then he shrugged self-deprecatingly. "Only working in a café kitchen and they're not promising anything permanent, but...well, it's enough to keep the wolf happy." When she looked blank for a moment, he added, "The one that's howling at my door."

By then she'd got it anyway, but didn't say so, just smiled.

"And we get free food," he said.

Her heart sank a little. Still smiling, she queried, "We?" And then wondered if she'd been nosy.

"Me and the wolf," he explained. "That's one hungry critter."

She laughed then, and he looked pleased. It struck her that he'd been aiming for that, trying to make her laugh with the corny joke. The thought warmed her cheeks, and she told herself not to be silly. Why would a guy like him be the least bit interested in a girl like her? And especially the way she looked now, in her uniform and with no makeup, her hair tied in those girly pigtails, the only way to keep it tidy and out of her eyes at school.

It wasn't as though he were some pathetic old man with a fetish about schoolgirls. He couldn't be much older than she was. He'd like *pretty* girls who matched his own spectacular good looks. Blondes with bouncy curls, brunettes with flowing, glossy manes, or blazing redheads—girls who wore bright, shiny lipstick to outline their luscious mouths, who colored their eyelids with the exact shadow to enhance eyes that were a clear blue or green or soft, sexy brown, instead of an indeterminate greenish-brown flecked with splashes of blue and gold. Girls who didn't have to wear glasses. Not plain-Jane girls like Paige Camden.

But, amazingly, he was looking at her as though he liked her a lot. And even more amazingly, he said, "What time do you finish here? Can we grab a coffee together afterward?"

CHAPTER SIX

PAIGE stared at him openmouthed, no doubt looking like a particularly stupid goldfish. When she found her voice she squeaked, "Me?"

"Me and you." His smile faded. "I owe you. I'd like to buy you a coffee."

The funny little flutterings inside her subsided. "No, you don't. There's no need to buy me anything."

That was the first time she saw his stubborn look. He looked up, away from her, and his chin thrust out. His eyes when they returned to her were darkened and stormy. "I want to," he said. "It's a debt, and I always pay my debts."

He smiled again, and she knew she was supposed to sprinkle a grain or two of salt on the words. But the smile was irresistible. Even as it occurred to her that he probably used it all the time to get what he wanted, she gave in. Because whatever the reason, at the moment what he wanted was her...or at least some of her time, and even if it was only out of gratitude, the prospect was decidedly alluring.

"Five o'clock," she murmured. "I'll meet you outside."

When the shop closed up and the woman who sometimes dropped her off on her own way home asked if she wanted a lift, she said, "Thanks, but I'm meeting someone."

And as the woman walked away Jager peeled himself away from the adjacent wall where he'd been lounging with his thumbs tucked into the pockets of his jeans, and came over to her, taking her hand.

His strong fingers closed around hers, and his eyes smiled, although his mouth stayed firm and straight. It was a wonderful mouth, she realized, fascinated by the clean outline of it, the indentation that softened the shape of his upper lip, the determined set of the lower one.

"What's your name?" Taking her with him, he started walking along the street. She had never held hands with a boy before, but he made it seem natural, comfortable and yet somehow exciting too.

"Paige," she answered him. "Paige Camden."

He repeated it, in a sexy undertone that made her toes tingle inside her regulation black lace-ups. "Paige. That's nice."

She was glad he thought so. "What's yours?"

"Jager." He spelled it out for her. *"J-a-g-e-r."* She guessed he'd had to do it for lot of people. "Jeffries," he added. "JJ, if you like."

She liked "Jager." But she asked, "Is that what your friends call you? JJ?"

"I don't have friends." As if aware that he'd shocked her, he added, "Some of my workmates up north called me that."

"You come from up north?"

"Yep." He halted outside a coffee shop. The

aroma of coffee floated out to the pavement where a few tables had been set to augment those inside.

"Will this do?"

"It's fine." Whatever he suggested would have been fine with her. Already just being with him was enough.

They had two cups of coffee each and Jager asked where she lived, if she had brothers and sisters, and were her parents still together. He seemed interested when she talked about her family, her home.

"How long have you been in Auckland?" she asked, and he said a few months. He was living in a cheap boardinghouse, but now that he had a job he'd be finding something better.

Jager stirred crystals into his second coffee and looked at her rather probingly. "How old are you, Paige?"

"Sixteen."

His eyelids flickered. "You wouldn't lie to me, would you?"

"Why should I?"

For a moment he regarded her somberly. Then a faint smile curved his beautiful mouth. "Yeah, why should you?"

She realized what worried him. Sixteen was over the legal age of consent. A strange mix of sensations—shock, pleasure, anticipation and righteous anger—sizzled through her blood. She ducked her head to hide a blush.

"What are you doing at school?" Jager asked.

She chose to take that literally, and listed the subjects she was studying—English, history, art. She was in her last year and planned to attend university.

"You're a smart girl," he said. "That's young for university, isn't it?"

Uncomfortably she shrugged that off, hunching over her coffee. "I'll be seventeen." She was a conscientious student and, not being pretty or vivacious, had fewer distractions than some of her schoolmates. "What did you do up north?" she asked him.

He talked about his first job on a fishing boat, interweaving scary stories of storms and dangerous machinery with anecdotes about colorful characters and minor mishaps at sea that made her burst into laughter.

He grinned back at her appreciatively. "I like making you laugh," he told her, sounding almost surprised, and she looked down into her coffee cup again, embarrassed, making him laugh in turn.

"You're shy!" he accused, as if the discovery delighted him. And she raised her eyes and said, "I am not!" And then, "Well, yes, I am really. But it's not funny."

He reached over the table for her hand and held it tightly. "I don't mean to laugh at you, Paige."

She muttered, "It's all right." And tried to withdraw her hand, but he held it tighter.

"It's not all right if I hurt you," he insisted. He let her go then. "Hit me if you like."

Her gaze flew up to his. He looked quite serious. "I don't want to hit you!"

He smiled at her—not the sexy smile this time, but an almost tentative one. "Good. But if I'm ever out of line, feel free. Or just tell me what I've done wrong."

She couldn't help the thrill that ran over her entire body. He'd offered her coffee, a thank-you gesture for a minor service. But now he was implying some kind of ongoing relationship.

"I don't hit people," she said. And then, because she was curious about him and also innately cautious and not a fool, she asked bluntly, "Do you?"

He shook his head. "Only if they hit me first. And never female people." He held her eyes. "Never."

She believed him. And her belief had not been misplaced. Even when they were tearing themselves and each other apart, when their ill-judged marriage was disastrously breaking up into shards of wounding words and bitter accusations, Jager had not once raised a hand to her.

When he lifted his hand now from its resting place on the couch back, it was to finger a strand of hair back from her cheek to behind her ear.

The movement startled her, and she stiffened.

"What are you thinking?" he said. "Should I be grateful that my old man suddenly remembered my existence?"

She didn't think gratitude was in his vocabulary. "You of all people should know everyone makes mistakes when they're young and…hormone-driven. He can't have been much older than you were when you…when we…"

"We got married," Jager said harshly. "There's a difference."

"Well, it turned out to be not such a hot idea," she reminded him.

"Yes." He got up rather suddenly. "If we start on that subject again..."

He was right. It could only lead to strife.

"Thanks again for your help." She followed him to the door.

"Anytime." He turned with his hand on the knob. "Anything. I mean that, Paige."

When he'd gone, the rooms with their newly gleaming floors seemed empty. She wandered through the house switching off lights and locking up, and found herself staring at her bed in the spare room and picturing Jager lying there against the pillows, waiting for her the way he had so often when they were married, hands behind his head, his magnificent chest bare as he watched her prepare to join him.

She'd been shy at first, and sometimes he'd taken pity and pretended to be absorbed in a book or magazine while she took off her clothes and donned a nightshirt or pajamas. But if she caught him peeking and scolded he'd laugh, then bound out of bed and catch her to him, smothering her protests with kisses, and take her back to the bed to complete undressing her himself.

Gradually she'd become less inhibited, even boldly, deliberately teasing him, treating him to their own private strip show. She knew her face could never compete with the girls he might have had, but her body was fine. At least it had never failed to arouse him.

He'd told her once, when they were lying close after making love, that the day he walked into the shop and saw her on the ladder, with her uniform hiked up her thighs as she reached for the vase on the top shelf, he'd wanted to drag her down and into his arms right then and there.

Half-mortified, half-delighted, she said, "You were looking up my skirt!"

"Couldn't help it," he said, smiling wickedly. "I thought, *Wow, great legs.* Then I started wondering what the rest of you looked like under that skirt and sweater."

"You did?" She'd have been horrified if she'd known what he was thinking.

"Until you came down and the penny dropped. You were wearing a uniform. I thought, Hell, a schoolgirl."

"Not, *Hell, the face doesn't live up to the legs?*"

"Don't be silly." He pinched her nose, and dropped a kiss on her mouth. "You've got a great face."

It was nice of him to say so, but she hadn't believed his offhand compliment. She was just grateful that he never reminded her she was no beauty.

The way he made love to her made her feel beautiful. He worshiped her body with his, just as it said in the marriage service. Inexperienced though she was, it hadn't been long before she matched his passion and his dedication to their mutual pleasure.

And when he buried his face against her neck and moaned his fulfillment, his arms wrapped around her, his thighs snug in the sweet cradle of hers, it didn't matter what she looked like. At that moment he was wholly given over to sensation, to the satisfaction of the need she'd created with her body.

And thinking about it so many years later, created a tension in her that she tried to shake off, moving briskly to get herself into bed—alone.

She'd bought a queen-size bed simply because she was used to it and no longer comfortable in a single one. She had no intention of sharing it with anyone, but for the first time it occurred to her that it was a big bed for one person. Lying there, she was conscious of the empty space beside her.

Irritated with herself, she plumped the pillows against the headboard, right in the middle, and reached for a book. But the story didn't hold her, and she sighed, letting the book drop to the floor, and switched off the light.

A pukeko screeched forlornly somewhere down by the beach. The birds had adapted to city life remarkably well—she'd seen them stalking on their long red legs right beside the busy motorway, undeterred by traffic roaring by. Faintly she could hear the water lapping on the shore. A lone morepork called from one of the neighbors' trees.

She was lonely. In the darkness she admitted it to herself. Over the past few weeks she'd had company almost every waking hour. Being with Maddie and Glen—and Jager—had helped her stave off the emptiness that lay in wait.

But it hadn't gone away.

She wondered if it ever would.

* * *

"Maddie tells me you've been working hard on your new home." Her mother had phoned her at work. "And Glen," Margaret added with an air of surprise.

"Glen's been a great help," Paige agreed. Had Maddie mentioned that Jager had pitched in too? Either she'd kept quiet about it or her mother preferred to ignore the fact.

"We haven't seen much of you."

Paige swallowed a pang of guilt, reminding herself that her parents knew they were welcome to visit her anytime.

"Why don't you come for dinner tonight?" Margaret said brightly.

Paige had been looking forward to an evening poring over wallpaper samples she'd picked up that day, but she said, "That would be nice."

"Good. We'll see you after work, then."

Paige arrived with a French loaf and a bottle of wine, which her mother assured her was welcome, if unnecessary.

After freshening up and shedding the jacket she'd been wearing with her ruby-red skirt and cream blouse, Paige entered the big formal sitting room where her father waited. He kissed her cheek and introduced her to a man who had risen at her entrance, putting down the glass in his hand.

He was solidly built and in his mid-thirties, a smooth-skinned executive type with a firm handshake and a direct stare behind authoritative horn-rims. "Philip is our new head of accounting," Henry said. "We've been talking over some of his projected strategies for the company. My daughter, Paige."

Philip was pleased to meet her, or so he said. Paige's antenna went up. Had her mother just wanted to even up the numbers at the table? Or was this a setup?

Over dinner she seized the opportunity when it arose of asking if he had a family.

Philip adjusted his glasses. "A boy who's ten, and a little girl, six. They live with their mother. We're divorced."

"I'm sorry."

"It's a couple of years now. One must go on."

Margaret said, mixing approval with understanding, "We can't live in the past." She glanced blandly at Paige. "Paige's husband died in America, you know. She's come home to start over."

Paige speared a piece of delicately grilled fish with unnecessary force. She was surprised at her mother. She'd have thought Margaret would expect her to observe a proper period of mourning for her husband before even thinking about other men.

Philip said quietly, "I'm very sorry, Paige."

Responding to the genuine sympathy, she said, "Thank you." It wasn't his fault that her parents thought he'd be good for her.

After dinner Paige showed her mother some of her wallpaper samples while the men talked business. Margaret went to make more coffee, declining Paige's help, and Philip strolled over to take her place on the sofa beside Paige. "You're redecorating?" he asked.

Surprisingly, he was an ardent do-it-yourselfer, with plenty of useful advice. When Margaret came back with the coffee he made to get up, but she gave him a pleased smile and told him not to move.

Paige left as soon as she decently could, though not before she'd been maneuvered into inviting Philip to call at the cottage and see for himself what she was doing with it.

At least she'd managed to avoid an actual date and time, leaving the invitation vague.

The following Saturday Paige rose early and prepared to hang wallpaper. Maddie and Glen were away for the weekend attending a friend's wedding in Taranaki, and Paige had assured them blithely that she could manage on her own. Anyway, she didn't want to monopolize all of Glen's weekends, knowing that Maddie didn't share his enthusiasm.

And she hadn't heard from Jager.

But when, a half hour after she'd hung the first drop in the sitting room, she heard a car stop outside, followed by a knock on the front door, her heart did a little skip as she called from her perch on a stepladder, "Come in." She'd left it on the latch after collecting the morning paper. Just in case, she'd told herself, without completing the thought. Just in case Jager arrived while she was unable to answer the door.

She heard it open tentatively, and a man's voice said, "Paige?"

Then Philip appeared in the sitting room doorway, his horn-rims turned enquiringly up to her. He was casually dressed and she supposed in his way he was quite good-looking. But he wasn't Jager.

To cover her sickening disappointment she gave

him a hugely welcoming smile. "Philip! How nice of you to drop in. Just a minute..."

"Don't move. Carry on." He crossed the room and stood with one hand on the ladder, just by her knees. "You're doing well," he told her. "And using paste too," he added approvingly. He'd told her even pre-pasted paper hung better with it. "But it'll be easier with two of us."

He was right. The work went much faster, and he was very good at managing the tricky bits about the doors and windows.

He was smoothing an intricately cut piece around the old tiled fireplace while Paige brushed paste onto the next drop when there was another knock on the door, a decisive double rap.

"Excuse me." She left the long strip of paper on the trestle table and hurried into the hallway. Jager was already pushing the door wide. It had probably opened when he knocked.

He stepped in, latching the door behind him, and scowled at her. "What's the use of having a burglar alarm if you're going to leave your damned door open?" he demanded.

"It's broad daylight, and I thought—"

"*I* thought you'd have had more sense. It might have been all right with Glen and me here, but when you're on your own—"

"I'm not."

That stopped him. "I thought the car outside belonged to the neighbors."

"You'd better come in," she said, despite the fact that he was already in, "and meet Philip." She turned and went back to the sitting room, leaving him to follow. "I can't leave what I'm doing."

"Who the hell is...?"

Philip put down the smoothing brush in his hand and straightened. Somehow he suddenly looked bigger, his chest deeper, his shoulders broader, although he couldn't match Jager's height. Like a puffer fish, Paige thought bemusedly, swelling to a larger size when threatened. Behind the glasses his eyes surveyed the invader with cool assessment. "That'd be me," he said mildly, but despite the thunder in Jager's gaze he wasn't intimidated.

Aware that the testosterone level in the room had just doubled—at least—Paige refrained from fanning a hand before her face, and introduced them.

When Philip stepped forward with his hand outstretched she almost expected the two of them to engage in arm-wrestling, but Jager merely gripped the other man's hand cursorily and then dropped it. His expression had become shuttered, only the narrowed gleam of his eyes indicating any emotion at all.

He cast a glance at the walls, then looked back at Philip. "You're a professional?" he asked. "Paige hired you..."

"Philip's a friend." Paige hoped he didn't mind being claimed as such when they barely knew each other. "He kindly offered to help."

"I told you, if you needed any more help—"

"He's experienced."

The gleam under Jager's black lashes altered slightly. "Is that so?" He looked at Paige. His gaze dropped over the paint-stained shirt that nearly covered the old shorts she wore with it, lingering on her legs before returning in leisurely fashion to her face. "I have some experience too," he said, sparing a glance for the other man. "Paige and I have been working on it for a while."

Philip wasn't stupid. His alert eyes went from Jager to Paige, and she said hurriedly, "My sister's husband brought Jager along to help. They're half brothers."

"So you're kind of related," Philip said, sorting that out, "by marriage."

Jager agreed, "You could say that." Paige felt the sting of his glance, but refused to meet it.

He looked around the room again. "You've been busy." Returning his gaze to Philip, he asked, "Been here long?"

Philip looked down at his watch, but before he could answer Paige said, "We've come a long way in a short time. Philip doesn't mess about."

The stormy green eyes lighted on her again. "I'm beginning to think that's what I've been doing."

Meeting his direct, gloves-off gaze, she said steadily, "You were very useful." Then recklessly she added, "All that male muscle was great. Now I'm into a different phase—Philip offered his skills and he's teaching me a lot."

For an instant longer he held her eyes, then he switched his attention to Philip. "You a teacher, Phil?"

Philip laid his elbow on a step of the ladder. "I'm an accountant...Jay."

Jager showed his teeth, but Paige wasn't certain the gesture could be called a smile. "A numbers man, huh? So how does an accountant get experience at…ah…home decorating?" He made it sound like needlepoint.

Philip answered equably, "My wife and I renovated three homes during our marriage."

"Uh-huh." Jager cocked his head, hands thrust into the pockets of his cotton casuals. "None of them satisfied you for long?"

"We sold them for good money and moved on."

"Is that what you do? Move on?"

Philip smiled. "We got a better house each time."

"You and your wife." Jager rocked slightly on his heels. "Uh…you're not married anymore?"

"No." A hint of regret colored Philip's tone. "She's selling real estate now, doing pretty well."

Jager's head tilted, as if he were sniffing the air for a foreign scent. He said, "And you…do you have your own practice?"

Philip stopped leaning on the ladder and adopted the same stance as Jager, his hands sliding into his pockets. "I'm head of accounting at Camden Industries," he said.

Jager too, looked at Paige before returning his gaze to Philip. He hadn't moved, but she was sure every one of his formidable muscles had tightened, as if he were a tiger ready to spring. *"Camden's."*

Paige could see his mind was working, probably overheating. Making two and two into at least five and a half. His quick glance stung her with contemptuous accusation. "So," he said to Philip, "you work for Paige's daddy."

Philip's jaw jutted. "I work for the firm. Paige and I met at Henry's house."

Paige didn't blame him for rising to Jager's bait. But he couldn't know that Jager had never been invited to use her father's first name, that he'd always meticulously called her parents Mr. and Mrs. Camden.

Taking advantage of the small silence that ensued, Philip asked Jager, "What do you do?"

His expression altered when Jager told him. Evidently he'd heard of JJ Communications. "You're *that* Jeffries?" he queried. "I thought you'd be older."

"I'm old enough."

"Married?" Philip didn't sound hopeful.

Jager's mocking gaze slid to Paige. "Not anymore."

She'd had enough of this. "You can see," she told Jager, "we're busy right now. I have to finish this before it dries." She picked up her abandoned brush and dipped it into the paste. "So unless you've come to help with the *home decorating...*" She let her gaze stray pointedly to the door.

His faint grin acknowledged the jibe she'd turned back on him.

Calling her bluff, he said, "Did you think I'd leave this without seeing it through? You know me better than that, Paige."

Paige's mouth tightened. Her brush slapped paste onto the back of the paper. She was aware of Philip's curious stare before he turned to shift the stepladder to a new position. She said, "Philip thinks we should have done the walls before the floors." She was, she realized, brandishing Philip at him like a shield.

"Does he?" Jager was standing by her now, and he leaned over and moved the piece of paper to allow her to reach the end. His tone implied that he didn't give a damn what Philip thought.

She carried the wet, sticky strip over to Philip and he ascended the ladder to align the paper carefully at the top and began smoothing it down with the wide brush Paige handed to him.

Behind her she sensed Jager quietly steaming as she helped Philip adjust the edges.

When she turned, Jager had the next piece ready.

"I have some experience too," he said. "Remember?"

His laser gaze and raised brows brought it all back. The dingy one-room "studio flat" they'd rented because it was all they could afford, with the landlord's grudging permission to redecorate, but at their own expense. They'd bought paint at a sale and started by slapping color on the tiny kitchen.

It had looked so good they'd become ambitious and found some cheap, cheerful paper to cover the other walls.

Given the quality of the paper and their own ignorance, maybe they hadn't made too bad a job of it but, "I don't think that counts," she said quellingly.

Jager folded the paper and carried it over to Philip. "We all learn from our mistakes," he said.

CHAPTER SEVEN

THE men appeared to have called a truce. When Philip began flexing his arms and grimacing at their stiffness, Jager took his turn on the ladder.

By the day's end they were working in tandem, exchanging male banter with a slight edge, and Paige felt like snapping someone's head off. Somehow she'd been shouldered out to the role of the Little Woman who provided tea and biscuits and rustled up lunch, handed smoothing brushes and trimming knives when they were needed, and was sometimes allowed to put paste on, but couldn't be trusted with anything important like climbing ladders or actually hanging the paper.

Unfair. The two of them were certainly getting through the job more quickly than she would have on her own, hardly pausing to eat, although they gratefully downed the drinks she made at frequent intervals. They seemed to be in competition to see who could work faster, longer, harder, an element of driving determination that had been absent when Glen and Jager worked together.

They finished the sitting room and a bedroom, then surveyed the hallway, smaller but tricky because of the doorways leading off it.

Paige decided to assert herself. "I'm tired," she announced truthfully, although her weariness had less to do with physical effort than coping with the palpable tension in the air. "And the light in here isn't very good. Thanks, guys, but let's leave it for tonight and I'll make you some dinner."

She thought there was a flicker of relief in Philip's expression. He took off his glasses and wiped the back of his hand across his forehead.

Jager cast her a searching look. "No need for you to cook for us. You'd better have an early night." He clapped a hand on Philip's shoulder and Paige thought she saw the other man control a wince. "Come on, Phil. We'll get out of here and let the lady rest, hmm?"

Since Paige wasn't arguing, Philip had to tacitly agree, his at first mulish stare becoming a rueful smile as he sketched a salute in Jager's direction, conceding him the point.

Paige kept her mouth shut, quietly seething. She wasn't about to throw herself between any swords. Or to make Philip an unwitting weapon, not even to give Jager the comeuppance that he richly deserved.

Somehow amid collecting jackets and saying their goodbyes, Jager managed to maneuver Philip out the door and send him down the steps first. Which allowed him to take a step back and say to Paige, "Make sure you get something to eat, yourself. Even if it's only a sandwich."

Not waiting for her to reply, he dipped his head and kissed her mouth, so briefly she had no chance to evade or respond. "See you tomorrow." And then he was bounding down the steps, jacket slung over his shoulder, to where Philip stood.

* * *

Philip too, had promised to return in the morning, but Jager arrived first.

Paige led him straight to the kitchen where she was making coffee. "You're early."

"You're up," he pointed out.

She picked up the toast she'd been eating. "Have you had breakfast?"

"Yeah. Is that all you're having?"

"It's all I need."

He ran his gaze over her old T-shirt and denim cutoffs. "That's open to argument."

"I'm not thin!"

His eyes were bland as they returned to her face. "I have no complaints about your figure, honey."

Exasperated, she turned her back on him to fiddle with the percolator.

He was leaning on the kitchen counter with a cup of coffee in his hand when she let Philip in later.

"I have to leave by lunchtime," Philip was telling her. "My w...ex-wife asked me to take the kids while she studies. She's getting herself a law degree." He sounded half-puzzled, half-proud. Seeing Jager, he nodded a wary greeting. "'Morning."

"You have kids?" Jager asked. Although he hadn't moved from his relaxed position, Paige sensed an undercurrent in the casual query.

"A boy and a girl," she remembered, bringing Jager's gaze to her face. "You didn't need to come today, Philip."

She couldn't read the oddly intent stare Jager gave her before he looked back at Philip. "We'd hate to take you away from your family," he said.

Even as Paige bridled at the possessive "we" Philip gave him a knowing grin. "Yeah, I know. But I've got all morning. And I don't like leaving anything halfway."

"Neither do I." Jager held the other man's gaze for a moment, then drained his cup. "And even though I was here before you, I guess I've been wasting time."

They had the hallway done before Philip left, apologizing again.

Paige shook her head. "You've been a huge help. I owe you. Why don't you come for dinner some time? Bring the children and we'll take them down to the beach for a swim."

He looked pleased. "Well, thanks. I may take you up on that."

Paige closed the door as he left, and turned to find Jager regarding her from the kitchen doorway, his shoulder propped against the frame. As she walked toward him he didn't move. "That's a step isn't it?" he said. "Inviting him to bring his kids. Have you met them?"

"No." She had to stop in front of him. He looked big and formidable. Telling him she hardly knew Philip was suddenly not an option. She had an overwhelming sensation of being gathered into the powerful male aura of Jager's sexuality, with scant hope of escape. Making a feeble effort at self-defense, she tilted her chin and said, "Not yet."

A muscle along his jaw tightened. The warning

glitter in his eyes made her heart thud. "Do you want children?"

The blunt question startled her. "Aidan and I hoped for a baby...but it never happened."

Her eyes stung and she bit on her lip to stop the tears. She'd thought she was all cried out for Aidan, and it was humiliating to be weeping for him in front of Jager.

His black brows had drawn together. He straightened away from the doorway, swearing under his breath, and took her arm to guide her into the kitchen where he pulled a chair from the table. "Sit down," he growled, almost forcing her to do so.

As if that would help. He'd never had any idea what to do with a weeping woman. Not that she'd done it often, preferring to keep her tears private.

She gulped down a sob, and gave a spurt of shaky laughter. "I'm all right."

"Sure." The bite in his voice was savage. "Can I get you a coffee? Or something stronger?"

"Coffee would be nice." She sat up, removed her glasses and pushed a few strands of hair from her face, brushing the incipient tears away in the same movement before replacing the glasses firmly on her nose.

She watched Jager make the coffee and find bread, butter, cheese and spreads. He added a pack of sliced ham, gave her a plate and knife, then poured the coffee and set a mug before her.

"Eat," he said, pulling up a chair himself.

When they had both done so he made more coffee

and sat again, pushing aside his empty plate to wrap his fingers around the mug he'd chosen. He seemed to be gripping it tightly despite the hot liquid inside, and his voice was deep and even when he said, "Tell me about Aidan."

Paige had begun to lift her own cup, but she put it down again so quickly a few drops spilled on the table. The surface coating was impermeable, but Jager silently got up and found a sponge, wiping up the spill before tossing the sponge into the sink. Then he resumed his seat and waited.

Paige glanced at him. He looked purposeful and intent and, except for a certain rigidity in his face, almost sympathetic. "Aidan," she said huskily, staring down at her coffee, "was a wonderful husband. A great person."

She fancied she heard Jager's teeth come together. "You met him in America?" His voice was gritty but carefully expressionless.

"Yes." Her parents had sent her there to visit her aunt and uncle who had settled in Pennsylvania, and to get to know her cousins, they said.

Of course it was really to help her recover from the debacle of her marriage. Which they'd insisted had been no real marriage at all, since Jager had falsified both their ages on the license application.

Despite their lack of consent, they had discovered—to Henry's chagrin and Margaret's horror—the bare civil ceremony was legally binding. Probably only the prospect of having a son-in-law with a criminal record had deterred Henry from making good his threat to have Jager jailed for making a false declaration.

"Aidan was a friend of my cousins. He was kind, when I needed kindness."

Once she had admitted to her parents that they were right, she *had* been too young to know what she was doing, it had been all too easy to slide back into letting them make the decisions. When her father brought her the divorce papers his lawyer had drawn up, she recoiled, but his patient reasoning wore her down, and she signed the document with shaking fingers before running to her room, where she'd wept into her lonely pillow all night.

"It won't be final for two years," Henry had warned her, not knowing that her stupid heart found that faintly hopeful. "But you'll be a free woman before you're twenty."

They had been supportive and understanding when she arrived tearfully on the doorstep and announced that her marriage was over. And not once had they said "We told you so." They enfolded her in warm love and sympathy, and with calm words of wisdom they had strengthened her resolve to separate herself from Jager and the roller coaster of their emotional life. And, noting her sensitivity on the subject, they had mostly refrained, with occasionally visible difficulty, from overtly criticizing him.

Overwhelmingly grateful, she'd begun, guiltily, to feel stifled by affection when her mother said her aunt in America would love to have her stay. And didn't she think that was what she needed? Her uncle, a college lecturer, would help get her a student visa. She could make up for some of her missed schooling.

Her very panic at the thought of leaving the country that held Jager told Paige it *was* what she needed. To get right away...away from the temptation to go flying back into his arms, back to the cycle of wild happiness and crushed hopes, of amazing, spontaneous sex and its aftermath of exhausted euphoria—and of heated, door-slamming, raised-voice quarrels that usually ended in bed with more sex, but left a legacy of simmering bitterness and an increasing, gnawing sense that nothing had really been resolved.

"Weren't your cousins kind?" Jager asked, digging a spoon into the sugar bowl on the table, although he didn't take sugar.

"Yes, they were nice." She watched him moodily lift the spoon and dig it in again. "And they were fun."

It was like living in an alternative universe where her runaway marriage had never happened. Where she'd never met a boy named Jager, never fallen madly in love, never defied her parents to be with him. Never finally admitted defeat.

She had hidden alternating bouts of despair and a bewildering, unfocused rage behind a brittle facade of feverish enjoyment, filled her days with new things, new activities and new people and, when she wasn't studying or discovering America, partied to the max with her cousins and their friends. It gave her less time to think. Less time to remember...to wish that things had turned out differently.

Sometimes she'd almost forgotten the aching void

deep down inside her. She paused to sip some coffee. "Aidan was part of a group my cousins and I used to go around with."

Jager stopped digging holes in the sugar and sat back, a hand hooking into his belt. "Was he good-looking?"

She couldn't help a slight smile. What did it matter? "He was nice-looking." Not like Jager, who would stand out in any company. She had scarcely noticed Aidan until the night she'd found herself standing alone in a corner at a party, while all about her people were drinking, laughing, dancing with their arms around each other.

She'd been attacked by a wave of longing. Longing for Jager, for his arms around her, his cheek against her temple, his thighs warming hers as they swayed in time to the music.

Holding a half-empty glass, she tried to stop tears from flowing down her cheeks, wondering what the hell she was doing in a strange land when everything she cared about was half a world away. And knowing it didn't make any difference, because Jager didn't love her anymore—he never had really loved her.

Aidan's hand touched her arm, and his gentle voice asked, "D'you want to dance, Paige?"

Unable to speak, she'd simply shaken her head, and he'd peered down into her face and said, "Let's go outside."

He shifted his hand to her waist and steered her to the door, and when they reached the quiet, tree-lined street he silently took her hand, and they walked like that for a long time.

"He had a gift of empathy," she said. "He always seemed to know what to do. Or when to do nothing. Say nothing."

"That's a talent." Jager's voice was dry but when she looked up, alert for signs of irony, his expression was sober.

"He was a special person," she said. "Everyone liked him."

"And you loved him."

"Yes, I did." She looked up at him, her eyes sad and clear. "I was lucky to be his wife."

It hadn't been the heedless, all-consuming emotion that burned so fiercely for Jager. But she'd valued the paler, steadier flame that she'd thought would last a lifetime. Until it was cruelly, abruptly snuffed out.

She sensed a leashed anger in Jager's tightened jaw and the flash of fire in his eyes. He turned his head and stared out the window, where the top of a ponga fern waved its lacy fronds in a breeze off the sea. His profile was strong and austere. It struck her again how very grown-up he looked now.

His eyes still on the window, he ground out, "I'm glad you were happy."

Tentatively she said, "What about you? Did you…? Have you been happy?"

"I've been busy. Too busy to think about it." He pushed his chair back and stood up. "If you want the rest of the papering done today…"

This time she got to do some of the real work. When they hung the last strip of silk-look gold paper in her bedroom, Jager swung her down from the ladder to the floor with his hands on her waist. "That's it. We're all done."

"It looks great. Thank you." She edged away from his hold, forgetting they'd moved the bed into the middle of the room to clear the walls. It caught the back of her legs and she fell onto the soft cover.

She saw the awareness in Jager's eyes, and held her breath as he stepped forward. But he only took her hand to help her up and a second later she was standing again.

"Do you want something to eat?" she asked to break the silence that followed. It was getting late and they hadn't eaten, intent on getting the job finished.

He released her. "If you're not too tired we could go out for a meal."

"Then I'm paying."

"Uh-uh." He shook his head.

"It's only fair."

"Too bad."

She knew that look. Argument, however rational, would only rebound off the rock wall of his stubborn will.

"We'll stay here then," she said, "and I'll make something."

The pugnacious thrust of his jaw showed his frustration, but all he said was, "I'll help."

She found a packet of pork strips in the freezer and thawed them in the microwave oven, and while she made a sweet-and-sour sauce and boiled a pot of rice Jager stir-fried vegetables.

They worked efficiently together, falling into a

rhythm established long ago, automatically moving aside to make room for each other.

Paige hadn't realized she was hungry, but she ate with relish, while Jager cleaned up an amount that would have done her for days.

She had asked him to open a bottle of wine, but noticed that like her he'd drunk sparingly. After they'd pushed aside their empty plates there was still some left in the bottle.

When she offered it to Jager he said, "I'm driving." Then he looked directly at her. "Unless you'd like me to stay."

She met his eyes and they were quite serious, probing hers.

It occurred to her that she *would* like him to stay, to take her to bed and make love to her, give her the gift of forgetfulness for one night, and be there in the morning when she woke.

She saw that he'd read her face, saw the triumphant leap of hope in his eyes. Then she remembered the last time he had woken in her bed, at her parents' house. It hadn't solved anything.

"No," she said.

The hope was replaced by a hard accusation. "What changed your mind?"

Paige stiffened. "I haven't changed my mind. I'm not interested."

He said softly, "Don't lie to me, Paige. I know you too well."

"You knew the stupid little teenager who nearly ruined her life for you. You don't know the person I am now at all."

"Nearly ruined your life?" he repeated slowly.

"I gave up everything for you. My schooling, my family, my home…"

She hadn't realized how hard it would be.

Her father had refused to finance her studies while she insisted on staying with Jager, and although both parents had assured her she was welcome at home anytime, they wouldn't extend the invitation to her husband. Paige wouldn't visit without him, and of course they hadn't ever set foot in the dingy rented flat.

She inquired about a student loan but it wasn't enough to live on, and the amount she was going to owe by the time she had a degree was frightening.

Instead she got a job, assuring Jager that university had been her parents' plan, not hers. She didn't care as long as she could be with him.

"You said it was worth it," Jager reminded her.

She had said so, determined to lie on the bed she'd made for herself, and when she shared it with Jager it did seem worth it.

For a while she hardly noticed how little money they had, although Jager had warned her he wasn't making much as a kitchen hand, and she'd conscientiously shopped for cheap cuts of meat and bargain vegetables to make their meals, even enjoying the challenge. Then he'd been promoted to barman and they'd celebrated by going out to dinner, the first time since their marriage.

And only a few weeks later he was sacked because he hadn't held onto his temper when an obnoxious customer became abusive.

Paige understood that his self-esteem couldn't withstand the man's malicious insults, but the sinking fear in her stomach wouldn't go away. The money she earned as a junior bookshop assistant would have to stretch far to keep them both. She economized further on meat and fish and cooked a lot of rice and pasta.

Sometimes she met her mother for a quick lunch in town, but as Margaret spent the time gently and insistently trying to "make her see sense" they were tense occasions, only adding to the estrangement. Her father phoned occasionally to gruffly inquire after her welfare, and she said she was fine.

She had never told them Jager was unemployed again.

Desperate, Paige answered an advertisement for nightclub dancers, promising good money but "No experience necessary" and was turned down. Her face, they told her bluntly, didn't match up to her figure. She wished she'd thought to leave her glasses behind and put on makeup, but it probably wouldn't have made any difference.

Jager found the newspaper where she'd ringed the ad, and she tried to make an amusing story of the interview. Only he didn't think it was funny. Whitefaced and furious, he'd told her he wasn't going to have her selling her damn body for him. And out of a simmering resentment she hadn't known was there, she'd retaliated that it wouldn't be necessary if he'd been less touchy about his stupid pride.

They made up later with frenzied lovemaking, both of them determined to close the frightening rift they'd revealed. *It's all right,* they'd told each other. *I didn't mean it. I'm sorry.*

Jager obtained temporary work laboring on a building site.

The day he came home lugging a secondhand computer, they had another row.

He put the machine down on the tiny kitchen table and Paige exclaimed, shocked into shrillness, "What on earth are we going to do with a computer?"

Accustomed to a home where the dishes went into a dishwasher, the washing machine and dryer worked perfectly, the hot water never ran out and she had no idea what the electricity bill came to, she'd been struggling to accustom herself to hand-washing dishes, dealing with an ancient and pernickety coin-operated communal washing machine, and saving money by drying clothes on a sagging outside wire in a cold, overgrown yard.

She hadn't had anything new to wear since she'd moved out of her parents' home, and earlier that day had yearned wistfully at a pretty skirt in a shop window and known there was no way she could justify buying it.

A computer seemed an indulgence, a luxury they couldn't afford.

"I'm not working for other people all my life," Jager said. "This could be my ticket to my own business."

"You dropped out of school!" she reminded him, unable to erase the scorn from her voice. "And what do you know about business?"

He'd become defensive and angry. "So I didn't

have a rich daddy to send me to a fancy private school—'' he sneered ''—and I left when I knew they couldn't teach me any more than I could learn off my own bat. But I'm not stupid. I'll learn.''

He had, and proved her wrong in the end. But she'd doubted him that night, and he'd lashed out in return. The wounds had never quite healed.

Throughout their short marriage she resented the computer almost as if it were another woman. She didn't understand the complex calculations he made on it for a digital communication system that he said was an improvement on anything on the market.

She knew he was smart and could probably have equaled or even surpassed her own exam results if he'd stayed at school. But she also knew that his youth and lack of qualifications, experience or contacts would make it difficult for him to succeed in business.

''Your parents could have made it easier on you.'' Jager's hand closed around his empty wineglass.

''They were doing what they thought best for me.''

''You still believe that?'' Hostility glittered in his eyes.

''Jager, I was seventeen. Far too young for marriage. Can you blame them?''

At the time Jager had wanted to try to talk them into giving consent.

''They'll stop us,'' she'd told him, alarmed at the thought. ''We can't tell them. Not until we're married.''

She'd told them she was spending the weekend

with a friend's family at their beach cottage. Lying to them felt wrong, but marrying Jager felt so right, and this was the only way. They'd been married quickly and quietly on Friday afternoon, and spent two magical nights and days together in a seaside motel they could ill afford.

She kept the secret until after her final high school exams, seeing Jager whenever she could, both of them frustrated by the constraints on their privacy, their time together. Then, having finished school, she announced that she wanted to live with her husband. And all hell broke loose.

She'd expected it, of course. But not that her parents would be so inflexible. With the optimism of youth she had thought that, presented with a fait accompli, after the initial shock they would accept Jager as the man she intended to spend her life with.

She hadn't been prepared for the suspicion and hostility they held toward him. Most of it she could brush off, but some things stuck, worming their way into her mind, her heart. Her mother saying bitterly, "He took one look at you and saw easy money—or so he thought. A rich man's daughter."

Paige had flared in his defense. "He didn't have any idea who I was! Or who my father was."

Margaret snorted. "Everyone knows the school uniform."

"Not all the pupils are from wealthy families." But people did tend to assume it. And she'd told Jager on that very first date what her father did, what his company was.

She despised herself for making an opportunity to ask Jager later if he'd recognized the uniform.

"Didn't have a clue," he'd answered. "I hadn't been in Auckland for long then. Why?"

"I just wondered." And then she felt guilty for lying to him.

Her father claimed angrily that Jager had asked him for money, and threatened him when he refused. She'd said she didn't believe that, and hung up on him. But her father wasn't a liar.

"I asked him for a loan," Jager admitted. "To help develop my ideas into a business, because the banks won't touch it without collateral and I thought for your sake he might. I drew up an agreement, with interest and everything. I'd have paid him back."

"You didn't mention it to me!"

"I wasn't going to tell you if he turned me down. I did it for you, Paige. Because you deserve better than this place, this life." He looked around the little flat, the meager furnishings.

She could imagine how much pride he had needed to swallow even to ask.

Jager said bitterly, "He wouldn't even look at the proposal. He'd rather see me drown, and take you with me. That's how much he loves his daughter!"

"He said you threatened him."

Jager frowned. "Things got a bit heated. I don't remember all the details. He accused me of using you to extort money from him. I told him what sort of a father I thought he was, and that he'd lose you completely the way he was carrying on."

Two versions. She believed Jager, of course she did. It was a misunderstanding.

But the misunderstandings proliferated, even after he landed a job with an electronics company, with better pay and better prospects. Perhaps by then it had been too late. She couldn't remember now what the final row had been about. Something unimportant, probably, but the last straw. She'd packed a bag and walked out with tears streaming down her face and fogging her glasses, and flagged down a cab to take her home.

CHAPTER EIGHT

JAGER pushed back his chair but didn't get up. "Did your parents approve of Aidan?"

"They liked him. I told you—"

"Oh, yeah. Everybody did. And it goes without saying they like Philip. Are you prepared to take second place to his ex-wife and his children? He hasn't cut loose from her...emotionally." Jager's expression was ruthless.

"I don't care!" she said, exasperated.

Fleetingly he looked furious, before his face went totally blank.

This was pointless. "I hardly know him!" Paige said, angry herself. "I met him at my parents' place and he offered me help with the decorating. He's just a nice man."

Jager was skeptical. "And he hopes you can help him get over his broken marriage. Not to mention it can't do his career any damage if he marries the boss's daughter."

"Not everyone has your eye for the main chance."

His head jerked back. "What?"

"Why did *you* really want to marry me? It certainly wasn't for my pretty face."

For once he appeared at a loss for words. "Why the hell do you think?" he demanded at last. "I was in love with you, dammit! I thought you were in love with me!"

"Would you have been so keen if my family hadn't had money?" The tormenting suspicion that she'd denied even to herself, buried deep in her subconscious out of fear and pride and wilful refusal to recognize the possibility, finally broke to the surface in all its stark ugliness.

For an instant he looked utterly blank, then almost murderous, before he wiped that expression too, from his face, and said in a deadly tone, "Would *you* have been so keen if I hadn't represented forbidden fruit? The bad boy from the wrong side of the tracks, the wrong side of the blanket? Your very own teenage rebellion? Well, it didn't last long once reality sank in, did it? When the going gets tough the rich little girls run back to Daddy."

"That's not fair!"

"What's fair?" he scoffed. "*Life* isn't fair, Paige. The way I feel about you isn't *fair!* Nothing in this whole damn wide world is *fair*. This—" he swooped to haul her from the chair and into his arms, the raging passion in his eyes making her gasp "—isn't fair." And then his mouth crushed hers, with the same bewildering mix of anger and desire.

She could hardly breathe, he held her so close, and his warmth and his scent, sexy and seductive, drowned her in sensation. Her parted lips accepted the thrust of his tongue, and the taste of him was exciting beyond bearing.

He was instantly aroused, letting her know it with the closeness of his hold, the explicit nudging of his body against hers. The blood in her veins raced, heating her skin, making her dizzy.

She loved him, had always loved him. Everything, everyone else in the world became a distant, unreal memory. This was what she was born for, what she had once known and had given up for a half-life, for a pale imitation.

She strained against him, yearning even closer, and felt a tremor run through his entire body. He broke the kiss and stared down at her flushed face, her glazed eyes, his own as brilliant as polished emeralds. With shaking hands he cupped her face, tipping back her head, and dropped hot, fierce kisses down the line of her throat.

"The hell with this," he muttered, and kissed her again, too swiftly. He swung her into his arms and strode through to the bedroom where a high full moon shone through the window and in the uneven light his face took on mysterious planes and shadows, gaunt and proud and taut, like a warrior going into battle.

Then they were lying on the bed, and he hauled off her shirt, and tore his own from his body. "I'm not offering you marriage this time," he said, the words grinding from his throat. He threw the shirt on the floor and pulled his jeans off, discarding them along with his underpants. She caught her breath as he turned back to her, magnificently naked.

Roughly he unzipped her shorts, and she lifted her hips to help him slide them off. "I won't promise you children," he said. His lips found her navel above her bikini panties, his hand splayed on her stomach and then moved lower, nudging the satin down. His fingers touched, lightly explored, and she writhed at the exquisite pleasure of it.

She pulled down the strap of her bra, silently begging, and Jager took the hint, his lips brushing the curve of her breast even as his hand went to the clasp, freeing her from the garment.

"All I can give you," he said, as it followed their other clothing to the floor, "is myself. And this…"

Then his mouth closed over her breast and she was spinning in the ether. His hands wove magic and his mouth intoxicated, and within a blessedly short time he was plunging into her and she was rising to meet him in an ecstasy of mutual need and fulfillment, a kaleidoscope of sensations so deep and so explosive she thought she'd break into a million glittering pieces before it was over.

And even as she lay panting in the aftermath, he began again, his hands gliding over her, his seduction sweet and slow this time, but knowing, remembering what she liked and exactly how she liked it. Bringing back poignant memories of other times, other places.

Paige reciprocated, touching him in the old ways, adoring him with her fingers, her lips, her tongue. Enjoying the guttural male purr of satisfaction he gave when she stroked him and tasted the salt musk of his skin.

This lovemaking was less frenetic, but even more satisfying, and the earth-shattering climax that clutched at her after she spread herself along his body and eased onto him until she held him deep and firm inside was enough to banish from her mind any thoughts of what tomorrow might bring.

* * *

When it came, she woke to see Jager coming into the room, freshly showered and wearing only his jeans.

He finger-combed damp hair from his forehead, and his jewel eyes lit on her. "Are you all right?"

"Yes." Her voice was husky. She tried to sit up without letting the sheet fall from her naked breasts, that still tingled from last night's ministrations. She lifted a hand to push fine hair out of her eyes and the sheet slipped.

Jager's eyes shifted, and she made a conscious effort not to coyly hitch the linen back into place. He swooped to pick up his shirt and shrug into it. "I've got to go," he said. "I have an early appointment, and I need to get home and change first." Already she could see him assuming his business persona, his expression becoming purposeful, remote, an intriguing and slightly unsettling transformation.

He glanced at his expensive watch. "I'll come back tonight, if that's okay." But he didn't sound as though he expected any argument. He sat on the bed to pull on his sneakers, then turned and brushed his lips across hers. For just an instant his eyes searched her face. "See you then," he said and left her. Seconds later she heard the slam of the front door.

Paige spent the day in a kind of daze. She must have got up and gone to work, because she found herself there, going through the motions of doing her job, apparently functioning normally. But she was on autopilot.

Until she'd driven home and desultorily tidied scraps of wallpaper and last night's dishes, and then Jager arrived, bringing a box of Chinese takeaways and a bottle of white wine. And suddenly she was alive again, every nerve end humming with anticipation and excitement.

He dished up the food, poured the wine and even produced a candle from a package he'd brought with him. A short, squat gold candle in a bubble-filled Venetian glass holder.

She remembered when they'd been just newly married he'd splashed out on fish and chips one night, produced a stub of a candle from somewhere and waxed it to a saucer disguised with leaves from a miserable, struggling grapevine in the neglected yard.

Blinking away tears of nostalgia, Paige took a sip of wine and spooned fragrant rice onto her plate, hardly making a dent in the feast spread before her. Jager had bought all her favorite Chinese dishes, things they'd scarcely ever been able to afford on their meager budget, and certainly not all at once. "We'll never eat all this!" she said.

"Give it a go," he answered, spearing a sweet-and-sour shrimp. "Anything we don't finish will keep."

They drank all the wine, and he toasted her with the last of it, his eyes full of promises. Promises of sweetness, of ecstasy, of physical fulfillment—and nothing more.

She couldn't complain that he hadn't warned her. Last night he'd been brutally frank about his intentions, and she hadn't made a murmur of protest.

And now it was too late to undo what they'd done. And what point was there in denying herself what Jager was willing to give? More than just sex, whatever he said.

He could withhold commitment, and even love. He could refuse to let her into his mind, and lock her out of his heart. But when he was in her arms and his body had become a part of hers, he couldn't wholly command his physical need for her, nor hide his emotions.

He might have had a much less complicated sexual relationship with any number of women—and very likely had, in the years they'd been apart. Paige bit her tongue on the unreasoning jealousy aroused at the thought. But he'd pursued her from the moment they met again. Despite her less than spectacular looks, despite the bitter failure of their marriage, and all the years between then and now, something had drawn him back to her.

All I can give you is myself...and this.

She'd settle for that. At least for a while. Lifting her glass, she returned the toast.

After the meal Jager made her stay in her chair while he cleaned up the table. And then wiped his hands, came to her and kissed her with a new gentleness, before leading her along the darkened passageway to her bedroom.

Paige was slipping into sleep when the bedroom phone rang. She had to get out of bed to find it because the room was still at sixes and sevens, but she crawled back under the sheets with the receiver in her hand. Jager turned and draped an arm over her midriff.

"Paige?" Maddie's voice queried. "You weren't asleep, were you?"

"No. Hi, how was the wedding?"

"Lovely, great fun. How's the decorating going?"

"Finished, really. All the wallpaper's hung."

"Finished?" Maddie's voice became muffled as she relayed the news to Glen in the background. "Did Jager help?"

"Yes, he's been...very useful." She smiled as Jager's lips nibbled her shoulder.

"Paige—I sort of let slip to Mother and Dad last week that he was...you know, helping out at the cottage."

So that was why their mother had been so anxious to introduce her to Philip. She couldn't help a small laugh. If anything, the plan had catapulted her into Jager's arms. One look at a potential rival and all his male territorial instincts had come to the fore. Within thirty-six hours he'd been in her bed.

He was in her bed now, feathering tiny kisses down her spine, his hand resting possessively on her hip.

Maddie said, "It's all right, then? You don't mind?"

"It's not a secret."

Jager sat up, raising his brows at her. "What?" he mouthed.

Paige shook her head. Maddie was saying, "I think they were wrong about him, anyway. I was too young at the time to have an opinion, and I hardly ever saw him, but I thought he was great-looking."

"He...he was," Paige agreed. His mouth was playing havoc with her, wandering in places that made her blood run hot.

"Mum and Dad can't say now that he's a no-hoper, can they? I mean, look at him!"

Paige was looking at him. He looked wonderful, all toned muscle and tanned skin. "No, they can't. Um, Maddie, I'm a bit tired...all that renovating...I need an early night."

After she'd switched off and put down the phone Jager said, "Tired?"

"Lazy." She slid down in the bed without dislodging the hand that had settled on her breast. "Oh, that's so good. Don't stop now."

"Maddie?" He sounded lazy too, but he didn't stop, his clever fingers making her skin tingle pleasurably. "What was that about?"

"You, mostly. She thinks you're terrific."

"I'm flattered. What about you?"

"Me?" She thought he was a superb lover and a complex human being, possibly a damaged one. And she suspected his motives.

Maybe her attraction for him was based on the fact that he'd once been considered not good enough to marry her. And maybe his determination to make her his mistress—implicit in the terms he'd spelled out—was a way to get back at all of them for past humiliation. "I think you don't need me to flatter your ego," she said, wondering if that was true. But if he needed her for anything but a bedmate, she knew he would be dragged by wild horses rather than admit it.

Philip phoned the following evening, while Paige and Jager were sharing her couch and listening to a CD he'd bought that day. She lay across his lap, her head cradled by his shoulder. If she closed her eyes she could imagine the years had fallen away and they were teenagers again, newly wed and still giddy with the novelty of being married.

The telephone bell shattered the mood, and she struggled up to go into the hallway and answer.

To hide her reluctance she greeted Philip warmly, and after telling him the job was finished thanked him again for his help and repeated her invitation. "When will you be having the children again? Sunday afternoon, then. Anytime. Yes, of course the dinner invitation stands. I'll look forward to it."

When she reentered the sitting room the music was over and Jager was taking the disk out of the machine. He closed the plastic case with a snap and put it aside. "Philip?"

"Yes." She went back to the sofa and sat down. "I invited him—"

"I heard."

Her eyes met his defiantly. "I'd promised. I can't go back on my word."

The silent lift of his brows and the sardonic curl of his mouth reminded her as surely as if he'd accused her that she had once gone back on her solemn marriage vows. Unconsciously her hands clenched against the fabric of the sofa.

Jager's voice was deceptively mild. "Do you hear me arguing?"

Loud and clear. But not in words. Resisting the urge to excuse or apologize, she said, "It wouldn't make any difference if you did." She wished he would come back to the sofa and pull her into his arms again instead of standing over her with that slightly forbidding expression.

"You realize you're giving him a misleading message?"

"I haven't given him any message at all," Paige snapped, "except one that says I appreciated his help. And I won't be." She would ensure Philip knew that any romantic involvement was out of the question.

"Thank you."

"It has nothing to do with you." She wasn't going to let him think he could order her life, her friendships. He had offered her so little of himself. "I'm not pandering to your wishes, Jager, just because we're sleeping together. So don't expect it."

A lambent flame flickered in his eyes. "Spoiling for a fight, darling?"

"No." She didn't want to fight him. She wanted to make love with him—fierce, all-consuming, mind-numbing love. "I just want you to know you can't steamroller me. You can't take over my life."

"Have I ever steamrollered you?"

Paige bit her lip. "No," she admitted. Even last night he'd given her every chance to repulse him if she'd wanted to. He was formidably self-assured and sexually confident, but that didn't make him a bully. If she'd been overwhelmed by him that was down to her own susceptibility. The stark fact was she wanted him, at least as much as he wanted her.

He strolled over to her, the fitful gleam in his eyes intensifying. "I'm glad we cleared that up. Now—" he bent and took both her hands in his, drawing her to her feet "—shall we go to bed?"

* * *

Philip's children were a nice, well-behaved pair, and the afternoon went pleasantly. When dinner was over Philip helped Paige wash up while the children watched a video in the sitting room.

"Thanks for this," he said, hanging up the tea towel, then coming close. "It's been nice, Paige."

"I'm glad." She moved unobtrusively further from him. "Like I said, I owed you."

He leaned against the sink counter and regarded her thoughtfully. "Seen Jager lately?"

"Yes, actually. I'm seeing quite a lot of him."

His lips pursed ruefully. He nodded. "I missed out there, then?"

"You're a very nice man, Philip."

"Thank you." He inclined his head. "And you're a nice woman." He paused. "I get the feeling there's not a lot of softness in Jager. I wouldn't want to see you hurt."

She was touched. "I appreciate your concern, but I can handle Jager." Even as she said it, she wondered if it was true. She could get badly burned...again.

"Okay. I'll mind my own business." Philip stepped forward to kiss her cheek. "I hope it works out for you."

Jager phoned later, after Philip and the children had left.

"Are you checking up on me?" Paige demanded.

"Don't be so touchy. I called to say good night. I could come round if you like."

Tempted, Paige decided not to give in. Jager was like a drug to her—the more she had of him the more she craved him. "I'm tired," she said. "Children have so much energy."

For a moment she thought he'd gone. Then he said, "How's Philip?"

"He seems fine."

"You let him down gently?"

"Stop fishing, Jager," she said crisply. "Will I see you tomorrow?"

"Is that an invitation?"

"If you like."

"Then I'll be there. Unless you'd like to come to my place?"

"No." She could barely cope with him on her own territory. She wasn't sure how she felt about venturing into his.

He laughed. "Okay. I'll bring dinner."

It didn't take Maddie long to figure out that Paige and Jager were sleeping together. Jager certainly made no effort to hide it, and pride wouldn't allow Paige to suggest they keep it secret.

"Do the parents know?" Maddie asked her, agog.

"Not yet." They were bound to find out, Paige supposed, but she wasn't anxious to break the news.

"I won't tell," Maddie promised.

"It doesn't really matter anymore, Maddie."

"Do you think...you might get married again?"

"It's not in our plans."

They had no plans, they were living wholly in the present. From day to day she didn't know if Jager would be sharing her bed that night or not. If she was going to be out she let him know. He scrupulously never asked where or why.

He'd begun to leave a toothbrush, shaver and comb in her bathroom, clothes in her wardrobe. She kept a couple of cans of his favorite beer in the fridge.

When she shopped for floor rugs Jager accompanied her. He helped her hang curtains and choose where the pictures should go on the walls. At a flea market they found an antique oval mirror for the bedroom, where the bed was now in pride of place and Paige had arranged an Indian sari, gleaming in red silk with delicate gold edges, in a graceful swathe on the silk-look gold-papered wall behind it.

She'd spent an extravagant amount on a lush wine velvet bedspread honeycombed with gold thread, and tossed silk cushions in gold and shades of red and purple against the pillows, the colors echoing the Persian rug on the floor. Colors of passion.

She fell for an ebony figurine of an almost life-size sleek, crouching black leopard with gleaming green glass eyes, and placed it beside a red velvet footstool in a corner of the room. Then, deciding she might as well go all the way, she hung several gold chains around its neck. And on the dressing table she crowded a dozen brass candlesticks of varying sizes and designs, furnishing them with red or gold candles.

"It looks like a love-nest!" Maddie exclaimed when she saw the room next. "Fantastic!"

When everything was in place Jager looked around the room, his gaze lingering on the leopard for a few seconds, then he reached for Paige, drew her toward the bed and pressed her down among the cushions, kissing her with passion and purpose. Later he dispensed with the bedspread and most of the cushions, but made good use of those that were left.

The next evening he arrived with a large flat parcel, and she unwrapped it to find a gilt-framed reproduction of Ingres' *Odalisque with a Slave,* the naked Eastern beauty in her sumptuous surroundings reclining against cushions that exactly matched Paige's bedroom walls.

He had trumped her leopard.

"Are you having a housewarming?" Maddie asked her.

Paige hadn't thought about it, but it might be as good a way as any to introduce their parents to the idea of her and Jager being a couple again.

She invited Philip, and a few people from her work, and the neighbors. The little house was full to overflowing, the guests spilling onto the porch and even into the garden, although the nights were cool now.

Jager greeted Paige's parents courteously, accepted their stiff nods, and found a chair for her mother.

"I'll take your coat," Paige offered as Margaret doffed the jacket she was wearing. "And Jager will get you a drink."

When she returned from the bedroom Jager and Glen were fiddling with the stereo while her parents, drinks in hand, talked with Philip.

She was distracted by some more arrivals and it wasn't until much later that her mother cornered her on the excuse of needing the bathroom, claiming she had forgotten where it was.

"That young man seems very much at home," Margaret commented as they edged through the crowd.

Paige said firmly, "Jager? Yes, he is. He spends a lot of time here."

Her mother cast her a look. "Your father says he's hugely successful, but leopards don't change their spots, and after Aidan...well, I hope you know what you're doing."

"Yes, I know what I'm doing."

"I see Philip's here," Margaret said hopefully. "I thought you and he got on rather well."

"He helped with the decorating. Actually he and Jager get on rather well too." They reached the bathroom and Paige opened the door. "Here you are."

"Good party," Jager said afterward, as they lay entwined in her bed. The leopard's glass eyes gleamed in the moonlight spilling into the room between filmy swathed curtains. A big moth flung itself against the window and blundered off into the night.

"I think so." Paige yawned.

His voice dry, he asked, "Do you think your parents got the message?"

She hadn't discussed that aspect with him at all. But he wasn't stupid. "They know we're...together."

"And...?"

"And what? I love my parents but they don't decide how I should run my life."

"How do they feel about it now that I'm not exactly on the poverty line?"

"Money had nothing to do with it. If we'd been older—"

"Do you really think that would have made much difference?"

She would never convince him. He had a blind spot as far as her parents were concerned, just as they did about him. "It's all in the past anyway. Can't we talk about something else?"

"Better still," he said, "let's not talk at all."

His mouth came down on hers, and within minutes she was incapable of talking, even of thinking, her whole being concentrated on the wonderful sensations he was creating, and the need to make him feel the same.

CHAPTER NINE

JAGER asked Paige to hostess a dinner party for him. "I'll get caterers in," he said, "but I'd like you to be there. By my side."

She hadn't ever set foot in his home. After the first couple of times when she'd evaded the suggestion, he had stopped asking. They went together to the theater or dinner or sporting events where they mixed with the sort of people her parents knew. Once they even attended the same social function as her mother and father and engaged in a short, formal chat. But wherever they went, afterward he returned her to the cottage and more often than not stayed the night.

She hadn't been wrong about the kind of relationship he'd offered her. She saw the satisfaction in his eyes when she dressed up, choosing clothes that without crossing the bounds of good taste instilled by her mother, emphasized her figure, distracting attention from her face. Dresses that hugged or flowed, were cut low in front or back; slit skirts, short skirts—though not too short; and for casual occasions, jeans that molded her neat bottom and hugged her long legs.

"This is Paige Camden," Jager would introduce her, his possessive arm encircling her waist, the pride in his eyes as they slipped over her proclaiming she was his. And more often than not, the other person said interestedly, "Oh...Henry's daughter?"

And she'd feel Jager's fingers on her waist as she acknowledged her parentage.

She was Jager's trophy, but no longer his wife.

"What sort of dinner party?" she inquired cautiously. They were dining at one of the exclusive—and expensive—restaurants he preferred. She picked up her wine from the impeccable linen tablecloth and sipped it to hide her trepidation.

"I owe some hospitality to a few people. You remember the Zimmermans? And the Hardys."

They had been guests of both couples. Married couples. She pushed the thought aside. "Anyone else?"

He shrugged. "I thought about ten people."

"It's quite a large party for dinner."

"I have a big dining table. The apartment is planned for entertaining."

She knew it was a serviced apartment in the central business district, a gracious old building converted at great cost to meet the demands of people like Jager who had the money to pay for service and style and preferred living near their city offices.

Paige put down the wineglass, watching the red liquid settle back into stillness, the light gleaming on it.

"And maybe Maddie and Glen," Jager persuaded. "We've eaten with them often enough."

They had, although sometimes her sister and brother-in-law dropped in at the cottage and stayed for an impromptu meal.

She looked up and found him regarding her intently. There was a tenseness about his shoulders, a tightening around his mouth. She saw this was important to him.

Paige had never analyzed her own reluctance to take this further step in their relationship. It was common knowledge now that they were lovers. They had appeared together in public often enough, and invitations frequently included them both. Even the Zimmermans, both in their sixties, had assigned them a double bedroom during a weekend visit to the couple's beach house.

"When do you plan to have this dinner party?" she asked. "And how formal will it be?"

Jager didn't smile but she sensed the easing of tension in him. He knew he'd won.

A few evenings later he arrived at the cottage with a plastic carrybag bearing the logo of a designer boutique. "I brought you a present," he said. "I hope it fits."

She opened the bag and took the carefully folded garment from its tissue wrapping, holding it by a pair of thin gold straps that cleverly curved around the front and turned into crisscrossed ties across a deep opening in the ruched black chiffon stretch bodice, and extended to an even lower one at the back. The bodice was thigh-length, and below that several soft layers of chiffon, each subtly edged with gold, flared into a short skirt.

It was beautiful and expensive and wildly sexy.

"I want you to wear it to my dinner party," Jager said. "Try it on."

Her fingers trembled. A small moth seemed to be fluttering in her throat. She let the dress drop back into the nest of tissue on the couch. "No," she said.

A frown appeared between his brows. "You don't like it? Black suits you. Believe me, you'll look great in that."

Paige knew she would. His instinct was unerring. In that dress she could be certain no one would be looking at her face.

She would look like his mistress.

Her hands tightened into fists. "I won't let you buy clothes for me, Jager."

The frown deepened. "I've bought you things before."

He'd bought lingerie for her, sexy undies and nightwear that she knew was as much for his pleasure as hers, but that she enjoyed wearing for him...in private. "This is different." The moth in her throat had turned into a hard, choking lump of ice.

"It's a dress," he said, impatiently, glancing at it. "What's so different about it? It's no more revealing than that green thing with the slit up to your thigh and the other slit in the front that drives me wild. Or that skimpy little black velvet top with the one button in front."

How could she explain her rejection of the concept of wearing a dress he'd chosen and paid for and asked her to wear? Her gut-level conviction that it would alter the carefully balanced status quo between them was unreasonable.

Intellectually she knew it didn't change anything. But somehow accepting his "gift" was accepting that she was no more to him than a sexual partner and a status symbol.

"It's...public," she said. "You want to show me off."

"It's a private dinner party," he argued. "I like showing you off. Any man would. Is that a crime?"

Paige gave up trying to make him understand. "I don't need another dress."

He looked thoughtful. "You haven't worn anything new lately."

That was true. She had spent most of Aidan's insurance money on the cottage and its refurbishment, keeping aside a small emergency fund. Her income was adequate and in time her father would leave her some money, but meantime she preferred to be independent, spending sensibly and cautiously. "I'm sorry if my wardrobe doesn't match up to your image," she said.

"When we were married one of your chief complaints was not having new things to wear."

She wished he hadn't reminded her. Unlike Jager, she'd never been able to bring herself to wear secondhand clothes. No doubt she'd been spoiled, as he'd scornfully told her.

Remembering how long he'd hung around outside the charity shop before entering, Paige had flung that at him, and he'd admitted that pride had warred with need. "But it's not so bad. And you were great. I watched how you handled the customers, friendly but respectful, just as if you were serving in some Queen Street store. That was class."

In the face of his patent admiration, the quarrel died then, and she'd even swallowed her misgivings and tried buying used clothes, but her revulsion at wearing something that had belonged to someone else—perhaps someone who had died—was uncontrollable.

This was a different emotion, but just as strong. "If you want me to wear something new," she said, "I'll buy it myself."

"That isn't the point."

"Then what is?"

He looked back at her in wordless anger. It seemed he was no more able to articulate his reasons than she was.

"Never mind," he said finally. "If you don't want it…" He shrugged, obviously baffled.

She'd spoiled his surprise, spurned his gift. And if she suspected his motives, she supposed they were subconscious and he was genuinely puzzled by her refusal. "I'm sure they'll take it back," she said, bending to replace the wrappings.

"I won't be taking it back," Jager said harshly. "Keep it, in case you change your mind. Or give it away."

She wouldn't be changing her mind, but perhaps forcing him to take it back would exacerbate any hurt he was feeling. Not that he showed hurt—only a tight-lipped frustration. She slipped the rewrapped dress into the bag. "How are the dinner plans going? Did you ask Glen if he and Maddie could come?"

"They're coming." The anger hadn't quite died

but his voice was neutral. "I haven't finalized yet with a couple of people. We'll probably be twelve in all."

Paige did buy a new dress. It wasn't as sexy nor as costly as the one that now sat at the back of a high shelf in her wardrobe, still in its bag. But it was soft and pretty, sage-green with a wide though modest neckline. And if Jager was disappointed when he opened the door to her after a whisper-quiet, mirrored elevator whisked her to his penthouse apartment, he didn't show it by a flicker of an eyelid.

He ushered her into a large, high-ceilinged room. A wall of windows looked out on the harbor, inky-black by night except where lights shimmered in snaking lines from anchored ships, the high arch of the Harbor Bridge, and shoreside buildings.

With a view like that the designer had wisely not tried to compete. The furniture was plain and almost stark, long couches covered in palest gray leather, occasional tables carved of light wood, with glass tops. Paige's high heels sank into unobtrusively gray-green carpet, and color was added by strategically placed rugs and large paintings.

A wide archway revealed the dining table, already set with gleaming cutlery and wineglasses.

She had arrived early, mindful of her hostess duties. "I see the table's fixed."

"The caterers did that first. They're in the kitchen now—come and meet them."

A pleasant middle-aged couple, the caterers seemed to have everything under control. Within minutes

Paige was back in the living room while Jager poured her a drink.

She couldn't help mentally comparing their surroundings to the cramped quarters they'd shared over ten years before. It was difficult to believe Jager was the same person.

They had both changed since then. He'd been the one who insisted on marriage, on commitment, a blind leap of faith in the future—their future. Security and permanence. Now she understood that he'd never had that from anyone, but at seventeen she hadn't comprehended how desperately he needed it from her. Under the surface brashness and stubbornness had been a deep-seated craving she'd been too young to understand, too inexperienced to fulfill.

Apparently he had found what he wanted in his career and his hard-earned wealth. This Jager no longer needed validation nor moral support from her. He didn't want her promises or her love. It was enough that he had access to her body, her company when he felt so inclined, her presence at his side when a presentable social partner was required.

"What's the matter?" Jager asked. Glass in hand, he was lounging on a sofa opposite her, and in the big room seemed distant, both physically and emotionally.

"Nothing." He must have read in her face the aching tug of regret for what might have been. She looked around them. "This is...impressive."

"More so than your parents' house?"

Theirs was large and architect-designed, with a pool and garden where Paige and Maddie had spent happy hours with their friends when they were growing up. It was a family home, the decor chosen by their mother with comfort as well as entertaining in mind achieving a balance of elegance and welcome.

"Do you need to compare?" she challenged him.

His gaze was enigmatic. "It's just an idle question."

Jager never asked idle questions, but she didn't want to start a fight before his guests arrived. She took some of her drink and changed the subject, commenting on the view.

When the doorbell chimed she was relieved. More people would dissipate the subtle tension in the air.

The Zimmermans had barely settled with their drinks when Maddie and Glen breezed in, holding hands. Every time their eyes met they smiled as though they simply couldn't help it. Marriage seemed to have made their feelings for each other even stronger, and Paige felt a pang of pure envy.

While Jager was handing Maddie a glass the doorbell sounded again and he went to answer it.

Paige was talking to Maddie on one of the sofas when he ushered in the new arrivals. Turning expectantly, she suffered a jolt when she saw her parents enter the room, restrained social smiles fixed on their faces.

White wine spilled over her hand as she stood up. Carefully she put down the glass and picked up a paper napkin to wipe it away. "You didn't tell me!" she accused Jager.

"I thought I'd surprise you."

Her mother wafted over and kissed her. "Aren't you pleased to see us?"

"Yes, of course." She returned the kiss and forced a smile for her father as he saluted her cheek too.

She looked at Jager, trying to divine why he'd done this, but he was asking Margaret what she wanted to drink, and then as the doorbell chimed yet again he asked Paige, "Would you pour a dry white for your mother, darling, while I get that?"

There was no chance to speak with him privately. At dinner she took her place opposite Jager and played the part he'd assigned her, keeping the conversations going, discreetly signaling to the caterers when the next course should be served, and making sure everyone was well fed and comfortable.

Afterward they had coffee and liqueurs. The caterers cleaned up and left, and while Paige talked with the Zimmermans she saw Jager approach her father, who was admiring the view from the window.

Henry turned, a little grim and wary, and she couldn't see Jager's expression, but she noted the way he inclined his head with a hint of respect for the older man.

That was a new tactic. When she'd first introduced them, after one of the women at the charity shop dropped a hint to her mother that she'd been "seeing some boy" and Margaret had suggested she bring her new friend to meet her parents, there had been no hint of deference in Jager.

He'd eyed the marble-floored foyer and graceful staircase with studied indifference, and when she ushered him into the comfortably though expensively furnished sitting room to meet her parents, his fast but comprehensive survey of the room seemed slightly disparaging.

He'd looked Henry squarely in the eye and called him "sir" but a note of irony in his voice made Henry glance at him sharply and Paige's nails dig into her palms. Her mother's careful smile of welcome elicited no more than a nod and a casual "Hi," as he took her outstretched hand.

He'd answered her mother's delicate questions about his background almost truculently, as if daring her to find fault with his lack of antecedents or education. And he seemed to go out of his way to emphasize the differences between his lifestyle and theirs. It hadn't been a comfortable visit, and Paige had braced herself for criticism later.

It had been veiled in slightly pained surprise that she could be attracted to "that type of boy" and patronizing pity at his upbringing and poor career prospects. But they hadn't really taken the relationship seriously until the bombshell of her marriage. After that her parents and Jager had become implacable enemies.

They didn't look like enemies now. Henry actually clapped Jager's shoulder as they left, and Margaret said with rather astonished sincerity, "We've had a very nice evening, Jager. I did enjoy talking with Serena Zimmerman."

Maddie and Glen were the last to leave, lingering when the other guests had gone.

They sat side by side on one of the sofas, Maddie snuggled into her husband's encircling arm. As soon as Jager returned to the room Maddie said, "Sit down, Jager. We have something to tell you two!"

Looking at her sister's radiant face, Paige guessed before Maddie blurted out, "We're pregnant!"

Ashamed of the split second of sheer jealousy that attacked her without warning, Paige jumped up to embrace her. "Congratulations, I can see you're thrilled. Do Mother and Dad know? They didn't say anything tonight."

"I phoned Mum yesterday when the test confirmed it, but she knew I wanted to tell you myself."

Jager rose to shake Glen's hand and kiss Maddie's cheek. "This calls for another drink," he said.

But Maddie shook her head. "I'm not allowed." She'd asked for a soft drink when she arrived, Paige recalled, and left her wineglass at dinner virtually untouched.

Glen declined too, saying they'd better get home as Maddie tired easily.

Closing the door behind them, Jager turned to Paige. "You're going to be an aunt."

"And you'll be an uncle."

Seemingly the thought hadn't occurred to him. A surprised smile curled his mouth. "I suppose so."

"Why didn't you tell me you'd invited my parents?" she demanded.

He looked slightly taken aback at the aggression in her tone, steering her back into the living room. "I wasn't sure they'd actually turn up. I didn't want you to be disappointed."

"Why did you ask them?"

"I thought you'd be pleased."

Or he'd wanted to flaunt her, their daughter, in their faces. She recalled the dress he'd bought—a statement if ever there was one. Inside her there was a hollow feeling. "How did you persuade them?"

A cynical curve to his mouth, he said, "I'm not beneath their standards of acceptability anymore. A few million dollars makes a difference."

"Why won't you believe me?" she snapped. "Money wasn't the issue."

He stopped in the middle of the room, and pulled her against him. "Let's not argue," he said huskily, his lips nuzzling her temple. He lifted a hand and turned her face up to him. "You were a wonderful hostess. Thank you."

For a thank-you kiss it was pretty devastating. He parted her lips and took full advantage of her compliance. As always, his kisses and the strength of his arms, the tender, arousing stroking of his hands, heated her body and quickened her breath, but this time her mind wouldn't be stilled.

She broke away, and he let her go. His mouth looked full and softer than usual, his eyes glittering, glazed. "You didn't bring a bag," he said.

"I'm not staying."

"You know I want you to."

"No. I haven't anything with me."

"I keep spare toothbrushes, and there's a heated towel rail in the bathroom. You can wash your undies and they'll dry before morning."

"I'm tired." And then she despised herself for making excuses.

"You can sleep here. If sleep is what you want."

When she made to object again he reached out and put his fingers over her mouth. "For some reason you're mad at me. I don't want you going away angry, Paige. We don't need to make love if you'd rather not. Just share my bed."

She *was* angry, in a confused, hurt way. Angry at herself as much as at him. And not quite sure why.

Part of it was because of what she saw as his one-upmanship over her parents and his determined refusal to see their point of view.

But part of it too was Maddie and Glen's announcement. Their delight in starting a family, that ultimate proof of a belief in a lasting bond between them, cruelly highlighted the nature of Jager and Paige's relationship. No promises, no ties except the ephemeral, easily broken one of sexual compatibility.

It wasn't enough.

The nagging little ache hadn't gone away. It was growing, filling her whole chest. Her eyes stung, and she put a hand up and bent her head into it to hide the incipient tears. The last thing she wanted was to cry in front of Jager.

"You *are* tired," he said. He lifted her into his arms, cradling her like a child. She squeezed her eyes shut while he carried into the hallway and through to the darkened master bedroom. Anger came to the fore again, stemming the tears. "Jager, I told you—"

"Shh." He lowered her to the bed, and when she tried to struggle up, held her wrists. "Rest. I'll sleep in the spare room if you like. I'm not asking anything of you, Paige, just giving you a bed for the night.

Now sit up and I'll unzip you and hang up that dress. It's too pretty to sleep in.''

It made any further insistence seem totally unreasonable. With a strong suspicion that his determination to have her stay was as irrational as her own reluctance to do so, she gave in. This pointless fight was only a symptom of much deeper issues at the heart of their relationship. Maybe the time had come to confront them. But not tonight.

She sighed, let him help her to sit up and bent forward for him to pull down the zip.

"I'll wash out your undies for you if you like," he offered.

Something caught in her throat. Stupid to be affected by that—a simple, practical but so intimate an action. She shook her head. "I'll change them when I get home tomorrow." She slid her feet under the cover as he pulled it aside for her, and took off her glasses to place them on the bedside table.

Jager was hanging up her dress. "Do you need the bathroom?" he asked her.

"No." She'd used it about an hour ago, and cleaned her teeth too. She always carried a toothbrush. For once her makeup could stay on overnight. "You don't need to sleep in the spare room," she said to his back, and saw him pause, his shoulders rigid, before he closed the wardrobe door. "But I do mean to sleep."

He kissed her nose. "I won't be long."

Although the bed was big enough for them to sleep comfortably without touching, Paige was glad when he slipped in beside her and she felt his body warm against her back, his arms around her. His breath feathered her nape in what sounded like a sigh of content.

Paige closed her eyes against the confusing mixture of emotions that threatened to overwhelm her, fighting tears. Fighting the growing conviction that they couldn't go on like this—*she* couldn't go on like this. And that this might be the last time they shared a bed.

She must have slipped into sleep quite quickly, despite the turmoil in her mind. When she woke she was alone. A black satin kimono lay at the end of the bed.

She took the kimono and went into the bathroom. Fifteen minutes later she had showered, and dried her newly washed panties with the hair dryer fixed to the wall, wondering if Jager ever used it, or if it was strictly for female visitors. But then, it was probably just one of the extra touches of luxury the designers had provided in all the apartments.

The dress she'd worn last night hardly seemed suitable for breakfast. She stepped into the panties and belted the roomy robe over them before going down the passageway.

The aroma of frying bacon met her. Besides the table in the center of the dining area, a small oval table and two chairs were set near the window. Last night it had served as a sideboard, but now it was laid for breakfast.

She entered the kitchen and Jager turned from putting bread into the toaster. "Just in time," he said, depressing the lever. "I heard you in the shower. If you want fruit, there are tinned peaches."

"Just juice, thanks." There were already glasses of it on the table.

He pulled the lid off a covered pan and slid crisp bacon and perfectly cooked eggs onto two plates, then added a slice of toast to each.

A plate in each hand, he came toward her, bent to press a kiss on her mouth and said, "You look great in my robe. Sexy. Come and eat."

CHAPTER TEN

PAIGE wasn't really hungry, but eating gave her an excuse to delay the inevitable. Even to consider the cowardly alternative of leaving things as they were, of accepting whatever crumbs of his life Jager was willing to share with her for as long as it suited him.

A bleak thought.

"You slept well," Jager commented, buttering his toast. "I was tempted to wake you, but you looked so peaceful I controlled myself."

"You want a medal?" she asked sardonically. Half of her wished he'd followed his instinct, made love to her one more time, while the other half told her it would only have made this even harder, maybe impossible.

"No medal, but I wouldn't turn down a reward."

His gaze slid over her and she looked away. Flirting wasn't on the menu this morning, and as for anything else... She concentrated on cutting into her bacon.

Later Jager took her plate away and made coffee. "You're very thoughtful," he said, placing her cup before her and resuming his seat.

Paige stirred sugar into her cup, taking her time. "I think we should talk."

"About what?"

She looked up at the wary expression on his face,

the slight frown. "About our relationship. About... what we want from each other."

Jager leaned back, his eyelids drooping so that his black lashes veiled his eyes. "What do you want?"

Paige replaced the spoon carefully in the saucer, glanced out at the view—the harbor in the morning light glittered blue and green, and yachts danced like white-winged birds on the waves.

Her hand crushed the silk of his borrowed robe in her lap. "I want things you can't give me," she said. *Or won't.* "I'm not blaming you, Jager. You didn't hold out any false hopes. But I'm—" she swallowed, because her heart was crying out against this "—I'm not willing to carry on with our...affair."

"Affair?"

"That's what it's called, Jager, when two people are sleeping together without commitment, without promises, free to break it off at anytime."

His face had gone oddly blank, his eyes lifeless. "Is that what you're doing? Breaking it off?"

She swallowed. "If it isn't...going anywhere, yes."

After a long moment he pushed back his chair and stood up. "You'd better get dressed," he said. "I'll take you home."

For a second or two she was stunned. That was it? No discussion, no protest, no attempt at persuasion, or even anger? Simply an acceptance that it was over? As if it didn't even *matter*.

She stared at the steaming, untouched coffee in front of her, stretched out a hand to pick up the cup, then realized her fingers were trembling, and let it clatter back into the saucer. A flash of sheer outrage took her to her feet, her shoulders stiff and straight. "I'll get a taxi," she said. She'd used one to come here, mindful of the fact that there would be drinks at dinner.

He didn't answer, but when she returned, dressed and with her head held high, he was standing in the doorway, his car keys in his hand. She didn't argue any further.

Neither of them spoke in the car. The ache in Paige's chest and throat was almost choking her. A tearing regret added itself to the ache. Why couldn't she have kept her mouth shut? Maybe with more time Jager would have...

He would have what? her mind jeered. Changed his mind? Decided to marry her after all? Vowed eternal love and devotion?

She reminded herself smartingly that fairy tales seldom happened in real life. She'd had her chance once with Jager and she'd blown it, bailed out when the going got rough. He wasn't going to forgive her for that, ever.

When he pulled up outside the cottage, she said, huskily, "Thank you," and gathered her bag and wrap with clumsy fingers.

"I'm coming in," Jager said.

Her heart gave a leap of hope, before she quelled it with stern reason. He probably just wanted to collect his things. "I'll send your stuff to you." She couldn't bear to watch him strip the cottage of every remnant of his frequent presence, every reminder of their time together.

"I'm coming in," he repeated, with a controlled ferocity that made her look at him, and what she saw stopped her heart. His face was white, pinched, and a tiny muscle throbbed near his jaw. He was quietly furious.

Curiously, she was more heartened than afraid. At least anger was an emotional reaction. It was his apparent indifference that had stunned her.

She led the way down the path and opened the door. "I want to change my clothes," she said. "I won't be long." Making it clear that she expected him to wait in the sitting room.

She stripped and pulled on fresh undies, jeans and a shirt. Then she took down the bag containing the dress Jager had bought. That strengthened her resolve. Two of his shirts hung in the wardrobe. She stuffed them in with the dress, followed them with a pair of trousers, a couple of pairs of socks, underpants. The bag was bulging.

In the bathroom she collected his shaving things, his toothbrush, and shoved them into a smaller bag, then lugged the lot into the sitting room.

"Here," she said, dumping the bags onto the couch. "You'd better take your CDs too."

He'd been standing at the window, looking out at the kowhai tree and the street beyond the hedge. He turned and looked at the bags as if he hadn't a clue what was in them. Comprehension dawned and slowly his gaze rose to her face. "There's no need for that."

"Isn't it what you came in for?"

Impatience creased his brow and darkened his eyes. "What the hell do I care about a few stupid clothes?"

Nothing, of course. What had once been a matter of vital importance was mere trivia to him now. "Then why insist on coming in?"

"To tell you that you've won," he said. "I can give you anything money can buy, Paige. I've given you myself—the new improved version that won't embarrass you before your family and friends. I've learned how to behave in the best company—even your parents must know that by now. But you want commitment, promises...? All right, you've got them. If that's what it takes to keep you."

Paige's head whirled at the unexpected, stunning turnabout. It should have made her happy. Instead she was filled with sick dismay. He didn't look as though he was making a declaration of love. More like a declaration of war. His voice was harsh, his eyes glittering with something akin to hostility. He paused, and then said, "So, my darling ex-wife...will you marry me...again?"

It shouldn't be like this, she thought. She should be in his arms, not facing him across the room as though they were enemies instead of lovers. He should be looking at her with tenderness, not that inimical, unrelenting green stare. Everything about the scene was wrong. This was far from a romantic dream coming true. It was a nightmare.

"No," she said. Self-preservation told her there was no other answer, although she could feel her heart splintering.

You've won, he'd said, but she hadn't won. If he

thought this was a battle, they were both losers. The latter part of their impetuous marriage, founded on love and ideals, had been bad enough. A second one, given Jager's clear resentment, his conviction that she'd forced him into a proposal, promised only another disaster.

"No?" He looked as if he'd been hit—hard.

She laughed—unsteadily, on the edge of crying. There was a kind of bitter humor in the situation. He was offering her exactly what she longed for, but in such a way that she'd be crazy to accept it. "No," she reiterated.

"What the hell kind of game are you playing now?" he demanded. "Ah—" he snapped his fingers "—I suppose you want your pound of flesh...my heart. All right, I love you! I admit it, freely. I loved you from the moment I set eyes on you, buzzing about that shop all earnest and purposeful and caring, and so damned efficient. I loved the purity of your profile when I first saw you serving at the counter—and when you looked at me through the window I loved the way your eyes were soft and misty and kind of vulnerable and yet wise behind those really serious glasses you wore. I've always loved you."

Paige didn't believe any of it. She folded her arms across herself as if she could ward off the barrage of his words, because he was throwing them at her like missiles rather than love-tokens.

"I'll love you till I die." Jager's eyes glowed like green fire. "Is that what you want to hear?"

She didn't, not if he didn't mean it. And everything in his tone suggested he didn't. Her throat felt raw.

Her whole body was shaking. "No," she managed to say again, scarcely more than a whisper. "Please go, Jager. Please."

A half-dozen expressions chased across his face. Rage, and chagrin, disbelief, briefly shock, and—surely not despair? For a moment he looked at her with piercing concern, until she stiffened her shoulders and met his gaze steadily, willing him to leave before she broke down.

He made an abrupt gesture, took a step toward her, but she quickly moved back and he stopped.

"All right," he said finally. "If that's what you want."

She didn't deny it, and after a few seconds he walked slowly past her and out of the front door.

Paige waited until she heard the car roar away before she collapsed onto the couch with a hand over her eyes, shivering despite the warmth of the sun streaming in the window, and trying to blot out thought, emotion, memory.

Her mother phoned later in the day to discuss Maddie's news. Margaret was ecstatic. Paige responded with as much enthusiasm as she could muster, but the events of the morning had left her feeling drained.

"And your father was quite impressed with Jager last night," Margaret said when she'd run out of comments on the prospect of a grandchild. "He says that young man has matured considerably."

"He *is* over thirty," Paige reminded her.

"Yes, well, apparently he has a good brain, Henry says."

"He always had a good brain." Paige couldn't seem to shake the habit of defending Jager.

"I suppose so," Margaret admitted. "But his manner left much to be desired. And I don't care what you say, you *were* too young to marry. He wasn't right for you then."

"I know, Mother," Paige agreed wearily.

"But...well, looking back, perhaps we might have helped a little. We did what we thought best at the time."

How ironic. Now, when it no longer made any difference, her parents were softening toward Jager. "It doesn't matter now."

Nothing mattered anymore.

She had to shake that feeling, Paige told herself in the following days. She got through them somehow, a matter of grim determination, getting out of bed, going through the motions of living and working, even eating regular meals, although nothing tasted as it should. It was like living in a thick, dreary fog; one that parted occasionally to give her glimpses of what real life was like, but she wasn't a participant.

She hadn't felt like this since the first few weeks after Aidan's death, nearly a year ago now. But she'd got over that, she realized with faint shock. Jager had helped her get over it.

And in some ways this was worse. Aidan was beyond human reach and nothing would bring him back. Jager was no more than a phone call away. She had only to dial his number and say one word—*yes*—to have him in her life again. But it would come with a cost. The cost of knowing that she'd backed him into a corner, made him feel emotionally blackmailed; and he might never get over his anger and resentment.

Relieved when the weekend came and she didn't need to drag herself to work and give an imitation of a living, breathing human being, she gave up trying to sleep in and tackled the garden instead. Already shrubs and perennials were flourishing, but weeds always threatened, and there was a warm, sheltered corner at the back of the house where she had decided to make a herb garden.

She was digging clods of earth and finding some satisfaction in chopping them with the sharp edge of the spade, when it was removed from her grasp and Jager said, "Here, let me do that."

Sheer happiness dizzied her for a golden moment before all the problems that beset them tumbled back into place. "I was doing all right," she said, wiping the back of a gloved hand over her damp forehead. Trust him to turn up when she was dirty and sweaty and in her oldest clothes, with not even her most minimal makeup on.

He glanced up, so briefly she had no time to see anything but the quick flash of his green eyes. "Sure," he said. "But I'll do it faster."

And with less effort, she acknowledged, watching the movement of his muscles under a white T-shirt and blue jeans. That's what he'd been wearing when she first saw him, but now the jeans had a designer label and the T-shirt wasn't threadbare.

Paige sat down on the back step and pulled off the gloves. Why was he here? She was afraid to ask.

He worked with an easy rhythm, and finished in half the time it would have taken her.

"Enough?" he queried her.

"Yes."

He lifted the spade and stuck it into the new garden bed, but stayed with his fingers curled around the handle, his eyes apparently studying the bare black earth. "I messed up the other night," he said. "Big time."

"Maybe we both did." Paige clasped her hands on her knees. "I didn't mean to make you feel trapped."

He looked up then but she had the feeling he wasn't really seeing her. "I suppose that's part of it."

"Part of it?"

"I was furious that you'd called my bluff." His eyes focused on her now. "I thought I'd got the upper hand, had you just where I wanted you."

Paige blinked. "You make it sound like a battle. What did you want, Jager, some kind of revenge?"

He altered his grip on the spade and looked down again, almost as though he planned to do more digging. "All I wanted was you. But I wanted—needed—to protect myself. I'd sworn I was never again going to descend to the hell you put me through when you left me, left our marriage. This time was going to be different. I was going to be in control. No vows, no promises to be broken. And if anybody dumped anybody, it was going to be me."

"I know you were holding back. You said you'd given me yourself, but you never really opened up to me." She asked with dull curiosity, "Did you plan to dump me?" It would have been a just revenge, she supposed.

"I tried not to plan at all, after the first time we slept together here in your bed. Before that...well, it was different then."

"Different, how?"

"It wasn't a coincidence, me being at your sister's wedding. After my father contacted me I had no particular reason to see him again. But on that first visit he told me about my brother and asked if I'd like to meet him. I let him talk, though I wasn't interested. Then he mentioned who Glen was marrying." He paused. "Glen still thinks it was his own idea to invite me to the wedding."

"You used him."

"I used him to get invited here too."

"Do you have *any* feelings for Glen, or your father?" she demanded.

He seemed to think about it. "Yes," he said finally. "My father's a good man who made a stupid, drunken mistake when he was young and is doing his best to make up for it. I respect him for that. Glen...he's a friend. He's a good guy, honest and caring and dependable. There aren't too many like him. And his mother..." With an air of surprise he said, frowning, "I suppose I've grown fond of her. Finding out her husband had another child must have been hard, and she's handled it with dignity and generosity."

"Were you using me too?"

His eyes darkened. "Did it feel that way?"

"I felt more like a mistress than a lover," she said.

"I didn't think of it like that. All I knew was that I wanted you—had to have you."

"In your bed? Mine?" she corrected.

"In my life, Paige. And it seemed to be working. When I finally got you to come to my place I felt you'd moved a step closer. You were with me, you wanted me, and I hadn't had to expose my feelings at all, I was still able to pretend that my world wouldn't end if you left me again. There were no more promises of undying love to be flung back in my face."

"No commitment," Paige murmured.

"And then you whipped the rug from under my feet. It hadn't occurred to me—stupidly—that all you had to do was threaten to leave me to have me fold like a melting jelly. I suppose I never thought you'd do it. When you did, I felt...helpless."

"You?" She swept an ironic gaze over him, from the six-foot-plus top of his head over the arrogant nose and iron jaw, the rock-hard muscles of his chest and arms, and right down to his size twelve feet.

"I didn't like the feeling," he said. "I lashed out. I'm sorry."

Paige didn't know what to say. The silence grew, and Jager put a foot on the spade, then lifted it off again. He finally let go his grip on the handle and took a step toward her. "I'll promise anything," he said, "do anything, to have you back, Paige. If marriage is what you want, you have it. I didn't mean those things I said." He shook his head impatiently, then went down on his haunches in front of her, taking her hands in his. "Or I should say, I did mean them, but not the way I said them."

"You said you loved me," she reminded him, looking down at their joined hands.

"And that I always will. It's true. I can't help it, and I warn you that if you walk out on me again you won't get away so easily. I'll be doing my damndest to bring you back."

"You said you loved me the first time you saw me."

He rubbed his thumb over the back of one of her hands. "A slight exaggeration, maybe. I was attracted to you. I wasn't sure why, because you weren't my usual type."

"I wasn't pretty."

"Pretty!" He dismissed that with a scornful jerk of his head, as if the word were "trash" or "trivia." "You had more than prettiness. Elegance. Class. I liked that about you from the start."

"Inner beauty?" she inquired, resignedly. How often had her mother reminded her it was more important than being pretty to look at?

"No!" Jager said. "Yes, that too, I guess. But not only that." He gave her a puzzled look. "Paige...you surely don't think you're ugly?"

"Not ugly. Just plain."

"You're not plain!" He shifted his hands to her shoulders and gave her a little shake. "Not that it matters, but you are going to be a beautiful old lady when all the *pretty* girls have lost their looks. Yours is the kind of beauty that lasts, that gets better with age. I've told you often enough, you're lovely!"

"I thought you were just being...kind."

The shocked disbelief in his eyes convinced her. Jager really did think she was beautiful! And although she knew it wasn't really important, she couldn't help a thrill of delight. If Jager believed it, even if he were deluded, who cared what the rest of the world thought?

It was a liberating thought. For the first time she believed he meant it. And if he really did love her...

She said, "I don't want you to feel pressured into marriage. If you like we can go on just as we are." He had made some revelations today that helped her understand him much better than before, in fact he'd come right out and told her how he felt. Such a giant step, for the first time she could hope their relationship might become permanent. That this time they would make it.

He leaned over and kissed her lips, gently. "I need you, Paige, my first and only love, and I don't care what I have to do to make you need me."

"You don't have to do anything." Nothing he could do could make her need him any more than she did.

His eyes searched her face. "Glen asked me to be godfather to his baby," he said. "It made me think for the first time about what having a baby means."

The question had hardly arisen when they were married. They'd known they were too young, and financially they couldn't possibly have coped. "A baby?" Paige whispered.

"I never wanted to be a father before," Jager said. "Until I saw his—my father's—family, and then

Glen and Maddie, I didn't believe people who said love expands to new people. It had never happened to me. But with those two—you can see it growing daily. They're more in love than ever. It's... awesome."

"You've been seeing them?" Paige felt slightly guilty. She'd spoken to Maddie a couple of times on the phone but she hadn't wanted to see anyone, hugging her hurt and pain to herself on the excuse that she didn't want to cloud Maddie's happiness with her own misery.

"I needed to talk to Maddie about you. I figured she knew you better than anyone."

"She never said."

"Because I asked her not to. My pride had taken enough of a beating without you knowing I was begging your sister to tell me what to do to get you back."

"What did she say?"

"She said, 'Be honest with her. And tell her you're sorry.' I'm being as honest as I can, Paige. And I'm asking you to forgive me. Can you?"

She loved him, and she was beginning to think that he truly loved her, despite her misgivings and his previous defensive attitude.

He'd been afraid of being hurt again. His mother had left him, then his aunt discarded him, and several foster homes had sent him away. All he'd known as a child was abandonment and betrayal. And when he thought he'd found his one true love and married her to prove that *he* was faithful and steadfast, she too had betrayed him, run away and repeated the cruel cycle.

"Can you forgive me?" she asked him. "For leaving you?" Because she knew he never had.

"You were barely more than a child," he said. "I asked too much of you. And your parents deliberately made it harder."

"My mother apologized for that, sort of, the other day."

He hesitated. "You always said they did it out of love."

"And you never believed that."

"It's an exclusive love," he said. "The kind that shuts out anyone who threatens what they want for you."

"Isn't that...?"

"Love of a kind," he conceded. "But did they care that they were hurting *you?* I won't do that to any child of mine. They wanted you to live the life they'd mapped out for you, not the one you wanted for yourself."

"I suppose," Paige acknowledged, "there's some truth in that. They could have been less...rigid. I hope I would be, that I'd support my children even when they made mistakes."

He stood up, taking her with him, so they stood face-to-face, as equals, even though he was taller. "Marry me again," he said quietly. "Bear my children, and love me all the days of my life, as I love you?"

It sounded like a solemn vow. She met his eyes. "If that's what you truly want."

"More than anything in the world. Ever since you left me I've been working toward this moment without knowing it. All my success, all the money I made, that fancy apartment I bought, was just to impress you."

"Oh, Jager!" she said, and almost apologetically, "I'm not impressed by that, you know."

Chagrin warred with his reluctant recognition of the truth. "I know," he confessed. "It doesn't mean anything to you, but it does to me."

"If it makes you happy," she said. "But if you lost it all tomorrow I'd still stick by you. Please believe that. I'm not seventeen and scared of real life anymore."

"I believe it, but it won't happen. I may not be as rich as Aidan, but—"

"Aidan wasn't rich!"

"Not by your father's standards, maybe—"

"Not by anyone's standards. He had a good job as an industrial chemist, but our home was mortgaged and...well, we weren't poor but we budgeted quite carefully. It was only with his insurance that I was able to buy this place."

He frowned down at her. "I assumed..."

"Wrong. But I suppose I can forgive you for that too. I've forgiven everything else."

"Everything?"

"Everything."

"So?"

She realized what he was waiting for. "Yes," she said. "I'll marry you."

He pulled her close and muttered into her hair,

"Thank you, darling, thank you!" Then he said, "It's a bit premature, but..."

And suddenly she was swung into his arms and carried through across the worn back doorstep, through the doorway and along the passageway to the bedroom.

"I'll miss this room," he said, depositing her on the bed and beginning to shuck his clothes.

"Miss it?" She watched him pull off the T-shirt, them, enjoying what he revealed.

"When we're married again." He unzipped his jeans and dropped them. Catching her inquiring look, he said, "You are going to live with me, aren't you?"

She sat up, and he perched on the bed and began to undress her too. Paige didn't stop him, lifting her arms to help him pull off her shirt, but said, "And give up the cottage?"

He undid her bra and tossed it aside. It landed on the leopard's ear and dangled. "I know you put a lot of work into it. *We* did."

"Then why can't we live here?"

Jager was looking rather greedily at her breasts, even as he unfastened her trousers and eased them down her legs. She didn't think he was listening. "Jager?" she insisted.

He pulled off the jeans and pushed her gently against the pillows, laying a hand on her breast as he kissed her, then lifted his head. "Don't you like the apartment? We can get another. Or a house. We'll need a house when the children arrive." He glanced down at what his hand was doing to her and smiled with satisfaction. "I'll find an architect—"

"Jager!" She gasped and wriggled, but held firm to her purpose. And his wrist. "I don't want to sell the cottage. Not yet anyway."

His hand finally stilled where it was. She said, "Why can't we live here?"

"Business," he said. "Entertaining. Besides..."

"Besides what?" she asked, and when he looked away, shrugging, she added fiercely, "Don't you dare clam up on me now! If I'm going to marry you I want to *know* what you're feeling."

"If?" he queried, his eyes narrowing.

"When we're married," Paige amended hastily, "and starting now! What is your problem?"

"I told you," he said unconvincingly. "But also—" he'd seen the threatening look on her face "—it was bought with your *other* husband's money."

"*My* money."

"From his insurance. It doesn't feel right."

"It seems to have felt perfectly all right until now."

"I didn't know then. And I haven't been living here. I can't," he said stubbornly. "Why do you think I've been trying to get you to my apartment since that first night?"

Exasperated, she said, "You can't be jealous of Aidan, Jager. He's dead."

"I'm not jealous." He scowled.

"Are you sure?" Paige reached up and smoothed back a strand of hair from the scowl. She hesitated, not wanting to denigrate Aidan, but decided to be honest. "I loved him, I won't pretend I didn't, but...it never felt the way it does with you."

The scowl lifted. "I've tried not to mind," he said. "I know I don't have any right."

She saw it had hurt him, but in time the hurt would ease. And she wouldn't let him ride roughshod over her. "I'm going to keep the cottage." She hoped he wasn't going to make it a bone of contention.

"You can. But I want our home to be *my* territory. Ours. Can you understand that?"

Yes, she could. He was sensitive about providing for her properly this time, showing her parents, with their old-fashioned values, that he could.

It might be a long while before he was utterly sure of her love, truly secure. She had a whole lifetime to prove it to him. Paige surrendered. "All right, I'll move into your apartment. But we could come here at weekends, maybe?"

"Done," he said promptly. "And I'll leave my cell phone behind. It'll be our secret hideaway, our love-nest in the suburbs."

She laughed softly. "Maddie said this room was like a love-nest."

"I'm glad I helped to create it," he said. "All that stripping and scraping away the years of covering up and neglect was worth it in the end." He looked around the room. "You've got rid of the accumulated rubbish and made it new and fresh again. Now—" he returned his attention to her, and lowered his mouth until it just touched her lips "—can we get on with what we're here for?"

He opened her mouth under his, and she arched into him, kissing him back without restraint, returning every caress, matching him in every way.

And when he gave her the ultimate physical delight and emotional fulfillment and she cried out against his mouth, and heard his answering groan, muffled in his throat, she knew that at last she had all of him, that he was wholly hers as she was wholly his. His wife again. Until the end of time.

MILLS & BOON
Special Edition

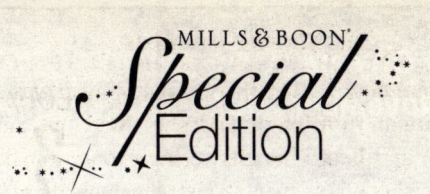

Life, love and family

6 brand-new titles each month

Available on the third Friday of every month
from WHSmith, ASDA, Tesco
and all good bookshops
www.millsandboon.co.uk

**On sale
2nd November 2007**

MILLS & BOON
BY REQUEST
3
NOVELS ONLY
£4.99

In November 2007 Mills & Boon present two bestselling collections, each featuring three wonderful romances by three of your favourite authors...

Pregnant Proposals

Featuring

His Pregnancy Ultimatum by Helen Bianchin
Finn's Pregnant Bride by Sharon Kendrick
Pregnancy of Convenience by Sandra Field

Available at WHSmith, Tesco, ASDA, and all good bookshops
www.millsandboon.co.uk

On sale 2nd November 2007

MILLS & BOON
BY REQUEST
3
NOVELS ONLY
£4.99

Don't miss out on these fabulous stories

Mistress by Consent

Featuring

Mistress by Agreement by Helen Brooks
The Unexpected Mistress by Sara Wood
Innocent Mistress by Margaret Way

Available at WHSmith, Tesco, ASDA, and all good bookshops
www.millsandboon.co.uk

MILLS & BOON
Romance

Pure romance, pure emotion

Needed: Her Mr Right
Barbara Hannay

Outback Boss, City Bride
Jessica Hart

4 brand-new titles each month

Available on the first Friday of every month
from WHSmith, ASDA, Tesco
and all good bookshops
www.millsandboon.co.uk

New York Times bestselling author

DIANA PALMER

is coming to

MILLS & BOON
Romance

Pure romance, pure emotion

Curl up and relax with her brand new *Long, Tall Texans* story

Winter Roses

Watch the sparks fly in this vibrant, compelling romance as gorgeous, irresistible rancher Stuart York meets his match in innocent but feisty Ivy Conley...

"Nobody tops Diana Palmer when it comes to delivering pure, undiluted romance. I love her stories."
—*New York Times* bestselling author Jayne Ann Krentz

On sale 2nd November 2007

Available at WHSmith, Tesco, ASDA, and all good bookshops
www.millsandboon.co.uk

MILLS & BOON
MEDICAL
Proudly presents

Brides of Penhally Bay

Featuring Dr Nick Tremayne

A pulse-raising collection of emotional, tempting romances and heart-warming stories – devoted doctors, single fathers, Mediterranean heroes, a Sheikh and his guarded heart, royal scandals and miracle babies…

Book One

CHRISTMAS EVE BABY
by Caroline Anderson

Starting 7th December 2007

A COLLECTION TO TREASURE FOREVER!
One book available every month

PENHALLY/LIST/1-3

MILLS & BOON
MEDICAL™
Proudly presents

Brides of Penhally Bay

A pulse-raising collection of emotional, tempting romances and heart-warming stories by bestselling Mills & Boon Medical™ authors.

January 2008
The Italian's New-Year Marriage Wish
by Sarah Morgan

Enjoy some much-needed winter warmth with gorgeous Italian doctor Marcus Avanti.

February 2008
The Doctor's Bride By Sunrise
by Josie Metcalfe

Then join Adam and Maggie on a 24-hour rescue mission where romance begins to blossom as the sun starts to set.

March 2008
The Surgeon's Fatherhood Surprise
by Jennifer Taylor

Single dad Jack Tremayne finds a mother for his little boy – and a bride for himself.

Let us whisk you away to an idyllic Cornish town – a place where hearts are made whole

COLLECT ALL 12 BOOKS!

Available at WHSmith, Tesco, ASDA, and all good bookshops
www.millsandboon.co.uk

MILLS & BOON
MEDICAL™

**Pulse-raising romance –
Heart-racing medical drama**

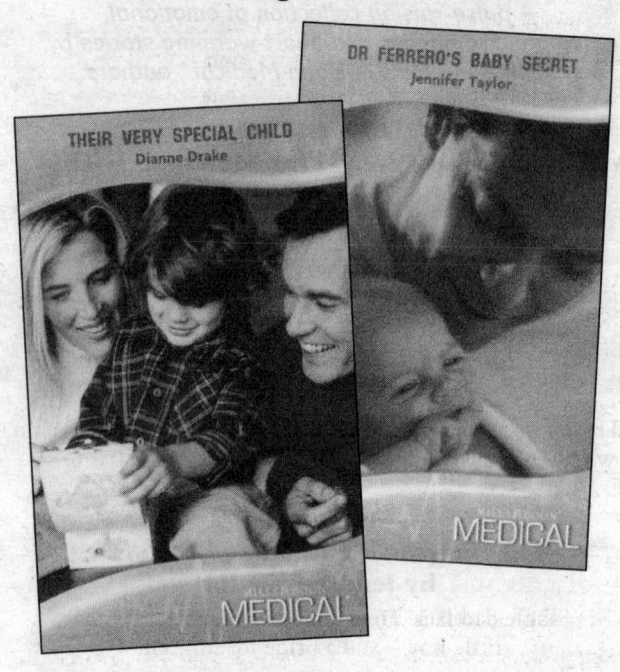

6 brand-new titles each month

Available on the first Friday of every month
from WHSmith, ASDA, Tesco
and all good bookshops
www.millsandboon.co.uk

GEN/03/RTL11